Praise for #1 *New York Times* Bestselling Author

NORA ROBERTS

"Roberts creates exceptional characters who...
live on in the reader's imagination and heart."
—*Publishers Weekly*

"Roberts is indeed a word artist, painting her story
and her characters with vitality and verve."
—*Los Angeles Daily News*

"With clear-eyed, concise vision and a sure pen,
Roberts nails her characters and settings with awesome precision,
drawing readers into a vividly rendered world of
family-centered warmth and unquestionable magic."
—*Library Journal*

"Move over, bestsellers.
The new 'top gun' of contemporary fiction has arrived."
—*Rave Reviews*

"The publishing world might be hard-pressed to find an author
with a more diverse style or fertile imagination than Roberts."
—*Publishers Weekly*

"Roberts has a warm feel for her characters
and an eye for the evocative detail."
—*Chicago Tribune*

"Romance will never die
as long as the megaselling Roberts keeps writing it."
—*Kirkus Reviews*

"Roberts' bestselling novels are some of the best
in the romance genre. They are thoughtfully plotted,
well-written stories featuring fascinating characters."
—*USA TODAY*

Dear Reader,

Enjoy the wonderful magic of two classics by Nora Roberts. This compilation features two couples who live by the rules—and love outside them.

In "Opposites Attract" Asher Wolfe is known for her exquisite beauty and incomparable precision on the tennis court. Ty Starbuck is the opposite—wild and passionate. Once a golden couple, they hadn't spoken for years, but their unexpected reunion is electric. Will the words that need to be spoken destroy them…or forge a remarkable rematch?

In "A Will and a Way" Pandora McVie's adored Uncle Jolley has passed away—but he's still making mischief. Pandora learns she's inherited one hundred and fifty million dollars—but there's a catch: she must manage to live with detestable Michael Donohue. Stuck in a Catskill mansion for six months with him is enough to make a sane person crazy. Or will it change two complicated people into perfect partners?

Happy reading!

The Editors
Silhouette Books

NORA ROBERTS

Chances

Silhouette® Books
Published by Silhouette Books
America's Publisher of Contemporary Romance

SILHOUETTE BOOKS

PLEASE RECYCLE THIS PRODUCT IS RECYCLABLE

Recycling programs for this product may not exist in your area.

CHANCES

ISBN-13: 978-0-373-28576-1
ISBN-10: 0-373-28576-0

This edition published by arrangement with Harlequin Books S.A.

Visit Silhouette Books at www.eHarlequin.com

Printed in U.S.A.

CONTENTS

Also available from Silhouette Books and Harlequin Books by

NORA ROBERTS

FALLING FOR RACHEL & CONVINCING ALEX
Two love stories about the Stanislaskis

WAITING FOR NICK & CONSIDERING KATE
The last two stories in the Stanislaski family saga

THE MACGREGOR GROOMS
Three stories featuring the irresistible patriarch Daniel MacGregor

REFLECTIONS & DREAMS
Two classic stories featuring characters from *Considering Kate*

FIRST IMPRESSIONS
A love story at Christmas time

CAPTIVATED & ENTRANCED
The first two books featuring the magical Donovans

LOVE BY DESIGN
Two books about the architecture of love

And coming soon
CHARMED & ENCHANTED

Opposites Attract

For Joan Schulhafer,
leader of tours, handler of details and good friend

Chapter One

"Advantage, Starbuck."

Isn't it always? Asher mused. For a moment the large arena held that humming silence peculiar to indoor sports events. There was an aroma of roasted peanuts and sweat. The overhead lights heated the scent somewhat pleasantly while the crush of bodies added enforced camaraderie. A small child sent up a babbling complaint and was hushed.

Seated several rows back at mid-court, Asher Wolfe watched Ty Starbuck—tennis master, Gypsy, eternal boy of summer and former lover. She thought again, as she had several times during more than two hours of play, that he'd changed. Just how wasn't yet completely clear. More than three years had passed since she'd seen him in the flesh. But he hadn't aged, or thickened, or lost any of his characteristic verve.

Rarely over the years had she watched a televised match—it was too painful. Too many faces were familiar, with his the most strictly avoided. If Asher had chanced to come across a write-up or picture of him in the sports pages or in a gossip column, she had immediately put it aside. Ty Starbuck was out of her life. Her decision. Asher was a very decisive woman.

Even her decision to come to the U.S. Indoor Tennis Championship had been a cool-headed one. Before making this trip, she had carefully weighed the pros and cons. In the end logic had won. She was getting back into the game herself. On the circuit, meetings with Ty would be unavoidable. She would see him now, letting the press, her colleagues and fans see clearly that there was nothing left of what had been three years before. Ty would see too, and, she hoped fervently, so would she.

Ty stood behind the baseline, preparing to serve. His stance was the same, she mused, as was his sizzling concentration. He tossed the ball up, coming back and over with the wicked left-handed serve that had become synonymous with his name, a Starbuck.

Asher heard the explosion of his breath that forced the power into it. She held her own. A lesser player than the Frenchman, Grimalier, would never have gotten a racket on the ball. His return was quick—force meeting force—and the rally began.

The crowd grew noisier as the ball smashed and thudded. Echoes bounced crazily. There were cries of encouragement, shouts of appreciation for the prowess of the two players. Ty's basic entertainment value hadn't decreased since Asher had been out of the game. Fans adored or detested him, but they never, never ignored him. Nor could she, though she was no longer certain which category she fell into. Every muscle of his body was familiar to her, every move, every expression. Her feelings were a confused jumble of respect, admiration and longing, which swirled to reach a vortex of pain, sharply remembered. Still, she was caught up in him again. Ty Starbuck demanded every last emotion and didn't really give a damn if it was love or hate.

Both men moved quickly, their eyes riveted on the small white sphere. Backhand, forehand, drop shot. Sweat poured down unheeded. Both the game and the fans demanded it. A tennis buff wanted to see the effort, the strain, wanted to hear the grunts and whistling breaths, wanted to smell the sweat. Despite her determination to remain dispassionate, Asher found herself watching Ty with the undiluted admiration she'd held for him for more than ten years.

He played with nonchalant flash—contradictory terms, but there it was. Strength, agility, form—he had them all. He had a long, limber body, seemingly elastic until the muscles flowed and bunched. His six-two height gave him an advantage of reach, and he could twist and turn on a dime. He played like a fencer—Asher had always thought a swashbuckler. Graceful sweeps, lunges, parries, with an almost demonic glint in his dusk-gray eyes. His face was that of the adventurer—narrow, rakish, with a hint of strong bone vying with an oddly tender mouth. As always, his hair was a bit too long, flowing wild and black around a white sweatband.

He was a set-up, and held advantage, but he played as though his life depended on this one point. That hadn't changed, Asher thought, as her heart pounded at double time. She was as involved in the match as if she were the one with the racket in her hand and the sweat rolling over her skin. Her palms were slick, her own muscles tight. Tennis involved its onlookers. Starbuck absorbed them. That hadn't changed either.

Ty smashed the ball crosscourt at the sideline. It careened away even as the Frenchman dove toward it. Asher sucked in her breath at the speed and placement of the ball.

"Wide," the line judge said dispassionately. A loud complaint poured out of the crowd. Asher fixed her eyes on Ty and waited for the explosion.

He stood, breathing hard from the punishing rally, his eyes fixed on the judge. The crowd continued to roar disapproval as deuce was called. Slowly, his eyes still on the judge, Ty swiped his wristband over his brow. His face was inscrutable but for his eyes, and his eyes spoke volumes. The crowd quieted to a murmur of speculation. Asher bit hard on her bottom lip. Ty walked back to the baseline without having uttered a sound.

This was the change, Asher realized with a jolt. Control. Her breath came out slowly as the tension in her shoulders diminished. In years past, Ty Starbuck would have hurled abuse—and an occasional racket—snarled, implored the crowd for support or berated them. Now he walked silently across the service court with temper smoldering in his eyes. But he held it in check. This was something new.

Behind the baseline Ty took his time, took his stance, then cracked an ace, like a bullet from a gun. The crowd screamed for him. With a quiet, insolent patience he waited while the scoring was announced. Again, he held advantage. Knowing him, and others like him, Asher was aware that his mind was occupied with his next move. The ace was already a memory, to be taken out and savored later. He still had a game to win.

The Frenchman connected with the next serve with a blazing forehand smash. The volley was sweating, furious and blatantly male. It was all speed and fire, two pirates blasting at each other across a sea of hardwood. There was the sound of the ball hitting the heart of the racket, the skid of rubber soles on wood, the grunts of the competitors as they drew out more force, all drowned beneath the echoes of cheers. The crowd was on its feet. Asher was on hers without even being aware of it. Neither man gave quarter as the seconds jumped to a minute, and a minute to more.

With a swing of the wrist the Frenchman returned a nearly impossible lob that drove him behind the baseline. The ball landed deep in the right court. With a forceful backhand Ty sent the ball low and away from his opponent, ending the two-and-a-half-hour match, three sets to one.

Starbuck was the U.S. Indoor Tennis champion, and the crowd's hero.

Asher let the enthusiasm pour around her as Ty walked to the net for the traditional handshake. The match had affected her more than she'd anticipated, but she passed this off as professional admiration. Now she allowed herself to wonder what his reaction would be when he saw her again.

Had she hurt him? His heart? His pride? The pride, she mused. That she could believe. The heart was a different matter. He would be angry, she concluded. She would be cool. Asher knew how to maintain a cool exterior as well as she knew how to smash an overhead lob. She'd learned it all as a child. When they met, she would simply deploy his temper. She had been preparing for the first encounter almost as religiously as she had been preparing to pick up her profession again. Asher was going to win at both. After he had finished with the showers and the press, she would make it a point to seek him out. To congratulate him—and to present the next test. It was much wiser for her to make the first move, for her to be the one prepared. Confident, she watched Ty exchange words with Grimalier at the net.

Then Ty turned his head very slowly, very deliberately. With no searching through the crowd, no hesitation, his eyes locked on hers. The strength of the contact had her drawing in a sharp, unwilling breath. His eyes held, no wavering. Her mouth went dry. Then he smiled, an unpleasant, direct challenge. Asher met it, more from shock than temerity as the crowd bellowed his name. *Starbuck* echoed from the walls like a litany. Ten seconds—fifteen—he neither blinked nor moved. For a man of action he had an uncanny ability for stillness. Boring into hers, his eyes made the distance between them vanish. The smile remained fixed. Just as Asher's palms began to sweat, he turned a full circle for the crowd, his racket above his head like a lance. They adored him.

He'd known, Asher thought furiously as people swarmed around her. He had known all along that she was there. Her anger wasn't the hot, logical result of being outmaneuvered, but small, silver slices of cold fury. Ty had let her know in ten seconds, without words, that the game was still on. And he always won.

Not this time though, she told herself. She had changed too. But she stood where she was, rooted, staring out at the now empty court. Her thoughts were whirling with memories, emotions, remembered sensations. People brushed by her, already debating the match.

She was a tall, reed-slim figure tanned gold from hours in the sun. Her hair was short, sculptured and misty-blond. The style flattered, while remaining practical for her profession. Over three years of retirement, Asher hadn't altered it. Her face seemed more suited to the glossy pages of a fashion magazine than the heat and frenzy of a tennis court. A weekender, one might think, looking at her elegant cheekbones in an oval face. Not a pro. The nose was small and straight above a delicately molded mouth she rarely thought to tint. Makeup on the courts was a waste of time, as sweat would wash it away. Her eyes were large and round, a shade of blue that hinted at violet. One of her few concessions to vanity was to darken the thick pale lashes that surrounded them. While other women competitors added jewelry or ribbons and bows to the court dress, Asher had never thought of it. Even off the court her attire leaned toward the simple and muted.

An enterprising reporter had dubbed her "The Face" when she had been eighteen. She'd been nearly twenty-three when she had retired from professional play, but the name had stuck. Hers was a face of great beauty and rigid control. On court, not a flicker of expression gave her opponent or the crowd a hint of what she was thinking or feeling. One of her greatest defenses in the game was her ability to remain unruffled under stress. The standard seeped into her personal life.

Asher had lived and breathed tennis for so long that the line of demarcation between woman and athlete was smudged. The hard, unbendable rule, imposed by her father, was ingrained into her—privacy, first and last. Only one person had ever been able to cross the boundary. Asher was determined he would not do so again.

As she stood staring down at the empty court, her face told nothing of her anger or turmoil—or the pain she hadn't been prepared for. It was calm and aloof. Her concentration was so deep that the leader of the small packet of people that approached her had to speak her name twice to get her attention.

She'd been recognized, she discovered. Though Asher had known it was inevitable, it still gave her a twist of pleasure to sign the papers and programs thrust at her. She hadn't been forgotten.

The questions were easy to parry, even when they skirted close to her relationship with Ty. A smile and double-talk worked well with fans. Asher wasn't naïve enough to think it would work with reporters. That, she hoped, was for another day.

As she signed, and edged her way back, Asher spotted a few colleagues—an old foe, a former doubles partner, a smattering of faces from the past. Her eyes met Chuck Prince's. Ty's closest friend was an affable player with a wrist of steel and beautiful footwork. Though the silent exchange was brief, even friendly, Asher saw the question in his eyes before she gave her attention to the next fan.

The word's out, she thought almost grimly as she smiled at

a teenage tennis buff. Asher Wolfe's picking up her racket again. And they'd wonder, and eventually ask, if she was picking up Ty Starbuck too.

"Asher!" Chuck moved to her with the same bouncy stride he used to cross a court. In his typical outgoing style he seized her by the shoulders and kissed her full on the mouth. "Hey, you look terrific!"

With a laugh Asher drew back the breath his greeting had stolen from her. "So do you." It was inevitably true. Chuck was average in almost every way—height, build, coloring. But his inner spark added appeal and a puckish sort of sexuality. He'd never hesitated to exploit it—good-naturedly.

"No one knew you were coming," Chuck complained, easing her gently through the thinning crowd. "I didn't know you were here until..." His voice trailed off so that Asher knew he referred to the ten seconds of potent contact with Ty. "Until after the match," he finished. He gave her shoulder a quick squeeze. "Why didn't you give someone a call?"

"I wasn't entirely sure I'd make it." Asher allowed herself to be negotiated to a clear spot in a rear hallway. "Then I thought I'd just melt into the crowd. It didn't seem fair to disrupt the match with any the-prodigal-returns business."

"It was a hell of a match." The flash of teeth gleamed with enthusiasm. "I don't know if I've ever seen Ty play better than he did in the last set. Three aces."

"He always had a deadly serve," Asher murmured.

"Have you seen him?"

From anyone else the blunt question would have earned a cold stare. Chuck earned a quick grimace. "No. I will, of course, but I didn't want to distract him before the match." Asher linked her fingers—an old nervous habit. "I didn't realize he knew I was here."

Distract Starbuck, she thought with an inner laugh. No one and nothing distracted him once he picked up his game racket.

"He went crazy when you left."

Chuck's quiet statement brought her back. Deliberately she unlaced her fingers. "I'm sure he recovered quickly." Because the retort was sharper than she had intended, Asher shook her head as if to take back the words. "How have you been? I saw an ad with you touting the virtues of a new line of tennis shoes."

"How'd I look?"

"Sincere," she told him with a quick grin. "I nearly went out and bought a pair."

He sighed. "I was shooting for macho."

As the tension seeped out of her, Asher laughed. "With that face?" She cupped his chin with her hand and moved it from side to side. "It's a face a mother could trust—foolishly," she added.

"Shh!" He glanced around in mock alarm. "Not so loud, my reputation."

"Your reputation suffered a few dents in Sydney," she recalled. "What was that—three seasons ago? The stripper."

"Exotic dancer," Chuck corrected righteously. "It was merely an exchange of cultures."

"You did look kind of cute wearing those feathers." With another laugh she kissed his cheek. "Fuchsia becomes you."

"We all missed you, Asher." He patted her slim, strong shoulder.

The humor fled from her eyes. "Oh, Chuck, I missed you. Everyone, all of it. I don't think I realized just how much until I walked in here today." Asher looked into space at her own thoughts, her own memories. "Three years," she said softly.

"Now you're back."

Her eyes drifted to his. "Now I'm back," she agreed. "Or will be in two weeks."

"The Foro Italico."

Asher gave him a brief smile that was more determination than joy. "I've never won on that damn Italian clay. I'm going to this time."

"It was your pacing."

The voice from behind her had Asher's shoulders stiffening. As she faced Chuck her eyes showed only the merest flicker of some secret emotion before they calmed. When she turned to Ty he saw first that his memory of her beauty hadn't been exaggerated with time, and second that her layer of control was as tough as ever.

"So you always told me," she said calmly. The jolt was over, she reasoned, with the shock of eye contact in the auditorium. But her stomach muscles tightened. "You played beautifully, Ty…after the first set."

They were no more than a foot apart now. Neither could find any changes in the other. Three years, it seemed, was barely any time at all. It occurred to Asher abruptly that twenty years wouldn't have mattered. Her heart would still thud, her blood would still swim. For him. It had always, would always be for him. Quickly she pushed those thoughts aside. If she were to remain calm under his gaze, she couldn't afford to remember.

The press were still tossing questions at him, and now at her as well. They began to crowd in, nudging Asher closer to Ty. Without a word he took her arm and drew her through the door at his side. That it happened to be a woman's rest room didn't faze him as he turned the lock. He faced her, leaning lazily back against the door while Asher stood straight and tense.

As he had thirty minutes before, Ty took his time studying her. His eyes weren't calm, they rarely were, but the emotion in them was impossible to decipher. Even in his relaxed stance there was a sense of force, a storm brewing. Asher met his gaze levelly, as he expected. And she moved him. Her power of serenity always moved him. He could have strangled her for it.

"You haven't changed, Asher."

"You're wrong." Why could she no longer breathe easily or control the furious pace of her heart?

"Am I?" His brows disappeared under his tousled hair for a moment. "We'll see."

He was a very physical man. When he spoke, he gestured. When he held a conversation, he touched. Asher could remember the brush of his hand—on her arm, her hair, her shoulder. It had been his casualness that had drawn her to him. And had driven her away. Now, as they stood close, she was surprised that Ty did not touch her in any way. He simply watched and studied her.

"I noticed a change," she countered. "You didn't argue with the referees or shout at the line judge. Not once." Her lips curved slightly. "Not even after a bad call."

He gave her a lightly quizzical smile. "I turned over that leaf some time ago."

"Really?" She was uncomfortable now, but merely moved her shoulders. "I haven't been keeping up."

"Total amputation, Asher?" he asked softly.

"Yes." She would have turned away, but there was nowhere to go. Over the line of sinks to her left the mirrors tossed back her reflection…and his. Deliberately she shifted so that her back was to them. "Yes," she repeated, "it's the cleanest way."

"And now?"

"I'm going to play again," Asher responded simply. His scent was reaching out for her, that familiar, somehow heady fragrance that was sweat and victory and sex all tangled together. Beneath the placid expression her thoughts shot off in a tangent.

Nights, afternoons, rainy mornings. He'd shown her everything a man and woman could be together, opened doors she had never realized existed. He had knocked down every guard until he had found her.

Oh God, dear God, she thought frantically. Don't let him touch me now. Asher linked her fingers together. Though his eyes never left hers, Ty noted the gesture. And recognized it. He smiled.

"In Rome?"

Asher controlled the urge to swallow. "In Rome," she agreed. "To start. I'll go in unseeded. It has been three years."

"How's your backhand?"

"Good." Automatically she lifted her chin. "Better than ever."

Very deliberately Ty circled her arm with his fingers. Asher's palms became damp. "It was always a surprise," he commented, "the power in that slender arm. Still lifting weights?"

"Yes."

His fingers slid down until they circled the inside of her elbow. It gave him bitter pleasure to feel the tiny pulse jump erratically. "So," he murmured softly, "Lady Wickerton graces the courts again."

"Ms. Wolfe," Asher corrected him stiffly. "I've taken my maiden name back."

His glance touched on her ringless hands. "The divorce is final?"

"Quite final. Three months ago."

"Pity." His eyes had darkened with anger when he lifted them back to hers. "A title suits you so well. I imagine you fit into an English manor as easily as a piece of Wedgwood. Drawing rooms and butlers," he murmured, then scanned her face as if he would memorize it all over again. "You have the looks for them."

"The reporters are waiting for you." Asher made a move to her left in an attempt to brush by him. Ty's fingers clamped down.

"Why, Asher?" He'd promised himself if he ever saw her again, he wouldn't ask. It was a matter of pride. But pride was overwhelmed by temper as the question whipped out, stinging them both. "Why did you leave that way? Why did you run off and marry that damn English jerk without a word to me?"

She didn't wince at the pressure of his fingers, nor did she make any attempt to pull away. "That's my business."

"*Your* business?" The words were hardly out of her mouth before he grabbed both her arms. "*Your* business? We'd been together for months, the whole damn circuit that year. One night you're in my bed, and the next thing I know you've run off with some English lord." His control slipped another notch as he shook her. "I had to find out from my sister. You didn't even have the decency to dump me in person."

"Decency?" she tossed back. "I won't discuss decency with you, Ty." She swallowed the words, the accusations she'd promised herself never to utter. "I made my choice," she said levelly, "I don't have to justify it to you."

"We were lovers," he reminded her tightly. "We lived together for nearly six months."

"I wasn't the first woman in your bed."

"You knew that right from the start."

"Yes, I knew." She fought the urge to beat at him with the hopeless rage that was building inside her. "I made my choice then, just as I made one later. Now, let me go."

Her cool, cultured control had always fascinated and infuriated him. Ty knew her, better than anyone, even her own father—certainly better than her ex-husband. Inside, she was jelly, shuddering convulsively, but outwardly she was composed and lightly disdainful. Ty wanted to shake her until she rattled. More, much more, he wanted to taste her again—obliterate three years with one long greedy kiss. Desire and fury hammered at him. He knew that if he gave in to either, he'd never be able to stop. The wound was still raw.

"We're not finished, Asher." But his grip relaxed. "You still owe me."

"No." Defensive, outraged, she jerked free. "No, I don't owe you anything."

"Three years," he answered, and smiled. The smile was the

same biting challenge as before. "You owe me three years, and by God, you're going to pay."

He unlocked the door and opened it, stepping back so that Asher had no choice but to meet the huddle of reporters head-on.

"Asher, how does it feel to be back in the States?"

"It's good to be home."

"What about the rumors that you're going to play professionally again?"

"I intend to play professionally beginning with the opening of the European circuit in Rome."

More questions, more answers. The harsh glare of a flash causing light to dance in front of her eyes. The press always terrified her. She could remember her father's constant instructions: Don't say any more than absolutely necessary. Don't let them see what you're feeling. They'll devour you.

Churning inside, Asher faced the pack of avid reporters with apparent ease. Her voice was quiet and assured. Her fingers were locked tightly together. With a smile she glanced quickly down the hall, searching for an escape route. Ty leaned negligently against the wall and gave her no assistance.

"Will your father be in Rome to watch you play?"

"Possibly." An ache, a sadness, carefully concealed.

"Did you divorce Lord Wickerton so you could play again?"

"My divorce has nothing to do with my profession." A half-truth, a lingering anger, smoothly disguised.

"Are you nervous about facing young rackets like Kingston and old foes like Martinelli?"

"I'm looking forward to it." A terror, a well of doubt, easily masked.

"Will you and Starbuck pair up again?"

Fury, briefly exposed.

"Starbuck's a singles player," she managed after a moment.

"You guys'll have to keep your eyes open to see if that changes." With his own brand of nonchalance, Ty slipped an arm around Asher's rigid shoulders. "There's no telling what might happen, is there, Asher?"

Her answer was an icy smile. "You've always been more unpredictable than I have, Ty."

He met the smile with one of his own. "Have I?" Leaning down, he brushed her lips lightly. Flashbulbs popped in a blaze of excitement. Even as their lips met, so did their eyes. Hers were twin slits of fury, his grimly laughing and ripe with purpose. Lazily he straightened. "The Face and I have some catching up to do."

"In Rome?" a reporter cracked.

Ty grinned and quite deliberately drew Asher closer. "That's where it started."

Chapter Two

Rome. The Colosseum. The Trevi fountain. The Vatican. Ancient history, tragedy and triumphs. Gladiators and competition. In the Foro Italico the steaming Italian sun beat down on the modern-day competitors just as it had on those of the Empire. To play in this arena was a theatrical experience. It was sun and space. There were lush umbrella pines and massive statues to set the forum apart from any other on the circuit. Beyond the stadium, wooded hills rose from the Tiber. Within its hedge trimmings, ten thousand people could chant, shout and whistle. Italian tennis fans were an emotional, enthusiastic and blatantly patriotic lot. Asher hadn't forgotten.

Nor had she forgotten that the Foro Italico had been the setting for the two biggest revelations in her life: her consuming love for tennis, her overwhelming love for Ty Starbuck.

She had been seven the first time she had watched her father win the Italian championship in the famed *campo central*. Of course she had seen him play before. One of her earliest memories was of watching her tall, tanned father dash around a court in blazing white. Jim Wolfe had been a champion before Asher had been born, and a force to be reckoned with long after.

Her own lessons had begun at the age of three. With her shortened racket she had hit balls to some of the greatest players of her father's generation. Her looks and her poise had made her a pet among the athletes. She grew up finding nothing unusual about seeing her picture in the paper or bouncing on the knee of a Davis Cup champion. Tennis and travel ruled her world. She had napped in the rear of limousines and walked across the pampered grass of Wimbledon. She had curtsied to heads of state and had her cheek pinched by a president. Before she began attending school she had already crossed the Atlantic a half dozen times.

But it had been in Rome, a year after the death of her mother, that Asher Wolfe had found a life's love and ambition.

Her father had still been wet and glowing from his victory, his white shorts splattered with the red dust of the court, when she had told him she would play in the *campo central* one day. And win.

Perhaps it had been a father's indulgence for his only child, or his ambition. Or perhaps it had been the quietly firm determination he saw in seven-year-old eyes. But Asher's journey had begun that day, with her father as her guide and her mentor.

Fourteen years later, after her own defeat in the semi-finals, Asher had watched Starbuck's victory. There had been nothing similar in the style of her father and the style of the new champion. Jim Wolfe had played a meticulous game—cold control with the accent on form. Starbuck played like a fireball—all emotion and muscle. Often, Asher had speculated on what the results would be if the two men were to meet across a net. Where her father brought her pride, Ty brought her excitement. Watching him, she could understand the sense of sexuality onlookers experienced during a bullfight. Indeed, there was a thirst for blood in his style that both alarmed and fascinated.

Ty had pursued her doggedly for months, but she had held him off. His reputation with women, his temper, his flamboyance and nonconformity had both attracted and repulsed her. Though the attraction was strong, and her heart was already lost, Asher had sensibly listened to her head. Until that day in May.

He'd been like a god, a powerful, mythological warrior with a strength and power that even the biased Italian crowd couldn't resist. Some cheered him, some cheerfully cursed him. He'd given them the sweat they had come to see. And the show.

Ty had taken the championship in seven frenzied sets. That night Asher had given him both her innocence and her love. For the first time in her life she had allowed her heart complete freedom. Like a blossom kept in the sheltered, controlled climate of a hothouse, she took to the sun and storm wildly. Days were steamier and more passionate—nights both turbulent and tender. Then the season had ended.

Now, as Asher practiced in the early morning lull on court five, the memories stirred, sweet and bitter as old wine. Fast rides on back roads, hot beaches, dim hotel rooms, foolish laughter, crazy loving. Betrayal.

"If you dream like that this afternoon, Kingston's going to wipe you out of the quarter-finals."

At the admonishment, Asher snapped back. "Sorry."

"You should be, when an old lady drags herself out of bed at six to hit to you."

Asher laughed. At thirty-three, Madge Haverbeck was still a force to be reckoned with across a net. Small and stocky, with flyaway brown hair and comfortably attractive features, she looked like an ad for home-baked cookies. She was, in fact, a world-class player with two Wimbledon championships, a decade of other victories that included the Wightman Cup and a wicked forehand smash. For two years Asher had been her doubles partner to their mutual satisfaction and success. Her husband was a sociology professor at Yale whom Madge affectionately termed "The Dean."

"Maybe you should sit down and have a nice cup of tea," Asher suggested while tucking her tongue in her cheek. "This game's rough on middle-aged matrons."

After saying something short and rude, Madge sent a bullet over the net. Light and agile, Asher sprang after it. Her concentration focused. Her muscles went to work. In the drowsy morning hum the ball thudded on clay and twanged off strings. Madge wasn't a woman to consider a practice workout incidental. She hustled over the court, driving Asher back to the baseline, luring her to the net, hammering at her by mixing her shots while Asher concentrated on adjusting her pace to the slow, frustrating clay.

For a fast, aggressive player, the surface could be deadly. It took strength and endurance rather than speed. Asher thanked the endless hours of weight lifting as she swung the racket again and again. The muscles in the slender arm were firm.

After watching one of Asher's returns scream past, Madge

shifted her racket to her left hand. “You’re pretty sharp for three years off, Face.”

Asher filled her lungs with air. “I’ve kept my hand in.”

Though Madge wondered avidly about Asher’s marriage and years of self-imposed retirement, she knew her former partner too well to question. “Kingston hates to play the net. It’s her biggest weakness.”

“I know.” Asher slipped the spare ball in her pocket. “I’ve studied her. Today she’s going to play my game.”

“She’s better on clay than grass.”

It was a roundabout way of reminding Asher of her own weakness. She gave Madge one of her rare, open smiles. “It won’t matter. Next week I’m playing center court.”

Slipping on a warm-up jacket, Madge gave a hoot of laughter. “Haven’t changed much, have you?”

“Bits and pieces.” Asher dabbed at sweat with her wristband. “What about you? How’re you going to play Fortini?”

“My dear.” Madge fluffed at her hair. “I’ll simply overpower her.”

Asher snorted as they strolled off the court. “You haven’t changed either.”

“If you’d told me you were coming back,” Madge put in, “we’d be playing doubles. Fisher’s good, and I like her, but…”

“I couldn’t make the decision until I was sure I wouldn’t make a fool of myself.” Slowly Asher flexed her racket arm. “Three years, Madge. I ache.” She sighed with the admission. “I don’t remember if I ached like this before.”

“We can trade legs any time you say, Face.”

Remembering, Asher turned with a look of concern. “How’s the knee?”

"Better since the surgery last year." Madge shrugged. "I can still forecast rain though. Here's to a sunny season."

"I'm sorry I wasn't there for you."

Madge hooked her arm through Asher's in easy comradeship. "Naturally I expected you to travel six thousand miles to hold my hand."

"I would have if…" Asher trailed off, remembering the state of her marriage at the time of Madge's surgery.

Recognizing guilt, Madge gave Asher a friendly nudge with her elbow. "It wasn't as big a deal as the press made out. Of course," she added with a grin, "I milked it for a lot of sympathy. The Dean brought me breakfast in bed for two months. Bless his heart."

"Then you came back and demolished Rayski in New York."

"Yeah." Madge laughed with pleasure. "I enjoyed that."

Asher let her gaze wander over the serene arena, quiet but for the thud of balls and hum of bees. "I have to win this one, Madge. I need it. There's so much to prove."

"To whom?"

"Myself first." Asher moved her shoulders restlessly, shifting her bag to her left hand. "And a few others."

"Starbuck? No, don't answer," Madge continued, seeing Asher's expression out of the corner of her eye. "It just sort of slipped out."

"What was between Ty and me was finished three years ago," Asher stated, deliberately relaxing her muscles.

"Too bad." Madge weathered Asher's glare easily. "I like him."

"Why?"

Stopping, Madge met the direct look. "He's one of the most alive people I know. Ever since he learned to control his temper, he brings so such emotion to the courts. It's good for the game. You don't have a stale tournament when Starbuck's around. He also brings that same emotion into his friendships."

"Yes," Asher agreed. "It can be overwhelming."

"I didn't say he was easy," Madge countered. "I said I liked him. He is exactly who he is. There isn't a lot of phony business to cut through to get to Starbuck." Madge squinted up at the sun. "I suppose some of it comes from the fact that we turned pro the same year, did our first circuit together. Anyway, I've watched him grow from a cocky kid with a smart mouth to a cocky man who manages to keep that wicked temper just under the surface."

"You like him for his temper?"

"Partly." The mild, homey-looking woman smiled. "Starbuck's just plain strung right, Asher. He's not a man you can be ambivalent about. You're either for him or against him."

It was as much inquiry as statement. Saying nothing, Asher began to walk again. Ambivalence had never entered into her feeling for Ty.

On his way home from his own practice court Ty watched them. More accurately he watched Asher. While she remained unaware of him, he could take in every detail. The morning sun glinted down on her hair. Her shoulders were strong and slender, her gait long, leggy and confident. He was grateful he could study her now with some dispassion.

When he had looked out and had seen her in the stands two weeks before, it had been like catching a fast ball with his stomach. Shimmering waves of pain, shock, anger, one sensation had raced after the other. He had blown the first set.

Then he had done more than pull himself together. He had used the emotions against his opponent. The Frenchman hadn't had a chance against Ty's skill combined with three years of pent-up fury. Always, he played his best under pressure and stress. It fed him. With Asher in the audience the match had become a matter of life and death. When she had left him she'd stolen something from him. Somehow, the victory had helped him regain a portion of it.

Damn her that she could still get to him. Ty's thoughts darkened as the distance between them decreased. Just looking at her made him want.

He had wanted her when she had been seventeen. The sharp, sudden desire for a teenager had astonished the then twenty-three-year-old Ty. He had kept a careful distance from her all that season. But he hadn't stopped wanting her. He had done his best to burn the desire out by romancing women he considered more his style—flamboyant, reckless, knowledgeable.

When Asher had turned twenty-one Ty had abandoned common sense and had begun a determined, almost obsessive pursuit. The more she had evaded him, the firmer she refused, the stronger his desire had grown. Even the victory, tasted first in Rome, hadn't lessened his need.

His life, which previously had had one focus, then had realigned with two dominating forces. Tennis and Asher. At the time he wouldn't have said he loved tennis, but simply that it was what and who he was. He wouldn't have said he loved Asher, but merely that he couldn't live without her.

Yet he had had to—when she'd left him to take another man's

name. A title and a feather bed, Ty thought grimly. He was determined to make Asher Wolfe pay for bringing him a pain he had never expected to feel.

By turning left and altering his pace Ty cut across her path, apparently by chance. "Hi, Madge." He gave the brunette a quick grin, flicking his finger down her arm before turning his attention fully to Asher.

"Hiya, Starbuck." Madge glanced from the man to the woman and decided she wasn't needed. "Hey, I'm late," she said by way of explanation, then trotted off. Neither Asher nor Ty commented.

From somewhere in the surrounding trees Asher heard the high clear call of a bird. Nearer at hand was the slumberous buzz of bees and dull thud of balls. On court three, someone cursed fluently. But Asher was conscious only of Ty beside her.

"Just like old times," he murmured, then grinned at her expression. "You and Madge," he added.

Asher struggled not to be affected. The setting had too many memories. "She hit to me this morning. I hope I don't have to face her in the tournament."

"You go against Kingston today."

"Yes."

He took a step closer. In her mind's eye Asher saw the hedge beside her. With Ty directly in her path, dignified retreat was impossible. For all her delicacy of looks, Asher didn't run from a battle. She linked her fingers, then dragged them apart, annoyed.

"And you play Devereux."

His acknowledgment was a nod. "Is your father coming?"

"No." The answer was flat and brief. Ty had never been one to be put off by a subtle warning.

"Why?"

"He's busy." She started to move by him, but succeeded only in closing the rest of the distance between them. Maneuvering was one of the best aspects of Ty's game.

"I've never known him to miss one of your major tournaments." In an old habit he couldn't resist nor she prevent, he reached for her hair. "You were always his first order of business."

"Things change," she responded stiffly. "People change."

"So it seems." His grin was sharp and cocky. "Will your husband be here?"

"Ex-husband." Asher tossed her head to dislodge his hand. "And no."

"Funny, as I recall he was very fond of tennis." Casually he set down his bag. "Has that changed too?"

"I need to shower." Asher had drawn nearly alongside of him before Ty stopped her. His hand slipped to her waist too quickly and too easily.

"How about a quick set for old times' sake?"

His eyes were intense—that oddly compelling color that was half night and half day. Asher remembered how they seemed to darken from the pupils out when he was aroused. The hand at her waist was wide-palmed and long-fingered—a concert pianist's hand, but it was rough and worked. The strength in it would have satisfied a prizefighter.

"I don't have time." Asher pushed to free herself and connected with the rock-hard muscles of his forearm. She pulled her fingers back as though she'd been burned.

"Afraid?" There was mockery and a light threat with the overtones of sex. Her blood heated to the force she had never been able to fully resist.

"I've never been afraid of you." And it was true enough. She had been fascinated.

"No?" He spread his fingers, drawing her an inch closer. "Fear's one of the popular reasons for running away."

"I didn't run," she corrected him. "I left." *Before you did,* she added silently. For once, she had outmaneuvered him.

"You still have some questions to answer, Asher." His arm slid around her before she could step back. "I've waited a long time for the answers."

"You'll go on waiting."

"For some," he murmured in agreement. "But I'll have the answer to one now."

She saw it coming and did nothing. Later she would curse herself for her passivity. But when he lowered his mouth to hers, she met it without resistance. Time melted away.

He had kissed her like this the first time—slowly, thoroughly, gently. It was another part of the enigma that a man so full of energy and turbulence could show such sensitivity. His mouth was exactly as Asher remembered. Warm, soft, full. Perhaps she had been lost the first time he had kissed her—drawn to the fury—captured by the tenderness. Even when he brought her closer, deepening the kiss with a low-throated groan, the sweetness never diminished.

As a lover he excelled because beneath the brash exterior was an underlying and deep-rooted respect for femininity. He enjoyed the softness, tastes and textures of women, and instinctively sought to bring them pleasure in lovemaking. As an inherent loner, it was another contradiction that Ty saw a lover as a partner, never a means to an end. Asher had sensed this from the first touch so many years ago. Now she let herself drown in the kiss with one final coherent thought. It had been so long.

Her arm, which should have pushed him away, curved up his back instead until her hand reached his shoulders. Her fingers grasped at him. Unhesitatingly she pressed her body to his. He was the one man who could touch off the passion she had so carefully locked inside. The only man who had ever reached her core and gained true intimacy—the meeting of minds as well as of bodies. Starved for the glimpses of joy she remembered, Asher clung while her mouth moved avidly on his. Her greed for more drove away all her reserve, and all her promises.

Oh, to be loved again, truly loved, with none of the emptiness that had haunted her life for too long! To give herself, to take, to know the pure, searing joy of belonging! The thoughts danced in her mind like dreams suddenly remembered. With a moan, a sigh, she pressed against him, hungry for what had been.

The purpose of the kiss had been to punish, but he'd forgotten. The hot-blooded passion that could spring from the cool, contained woman had forced all else from his mind but need. He needed her, still needed her, and was infuriated. If they had been alone, he would have taken her and then faced the consequences. His impulses were still difficult to control. But they weren't alone.

Some small part of his mind clung to reality even while his body pulsed. She was soft and eager. Everything he had ever wanted. All he had done without. Ty discovered he had gotten more answers than he'd bargained for.

Drawing her away, he took his time studying her face. Who could resist the dangerous power of a hurricane? The wicked, primitive rumblings of a volcano? She stared at him, teetering between sanity and desire.

Her eyes were huge and aware, her lips parted breathlessly. It was a look he remembered. Long nights in her bed, hurried afternoons or lazy mornings, she would look at him so just before loving. Hot and insistent, desire spread, then closed like a fist in his stomach. He stepped back so that they were no longer touching.

"Some things change," he remarked. "And some things don't," he added before turning to walk away.

There was time for deep breathing before Asher took her position for the first serve. It wasn't the thousand pairs of eyes watching around the court that had her nerves jumping. It was one pair, dark brown and intense, seventy-eight feet away. Stacie Kingston, age twenty, hottest newcomer to the game in two years. She had energy, force and drive, along with a fierce will to win. Asher recognized her very well. The red clay spread out before her, waiting.

Because she knew the importance of mastering the skittish nerves and flood of doubts, she continued to take long, deep breaths. Squeezing the small white ball, Asher discovered the true meaning of trial by fire. If she won, here where she had never won before, three years after she had last lifted a racket professionally, she would have passed the test. Rome, it seemed, would always be her turning point.

Because it was the only way, she blocked out the past, blocked out tomorrow and focused wholly on the contest. Tossing the ball up, she watched the ascent, then struck home. Her breath came out in a hiss of effort.

Kingston played a strong, offensive game. A studied, meticulous player, she understood and used the personality of clay to her advantage, forcing Asher to the baseline again and again. Asher found the dirt frustrating. It cut down on her speed. She was hurrying, defending herself. The awareness of this only made her rush more. The ball eluded her, bouncing high over her head when she raced to the net, dropping lazily into the forecourt when she hugged the baseline. Unnerved by her own demons, she double-faulted. Kingston won the first game, breaking Asher's serve and allowing her only one point.

The crowd was vocal, the sun ferocious. The air was thick with humidity. From the other side of the hedge Asher could hear the games and laughter of schoolchildren. She wanted to throw aside her racket and walk off the court. It was a mistake, a mistake, her mind repeated, to have come back. Why had she subjected herself to this again? To the effort and pain and humiliation?

Her face was utterly passive, showing none of the turmoil. Gripping the racket tightly, she fought off the weakness. She had played badly, she knew, because she had permitted Kingston to set the pace. It had taken Asher less than six minutes from first service to defeat. Her skin wasn't even damp. She hadn't come back to give up after one game, nor had she come back to be humiliated. The stands were thick with people watching, waiting. She had only herself.

Flicking a hand at the short skirt of her tennis dress, she walked back to the baseline. Crouched, she shifted her weight to the balls of her feet. Anger with herself was forced back. Fear was conquered. A cool head was one of her greatest weapons, and one she hadn't used in the first game. This time, she was determined. This time, the game would be played her way.

She returned the serve with a drop shot over the net that caught Kingston off balance. The crowd roared its approval as the ball boy scurried across the court to scoop up the dead ball.

Love-fifteen. Asher translated the scoring in her head with grim satisfaction. Fear had cost her the first game. Now, in her own precise way, she was out for blood. Kingston became more symbol than opponent.

Asher continued to draw her opponent into the net, inciting fierce volleys that brought the crowd to its feet. The roar and babble of languages did not register with her. She saw only the ball, heard only the effortful breathing that was hers. She ended that volley with a neatly placed ball that smacked clean at the edge of the baseline.

Something stirred in her—the hot, bubbling juice of victory. Asher tasted it, reveled in it as she walked coolly back to position. Her face was wet now, so she brushed her wristband over her brow before she cupped the two service balls in her hand. Only the beginning, she told herself. Each game was its own beginning.

By the end of the first set the court surface was zigzagged with skid marks. Red dust streaked the snowy material of her dress and marked her shoes. Sweat rolled down her sides after thirty-two minutes of ferocious play. But she'd taken the first set six-three.

Adrenaline was pumping madly, though Asher looked no more flustered than a woman about to hostess a dinner party. The competitive drives she had buried were in complete control. Part of her sensed Starbuck was watching. She no longer cared. At that moment Asher felt that if she had faced him across the net, she could have beaten him handily. When Kingston returned her serve deep, Asher met it with a topspin backhand that brushed the top of the net. Charging after the ball, she met the next return with a powerful lob.

The sportswriters would say that it was at that moment, when the two women were eye to eye, that Asher won the match. They remained that way for seconds only, without words, but communication had been made. From then Asher dominated, forcing Kingston into a defensive game. She set a merciless pace. When she lost a point she came back to take two. The aggressiveness was back, the cold-blooded warfare the sportswriters remembered with pleasure from her early years on the court.

Where Starbuck was fire and flash, she was ice and control. Never once during a professional match had Asher lost her iron grip on her temper. It had once been a game among the sportswriters—waiting for The Face to cut loose.

Only twice during the match did she come close to giving them satisfaction, once on a bad call and once on her own poor judgment of a shot. Both times she stared down at her racket until the urge to stomp and swear had passed. When she had again taken her position, there had been nothing but cool determination in her eyes.

She took the match six-one, six-two in an hour and forty-nine minutes. Twice she had held Kingston's service to love. Three times she had served aces—something Kingston with her touted superserve had been unable to accomplish. Asher Wolfe would go on to the semi-finals. She had made her comeback.

Madge dropped a towel over Asher's shoulders as she collapsed on her chair. "Good God, you were terrific! You destroyed her." Asher said nothing, covering her face with the towel a moment to absorb sweat. "I swear, you're better than you were before."

"She wanted to win," Asher murmured, letting the towel drop limply again. "I *had* to win."

"It showed," Madge agreed, giving her shoulder a quick rub. "Nobody'd believe you haven't played pro in three years. I hardly believe it myself."

Slowly Asher lifted her face to her old partner. "I'm not in shape yet, Madge," she said beneath the din of the still-cheering crowd. "My calves are knotted. I don't even know if I can stand up again."

Madge skimmed a critical glance over Asher's features. She couldn't detect a flicker of pain. Bending, she scooped up Asher's warm-up jacket, then draped it over Asher's shoulders. "I'll help you to the showers. I don't play for a half hour. You just need a few minutes on the massage table."

Exhausted, hurting, Asher started to agree, then spotted Ty

watching her. His grin might have been acknowledgment of her victory. But he knew her, Asher reflected, knew her inside as no one else did.

"No thanks, I'll manage." Effortfully she rose to zip the cover around her racket. "I'll see you after you beat Fortini."

"Asher—"

"No, really, I'm fine now." Head high, muscles screaming, she walked toward the tunnel that led to the locker rooms.

Alone in the steam of the showers, Asher let herself empty, weeping bitterly for no reason she could name.

Chapter Three

It was the night after her victory in the semi-finals that Asher confronted Ty again. She had kept herself to a rigorous schedule of practice, exercise, press, and play. Her pacing purposely left her little time for recreation. Practice was a religion. Morning hours were spent in the peaceful tree-shaded court five, grooving in, polishing her footwork, honing her reflexes.

Exercise was a law. Push-ups and weight lifting, stretching and hardening the muscles. Good press was more than a balm for the ego. Press was important to the game as a whole as well as the individual player. And the press loved a winner.

Play was what the athlete lived for. Pure competition—the testing of the skills of the body, the use of the skills of the mind. The best played as the best dancers danced—for the love of it. During the days of her second debut, Asher rediscovered love.

In her one brief morning meeting with Ty she had rediscovered passion. Only her fierce concentration on her profession kept her from dwelling on a need that had never died. Rome was a city for lovers—it had been once for her. Asher knew that this time she must think of it only as a city for competition if she was to survive the first hurdle of regaining her identity. Lady Wickerton was a woman she hardly recognized. She had nearly lost Asher Wolfe trying to fit an image. How could she recapture herself if she once again became Starbuck's lady?

In a small club in the Via Sistina where the music was loud and the wine was abundant, Asher sat at a table crowded with bodies. Elbows nudged as glasses were reached for. Liquor spilled and was cheerfully cursed. In the second and final week of the Italian Open, the tension grew, but the pace mercifully slowed.

Rome was noise, fruit stands, traffic, outdoor cafés. Rome was serenity, cathedrals, antiquity. For the athletes it was days of grueling competition and nights of celebration or commiseration. The next match was a persistent shadow over the thoughts of the winners and the losers. As the music blared and the drinks were poured, they discussed every serve, every smash and error and every bad call. Rome was blissfully indolent over its reputation for bad calls.

"Long!" A dark, lanky Australian brooded into his wine. "That ball was inside by two inches. Two bloody inches."

"You won the game, Michael," Madge reminded him philosophically. "And in the second game of the fifth set, you had a wide ball that wasn't called."

The Australian grinned and shrugged. "It was only a little wide." He brought his thumb and forefinger close together at the good-natured razzing of his peers. "What about this one?" His gesture was necessarily shortened by the close quarters as he lifted a drink toward Asher. "She beats an Italian in the Foro Italico, and the crowd still cheers her."

"Breeding," Asher returned with a mild smile. "The fans always recognize good breeding."

Michael snorted before he swallowed the heavy red wine. "Since when does a bloody steamroller need breeding?" he countered. "You flattened her." To emphasize his point he slammed a palm down on the table and ground it in.

"Yeah." Her smile widened in reminiscent pleasure. "I did, didn't I?" She sipped her dry, cool wine. The match had been longer and more demanding than her first with Kingston, but her body had rebelled a bit less afterward. Asher considered it a double victory.

"Tia Conway will go for your jugular," he said pleasantly, then called to his countrywoman at a nearby table. "Hey, Tia, you gonna beat this nasty American?"

A dark, compact woman with striking black eyes glanced over. The two women measured each other slowly before Tia lifted her glass in salute. Asher responded in kind before the group fell back to its individual conversations. With the music at high volume, they shouted to be heard, but words carried only a foot.

"A nice woman," Michael began, "off the court. On it, she's a devil. Off, she grows petunias and rosemary. Her husband sells swimming pools."

Madge chuckled. "You make that sound like a misdemeanor."

"I bought one," he said ruefully, then looked back at Asher. She was listening with half an ear to the differing opinions on either side of her of a match by two players. "Still, if I played mixed doubles, I'd want Face for a partner." Asher acknowledged this with a curious lift of a brow. "Tia plays like a demon, but you have better court sense. And," he added as he downed more wine, "better legs."

For this Madge punched him in the shoulder. "What about me?"

"You have perhaps the best court sense of any female world-class player," Michael decided slowly. "But," he continued as Madge accepted her due with a regal nod, "you have legs like a shotputter."

A roar of laughter rose up over Madge's indignation. Asher leaned back in her chair, enjoying the loosening freedom of mirth as Madge challenged Michael to show his own and be judged. At that moment Asher's eyes locked with Ty's. Her laughter died unnoticed by her companions.

He'd come in late and alone. His hair was unruly, as though he had ridden in a fast car with the top down. Even completely relaxed, dressed in jeans, his hands in his pockets, some aura of excitement swirled around him. In the dim light his face was shadowed, all hollows and planes, with his eyes dark and knowing. No woman could be immune to him. A former lover was helpless not to remember what magic his mouth could perform.

Asher sat still as a stone—marble, pale and elegant in the rowdy, smoke-curtained bar. She couldn't forget any more than she could stop wanting. All she could do was refuse, as she had three years before.

Without taking his eyes from hers Ty crossed the room, skirted crowded tables. He had Asher by the arm, drawing her to her feet before the rest of the group had greeted him.

"We'll dance." It was a command formed in the most casual tones. As on court, Asher's decision had to be made in a tenth of a second. To refuse would have incited speculative gossip. To agree meant she had her own demons to deal with.

"I'd love to," she said coolly, and went with him.

The band played a slow ballad at ear-splitting volume. The vocalist was flat, and tried to make up for it by being loud. Someone knocked a glass off a table with a splintering crash. There was a pungent scent of spilled wine. A bricklayer argued with a Mexican tennis champion on the proper way to handle a topspin lob. Someone was smoking a pipe filled with richly sweet cherry tobacco. The floorboards were slightly warped.

Ty gathered her into his arms as though she had never been away. "The last time we were here," he murmured in her ear, "we sat at that corner table and drank a bottle of Valpolicella."

"I remember."

"You wore the same perfume you're wearing now." His lips grazed her temple as he drew her closer. Asher felt the bones in her legs liquefy, the muscles in her thighs loosen. "Like sun-warmed petals." Her heartbeat was a light, uncertain flutter against his. "Do you remember what we did afterward?"

"We walked."

The two hoarsely spoken words seemed to shiver along his skin. It was impossible to keep his mouth from seeking small tastes of her. "Until sunrise." His breath feathered intimately at her ear. "The city was all rose and gold, and I wanted you so badly, I nearly exploded. You wouldn't let me love you then."

"I don't want to go back." Asher tried to push away, but his arms kept her pressed tight against him. It seemed every line of his body knew every curve of hers.

"Why? Because you might remember how good we were together?"

"Ty, stop it." She jerked her head back—a mistake as his lips cruised lazily over hers.

"We'll be together again, Asher." He spoke quietly. The words seemed to sear into the tender flesh of her lips. "Even if it's only once…for old times' sake."

"It's over, Ty." The claim was a whisper, the whisper unsteady.

"Is it?" His eyes darkened as he pressed her against him almost painfully. "Remember, Asher, I know you, inside out. Did your husband ever find out who you really are? Did he know how to make you laugh? How," he added in a low murmur, "to make you moan?"

She stiffened. The music whirled around them, fast now with an insistent bass beat. Ty held her firmly against him, barely swaying at all. "I won't discuss my marriage with you."

"I damn well don't want to know about your *marriage*." He said the word as if it were an obscenity as his fingers dug into the small of her back. Fury was taking over though he'd sworn he wouldn't let it. He could still get to her. Yes, yes, that was a fact, he knew, but no more than she could still get to him. "Why did you come back?" he demanded. "Why the hell did you come back?"

"To play tennis." Her fingers tightened on his shoulder. "To win." Anger was growing in her as well. It appeared he was the only man who could make her forget herself enough to relinquish control. "I have every right to be here, every right to do what I was trained to do. I don't owe you explanations."

"You owe me a hell of a lot more." It gave him a certain grim satisfaction to see the fury in her eyes. He wanted to push. Wanted to see her anger. "You're going to pay for the three years you played lady of the manor."

"You don't know anything about it." Her breath came short and fast. Her eyes were nearly cobalt. "I paid, Starbuck, I paid more than you can imagine. Now I've finished, do you understand?" To his surprise, her voice broke on a sob. Quickly she shook her head and fought back tears. "I've finished paying for my mistakes."

"What mistakes?" he demanded. Frustrated, he took her by the shoulders. "What mistakes, Asher?"

"You." She drew in her breath sharply, as if stepping back from a steep edge. "Oh, God, you."

Turning, she fought her way through the swarm of enthusiastic dancers. Even as she sprang out into the sultry night Ty whirled her around. "Let me go!" She struck out blindly, but he grabbed her wrist.

"You're not going to walk out on me again." His voice was dangerously low. "Not ever again."

"Did it hurt your pride, Ty?" Emotion erupted from her, blazing as it could only from one who constantly denied it. "Did it hurt your ego that a woman could turn her back on you and choose someone else?"

Pain ripped through him and took over. “I never had your kind of pride, Asher.” He dragged her against him, needing to prove he had some kind of power over her, even if it was only physical. “The kind you wear so that no one can see you’re human. Did you run because I knew you? Because in bed I could make you forget to be the perfect lady?”

“I left because I didn’t want you!” Completely unstrung, she shouted, pounding with her free hand. “I didn’t want—”

He cut her off with a furious kiss. Their tempers soared with vivid passion. Anger sizzled in two pairs of lips that clung because they were helpless to do otherwise. There was never any choice when they were together. It had been so almost from the first, and the years had changed nothing. She could resist him, resist herself, for only so long. The outcome was inevitable.

Suddenly greedy, Asher pressed against him. Here was the sound and the speed. Here was the storm. Here was home. His hair was thick and soft between her questing fingers, his body rock-hard against the firmness of hers. His scent was his “off-court” fragrance—something sharp and bracing that she’d always liked.

The first taste was never enough to satisfy her, so she probed deeper into his mouth, tongue demanding, teeth nipping in the way he himself had taught her. A loud crash of brass from the band rattled the windows behind them. Asher heard only Ty’s moan of quiet desperation. Between the shadows and the moonlight they clung, passion building, old needs merging with new.

Her breath trembled into the night as he took a crazed

journey of her face. His hands slid up until his thumbs hooked gently under her chin. It was a familiar habit, one of his more disarming. Asher whispered his name half in plea, half in acceptance before his mouth found hers again. He drew her into him, slowly, inevitably, while his fingers skimmed along her cheekbones. The more tempestuous the kiss, the more tender his touch. Asher fretted for the strong, sure stroke of his hands on her body.

Full circle, she thought dizzily. She had come full circle. But if once before in Rome she had been frightened when his kisses had drained and exhilarated her, now she was terrified.

"Please, Ty." Asher turned her head until her brow rested on his shoulder. "Please, don't do this."

"I didn't do it alone," he muttered.

Slowly she lifted her head. "I know."

It was the vulnerability in her eyes that kept him from dragging her back to him. Just as it had been her vulnerability all those years before that had prevented him taking her. He had waited for her to come to him. The same would hold true this time, he realized. Cursing potently under his breath, Ty released her.

"You've always known how to hold me off, haven't you, Asher?"

Knowing the danger had passed, she let out an unsteady breath. "Self-preservation."

Ty gave an unexpected laugh as his hands dove for his pockets. "It might have been easier if you'd managed to get fat and ugly over the last three years. I wanted to think you had."

A hint of a smile played on her mouth. So his moods could

change, she thought, just as quickly as ever. "Should I apologize for not accommodating you?"

"Probably wouldn't have made any difference if you had." His eyes met hers again, then roamed her face. "Just looking at you—it still takes my breath away." His hands itched to touch. He balled them into fists inside his pockets. "You haven't even changed your hair."

This time the smile bloomed. "Neither have you. You still need a trim."

He grinned. "You were always conservative."

"You were always unconventional."

He gave a low appreciative laugh, one she hadn't heard in much too long. "You've mellowed," he decided. "You used to say radical."

"*You've* mellowed," Asher corrected him. "It used to be true."

With a shrug he glanced off into the night. "I used to be twenty."

"Age, Starbuck?" Sensing a disturbance, Asher automatically sought to soothe it.

"Inevitably." He brought his eyes back to hers. "It's a young game."

"Ready for your rocking chair?" Asher laughed, forgetting caution as she reached up to touch his cheek. Though she snatched her hand away instantly, his eyes had darkened. "I—" She searched for a way to ease the fresh tension. "You didn't seem to have any problem smashing Bigelow in the semi-finals. He's what, twenty-four?"

"It went to seven sets." His hand came out of his pocket. Casually he ran the back of it up her throat.

"You like it best that way."

He felt her swallow quickly, nervously, though her eyes remained level. "Come back with me, Asher," he murmured. "Come with me now." It cost him to ask, but only he was aware of how much.

"I can't."

"Won't," he countered.

From down the street came a high-pitched stream of Italian followed by a bellow of laughter. Inside the club the band murdered a popular American tune. She could smell the heat-soaked fragrance of the window-box geraniums above their heads. And she could remember, remember too well, the sweetness that could be hers if she crossed the line. And the pain.

"Ty." Asher hesitated, then reached up to grasp the hand that lingered at her throat. "A truce, please. For our mutual benefit," she added when his fingers interlaced possessively with hers. "With us both going into the finals, we don't need this kind of tension right now."

"Save it for later?" He brought her reluctant hand to his lips, watching her over it. "Then we pick this up in Paris."

"I didn't mean—"

"We deal now or later, Face, but we deal." He grinned again, tasting challenge, tasting victory. "Take it or leave it."

"You're just as infuriating as ever."

"Yeah." The grin only widened. "That's what keeps me number one."

On an exasperated laugh, Asher let her hand relax in his. "Truce, Starbuck?"

He let his thumb glide back and forth over her knuckles.

"Agreed, on one condition." Sensing her withdrawal, he continued. "One question, Asher. Answer one question."

She tried to wrest her hand away and failed. "What question?" she demanded impatiently.

"Were you happy?"

She became very still as quick flashes of the past raced through her head. "You have no right—"

"I have every right," he interrupted. "I'm going to know that, Asher. The truth."

She stared at him, wanting to pit her will against his. Abruptly she found she had no energy for it. "No," she said wearily. "No."

He should have felt triumph, and instead felt misery. Releasing her hand, he stared out at the street. "I'll get you a cab."

"No. No, I'll walk. I want to walk."

Ty watched her move into the flood of a streetlight and back into the dark. Then she was a shadow, disappearing.

The streets were far from empty. Traffic whizzed by at the pace that seemed the pride of European cities. Small, fast cars and daredevil taxis. People scattered on the sidewalks, rushing toward some oasis of nightlife. Still, Ty thought he could hear the echo of his own footsteps.

Perhaps it was because so many feet had walked the Roman streets for so many centuries. Ty didn't care much for history or tradition. Tennis history perhaps—Gonzales, Gibson, Perry, these names meant more to him than Caesar, Cicero or Caligula. He rarely thought of his own past, much less of antiquity. Ty was a man who focused on the present. Until Asher had come back into his life, he had thought little about tomorrow.

In his youth he had concentrated fiercely on the future, and what he would do if… Now that he had done it, Ty had come to savor each day at a time. Still, the future was closing in on him, and the past was never far behind.

At ten he had been a hustler. Skinny and streetwise, he had talked his way out of trouble when it was possible, and slugged his way out when it wasn't. Growing up in the tough South Side of Chicago, Ty had been introduced to the seamier side of life early. He'd tasted his first beer when he should have been studying rudimentary math. What had saved him from succumbing to the streets was his dislike and distrust of organized groups. Gangs had held no appeal for Ty. He had no desire to lead or to follow. Still, he might have chosen a less honorable road had it not been for his unquestioning love for his family.

His mother, a quiet, determined woman who worked nights cleaning office buildings, was precious to him. His sister, four years his junior, was his pride and self-assumed responsibility. There was no father, and even the memory of him had faded before Ty reached mid-childhood. Always, he had considered himself the head of the family, with all the duties and rights that it entailed. No one corrected him. It was for his family that he studied and kept on the right side of the law—though he brushed the line occasionally. It was for them that he promised himself, when he was still too young to realize the full extent of his vow, to succeed. One day he would move them out, buy them a house, bring his mother up off her knees. The picture of how hadn't been clear, only the final result. The answer had been a ball and racket.

Ada Starbuck had given her son a cheap, nylon-stringed racket for his tenth birthday. The gift had been an impulse. She had been determined to give the boy something other than the necessary socks and underwear. The racket, such as it was, had been a gesture of hope. She could see too many of her neighbors' children fall into packs. Ty, she knew, was different. A loner. With the racket he could entertain himself. A baseball or football required someone to catch or pass. Now Ty could use a concrete wall as his partner. And so he did—at first for lack of something better to do. In the alley between apartment buildings he would smash the ball against a wall scrawled with spray paint. DIDI LOVES FRANK and other less romantic statements littered his playing field.

He enjoyed setting his own rhythm, enjoyed the steady thud, thump, smash he could make. When he became bored with the wall, he began haunting the neighborhood playground courts. There, he could watch teenagers or middle-aged weekenders scramble around the courts. He hustled pennies retrieving balls. Deciding he could do better than the people he watched, Ty badgered an older boy into a game.

His first experience on a court was a revelation. A human forced you to run, sent balls over your head or lined them at you with a speed a stationary wall couldn't match. Though he lost handily, Ty had discovered the challenge of competition. And the thirst to win.

He continued to haunt the courts, paying more attention to details. He began to select the players who took the game seriously. Possessing quite a bit of charm even at that age, Ty talked himself into more games. If someone took the time to teach, he listened and adjusted the advice to suit his own style. And he was developing a style. It was rough and untutored, with the flash the sportwriters would later rave about just a spark. His serve was a far cry from a grown Starbuck's, but it was strong and uncannily accurate. He was still awkward, as growing boys are, but his speed was excellent. More than anything else, his fierce desire to win had his game progressing.

When the cheap racket simply disintegrated under constant use, Ada raided the household budget and bought Ty another. Of the hundreds of rackets he had used in his career, some costing more than his mother had made in a week, Ty had never forgotten that first one. He had kept it, initially from childhood sentiment, then as a symbol.

He carved out a name for himself in the neighborhood. By the time he was thirteen it was a rare thing for anyone, child or adult, to beat Ty Starbuck on the courts. He knew his game. He had read everything he could get his hands on—tennis as a sport, its history, its great players. When his contemporaries were immersed in the progress of the White Sox or the Cubs, Ty watched the Wimbledon matches on the flickering black-and-white TV in his apartment. He had already made up his mind to be there one day. And to win. Again, it was Ada who helped the hand of fate.

One of the offices she cleaned belonged to Martin Derick, a lawyer and tennis enthusiast who patronized a local country club. He was an offhandedly friendly man whose late hours brought him in contact with the woman who scrubbed the hall outside his door. He called her Mrs. Starbuck because her dignity demanded it, and would exchange a word of greeting on his way in or out. Ada was careful to mention her son and his tennis abilities often enough to intrigue and not often enough to bore. Ty had come by his shrewdness naturally.

When Martin casually mentioned he would be interested in seeing the boy play, Ada told him there was an informal tournament set for that Saturday. Then she hurriedly arranged one. Whether curiosity or interest prompted Martin to drive to the battered South Side court, the results were exactly as Ada hoped.

Ty's style was still rough, but it was aggressive. His temper added to the spark, and his speed was phenomenal. At the end of a set, Martin was leaning against the chain-link fence. At the end of the match, he was openly cheering. Two hours on the manicured courts of his club had never brought him quite this degree of excitement. Ideas humming in his brain, he walked over to the sweaty, gangly teenager.

"You want to play tennis, kid?"

Ty spun the racket as he eyed the lawyer's pricey suit. "You ain't dressed for it." He gave the smooth leather shoes a mild sneer.

Martin caught the insolent grin, but focused on the intensity of the boy's eyes. Some instinct told him they were champion's eyes. The ideas solidified into a goal. "You want to play for pay?"

Ty kept spinning the racket, wary of a hustle, but the question had his pulse leaping. "Yeah. So?"

This time Martin smiled at the deliberate rudeness. He was

going to like this kid, God knew why. "So, you need lessons and a decent court." He glanced at Ty's worn racket. "And equipment. What kind of power can you get out of plastic strings?"

Defensive, Ty tossed up a ball and smashed it into the opposing service court.

"Not bad," Martin decided mildly. "You'd do better with sheep gut."

"Tell me something I don't know."

Martin drew out a pack of cigarettes and offered one to Ty. He refused with a shake of his head. Taking his time, Martin lit one, then took a long drag.

"Those things'll mess up your lungs," Ty stated idly.

"Tell me something I don't know," the lawyer countered. "Think you can play on grass?"

Ty answered with a quick, crude expletive, then sliced another ball over the net.

"Pretty sure of yourself."

"I'm going to play Wimbledon," Ty told him matter-of-factly. "And I'm going to win."

Martin didn't smile, but reached into his pocket. He held out a discreet, expensively printed business card. "Call me Monday," he said simply, and walked away.

Ty had a patron.

The marriage wasn't made in heaven. Over the next seven years there were bitter arguments, bursts of temper and dashes of love. Ty worked hard because he understood that work and discipline were the means to the end. He remained in school and studied only because his mother and Martin had a conspiracy against him. Unless he completed high school with decent grades, the patronage would be removed. As to the patronage itself, Ty accepted it only because his needs demanded it. But he was never comfortable with it. The lessons polished his craft. Good equipment tightened his game. He played on manicured grass, well-tended clay and wood, learning the idiosyncrasies of each surface.

Every morning before school he practiced. Afternoons and weekends were dedicated to tennis. Summers, he worked part-time in the pro shop at Martin's club, then used the courts to hone his skill. By the time he was sixteen the club's tennis pro could beat him only if Ty had an off day.

His temper was accepted. It was a game of histrionics. Women found a certain appeal in his lawlessness. Ty learned of female pleasures young, and molded his talent there as carefully as he did his game.

The only break in his routine came when he injured his hand coming to the defense of his sister. Ty considered the two-week enforced vacation worth it, as the boy Jess had been struggling with had a broken nose.

He traveled to his first tournament unknown and unseeded. In a lengthy, gritty match heralded in the sports pages, he found his first professional victory. When he lost, Ty was rude, argumentative and brooding. When he won, he was precisely the same. The press tolerated him because he was young, brilliant and colorful. His rise from obscurity was appreciated in a world where champions were bred in the affluent, select atmosphere of country clubs.

Before his nineteenth birthday Ty put a down payment on a three-bedroom house in a Chicago suburb. He moved his family out. When he was twenty he won his first Wimbledon title. The dream was realized, but his intensity never slackened.

Now, walking along the dark streets of Rome, he thought of his roots. Asher made him think of them, perhaps because hers were so markedly different. There had been no back alleys or street gangs in her life. Her childhood had been sheltered, privileged and rich. With James Wolfe as a father, her introduction to tennis had come much earlier and much easier than Ty's. At four she had a custom-made racket and had hit balls on her father's private courts. Her mother had hired maids to scrub floors, not been hired out to scrub them.

At times Ty wondered if it was that very difference that had attracted him to her. Then he would remember the way she felt in his arms. Backgrounds were blown to hell. Yet there was something about her reserve that had drawn him. That and the passion he had sensed lay beneath.

The challenge. Yes, Ty admitted with a frown, he was a man who couldn't resist a challenge. Something about the cool, distant Asher Wolfe had stirred his blood even when she had been little more than a child. He'd waited for her to grow up. And to thaw out, he reminded himself ruefully. Turning a corner without direction, Ty found himself approaching one of Rome's many fountains. The water twinkled with light gaiety while he watched, wishing his blood were as cool.

God, how he wanted her still. The need grated against pride, infuriating and arousing him. He would have taken her back that night even knowing she had been another man's wife, shared another man's bed. It would have been less difficult to have thought about her with many lovers than with one husband—that damn titled Englishman whose arms she had run to straight from his own. *Why?* The question pounded at him.

How many times in those first few months had he relived their last few days together, looking for the key? Then he'd layered over the hurt and the fury. The wound had healed jaggedly, then callused. Ty had gone on because he was a survivor. He'd survived poverty, and the streets, and the odds. With an unsteady laugh he raked a hand through his thick mop of hair. But had he really survived Asher?

He knew he had taken more than one woman to bed because her hair was nearly the same shade, her voice nearly the same tone. Nearly, always nearly. Now, when he had all but convinced himself that what he remembered was an illusion, she was back. And free. Again, Ty laughed. Her divorce meant nothing to him. If she had still been legally tied to another man, it would have made no difference. He would still have taken her.

This time, he determined, he'd call the shots. He was out of patience. He would have her again, until he decided to walk away. Challenge, strategy, action. It was a course he had followed for half his life. Taking out a coin, he flipped it insolently into the rippling waters of a fountain, as if daring luck to evade him. It drifted down slowly until it nestled with a hundred other wishes.

His eyes skimmed the streets until he found the neon lights of a tiny bar. He wanted a drink.

Chapter Four

Asher had time to savor her title as Italian Woman's Champion on the flight between Rome and Paris. After the match she had been too exhausted from nearly two hours of unrelenting competition to react. She could remember Madge hugging her, the crowd cheering for her. She could remember the glare of flashbulbs in her face and the barrage of questions she had forced herself to answer before she all but collapsed on the massage table. Then the celebrations had run together in a blur of color and sound, interviews and champagne. Too many faces and handshakes and hugs. Too many reporters. Now, as the plane leveled, reaction set in. She'd done it.

For all of her professional career, the Italian clay had beaten her. Now—now her comeback was viable. She had proven herself. Every hour of strain, every moment of physical pain during the last six months of training had been worth it. At last Asher could rid herself of all the lingering doubts that she had made the right decision.

Though there had been no doubts about her choice to leave Eric, she mused, feeling little emotion at the dissolution of her marriage—a marriage, Asher remembered, that had been no more than a polite play after the first two months. If she had ever made a truly unforgivable mistake, it had been in marrying Lord Eric Wickerton.

All the wrong reasons, Asher reflected as she leaned back in her seat with her eyes closed. Even with her bitter thoughts of Eric, she could never remove the feeling of responsibility for taking the step that had legally bound them. He had known she hadn't loved him. It hadn't mattered to him. She had known he wanted her to fit the title of Lady. She hadn't cared. At the time the need to escape had been too overpowering. Asher had given Eric what he had wanted—a groomed, attractive wife and hostess. She had thought he would give her what she needed in return. Love and understanding. The reality had been much, much different, and almost as painful as what she had sought to escape. Arguments were more difficult, she had discovered, when two people had no mutual ground. And when one felt the other had sinned…

She wouldn't think of it, wouldn't think of the time in her life that had brought such pain and disillusionment. Instead, she would think of victory.

Michael had been right in his assessment of Tia on the court. She was a small, vibrant demon who played hard and never seemed to tire. Her skill was in picking holes in her opponent's game, then ruthlessly exploiting them. On court she wore gold—a thin chain around her neck, swinging hoops at her ears and a thick clip to tame her raven hair. Her dress was pastel and frilled. She played like an enraged tigress. Both women had run miles during the match, taking it to a full five sets. The last one had consisted of ten long, volatile games with the lead shooting back and forth as quickly as the ball. Never had it been more true that the match wasn't over until it was over.

And when it was over, both women had limped off the court, sweaty, aching and exhausted. But Asher had limped off with a title. Nothing else mattered.

Looking back at it, Asher found herself pleased that the match had been hard won. She wanted something the press would chatter about, something they would remember for more than a day or two. It was always news when an unseeded player won a world title—even considering Asher's record. As it was, her past only made her hotter copy. She needed that now to help keep the momentum going.

With Italy behind her, Paris was next. The first leg of the Grand Slam. She had won there before, on clay, the year she had been Starbuck's lady. As she had with Eric, Asher tried to block Ty out of her mind. Characteristically he wasn't cooperative.

We pick this up in Paris.

The words echoed softly in her head, part threat, part promise. Asher knew him too well to believe either was idle. She would have to deal with him when the time came. But she wasn't naïve or innocent any longer. Life had taught her there weren't any easy answers or fairy-tale endings. She'd lost too much to believe happy-ever-after waited at the end of every love affair—as she had once believed it had waited for her and Ty. They were no longer the prince and princess of the courts, but older, and, Asher fervently hoped, wiser.

She was certain he would seek to soothe his ego by trying to win her again—her body if not her heart. Remembering the verve and depth of his lovemaking, Asher knew it wouldn't be easy to resist him. If she could have done so without risking her emotions, Asher would have given Ty what he wanted. For three colorless years she had endured without the passion he had brought to her life. For three empty years she had wondered and wanted and denied.

But her emotions weren't safe. On a sigh, Asher allowed herself to feel. She still cared. Not a woman to lie to herself, Asher admitted she loved Ty, had never once stopped loving him. It had never been over for her, and deep within she carried the memory of that love. It brought guilt.

What if he had known? she thought with the familiar stir of panic. How could she have told him? Asher opened her eyes and stared blindly through the sunlight. It was as harsh and unforgiving as the emotions that raged through her. Would he have believed? Would he have accepted? Before the questions were fully formed, Asher shook her head in denial. He could never know that she had unwittingly married another man while she carried Ty's child. Or that through her own grief and despair she had lost that precious reminder of her love for him.

Closing her eyes, Asher willed herself to sleep. Paris was much too close.

"Ty! Ty!"

Pausing in the act of zipping the cover on his racket, Ty turned. Pleasure shot into his eyes. In a quick move he dropped his racket and grabbed the woman who had run to him. Holding her up, he whirled her in three dizzying circles before he crushed her against him. Her laughter bounced off the air in breathless gasps.

"You're breaking me!" she cried, but hugged him tighter.

Ty cut off her protest with a resounding kiss, then held her at arm's length. She was a small woman, nearly a foot shorter than he, nicely rounded without being plump. Her gray-green eyes were sparkling, her generous mouth curved in a dazzling smile. She was a beauty, he thought—had always been a beauty. Love surrounded him. He tousled her hair, dark as his own, but cut in a loose swinging style that brushed her shoulders. "Jess, what are you doing here?"

Grinning, she gave his ear a sisterly tug. "Being mauled by the world's top tennis player."

Ty slipped an arm around her shoulders, only then noticing the man who stood back watching them. "Mac." Keeping his arm around Jess, Ty extended a hand.

"Ty, how are you?"

"Fine. Just fine."

Mac accepted the handshake and careful greeting with light amusement. He knew how Ty felt about his little sister—the little sister who was now twenty-seven and the mother of his child. When he had married Jess, over two years before, Mac had understood that there was a bond between brother and sister that would not be severed. An only child, he both respected and envied it. Two years of being in-laws had lessened Ty's caution with him but hadn't alleviated it. Of course, Mac mused ruefully, it hadn't helped that he was fifteen years Jess's senior, or that he had moved her across the country to California, where he headed a successful research and development firm. And then, he preferred chess to tennis. He'd never have gotten within ten yards of Jessica Starbuck if he hadn't been Martin Derick's nephew.

Bless Uncle Martin, Mac thought with a glance at his lovely, adored wife. Ty caught the look and relaxed his grip on his sister. "Where's Pete?" he asked, making the overture by addressing Mac rather than his sister.

Mac acknowledged the gesture with a smile. "With Grandma. They're both pretty pleased with themselves."

Jess gave the bubbling laugh that both men loved. "Hardly more than a year old and he can move like lightning. Mom's thrilled to chase him around for a few weeks. She sends her love," she told Ty. "You know how she feels about long plane flights."

"Yeah." He released his sister to retrieve his bag and racket. "I talked to her just last night; she didn't say anything about your coming."

"We wanted to surprise you." Smug, Jess hooked her hand into Mac's. "Mac thought Paris was the perfect place for a second honeymoon." She sent her husband a brief but intimate look. Their fingers tightened.

"The trick was getting her away from Pete for two weeks." He gave Ty a grin. "You were a bigger incentive than Paris." Bending, he kissed the top of his wife's head. "She dotes on Pete."

"No, I don't," Jess disagreed, then grinned. "Well, I wouldn't if Pete weren't such a smart baby."

Mac began to unpack an old, favored pipe. "She's ready to enroll him in Harvard."

"Next year," Jess responded dryly. "So, you're going in as top seed," she continued, giving her full attention to her brother. Was there some strain around his eyes? she wondered, then quickly discounted it. "Martin's proud enough to bust."

"I was hoping he might make it out for the tournament." Ty glanced toward the empty stands. "Funny, I still have a habit of looking for him before a match."

"He wanted to be here. If there had been any way for him to postpone this trial, but..." Jess trailed off and smiled. "Mac and I will have to represent the family."

Ty slung the bag over his shoulder. "You'll do fine. Where are you staying?"

"At the—" Jess's words came to a stop as she spotted a slender blonde crossing an empty court a short distance away. Reaching up, she brushed at her brow as if pushing aside an errant strand of hair. "Asher," she murmured.

Ty twisted his head. Asher wasn't aware of them, as Chuck was keeping her involved in what appeared to be a long, detailed description of a match. "Yes," Ty said softly. "Asher." He kept his eyes on her, watching the movements of her body beneath the loosely fitting jogging suit. "Didn't you know she was here?"

"Yes, I—" Jess broke off helplessly. How could she explain the flurry of feelings that she experienced in seeing Asher Wolfe again. The years were winked away in an instant. Jess could see the cool blue eyes, hear the firmly controlled voice. At the time there'd been no doubt in her mind about right and wrong. Even the chain reaction that had begun on a hazy September afternoon had only served to cement Jess's certainty. Now there'd been a divorce, and Asher was back. She felt her husband's warm palm against hers. Right and wrong weren't so clearly defined any longer.

A bubble of nausea rose as she turned to her brother. He was still watching Asher. Had he loved her? Did he still? What would he do if he ever learned of his sister's part in what had happened three years before? Jess found the questions trembling on her tongue and was afraid of the answers. "Ty…"

His eyes were dark and stormy, a barometer of emotion. Something in them warned Jess to keep her questions to herself. Surely there would be a better time to bring up the past. She had both a sense of reprieve and a feeling of guilt.

"Beautiful, isn't she?" he asked lightly. "Where did you say you were staying?"

"And because he's eighteen and played like a rocket in the qualifying rounds, they're muttering about an upset." Chuck tossed a tennis ball idly, squeezing it when it returned to his palm. "I wouldn't mind if he weren't such a little twerp."

Asher laughed and snatched the ball as Chuck tossed it again. "And eighteen," she added.

He gave a snort. "He wears designer underwear, for God's sake. His mother has them dry cleaned."

"Down boy," Asher warned good-naturedly. "You'll feel better once you wipe him out in the quarter-finals. Youth versus experience," she added because she couldn't resist. Chuck twisted a lock of her hair around his finger and pulled.

"You meet Rayski," he commented. "I guess we could call that two old pros."

Asher winced. “Your point,” she conceded. “So, what’s your strategy for this afternoon?”

“To beat the tar out of him,” Chuck responded instantly, then grinned as he flexed his racket arm. “But if he gets lucky, I’ll leave it up to Ty to smash him in the semis or the finals.”

Asher bounced the ball on the clay. Her fingers closed over it, then released it again. “You’re so sure Ty will get to the finals?”

“Money in the bank,” he claimed. “This is his year. I swear, I’ve never seen him play better.” Pleasure for his friend with the light lacing of envy gave the statement more impact. “He’s going to be piling up titles like dominoes.”

Asher said nothing, not even nodding in agreement as Chuck sought to prove his point by giving her a replay of Ty’s qualifying match. A breeze stirred, sending blossoms drifting to the court at her feet. It was early morning, and the Stade Roland Garros was still drowsily charming and quiet. The thump of balls was hardy noticeable. In a few hours the fourteen thousand seats around the single center court would be jammed with enthusiasts. The noise would be human and emotional, accented by the sounds of traffic and squealing brakes on the highway that separated the stadium from the Bois de Boulogne.

Asher watched the breeze tickle a weeping willow as Chuck continued his rundown. In this first week of the games, tennis would be played for perhaps eleven hours a day so that even the first-round losers used the courts enough to make the trip worthwhile. It was considered by most pros the toughest championship to win. Like Ty, Asher was after her second victory.

Paris. Ty. Was there nowhere she could go that wasn't so firmly tied in with memories of him? In Paris they'd sat in the back of a darkened theater, necking like teenagers while an Ingmar Bergman film had flickered on the screen unnoticed. In Paris he had doctored a strained muscle in her calf, pampering and bullying so that she had won despite the pain. In Paris they had made love, and made love, and made love until they were both weak and exhausted. In Paris Asher had still believed in happy endings.

Fighting off memories, Asher glanced around the stadium. Her eyes locked with Jess's. Separated by a hundred yards, both women endured a jolt of shock and distress. They stared, unable to communicate, unable to look away.

"Hey, it's Jess!" Chuck interrupted himself to make the announcement. He waved, then grabbed Asher's hand to drag her with him. "Let's go say hi."

Panicked, Asher dug in her heels. "No, I—I have to meet..." Her mind was devoid of excuses, but she snatched her hand from Chuck's. "You go ahead, I'll see you later." Over Chuck's protest, she dashed in the opposite direction.

Breathless, Asher found herself in the Jardin des Plantes with its sweet, mingling scents, little plaques and poetry. It seemed an odd setting for jangled nerves. Making an effort to calm herself, she slowed her pace.

Silly to run, she told herself. No, she corrected herself, stupid. But she hadn't been prepared to see Ty's sister, the one person who knew all the reasons. To have confronted Jess then, when her mind was already so crowded with Ty, would have been disastrous. Steadying, Asher told herself she just needed a little time to prepare. And it had been obvious Jess had been just as stunned as she. At the moment, Asher was too busy calming herself to wonder why.

She wouldn't, couldn't, think about the last time she'd seen Jessica Starbuck—that hot, close Indian summer afternoon. It would be too easy to remember each word spoken in the careless disorder of the hotel room Asher had shared with Ty. She would remember the hurt, the frantic packing, then her irrevocable decision to go to Eric.

Oh, Ty had been right, she had run away—but she hadn't escaped. So little had changed in three years, and so much. Her heart had remained constant. With a sigh Asher admitted it had been foolish to believe she could take back what she had given so long ago. Ty Starbuck was her first lover, and the only man she had ever loved.

A child had been conceived, then lost before it could be born. She'd never forgiven herself for the accident that had taken that precious, fragile life from her. Perhaps more than a lack of love and understanding, it had been the loss of Ty's child that had destroyed any hope for her marriage.

And if the child had lived? she asked herself wearily. What then? Could she have kept it from him? Could she have remained the wife of one man while bearing the child of another? Asher shook her head. No, she would no longer dwell on possibilities. She'd lost Ty, his child, and the support of her own father. There could be no greater punishments to face. She would make her own future.

The touch of a hand on her shoulder had her whirling around. Asher stared up at Ty, her mind a blank, her emotions in turmoil. A hush seemed to spread over the garden, so she could hear the whisper of air over leaves and blossoms. The scent that reached her was sweet and heady—like a first kiss. He said nothing, nor did she until his hand slid down her arm to link with hers.

"Worried about the match?"

Almost afraid he would sense them, Asher struggled to push all thoughts of the past aside. "Concerned," she amended, nearly managing a smile. "Rayski's top seed."

"You've beaten her before."

"And she's beaten me." It didn't occur to her to remove her hand from his or to mask her doubts. Slowly the tension seeped out of her. Through the link of hands Ty felt it. They had stood here before, and the memory was sweet.

"Play her like you played Conway," he advised. "Their styles are basically the same."

With a laugh Asher ran her free hand through her hair. "That's supposed to be a comfort?"

"You're better than she is," he said simply, and earned an astonished stare. Smiling, he brushed his fingers carelessly over her cheek. "More consistent," he explained. "She's faster, but you're stronger. That gives you an advantage on clay even though it isn't your best surface."

At a loss, Asher managed a surprised, "Well."

"You've improved," Ty stated as they began to walk. "Your backhand doesn't have the power it should have, but—"

"It worked pretty well on Conway," Asher interrupted testily.

"Could be better."

"It's perfect," she disagreed, rising to the bait before she caught his grin. Her lips curved before she could stop them. "You always knew how to get a rise out of me. You're playing Kilroy," she went on, "I've never heard of him."

"He's been around only two years. Surprised everyone in Melbourne last season." He slipped an arm around her shoulders in a gesture so familiar, neither of them noticed. "What's that flower?"

Asher glanced down. "Lady's slipper."

"Silly name."

"Cynic."

He shrugged. "I like roses."

"That's because it's the only flower you can identify." Without thinking, she leaned her head on his shoulder. "I remember going in to take a bath one night and finding you'd filled the tub with roses. Dozens of them."

The scent of her hair reminded him of much more. "By the time we got around to clearing them out, it took over an hour."

Her sigh was wistful. "It was wonderful. You could always surprise me by doing something absurd."

"A tub of lady's slippers is absurd," he corrected. "A tub of roses is classy."

Her laughter was quick and appreciative. Her head still rested on his shoulders. "We filled everything in the room that could pass for a vase, including a bottle of ginger ale. Sometimes when I—" She cut herself off, abruptly realizing she would say too much.

"When you what?" Ty demanded as he turned her to face him. When she only shook her head, he tightened his grip. "Would you remember sometimes, in the middle of the night? Would you wake up and hurt because you couldn't forget?"

Truth brought tension to the base of her neck. In defense, Asher pressed her palms against his chest. "Ty, please."

"I did." He gave her a frustrated shake that knocked her head back. "Oh, God, I did. I've never stopped wanting you. Even hating you I wanted you. Do you know what it's like to be awake at three o'clock in the morning and need someone, and know she's in another man's bed."

"No, no, don't." She was clinging to him, her cheek pressed against his, her eyes tightly shut. "Ty, don't."

"Don't what?" he demanded as he drew her head back. "Don't hate you? Don't want you? Hell, I can't do anything else."

His eyes blazed into her, dark with fury, hot with passion. She could feel the race of his heart compete with hers. Abandoning pride, she pressed her lips to his.

At the instant of contact he stood still, neither giving nor taking. On a moan she drew him closer, letting her lips have their way. A shudder coursed through him, an oath ripped out, then he was responding, demanding, exciting. Why had he tried to resist? Nothing was clear to him as her lips raced crazily over his face. Wasn't this what he wanted? To have her again, to prove he could, to purge his system of her once and for all. Motives dimmed in desire. There was only Asher—the sweet taste of her, her scent more heady, more seductive than the garden of flowers. He couldn't breathe and not fill himself on her. So he surrendered to the persuading lips and soft body that had haunted his dreams.

Dragging his lips from hers only a moment, Ty pulled her through the fragile branches of a willow. The sun filtered through the curtain of leaves, giving intermittent light. In the cool dimness his mouth sought hers again and found it yielding. The blood pounded in his veins.

He had to know if her body was the same, unchanged during the years he'd been denied her. As his hand took her breast he groaned. She was small and firm and familiar. Through the material of her jacket he felt the nipple harden in quick response. Impatient, he tugged the zipper down, then dove under her shirt until he found the smooth tender flesh that had always made him feel his hands were too rough. Yet she didn't draw away as his calluses met her. She pressed against him. Her moan was not one of discomfort, but of unmistakable pleasure.

Trembling, her fingers reached for his hair. He could feel the urgency in them just as he could taste it on her heated lips. He broke his kiss only to change angles, then deepened it, allowing his tongue to drink up all the dark flavors of her mouth. Against his palm her heart thudded wildly, but only his fingers moved to arouse her.

Slowly his other hand journeyed to her hip to mold the long, slender bone. He was lost somewhere between yesterday and today. The heavy fragrance of flowers still wet with morning dew was more seductive than perfume. Half dreaming, Ty took his mouth to her throat. He heard her sigh float off on the scented air. Was she dreaming too? Was the past overlapping this moment for her as well as for him? The thoughts drifted into his mind, then out again before they could be answered. Nothing mattered but that he was holding her again.

From far off came a ripple of laughter. Ty brought his mouth back to Asher's. A rapid smattering of French drifted to him. Ty drew her closer until their bodies seemed fused. Footsteps and a giggle. Like a dreamer, he sensed the intrusion and swore against it. For another moment he clung, drawing on her lingering passion.

When he released her, Asher was breathless and swaying. Wordlessly he stared down at her with eyes nearly black with emotion. Her lips were parted, swollen from his, and he gave in to need and kissed her one long last time. Gently now, slowly, to store up every dram of sweetness. This time she trembled, her breath coming harsh and fast like a diver's who breaks surface after a long submersion. Disoriented, she gripped his arms.

How long had they been there? she wondered. It could have been seconds or days. All she was sure of was that the longing had intensified almost beyond control. Her blood was racing in her veins, her heart pounding desperately. She was alive. So alive. And no longer certain which path she would take.

"Tonight," Ty murmured, bringing her palm to his lips.

The vibration shot up her arm and into her core. "Ty…" Asher shook her head as she tried to draw her hand away. His fingers tightened.

"Tonight," he repeated.

"I can't." Seeing the temper shoot into his eyes, Asher covered their joined hands with her free one. "Ty, I'm frightened."

The quiet admission killed his anger. He let out a weary sigh. "Damn you, Asher."

Saying nothing, she wrapped her arms around his waist, pressing her cheek to his chest. Automatically Ty reached to smooth her hair. His eyes closed. "I'm sorry," she whispered. "I was frightened of you once before. It seems to be happening again." And I love you, she told him silently. As much as ever. More, she realized. More, because of the years of famine.

"Asher." He held her away from him. She felt the passion swirling around him. "I won't promise to wait for you to come to me this time. I won't promise to be gentle and patient. Things aren't the same."

She shook her head, but in agreement. "No, things aren't the same. It might be better, much better for both of us if we just stayed away from each other."

Ty laughed shortly. "We won't."

"If we tried," Asher began.

"*I* won't."

She let out a breath of exasperation. "You're pressuring me."

"Damn right." Before she could decide whether to laugh or to scream, she was in his arms again. "Do you think I don't feel pressured too?" he demanded with a sudden intensity that kept Asher from answering. "Every time I look at you I remember the way things were for us and drive myself crazy trying to figure out why you left me. Do you know what that does to me?"

She gripped his upper arms with strong hands. "You have to

understand, I won't go back. Whatever happens to us now begins now. No questions, no whys." She saw the anger boiling in his eyes, but kept hers level. "I mean that, Ty. I can't give you explanations. I won't dig up the past."

"You expect me to live with that?"

"I expect nothing," she said quietly. The tone caused him to look deeper for the answers she refused to give. "And I've agreed to nothing. Not yet."

"You ask for too much," he bit off as he released her. "Too damn much."

She wanted to go to him, go back to his arms and beg him to forget the past. Perhaps it was possible to live for the moment if one wanted to badly enough. It might have been pride that stopped her, or the deeply ingrained survival instinct she had developed since that long-ago September afternoon when she had fled from him and the prospect of pain. Asher laced her fingers together and stared down at them. "Yes, I know. I'm sorry, Ty, we'll only hurt each other."

Tense and tormented, he turned back. "I've never wanted to hurt you, Asher. Not even when I thought I did."

The ache spread so quickly, she almost gasped from it. Isn't that what Jess had said that day? *He'd never want to hurt you...never want to hurt you.* Asher could hear the words echoing inside her head. "Neither of us wanted to," she murmured. "Both of us did. Isn't it foolish to do it again?"

"Look at me." The command was quiet and firm. Bracing herself, Asher obeyed. His eyes were locked on hers—those dark, penetrating eyes that conveyed such raw feeling. Gently he touched her cheek. Without hesitation her hand rose to cover his. “Now,” he whispered, “ask me again.”

A long, shuddering breath escaped. “Oh, Ty, I was so sure I could prevent this. So sure I could resist you this time.”

“And now?”

“Now I’m not sure of anything.” She shook her head before he could speak again. “Don’t ask now. Give us both some time.”

He started to protest, then managed to restrain it. He’d waited three years, a bit longer wouldn’t matter. “Some time,” he agreed, lowering his hand. But as she started to relax, he took her wrist. The grip was neither gentle nor patient. “The next time, Asher, I won’t ask.”

She nodded, accepting. “Then we understand each other.”

His smile was a trifle grim. “That we do. I’ll walk you back.” He drew her through the curtain of leaves.

Chapter Five

Fifth set. Seventh game. At the baseline Ty crouched, ready to spring for Michael's serve. The air was heavy, the sky thick with rain-threatening clouds so that the light was dreary. Ty didn't notice. He didn't notice the stadium full of people, some dangling through the railing, some hanging from the scoreboard. He didn't notice the shouts and whistles that were either for or against him.

Tennis was a game of the individual. That was what had drawn him to it. There was no one to blame for a loss, no one to praise for a win but yourself. It was a game of motion and emotion, both of which he excelled in.

He had looked forward to meeting Michael in the semis. The Australian played a hot, passionate game full of dramatic gestures, furious mutters and pizzazz. There were perhaps five competitors Ty fully respected, Michael being one of them. Wanting to win was only a step below wanting a challenge. A fight. He'd grown up scrapping. Now the racket was merely an extension of his arm. The match was a bout. The bout was one on one. It had never—would never—be only a game.

The Australian was a set up, with his momentum still flowing. Ty's only thought at the moment was to break his serve and even the match. Thus far he had spotted no weaknesses in his opponent's game. Like a boxer, he watched for the opening.

He heard the sound of the ball hitting the sweet spot of the racket before it rocketed toward him. It landed deep in the corner of the service court, beautifully placed. Ty's mind and body moved as one as he sprang for the return. Defense, offense, strategy all had to be formulated in a fraction of a second. Strength had to be balanced with form. Both men sprinted over the court for the rally, faces glowing with concentration and sweat. The roar of the crowd rose to meet the distant thunder.

Thus far, the ratio had been nearly ten to one in favor of ground strokes. Ty decided to alter the pace and go with power. Using a vicious left-to-right slice, he shook Michael's balance. Ty blasted away at the attempted passing shot, barely shortening his backswing. Michael couldn't reach the backhand volley, let alone return it. Love-fifteen.

Shaking the damp hair back from his face, Ty returned to the baseline. A woman in the crowd called out what could have been a congratulations or a proposition. Ty's French wasn't strong enough to decipher the phrase. Michael's serve sent up a puff of smoke. Before his return was over the net, Ty was at mid-court and waiting. A testing ground stroke, a sharp return. A tricky topspin, a slice. Michael's decision to try to lob over Ty was a mistake. The smoking smash careened off the court and into the grandstands. Love-thirty.

Michael walked a complete circle, cursing himself before he took his position again. Casting off impatience, Ty waited. Crouched, swaying side to side, unblinking, he was ready. Both players exploited angles and depths with ground strokes. There was a long, patient rally as each watched for the chance to smash a winner. It might have been pure showmanship if it hadn't been for the sounds of exertion coming from the two players.

A UPI photographer had his motor drive humming as he recorded the game. He framed Ty, arms extended for balance, legs spread for the stretch, face fierce. It crossed his mind as he continued to snap that he wouldn't want to face that American on any playing field.

Gracefully, with an elegance belied by his expression, Ty executed a backhand with a touch of underspin. Michael's return thudded against the net. Love-forty.

Angry and shaken, Michael punched his first serve into the net. Having no choice at game point, he placed his next serve carefully. Ty went straight for the volley and took the net. The exchange was fast and furious, the players moving on instinct, the crowd screaming in a mixture of languages. Ty's wrist was locked. The ball whipped from racket to racket at terrifying speed. There were bare seconds between contact, making both men anticipate flight rather than see it. Changing tactics in the wink of an instant, Ty brought the racket face under at the moment of impact. With a flick of a wrist he dropped a dump shot over the net. Risky, experts would say. Gutsy, fans would claim. Ty would ignore both. Game and set.

"Oh, Mac!" Jess leaned back and expelled a long breath. "I'd nearly forgotten what it was like to watch Ty play."

"You watched him just a few weeks ago," he pointed out, using a damp handkerchief to wipe his neck. The wish for his air-conditioned office flitted only briefly into his mind.

"On television," Jess returned. "That's different. Being here…can't you feel it?"

"I thought it was the humidity."

Laughing, Jess shook her head. "Always down to earth, Mac. That's why I love you."

Her smile seemed to open just for him. It could still make his blood sing. "Then I intend to stay there," he murmured, kissing her knuckles. Feeling her hand tense, he looked up, puzzled. Her eyes were aimed over his shoulder. Curious, he turned, spotting a few tennis faces he recognized. Among them was Asher Wolfe. It was on her that his wife's gaze was locked.

"That's the former Lady Wickerton, isn't it?" he asked casually. "She's stunning."

"Yes." Jess tore her eyes away, but the tension in her fingers remained. "Yes, she is."

"She won her match this morning. We'll have an American going into the women's finals." Jess said nothing as Mac stuffed the handkerchief back into his pocket. "She was away from the game for a while, wasn't she?"

"Yes."

Intrigued by his wife's flat answer, Mac probed. "Didn't she and Ty have something going a few years back?"

"It was nothing." With a nervous swallow Jess prayed she spoke the truth. "Just a passing thing. She's not Ty's type. Asher's very cool, much more suited to Wickerton than to Ty. He was attracted to that for a while, that's all." She moistened her lips. "And it was obvious she wasn't serious about him, otherwise she'd never have married Wickerton so quickly. She was making Ty unhappy, very unhappy."

"I see," Mac murmured after a moment. Jess had spoken too quickly and too defensively. Studying his wife's profile, he wondered. "I suppose Ty's too involved in his career to be serious about a woman?"

"Yes." The look Jess gave him was almost pleading. "Yes, he'd never have let her go if he'd been in love with her. Ty's too possessive."

"And proud," he reminded her quietly. "I don't think he'd run after any woman, no matter how he felt about her."

Feeling her stomach roll, Jess said nothing. She turned to watch her brother take the position for his first serve.

Instead of the hazy afternoon she saw a brilliant morning. Instead of the clay of Roland Garros she saw the newly empty grass courts of Forest Hills. Ty was leaning over the rail, staring out at center court. She had a fanciful thought that he looked like the captain of a ship with his eyes on the open, endless sea. In her world she loved no one more than him, could conceive of loving no one more. He was brother and father and hero. He'd provided her with a home, clothes and an education, asking nothing in return. As a result, she would have given him anything.

Crossing to him, she slipped her arm around him, nestling her head in the crook of his shoulder.

"Thinking about this afternoon?" she murmured. He was slated to face Chuck Prince in the finals of the U.S. Open.

"Hmm?" Distracted, Ty shrugged. "No, not really."

"It must feel odd to compete against your closest friend."

"You must forget you're friends for a couple hours," Ty returned.

He was brooding; she sensed it. And unhappy. There was no one, including her mother, Jess felt more loyalty to. Her grip around him tightened. "Ty, what is it?"

"Just restless."

"Have you fought with Asher?"

Absently he tousled her hair. "No, I haven't fought with Asher."

He lapsed into silence for so long that Jess began to suspect he wasn't telling the entire truth. She was already worried about him and Asher. The relationship had lasted longer than was habitual for Ty. Jess saw Asher's reserve as coldness, her independence as indifference. She didn't hang on Ty as other women did. She didn't listen raptly to every word he spoke. She didn't adore him.

"Do you ever think back, Jess?" he asked suddenly.

"Think back?"

"To when we were kids." His eyes skimmed over the manicured courts, but didn't see them. "That crummy apartment with the paper walls. The DeMarcos next door screaming at each other in the middle of the night. The stairwell always smelled of old garbage and stale sweat."

The tone of his voice disturbed her. Seeking comfort as much as to comfort, she turned her face into his chest. "Not often. I guess I don't remember it as well as you. I hadn't turned fifteen when you got us out."

"I wonder sometimes if you can ever escape that, if you can ever really turn your back on it." His eyes were focused on something

Jess couldn't see. She strained to share the vision. "Old garbage and stale sweat," he repeated quietly. "I can't forget that. I asked Asher once what smell she remembered most from her childhood. She said the wisteria that hung over her bedroom window."

"Ty, I don't understand."

He swore softly. "Neither do I."

"You left all that behind," she began.

"I left it," he corrected her. "That doesn't mean I left it behind. We were having dinner last night. Wickerton stopped by the table and started a conversation about French Impressionists. After five minutes I didn't know what the hell they were talking about."

Jess bristled. She knew because Ty had sent her to college. She knew because he had provided the opportunity. "You should have told him to get lost."

With a laugh Ty kissed her cheek. "That was my first thought." Abruptly he sobered. "Then I watched them. They understand each other, speak the same language. It made me realize there are some fences you just can't climb."

"You could if you wanted to."

"Maybe. I don't." He let out a long breath. "I don't really give a damn about French Impressionists. I don't give a damn about the mutual friends they have that are distant cousins of the Queen of England, or who won at Ascot last month." Storm warnings were in his eyes, but he shrugged. "Even if I did, I wouldn't fit into that kind of life because I'd always remember the garbage and sweat."

"Asher has no business encouraging that man," Jess stated heatedly. "He's been following her around since Paris."

Ty gave a grim laugh. "She doesn't encourage or discourage. Drawing room conversation," he murmured. "Ingrained manners. She's different from us, Jess, I've known that all along."

"If *she'd* tell him to get lost—"

"She couldn't tell anyone to get lost any more than she could sprout wings and fly."

"She's cold."

"She's different," Ty returned immediately but without heart. He cupped his sister's chin in his hand. "You and me, we're the same. Everything's up front. If we want to shout, we shout. If we want to throw something, we throw it. Some people can't."

"Then they're stupid."

This time his laugh was warm and genuine. "I love you, Jess."

Throwing her arms around him, she hugged him fiercely. "I can't bear to see you unhappy. Why do you let her do this to you?"

Frowning, Ty stroked her hair. "I've been trying to figure that out. Maybe…maybe I just need a shove in the right direction."

Jess held him tighter, searching her mind for the answer.

Seventh set. Tenth game. The crowd was as vocal, as enthusiastic and as hungry as it had been an hour before. Leaning forward in his seat, his eyes glued to the ball, Chuck sat between Asher and Madge.

"You've got something riding on this one, don't you, cowboy?" Madge commented dryly though her own heart was pumping. Chuck would face the winner in the finals.

"It's the best match I've seen in two years." His own face was damp, his own muscles tense. The ball traveled at such speeds, it was often only a white blur.

Asher spoke to neither of them. Her objectivity had been long since destroyed. Ty enthralled her. Both men possessed the raw athletic ability competitors admired and envied. Both were draining the other's resources without mercy. But it was Ty, always Ty, who ripped the emotion from her.

She could admire Michael, admit his brilliance, but he didn't cause that slow, churning ache in her stomach. Had she not once been Ty's lover, had she not even known him, would she still be so drawn? Controlled rage. How was it a woman raised in such an ordered, sheltered existence would be pulled irresistibly to a man with such turbulent passion? Opposites attract? she wondered. No, that was much too simple.

Sitting in the crowded stadium, Asher felt the thrill of desire as clearly as though she had been naked in his arms. She felt no shame. It was natural. She felt no fear. It was inevitable. Years made up of long, unending days vanished. What a waste of time, she thought suddenly. No, a loss, she corrected herself. A loss of time—nothing's ever wasted. *Tonight.* The decision came to her as effortlessly as it had the first time. Tonight they would be together. And if it was only once—if once was all he wanted—it would have to be enough. The long wait was over. She laughed out loud in relief and joy. Chuck sent her an odd look.

"He's going to win," Asher said on a second laugh. Leaning on the rail, she rested her chin on her folded hands. "Oh, yes, he's going to win."

There was a dull ache in his racket arm that Ty ignored. The muscles in his legs promised to cramp the moment he stopped moving. He wouldn't give in to them any more than he would give in to the man across the net. One thing hadn't changed in twenty years. He still hated to lose.

A point away from the match, he played no less tigerishly than he had in the first game. The rallies had been long and punishing. The ball whistled. Sweat dripped. For the last twenty minutes Ty had forsaken artistry for cunning. It was working.

Power for power, they were in a dead heat, so that Ty chose to outmaneuver the Australian. He worked him over the court, pacing him, some might say stalking him. The game went to deuce three times while the crowd grew frantic. An ace gave him advantage—a screeching bullet that brought Ty the final impetus he needed. Then Ty played him hot-bloodedly. The men drove from side to side, their faces masks of effort and fury. The shot came that he'd been waiting for. Michael's awesome backhand drove crosscourt to his southpaw forehand. The ball came to Ty at waist level. Michael didn't even have to see the return to know it was over.

Game, set and match.

The heat hit him then, and the fatigue. It took an effort not to stagger. Simply to have fallen to his knees would have been a relief. He walked to the net.

Michael took his hand, then draped his free arm around Ty's shoulder. "Damn you, Starbuck," he managed breathlessly. "You nearly killed me."

Ty laughed, using his opponent for balance a moment. “You too.”

“I need a bloody drink.” Michael straightened, giving Ty a glazed grin. “Let’s go get drunk.”

“You’re on.”

Turning, they separated, victor and vanquished, to face the press, the showers and the massage tables. Ty grabbed the towel someone handed him, nodding at the questions and congratulations being hurled at him. Behind the cloth he could hear the click and whir of cameras. He was too weary to curse them. Someone was gathering his rackets. He could hear the clatter of wood on wood. The strength that had flowed freely through him only moments before drained. Exhausted, he let the drenched towel fall. His eyes met Asher’s.

So blue, he thought. Her eyes are so blue. And cool, and deep. He could drown in them blissfully. The unbearable heat vanished, as though someone had opened a window to a fresh spring breeze.

“Congratulations.” When she smiled, his fatigue slid away. Strangely it wasn’t desire that replaced it, but comfort, sweet simple comfort.

“Thanks.” He took the racket bag from her. Their hands barely brushed.

“I suppose the press is waiting for you inside.”

The short retort Ty made was both agreement and opinion. On a low laugh she stepped closer.

“Can I buy you dinner?”

The quirk of his brow was the only indication of surprise. “Sure.”

"I'll meet you at seven in the lobby of the hotel."

"All right."

"Starbuck, what do you feel was the turning point of the match?"

"What strategy will you use playing Prince in the finals?"

Ty didn't answer the reporters, didn't even hear them as he watched Asher weave her way through the crowd. From overhead Jess watched with a small, fluttering sensation of déjà vu.

Ty got under the stream of the shower fully dressed. He let the cool water sluice over him while he stripped. A reporter from *World of Sports* leaned against a tiled wall, scribbling notes and tossing questions. Naked, with his clothes in a soggy heap at his feet, Ty answered. Always, he handled the press naturally because he didn't give a damn what they printed. He knew his mother kept a scrapbook, but he never read the articles or interviews. Lathering the soap over his face with both hands, he washed the sticky sweat away. Someone passed him a plastic jug of fruit juice. With the water streaming over him, he guzzled it down, replacing lost fluid. The weakness was seeping back, and with it the pain. He made his way to the massage table by instinct, then collapsed onto it.

Strong fingers began to work on him. Questions still hammered in his ear, but now he ignored them. Ty simply closed his eyes and shut them out. A line of pain ran up his calf as the muscles were kneaded. He winced and held on, knowing relief would follow. For ten agonizing minutes he lay still while his body was rubbed and pounded. He began to drift. Like a mother's memory of the pain of childbirth, his memory of the pain began to dim.

He could remember winning. And he could remember dark blue eyes. With those two visions tangling in his mind, he slept.

The floor of the lobby was marble. White marble veined with pink. Madge had commented that it would be the devil to keep clean. Her husband had dryly commented that she wouldn't know one end of the mop from the other. Asher sat, listening to their comfortable banter while she told herself she wasn't nervous. It was six-fifty.

She'd dressed carefully, choosing a simple crêpe de Chine as pale as the inside of a peach. Her hair fluffed back from her face, exposing the tiny pearl and coral drops at her ears. Her ringless fingers were interlaced.

"Where are you eating?"

Asher brought her attention back to Madge. "A little place on the Left Bank." There was an enthusiastic violinist, she remembered. Ty had once passed him twenty American dollars and cheerfully told him to get lost.

At the bellow of thunder Madge glanced toward the lobby doors. "You're going to play hell getting a cab tonight." She leaned back. "Have you seen Ty since the match?"

"No."

"Chuck said both he and Michael were sleeping on the tables like babies." A chuckle escaped as she crossed strong, short legs. "Some industrious stringer for a French paper got a couple of classic shots."

"Athletes in repose," her husband mused.

"It kind of blows the tough-guy image."

Asher smiled, thinking how young and vulnerable Ty looked in sleep. When the lids closed over those dramatic eyes, he reminded her of an exhausted little boy. It was the only time the frenetic energy stilled. Something stirred in her. If the child had lived… Hurriedly she censored the thought.

"Hey, isn't that Ty's sister?"

Asher turned her head to see Jess and Mac crossing the lobby. "Yes." Their eyes met, leaving no choice. Gripping her husband's hand, Jess walked across the white marble.

"Hello, Asher."

"Jess."

A quick moistening of lips betrayed nerves. "I don't think you know my husband. Mackenzie Derick, Lady Wickerton."

"Asher Wolfe," she replied smoothly, taking Mac's hand. "Are you related to Martin?"

"My uncle," Mac informed her. "Do you know him?"

The smile brought warmth to her eyes. "Very well." She made the rest of the introductions with a natural poise Mac approved of. Cool, yes, he mused, remembering his wife's description. But with an underlying vibrancy perhaps a man would discern more quickly than another woman. He began to wonder if Jess's opinion of Ty's feelings was accurate.

"Are you a tennis fan, Mr. Derick?" Asher asked him.

"Mac," he supplied. "Only by marriage. And no, I don't play, much to Uncle Martin's disgust."

Asher laughed, appreciating the humor in his eyes. A strong man, she thought instantly. His own man. He wouldn't take second place to Ty in his wife's life. "Martin should be satisfied having cultivated one champion." Her eyes drifted to Jess, who was sitting straight and tense beside Madge. "Is your mother well?"

"Yes, yes, Mom's fine." Though she met the cool, clear gaze, her fingers began to pleat the material of her skirt. "She's at home with Pete."

"Pete?"

"Our son."

Asher's throat constricted. Mac noticed with some surprise that her knuckles whitened briefly on the arm of her chair. "I didn't know you'd had a baby. Ada must be thrilled to have a grandchild." The pressure on her heart was unbearable. Her smile was casual. "How old is he?" she made herself ask.

"Fourteen months." As the tension built in one woman, it flowed out of the other. Jess was already reaching into her purse for her wallet. "I swear he never walked, he started out running. Mom says he's like Ty. He has his coloring too." She was offering a picture. Asher had no choice but to accept it.

There was some of his father in him—the shape of the face. But the Starbuck genes were strong. The baby's hair was dark and thick, like his mother's. Like Ty's. The eyes were large and gray. Asher wondered if she could actually feel the air of perpetual motion around the child, or if she imagined it. Another baby would have had dark hair and gray eyes. Hadn't she pictured the face countless times?

"He's beautiful," she heard herself say in a calm voice. "You must be very proud of him." When she handed the snapshot back her hands were perfectly steady.

"Jess thinks he should wait until he's twelve before he runs for president."

Asher smiled, but this time Mac didn't find the reflected warmth in her eyes. "Has Ty bought him a racket yet?"

"You know him very well," Mac observed.

"Yes." She looked back at Jess steadily. "Tennis and his family come first, always."

"I hate to admit it," Madge put in with a sigh, "but I can remember a dozen years ago when this one was a skinny teenager, chewing her fingernails at every one of Ty's matches. Now you're a mother."

Jess grinned, holding out her hands for inspection. "And I still bite my nails at Ty's matches."

It was Asher who saw him first. But then, her senses were tuned for him. Ty stepped off the elevator dressed in slim black slacks and a smoke-gray shirt. He wouldn't have chosen the shirt because it matched his eyes so perfectly. Asher knew he wore it because it would have been the first thing his hand had grabbed from the closet. He wore clothes with the casual style of one who gave no thought to them and still looked marvelous. A disciplined body and trained grace made it inevitable. His hair had been combed, but defied order. He paused briefly, even in stillness communicating motion. Asher's heartbeat was a dull, quick thud.

"Oh, there's Ty!" Jess sprang up, hurrying across the lobby to meet him. "I didn't get to congratulate you. You were absolutely wonderful."

Though his arm slipped around her, Jess saw that his eyes had drifted over her head. Without turning, she knew who they focused on.

Asher didn't see, nor did she speak.

"Well, Starbuck, you earned your pay today," Madge commented. "The Dean and I are going to the Lido to hold Michael's hand."

"Tell him I lost three pounds on the court today." He spoke to her, lightly enough, but his eyes never left Asher's.

"I don't think that's going to make him feel a hell of a lot better," she returned, giving her husband a nudge as she rose. "Well, we're off to fight for a taxi. Anyone going our way?"

"As a matter of fact," Mac began, picking up the hint easily, "Jess and I were on our way out too."

"Want a lift, Ty?" Madge's husband gave her an offended look as she ground her heel into his foot. But he shut his mouth firmly when Madge shot him a deadly glance.

Even to a man who rarely comprehended subtleties, it became obvious there were things being said without words. The little group had simply ceased to exist for Ty and Asher. After a hard look at the silent couple The Dean straightened his glasses and grinned at his wife.

"I guess not, huh?"

"You're so quick, babe." Madge began shepherding the rest toward the doors. "Anyone know some French obscenities? It's the best way to get a cab in the rain."

Asher rose slowly. From behind her she could hear the ding of a bell on the desk and the whoosh of the storm as the doors were opened then quickly closed. For a moment Ty thought she looked like something that should be enclosed in glass. Not to be touched, not to be soiled. She reached out her hand.

When he took it, it was warm. Flesh and blood.

In unspoken agreement they turned away from the doors and walked to the elevator.

Chapter Six

They didn't speak, but then they didn't need to. With one hand still holding hers, Ty pushed the button for his floor. The elevator began its silent rise. Once, the hand in his trembled lightly. He found it unbearably exciting. The numbers above their heads flashed ponderously until at last the car stopped. When the doors slid open they stepped into the carpeted hall together.

Asher heard the key jingle against loose change as Ty reached into his pocket. She heard the click of the lock before he released her hand. The choice was still hers. She stepped out of the light into the dimness of the room.

It smelled of him. That was her first thought. The air carried Ty's lingering fragrance. Something sharp, something vital. Something she had never forgotten. All at once her nerves began to jump. The poise that had carried her this far fell away. Searching for something to say, she wandered the room. It was untidy, with a shirt thrown here, shoes tossed there. She knew if she opened the closet, she would find a neat stack of rackets, the only semblance of order. Instead, she moved to the window. Rain ran like tears down the glass.

"It's going to storm all night."

As if to accent her words, lightning split the sky. Asher counted to five, then heard the thunder answer. Hundreds of lights spread through the darkness. The city was there, crowded, moving—distant. Staring through the wet glass, she waited for Ty to speak.

Silence. The patter of rain on the window. The distant hum of traffic. Another moan of thunder. Unable to bear it, Asher turned.

He was watching her. The small bedside lamp threw both light and shadow into the room. His stance was neither relaxed nor threatening, and she understood. He had given her a choice before she entered. Now he wouldn't let her go. A bridge had been burned. Asher felt nothing but relief that the decision was already made. But her fingers were numb as she reached to loosen the thin belt at her waist.

Crossing to her, Ty laid his hands over hers, stopping the movement. Asher stared up at him, unsure, as nervous as the first time. Without speaking he took her face in his hands to study her. He wanted to remember her this way—in shadowed light with the fury of a storm at her back. Her eyes were dark with traces of fear, traces of desire. In a gesture of surrender her arms had dropped to her sides. But he didn't want surrender—perhaps she had forgotten.

As he lowered his head Ty watched her lids shut, her lips part in anticipation. Gently he kissed her temple, then the other, then the delicate curve of an eyebrow. Without haste, his eyes closed. He reacquainted himself with her face through taste and touch.

Her lips beckoned, but he nibbled along the line of her jaw, on the hollow of her cheek.

His thumb brushed her bottom lip as he whispered kisses over her face. He remembered every curve. Her breath shuddered out as he kissed the corners of her mouth. He brushed his over it, retreating when Asher sought more pressure. There was only the fleeting promise of more. With a moan she gripped his forearms. He'd waited for the strength. He'd waited for the demands. Again he touched his lips to hers, allowing his tongue a brief taste. Now her arms wrapped possessively around him. Now passion exploded, mouth against mouth. Lightning flashed, illuminating them as one form in the ageless wonder of lovers.

"Undress me," she whispered breathlessly, hardly able to speak as her lips fused again and again with his. "I want you to undress me."

In answer, he lowered the zipper slowly, allowing his fingers to trail along her bare skin. He found more silk, something thin and fragile. The dress slithered down her body to lie at her feet. Growing impatient, Asher worked her hands between them to deal with the buttons of his shirt while her mouth continued to cling to his. She felt the hard muscle, the line of ribs, the mat of hair. A moan wrenched from her out of deep, desperate need.

The thigh-length chemise was too much of a barrier. Longing for the intimacy of flesh against flesh, Asher reached to draw down the strap. Again Ty stopped her.

"Don't rush," he murmured, then tore at her control with a deep, lingering kiss. The pressure was hard and demanding, the lips soft and heated. "Come to bed."

In a haze she let him lead her, felt the mattress give under her weight, then his. Anticipation shivered along her skin. "The light," she whispered.

As he circled her throat with his hand, Ty's eyes met hers. "I need to see you." Thunder exploded as his mouth crushed down on hers.

When she would have hurried, he set the pace. Languorous, sleepy, enervating. It seemed her lips alone would pleasure him enough for a lifetime. She was so soft, so moist. Far from pliant, Asher moved against him, inviting, insisting. Her urgency excited him, but Ty chose to savor. Over the silk his hands roamed to trace her shape from thigh to breast. The peaks strained against the sheer material.

He took his mouth to her shoulder, catching the narrow strap of the silk with his teeth. Inch by inch he lowered it until her flesh was exposed to him. She was firm and creamy-white in contrast to the tan of her arms and shoulders.

"So lovely," he whispered while his fingertip brought down the second strap.

When she was naked to the waist, his mouth ranged down slowly, though with her hands in his hair she urged him down. With lips parted, Ty sought the peak of her breast. Asher arched, pressing him down. She wanted him to be greedy, wanted to feel the rough scrape of his tongue. When she did she could no longer be still. Her body vibrated with the beat of a hundred tiny pulses. Desire, raw and primitive, tore through her with the power to obliterate all but one thought. She was woman; he was man. Seeking pleasure, Asher moved under him, letting her hands roam.

He abandoned gentleness because she wanted none. It had always driven him wild when her passion was unleashed. She had no inhibitions, no shame. When they came together like this she was all fire, and as dangerous as the lightning in the night sky. Ty wasn't even aware of his control slipping away. Hard-palmed hands ran bruisingly over tender skin. Short, manicured nails dug into strong shoulders.

His breathing was ragged when he tore the garment from her. She gave him no time to view her nakedness. Her fingers were busy, struggling to remove the last barrier of his clothing. Their frantic movements took them over the bed, tangling in the sheets. Her skin was damp and trembling, but her hands were so strong, and so certain. There could be no more waiting.

A pain stabbed into him as he entered her. It was sharp, then sweet. He thought he heard her cry out as she had that first night when he had taken her innocence. Then she was wrapped around him—legs, arms. Her mouth fastened on his. The storm crashed directly overhead. They rose with it.

His hand lay lightly on her breast. Asher sighed. Had she ever known such pure contentment? she wondered. No, not even when they had been together before. Then she hadn't known what it would be like to do without him. She shuddered, then moved closer.

"Cold?" Ty drew her to him until her head rested on the curve of his shoulder.

"A little. Where's my chemise?"

"Devoured."

She laughed, flinging her arms around him as though she

would never let go. Free, she thought. How wonderful to be free—to love, to laugh. Supporting herself on his chest, she stared down into his face. For once his eyes were calm. A faint smile curved his lips. Beneath her his breathing was even and slow, to match hers. To match, her mind repeated. They had always been like two halves of the same whole.

"Oh, God, I missed you, Ty." On those words she buried her face against his throat. Empty, empty, she thought. It seemed like a lifetime of emptiness had been wiped away with an hour of fulfillment.

"Asher—"

"No, no questions. No questions." Wildly she rained kisses over his face. "Just feel, just be with me. I need to laugh tonight, the way we used to."

He stopped her hurried movements by taking her head in his hands. There was a plea in her eyes and a light trace of desperation. No, he didn't want to see that now. Pushing away the questions that drummed in his head, he smiled at her.

"I thought you were going to buy me dinner."

Relief washed over her before she grinned. "I have no idea what you're talking about."

"You asked me for a date."

Tossing her head back, she arched an elegant brow. "*I* asked you? You've been out in the heat too long, Starbuck."

"Dinner," he repeated, rolling her over until he loomed above her.

"As far as I can tell, you've already eaten a sixty-dollar silk chemise. Are you still hungry?"

For an answer, he lowered his mouth to her neck and bit, none too gently. Laughing, she tried to twist away. "Food," he muttered. "I have to eat."

Remembering a weakness, she found the spot on his ribs and squeezed. His body jerked, giving her the opportunity to slither away. She was giggling like a girl when he grabbed her and pulled her back. "How many people know the indomitable Starbuck is ticklish?" she demanded when he pinned her arms over her head. "What would the press pay to find out?"

"About the same as they'd pay to find out elegant Asher Wolfe has a heart-shaped birthmark on her very attractive bottom."

Asher considered this a moment. "Even," she decided. Her smile slanted seductively. "Do you really want to go out to eat?"

Desire fluttered lightly in the pit of his stomach as he looked down at her. The light angled across her face, accenting the smooth, glowing skin and darkened eyes. The thunder was a distant rumble now, but he felt it vibrate in his head.

"There's always room service," he murmured, tasting her lips. He kept her arms pinned as he dropped light, teasing kisses over her face. Nestling in the vulnerable curve of her neck, he used his tongue to stir and arouse.

"Ty," she moaned, unable to struggle against the captivity. "Make love to me."

His chuckle was low and he was pleased. "Oh, I am. This time," he whispered into her ear, "we won't hurry. Hours, love." His tongue darted to her ear, making her squirm in agonized delight. "Hours and hours." Then he shifted, bringing her close to his side. Cradling her, he felt her heart pounding against him. When he reached for the phone, Asher glanced up, puzzled. "Food," he reminded her.

She gave a weak laugh. "I should have remembered your stomach comes first."

His hand grazed over her breast. "Not necessarily." Her nipple was already taut. He flicked his thumb over it lazily.

"Ty—" With a kiss he silenced her.

"Champagne," he said into the phone while driving Asher mad with careless strokes and fondling. "Dom Pérignon. Caviar," he went on, sending her a questioning look that she was powerless to answer. "Beluga." He gave her a light kiss, running his hand down to the flat of her stomach. She quivered, turning into him. Legs tangled as he brushed his lips over her shoulder. "Cold shrimp." He bit her tender bottom lip. "Mmm, that'll do. Yes, for two." As he dropped the phone back on its cradle, Asher found his mouth in a desperate, yearning kiss. "Food excites you?" he mumbled against the hungry lips. Struggling not to take her instantly, he ran his hand to her hip, kneading warm flesh.

"I want you." Her voice was low and throaty, her hands questing. "I want you now."

"Shh." Slow, patient, his stroking aroused rather than subdued. "Relax. There's time. I want to see you again." He drew away from her. "Really see you."

She was burning for him. Now she lay naked and vulnerable under his gaze. As she watched, his eyes darkened, grew stormy. Her breathing quickened. When she reached out he took her hand, burying his lips in the palm.

"You're more beautiful than ever," he said huskily. "It shouldn't be possible. I've looked at you so many times and have been afraid to touch."

"No." Asher pulled him to her until they were heart to heart. "I'm never more alive than when you touch me." With a sigh Ty nestled down until his head rested between her breasts. Asher combed her fingers through his hair as contentment layered over desire. "Today, when I watched you playing Michael, I wanted you. Sitting there, surrounded by thousands of people in the middle of the afternoon, all I could think about was being with you like this." She gave a gurgle of laughter. "Wicked thoughts, such wonderfully wicked thoughts."

"So your invitation to dinner carried an ulterior motive."

"In your weakened condition I knew you'd be a pushover, though I had thought I'd have to take you out and ply you with food and wine first."

"And if I'd refused?"

"I'd have come up with something else."

Grinning, he lifted his head. "What?"

Asher shrugged. "I could have come up here and seduced you before you'd gotten your strength back."

"Hmm...I almost wish I'd said no."

"Too late. I have you now."

"I could get stubborn."

Slowly she smiled. "I know your weaknesses," she whispered, running a fingertip up the nape of his neck. His shudder was quick and uncontrollable. Leaning up, she took his face in her hands. Lazily she rubbed her lips over his, then deepened the touch into a kiss—a long, draining taste that left him weak. Her tongue glided over his, then retreated.

"Asher." On an oath he crushed her beneath him, savaging her mouth with a need that had risen so quickly, it left him dazed. He didn't hear the discreet knock on the door, nor did he understand her murmurs.

"The door," she managed. "Ty, it's room service."

"What?"

"The door."

Laying his forehead on hers, he struggled to recapture his control. "They're awful damn quick," he muttered. He found he was trembling. How could he have forgotten that she could make him tremble? After letting out a long breath, he rose. Asher pulled the sheets up to her chin and watched him cross to the closet.

A beautiful body, she thought, both proud and admiring. Long and lean, with a network of muscle. She looked her fill as he rummaged through his closet for a robe. Strong shoulders, trim waist, narrow hips and long legs. An athlete's body, or a dancer's. He was made to compete.

He shrugged into the robe, belting it carelessly. Grinning, he turned to her. Asher's heart lodged in her throat. "Ty, you're so beautiful."

His eyes widened in astonishment. Torn between amusement and masculine discomfort, he headed for the door. "Good God," he said, making Asher smother a giggle. She brought her knees up to her chest as he signed the check at the door. In some ways, she mused, he was a little boy. To his way of thinking, the word *beautiful* applied only to a woman—or to an ace. He'd be more insulted than complimented having it applied to himself. Yet she saw him that way—not only physically. He was a man capable of lovely gestures, a man unashamed of his deep love for his mother, unafraid to show tenderness. He had no cruelty in him, though on the court he was unmerciful. His temper was explosive, but he was incapable of holding a grudge. Asher realized that it was his basic capacity for feeling that she had missed most of all. And still he had never, in all their closeness, in all the months of intimacy, told her that he loved her. If he had once said the words, she would never have left him.

"Where have you gone?"

Asher turned her head to see him standing beside a tray, a bottle of champagne in his hands. Quickly she shook her head and smiled again. "Nowhere." She cocked her head at the bottle. "All that just for us?"

He walked to the bed and sat on the edge. "Did you want some too?" The cork came off with a resounding pop as she cuffed his shoulder. With an easy stretch he rolled the tray toward them. "Here, hold the glasses." Without ceremony he poured champagne until it nearly ran over the rims.

"Ty, it'll spill on the bed."

"Better be careful then," he advised as he set the bottle back in the ice. He grinned as she sat cross-legged, balancing two glasses in her hands. The sheet was held in place over her breasts by arms pressed tightly to her sides.

She returned the grin with a glance of exasperation. "Aren't you going to take one?"

"Oh, I don't know." Hooking a finger under the sheet, he nudged it downward, exposing creamy flesh.

"Ty, cut it out, I'll spill it!"

"Better not, we have to sleep here." He urged the sheet a trifle lower. Frustrated, Asher looked from glass to glass. Wine swayed dangerously.

"This is a dirty trick, Starbuck."

"Yeah, I like it."

Asher narrowed her eyes. "I'm going to pour both glasses into your lap."

"Terrible waste," he decided, kissing her. "It's good stuff. I always found it strange," he began, lazily kissing her face as he spoke, "that I was bred for beer and you were bred for champagne, but you haven't any head for it."

"I have a perfectly good head for champagne."

Chuckling, he brushed his lips over her throat. "I remember one very memorable night when we shared a bottle. Three glasses make you crazy. I like you crazy."

"That's absurd." The lift of brow challenged him. Without hesitation Asher brought a glass to her lips, losing the sheet as she drank it. Ty watched the linen pool into her lap before she drained the last drop. "That's one," Asher announced, lifting the second glass. Ty plucked it from her fingers.

"Let's spread it out a little," he advised, amused. He drank, more conservatively, then reached for the tray of caviar. "You like this stuff."

"Mmm." Suddenly hungry, Asher spread a generous amount on a toast point. Ty settled down to the bowl of cold shrimp and spicy sauce. "Here, it's good." Though he allowed her to feed him a bite, he wrinkled his nose.

"Overrated," he stated. "This is better." He popped a shrimp into Asher's mouth.

"'S wonderful," she agreed with a full mouth, then chose another. "I didn't know I was so hungry."

Ty filled her glass again. Could anyone else imagine her, he wondered, sitting naked in bed, licking sauce from her finger? Did anyone else know how totally open she could be? She was talking now, in fits and starts as she ate, replaying her match. Ty let her ramble, pleased just to hear her voice, to see her animation. She was satisfied with her serve, worried about her backhand volley.

Publicly she chose her words with care, and made certain there were few of them. If a reporter could see her now, Ty mused, he'd wear a pencil down to the nub. She was full of joy and doubt, fear and self-congratulation. Words tumbled out without discretion. Her face was animated, her hands gestured. By the time she had slowed down, her second glass was empty. Perhaps she was completely happy, because she wasn't even aware of the sensation. She was simply at ease, completely herself. Comfortably full, she toyed with the last of the caviar.

"Are you worried about playing Chuck in the finals?"

Ty bit into a shrimp. "Why?"

"He was always good," Asher began, frowning a bit. "But he's developed over the past few years."

Grinning, Ty tilted more wine into her glass. "Don't you think I can beat him?"

She sent him a long, considering look. "You were always good too."

"Thanks." After setting the caviar on the tray, he stretched lengthwise on the bed.

"Chuck plays a bit like my father did," Asher mused. "Very clean, very precise. His talent's polished rather than raw."

"Like mine."

"Yes. That raw athletic ability is something every competitor envies. My father used to say that you had more natural talent than any player he'd seen in his career." Over the rim of her glass she smiled down at him. "Yet he always wanted to smooth out your form. Then there were your…antics on the court."

Ty laughed, kissing her knee through the sheet. "It used to drive him crazy."

"I imagine he'd be more pleased if he saw you play now."

"And you?" Ty countered. "How would he feel if he saw you play now?"

Asher shifted her eyes from his to stare into her glass. "He won't."

"Why?"

As if to erase the question, she lifted her hand. "Ty, please."

"Asher," he said quietly, grasping her fingers. "You're hurting."

If she could have held it back, she would have. But the words tumbled out. "I let him down. He won't forgive me."

"He's your father."

"And he was my coach."

Unable to comprehend, Ty shook his head. "What difference does that make?"

"All the difference." The pain slipped out. As if to numb it, she swallowed more wine. "Please, not tonight. I don't want anything to spoil tonight."

Her fingers had tightened on his. One by one Ty kissed them until he felt the tension relax. "Nothing could." Over their joined hands, dark, intense eyes met hers. Spontaneously her pulse began to race. "I never got you completely out of my mind," he confessed. "Too many things reminded me—a phrase, a song. Silence. There were times alone at night I would have sworn I heard you breathing in the quiet beside me."

The words moved her…hurt her. "Ty, those were yesterdays. We can start now."

"Now," he agreed. "But we'll have to deal with yesterday sooner or later."

Though she opened her mouth to disagree, she knew. "Later then. Right now I don't want to think about anything but being with you."

He grinned, brushing a stray curl from her cheek. "It's difficult to argue with that."

"Don't get cocky," she told him, then tossed off the rest of her champagne. "That was three," Asher said haughtily. "And I'm not the least affected."

Ty had no trouble recognizing the signs—the flushed cheeks, the glowing eyes and misty smile. Whatever she might say, he knew the champagne was swimming in her head. And when they loved again, she would be soft and strong and passionate.

He found himself wanting to simply look at her for a few minutes more. Once they touched, the fire would take them.

"Want another?" he offered.

"Sure."

Wisely he filled her glass only halfway before he replaced the bottle. "I caught your interview today," Ty commented. "It was on while I was changing."

"Oh?" Asher shifted to lie on her stomach, propping herself on her elbows. "How'd I do?"

"Hard to say. It was all in French."

She laughed, adjusting her position so that she could take another sip. "I'd forgotten."

"How about a translation?"

"He asked things like—Mademoiselle Wolfe, do you find any changes in your style after your temporary retirement? And I said something like I feel I've tightened my serve." She chuckled into her wine. "I didn't mention that my muscles beg for me to give them a break after two sets. He asked how I felt about playing the *young* Miss Kingston in the finals and I refrained from punching him in the mouth."

"That was diplomatic," Ty answered, slipping the glass from her fingers.

"I'm a hell of a diplomat," Asher agreed. Rolling over on her back, she looked up at him. He lounged just behind her so that she had to tilt her head at an odd angle to make eye contact. "You stole my glass."

"Yes, I did." After setting it on the tray, Ty gave the wheeled table a slight shove.

"Did we finish dinner?" Reaching up and back, she locked her arms around his neck.

"We've definitely finished dinner." He allowed her to urge him down until his mouth hovered above hers.

"Got any suggestions about what we should do now?" She liked the strangeness of having his face upside down over hers. Playfully she nipped at his lip.

"No. Do you?"

"Got a deck of cards?"

"Uh-uh."

"Then I guess we'll have to make love." She gave a rich, low laugh before she kissed him again. "All night—just to pass the time."

"It's something to do. Rainy nights are so boring."

Eyes dancing, she nodded. "Mmm, yes. Let's make the best of it."

Her lips were curved in a smile as his met them, but they parted eagerly. She found it strangely seductive to have his tongue meet hers this way. On a gurgle of laughter, she closed her teeth gently, capturing him. In response, he trailed his fingers over her breast until her moan freed him.

"I get dizzy kissing you upside down," Asher murmured.

"I like you dizzy." Leaning forward, he trailed moist kisses over her throat. The tip of his tongue picked up her flavor, then lingered over it. He could feel pulse beats both with his hand and his lips. Finding the curve of his neck vulnerable, Asher began to give him the same pleasure he was bringing her.

"I want to touch you," she complained. "I can't touch you this way."

But he continued to explore from where he was, enjoying

the freedom his hands had over her body. The scent of the rich sauce still lingering in the air, and the zing of champagne clung to two tongues as they joined. The mattress groaned quietly as she shifted. Then she was on her knees, pressed body to body. In a quick move she had stripped the robe from him so he was as naked as she. With a half laugh, half sigh, she ran her palms up his strong back.

Entwined, enchanted, neither noticed that the rain had ceased. Inside the quiet room, pleasure built. Strong thigh pressed against strong thigh, hungry lips sought hungry lips. Their passion was equal, their needs the same. Together, they lay down.

Soft sighs became moans. Before long, gentle caresses became demanding. Both seemed desperate to touch and be touched, to have their own weaknesses exploited. With instinctive understanding they held back the final gift. The inner fire built, dampening their flesh, but still they lingered over each other. There was so much to make up for, so much time to recapture. Though passion was flaring, this thought hovered in the back of both their minds. Tonight was a fresh beginning. They wanted all of it.

Asher thought her lungs would burst. The combination of wine and passion buzzed in her head. A laugh, smoky with desire, floated from her as he gasped her name. She wanted to tempt him, torment him, give to him. His stomach was hard and flat with muscle, yet the touch of her fingertip could make it quiver. Asher had forgotten this sense of power and exulted in it. Her small hands could make him weak. Her shapely, serious mouth could drive him wild.

The power shifted so abruptly, she was helpless. He found

her greatest vulnerability and used his tongue to destroy her last vestige of control. Half wild, she called for him, struggling to have more, desperate to have all. Arching, she pressed him closer, cresting on a wave of delight that had no chance to recede. She thrashed as if in protest, yet arched again in invitation. As she built toward a higher peak, Ty slid up her body. Greedy, she drew him inside of her, hearing his gasp for breath before there was only feeling.

Later, they still clung together, damp, spent, fulfilled. He shifted only to turn out the light. In the midnight darkness they molded to each other, drifting toward sleep.

"You'll move in with me."

The murmur was a statement rather than a question. Asher opened her eyes before she answered. She could just see the outline of his face. "Yes, if you want me."

"I never stopped wanting you."

Without the light he didn't see the flicker of doubt in her eyes before he slept.

Chapter Seven

She was afraid of London. Lady Wickerton had lived there—hostessing parties in the elegant three-story house in Grosvenor Square, attending the ballet at the Royal Opera House, the theater in Drury Lane, shopping in the West End. Lady Wickerton had played bridge with members of Parliament and had sipped tea at Buckingham Palace. Lady Wickerton had been a quiet, dutiful wife, a woman of intelligence, breeding and control. She had nearly suffocated in London.

Perhaps if Ty hadn't come between Jim Wolfe's daughter and Eric Wickerton's wife, Asher would have accepted her role with ease. She'd wanted to, had struggled to. Too much passion simmered inside her. It had been there all of her life, but the months with Ty had liberated it. Controlling something dormant was entirely different from harnessing something that pulsed with life. There had not even been her profession as an outlet for the energy that drove her.

Coming back to London was the most difficult step yet. There she would not only have to face memories of Ty, but the ghost of a woman she had pretended to be. It was all so familiar—Westminster Abbey, Trafalgar Square, the smells, the voices. Even the anticipation of Wimbledon couldn't block them out. There would be faces here that would remember the coolly elegant Lady Wickerton. And there would be questions.

Publicly she would remain aloof, distant and uninformative. Asher felt she owed Eric that much. She would simply refuse to discuss her marriage or its demise. Her early training, her years of following her father's rules, would serve her now more than ever.

She would give them tennis. With two straight championships now under her belt, Asher would have been spotlighted in any case. It was up to her to sway the press away from her personal life toward her professional resurgence. What was growing between her and Ty was still too fragile to be shared.

Happiness. She had nearly forgotten how simple and overwhelming the feeling was. Lazy midnight talks, crazy loving, quiet walks. They shared a hotel room and made it home for the days and nights they were there. She felt as much a gypsy as he, and was content to be so. Once she had looked for roots, stability, commitment. She'd learned that they meant nothing without the fullness of love. His spontaneity had always fascinated her. This time Asher would resolve the lingering fear of it and enjoy.

"Aren't you dressed yet?"

At the question Asher stopped tying her tennis shoe and glanced up. Ty stood in the doorway between the small parlor and bedroom. Fully dressed, impatient, he frowned at her. His hair fell over his forehead as unruly as ever and still slightly damp from his shower. Waves of love radiated through her.

"Nearly," Asher tossed back. "Not everyone can move quickly in the morning, you know—especially on six hours sleep."

The frown became a grin. "Something keep you up?" He caught the shoe she hurled at him in one hand, his eyes never leaving her face. Apparently the late night hadn't affected him. He looked well rested and full of barely controlled energy. "You can always take a nap after morning practice."

"Awfully pleased with yourself this morning, aren't you?"

"Am I?" Still grinning, he came toward her, tossing her shoe lightly. "It probably has something to do with trouncing that British kid in the quarter-finals yesterday."

"Oh?" Lifting a brow, Asher looked up at him. "Is that all you're pleased about?"

"What else?"

"Let me have my shoe," she demanded. "So I can throw it at you again."

"Did you know you have a poor morning attitude?" he asked, holding the shoe out of reach.

"Did you know you've been insufferable ever since you won the French?" she countered sweetly. "Remember, it's only one quarter of the Grand Slam."

He moved the shoe farther out of reach as she made a grab for it. "For you too, Face," he reminded her.

"The rest's on grass." In an attempt to hold him still, Asher grabbed the waistband of his warm-up pants.

"The woman's insatiable," he sighed. Diving, he pinned her beneath him on the bed.

"Ty! Stop!" Laughing, Asher pushed against him as he nuzzled at her neck. "We'll be late for practice."

"Oh. You're right." Giving her a quick kiss, he rolled away from her.

"Well," Asher muttered as she sat up, "you didn't take much persuading." Even as she started to tidy her hair, she was spun back into his arms. Her startled exclamation was smothered by his lips.

Long, deep, infinitely tender, smolderingly passionate. His arms circled her. Asher felt her bones soften, then dissolve. Her head fell back, inviting him to take more. Cradling her, Ty went on a slow exploration of her mouth. For the moment he enjoyed the sense of total domination. If they continued, he knew she would begin her own demands. Then it would be power for power. The knowledge excited him. Still, he laughed against her lips. There was time. A lifetime.

"You awake yet?" he asked her as he ran a hand lightly over her breast.

"Mmm-hmm."

"Good. Let's go." After setting her on her feet, he gave Asher's bottom a friendly pat.

"I'll get you for that," she promised. Needs stirred inside her, not quite under control.

"I certainly hope so." With an easy smile Ty slipped an arm around her shoulders. "You need to work on your backhand volley," he began as they walked from the room.

Insulted, Asher tossed her head back. "What are you talking about?"

"If you'd shorten your swing a bit more—"

"Shorten your own swing," she retorted. "And while you're at it," she continued, "you weren't exactly Mr. Speed yesterday."

"Gotta save something for the finals."

Asher snorted as she punched the elevator button. "Your conceit never wavers."

"Confidence," Ty contradicted. He liked seeing her this way—relaxed, but ready to laugh or to slap back. Briefly he wondered if she realized she was even more beautiful when she forgot caution. "What about breakfast?"

"What about it?"

"Want to grab some eggs after practice?"

She slid her eyes to his as the doors opened. "Is that your best offer?"

Ty lifted a brow as he followed her into the elevator. Asher exchanged a polite nod with a middle-aged couple in tweed. "Maybe you'd like to take up where we left off last night?" Ty lounged against an elevator wall as Asher gaped at him. "What did you say your name was again?"

Asher could feel two pairs of shocked and interested eyes boring into her back. "Misty," she replied, allowing a trace of cockney to color her voice. "Will you spring for champagne again, Mr. Starbuck? It was ever so good."

He recognized the light of challenge in her eyes and grinned. "So were you, sweetie."

When the doors opened to the lobby, the older couple moved out reluctantly. Asher punched Ty in the arm before she followed.

In less than an hour they were both concentrating on form and speed and the capricious bounces a ball could take on grass. Was she playing better? Asher wondered as she sprang for Madge's slice. She felt looser, less encumbered. Indeed, she felt as though losing were not even a possibility. At Wimbledon she could forget the city of London.

Instead, she could remember the qualifying games at Roehampton, with their anything-goes attitude. Both bad language and rackets had flown. It was a contrast to the elegance and glamour of Wimbledon. Here both the players and the crowd were steeped in tradition. Hydrangeas against a backdrop of rich green grass, ivy-covered walls, limos and chauffeurs. Colors were soothing, mauve and green, as if time itself had sobered them.

Here spectators would be well-mannered, quiet between points, applauding after them. Even those in standing room would behave, or the chair judge would tell them politely to quiet down. No one hung from the scoreboards at Wimbledon. It was as revered as the changing of the guards, as English as double-decker buses.

There was no doubt, as one gazed around the immaculately tended velvet lawns, the pampered roses, the dollhouse kiosks and the stands that could accommodate more than twenty-five thousand, that Wimbledon *was* tennis. It was here former players migrated to. It was here future players aspired to. Asher remembered Ty telling her about watching the matches one long-ago July Fourth and making a vow. He had kept it, not once, but four times. More than anything she had wanted before, Asher wanted them to both walk away from Centre Court as champions.

Behind the baseline, Asher stood with a racket and a ball, staring off into space.

"Had enough?" Madge called out.

"Hmm...what?" Asher's head snapped around. Seeing Madge standing with her legs spread, hand on hips, had her laughing. "I suppose I have, I was daydreaming."

From opposite ends of the court, they walked toward their bags and jackets. "No sense asking if you're happy," Madge began conversationally. "You look absolutely miserable floating two inches off the ground."

"That obvious, huh?"

"I won't pretend not to be pleased," Madge added smugly. "I've always thought you two made a great team. Going to make it official?"

"I— No, we're just taking it one day at a time." Asher kept her eyes lowered as she packed her racket. "Marriage is just a formality, after all."

"And pigs fly," Madge countered calmly. When Asher glanced up with a cautious smile, she went on. "For some, yes, you're right. Not for you, Face. Why did you stay in an unhappy marriage for three years?" When Asher started to speak, Madge lifted a hand. "Because to you marriage is a promise, and you don't break promises."

"I failed once," she began.

"Oh, all by yourself? Isn't that being a bit self-absorbed?" Impatient, Madge settled her hands on her hips again. "Listen, you aren't going to let one mistake keep you from being happy, are you?"

"I am happy," Asher assured her, punctuating the statement by touching Madge's shoulder. "Ty's all I've ever wanted, Madge. I can't risk losing him again."

Her brow puckered in confusion. "But you left him, Asher, not the other way around."

"I'd already lost him," she said flatly.

"Asher, I don't—"

"It's a new day," she interrupted, then took a deep breath of scented morning air. "A fresh start. I know what mistakes I made and have no intention of repeating them. There was a time in my life that I thought I had to come first, before this." Holding up the small white ball, Asher examined it. "Before anything. I looked on tennis as a competitor, his family as a rival. That was stupid." Dropping the ball into a can, Asher closed it.

"That's funny," Madge mused. "There was a time in my life I thought The Dean's work came first. He thought the same about me. It wasn't true in either case."

With a smile Asher slung her bag over her shoulder. "Ty won't ever forget that tennis took him out of that tenement. Maybe he shouldn't. That's the thing that brings fire to his game."

She knows him so well in some ways, Madge thought, and not at all in others. "And what brings the ice to yours?"

"Fear," Asher answered before she thought. For a moment she gave Madge a blank look, then shrugged. Saying it aloud made it seem rather unimportant. "Fear of failure, or exposure." Laughing, she began to walk. "Thank God you're not a reporter."

The gravel crunched underfoot as they moved down the path. It was a sound Asher associated with the tidiness of English courts. "Remind me to tell you sometime what goes through my head five minutes before a match."

With a sigh Asher hooked her arm through her old partner's. "Let's hit the showers."

* * *

There was no dream. Asher slept as deeply as a child, with no worries, no nagging fears. The curtains were drawn closed so that the afternoon sun filtered through lazily. Traffic sounds muffled through it, coming as a quiet drone. She wore only a short terry robe and lay on top of the spread. Ty would come back to wake her so that they could spend some time sightseeing before nightfall. Because they were both scheduled to play the following day, they would go to bed early.

The knock on the door wakened her. Sitting up, Asher ran a hand through her tousled hair. He'd forgotten his key, she thought groggily. She stepped from the dim bedroom into the brighter parlor, wincing against the change of light. Absently she wondered what time it was as she opened the door. Shock took a moment to penetrate.

"Eric," she whispered.

"Asher." He gave her what was nearly a bow before he elbowed his way into the room. "Did I wake you?'

"I was napping." She closed the door, trying to recover her scattered wits. He looked the same, she thought. Naturally he would. Eric would see no reason to change. He was tall, slim, with a military carriage. He had a sharp-featured European face, a bit haughty and remote. Dark blond hair was cut and groomed to indicate wealth and conservatism. Light eyes in a pale face—both romantic, yet intelligent and cold. Asher knew that his mouth could twist into a hard line when he was crossed. As a suitor he had been charming, as a lover, meticulous. As a husband he'd been unbearable. She drew herself straight. He was no longer her husband.

"I didn't expect to see you, Eric."

"No?" He smiled. "Did you think I wouldn't drop by while you were in town? Lost a bit of weight, Asher."

"Competition tends to do that."Years of training had her gesturing toward a chair. "Please, sit down. I'll get you a drink."

There was no reason to be upset by him now, she told herself. No need to feel fear or guilt. Divorced couples managed to be civilized more often than not. Eric, Asher thought with a grim smile, was a very civilized man.

"Have you been well?" She poured his scotch neat, then added ice to Perrier for herself.

"Quite well. And you?"

"Yes. Your family?"

"Doing wonderfully." Eric accepted the glass she offered, then eyed her over the rim. "And your father?" He watched for the flash of pain, and was satisfied.

"As far as I know, he's fine." Quite consciously Asher drew on the mask as she sat.

"Still hasn't forgiven you for giving up your career."

Her eyes were level now and expressionless. "I'm sure you're aware he hasn't."

Mindful of the crease in his pants, Eric crossed his legs. "I thought perhaps now that you're competing again..." He allowed the sentence to die.

Asher watched the bubbles rise in her glass, but left them

untasted. “He no longer acknowledges me,” she said flatly. “I’m still paying, Eric.” She lifted her eyes again. “Does that satisfy you?”

He drank leisurely for a moment. “It was your choice, my dear. Your career for my name.”

“For your silence,” Asher corrected. “I already had your name.”

“And another man’s child in your belly.”

Ice clinked against ice as her hands shook. Quickly she controlled the tremor. “One would have thought it would have been enough that I lost the child,” she murmured. “Did you come all this way to remind me?”

“I came,” Eric said as he leaned back, “to see how my ex-wife was adjusting. You’re victorious on the courts, Asher, and as lovely as ever.” She didn’t speak as his eyes roamed the room. “Apparently you didn’t waste too much time picking up with your old lover.”

“My mistake was in leaving him, Eric. We both know that. I’m very, very sorry.”

He sent her an icy look. “Your mistake was in trying to pass his bastard off on me.”

Furious and trembling, Asher sprang to her feet. “I never lied to you. And by God, I’ll never apologize again.”

He remained seated, swirling liquor. “Does he know yet?”

Her color drained dramatically enough to make him smile genuinely. Hate ate at him. “No, I see he doesn’t. How interesting.”

“I kept my word, Eric.” Though her hands were laced tightly together, Asher’s voice was strong. “As long as I was your wife, I did everything you asked of me.”

He acknowledged this with a slight nod. Her honesty hadn't been enough—nor had her three years of penance. "But you're not my wife any longer."

"We agreed. The marriage was intolerable for both of us."

"What are you afraid he'd do?" Eric mused, frowning up at the ceiling. "He's a very physical man as I remember, with a primitive sort of temper." Lowering his eyes, he smiled again. "Do you think he'd beat you?"

Asher gave a short laugh. "No."

"You're very confident," he murmured. "What exactly are you afraid of?"

Wearily she dropped her hands to her sides. "He wouldn't forgive me, Eric, any more than you have. I lost the child, I lost my father. My self-esteem. I'll never lose the guilt. I hurt nothing but your pride, Eric, haven't I suffered enough for that?"

"Perhaps...perhaps not." Rising, he stepped toward her. She remembered the scent of his crisp, dignified cologne very well. "Perhaps the most perfect punishment might be in never knowing your secret is safe. I'll make you no promises, Asher."

"It astonishes me that I was ever naïve enough to think of you as a kind man, Eric," she said softly.

"Justice," he returned, toasting her.

"Revenge has little to do with justice."

He shrugged an elegant shoulder. "All in your viewpoint, my dear."

She wouldn't give him the satisfaction of breaking down—of weeping, of screaming or begging. Instead, Asher stood perfectly still. "If you've said all you've come to say, I'd like you to go."

"Of course." After finishing off the liquor, he set down the glass. "Sleep well, darling. Don't bother, I'll let myself out." Eric turned the doorknob and found himself face-to-face with Ty. Nothing could have pleased him more.

Ty noted his cold, satisfied smile before his gaze shifted to Asher. Standing in the center of the room, she seemed frozen. There was anguish, and, he thought, fear in her eyes. Her face was dead-white and still. Even as he wondered what it was she feared, Ty took in the rest of her appearance. The tousled hair, the brief robe and exposed skin had rage boiling in him. Asher could feel it from where she stood.

His eyes whipped back to Eric's. There was murder in them. "Get the hell out of here."

"Just on my way," Eric said equably, though he had inched back against the door in instinctive defense. His last thought as he shut it behind him was that Asher would bear the brunt of the fury in Ty's eyes. That alone had made it worth the trip.

The room vibrated with the silent storm. Asher didn't move. It seemed Ty would stare at her for eternity. The trembling was difficult to control, but she forced herself. If she made light of the incident, perhaps so would he.

"What the hell was he doing here?"

"He just dropped by…I suppose to wish me luck." The lie sliced at her.

"Cozy." Crossing to her, Ty caught the lapel of her robe in his hand. "Don't you usually dress for visitors, Asher? Then again, I suppose it isn't necessary for ex-husbands."

"Ty, don't."

"Don't what?" he demanded. Though he struggled against the words, the accusations, the feelings, he knew it was a losing battle. Against the unknown he would always attack. "Wouldn't it be better form to meet him somewhere else? It's a little sticky here, isn't it?"

The cold sarcasm hurt more than his fury would have. With so much to hide, she could only shake her head. "Ty, you know there's nothing between us. You know—"

"What the hell do I know?" he shouted, grasping the other lapel. "Don't ask, don't question. Then I walk in and find you entertaining the bastard you left me for."

"I didn't know he was coming." She gripped his arms for balance as he nearly lifted her off her feet. "If he had called, I would have told him to stay away."

"You let him in." Enraged, he shook her. "Why?'

Despair rather than fear clutched at her. "Would you be happier if I had slammed the door in his face?"

"Yes, damn it."

"I didn't." She pushed at him now, as furious as he. "I let him in, I gave him a drink. Make what you like of it. I can't stop you."

"Did he want you back?" he demanded, ignoring her struggles. "Is that why he came?"

"What does it matter?" Impotently she slammed her fists into his chest. "It's not what *I* want." She threw back her head, her eyes burning.

"Then tell me, tell me now why you married him." When she tried to pull away, he dragged her back. "I'll have that much, Asher, and I'll have it now."

"Because I thought he was what I needed," she cried out. Roaring in her ears was the anger, the fear she had felt for Eric.

"And was he?" To prevent her from striking out, Ty grasped her wrist.

"No!" She jerked but couldn't free herself. Frustration added to an almost unreasonable fury. "No, I was miserable. I was trapped." Her voice was both strong and harsh. "I paid in ways you can't imagine. There wasn't a day I was happy. Does that satisfy you?"

She did something he had never seen her do before. She wept. His grip on her wrists loosened as he watched tears flood her eyes and spill onto her cheeks. Never in all the years he'd known her had he seen that kind of torment on her face. Tearing herself from his grip, Asher fled into the bedroom, slamming the door at her back.

She wanted peace. She wanted privacy. The grief had hit her unexpectedly. If the tears hadn't clogged her throat, she would have told him about the baby. The words had been there, ready to spill out in anger. Then speech had been impossible. Now she needed to weep it out.

Ty stared at the closed door for a long time. The wrenching sound of sobbing came to him. It was a reaction he hadn't expected. His anger was justified, as were his questions. Anger for anger he could have comprehended, but the pain he heard was altogether different. Having come from a family of women, he understood a woman's tears. Over the years he'd done his share of comforting and soothing. But these sobs were hot and bitter—and Asher never wept.

Jess cried easily, quiet, feminine tears. His mother wept with joy or silent sadness. These he could handle. A shoulder could be offered, a few sympathetic words, a teasing comment. Instinctively he knew none of those were the prescription for raw grief.

He still had questions. He still had anger. But the sounds from the bedroom forced him to put them aside. Ty recognized when tears were used as a weapon or a defense. These were being torn from her unwillingly. Dragging a hand through his hair, he wondered if it was Eric or himself who was responsible for them. Or something he knew nothing about. Cursing softly, he went to the door and opened it.

She lay curled on the bed in a ball of misery. Her body shook. When he touched her she jerked away. Saying nothing, Ty lay down beside her, gathering her close. For another moment she fought him. *Alone.* Her tears were not to be observed, not to be shared. *Private.* Ty dealt with her struggles by merely holding her tighter in arms that were both strong and gentle.

"I'm not going anywhere," he murmured.

With no more protest, Asher clung to his comfort and let her grief run its course.

It had grown dark and her body was weak. There were no more tears left in her. Ty's arms were strong around her. Beneath her damp cheek she could hear the steady beat of his heart. Gently, almost absently, his fingers stroked the base of her neck.

She'd nearly told him. Asher closed her eyes, too weary to feel fear or regret. If she could have summoned up the energy, she would have been grateful for the tears that had prevented her confession.

I lost your baby. Would he be holding her now if those words had spilled out? What good would it do to tell him? she asked herself. Why make him grieve for something he had never known? And grieve he would, she knew, after the anger passed. It came to her suddenly that it wasn't only fear that kept the secret locked inside her. She couldn't bear to see Ty hurt as she had hurt.

How could she explain to him about Eric without dragging up old bitterness, opening old wounds? Ty hadn't wanted her any longer—Jess had made that abundantly clear. But Eric had. It had been her pride that had turned to Eric, then her sense of duty that had kept her with him. Perhaps if she had been stronger after the accident she would never have made those promises to him....

Asher had floated to consciousness on a wave of pain. What reason was there to wake up and hurt? she thought groggily. Sleep, sleep was so peaceful.

She remembered the shouting, the fall, the swimming darkness. The baby...Ty's baby. Panic—the panic pierced by lethargy. Her eyelids seemed weighted with lead, but she forced them open even as she reached a protective hand to her stomach. Stern and cold, Eric's face floated in front of her eyes.

"The baby," she managed through dry lips.

"Dead."

Tearing, burning grief replaced the pain. "No." Moaning, she closed her eyes again. "Oh, God, no. My baby, not my baby. Ty—"

"Listen to me, Asher." Eric spoke briskly. For three days he had waited while Asher drifted in and out of consciousness. She had lost the baby and a great deal of blood. Once she had nearly slipped away, but he had willed her to live. The love he had once felt had turned to resentment that bordered on hate. She had deceived him, made a fool of him. Now he would have his payment.

"My baby..."

"The baby's dead," he said flatly, then gripped her hand. "Look at me." She obeyed with eyes glazed with sorrow. "You're in a private clinic. The reason for your being here will never be known beyond the front doors. If you do what I say."

"Eric..." A spark of hope flickered. With what strength she had, Asher tightened her fingers on his. "Are they sure? Couldn't there be a mistake? Please—"

"You miscarried. The servants will be discreet. As far as anyone knows, we've slipped away for a few days."

"I don't understand." She pressed her hand against her stomach as if to make the truth a lie. "The fall...I fell down the stairs. But—"

"An accident," he stated, making the loss of the child sound like a broken glass.

Insidiously the pain slipped through. "Ty," Asher moaned, shutting her eyes.

"You're my wife, and will remain so until I say differently." Eric waited until her eyes focused on him again. "Would you have me call your lover and tell him you married me while carrying his child?"

"No." She could only whisper the word. *Ty.* She ached for him. He was lost to her—as lost as the child they'd made together.

"Then you'll do as I say. You'll retire from professional tennis. I won't have the press speculating about the two of you and dragging my name through the mud. You'll behave as I expect Lady Wickerton to behave. I will not touch you," he continued with a trace of disgust. "Any physical desire I felt for you is gone. We will live in the manner I designate or your lover will hear from me about this game you played. Is this understood?"

What did it matter how she lived? Asher asked herself. She was already dead. "Yes. I'll do whatever you want. Please, leave me alone now."

"As you wish." He rose. "When you're stronger, you'll give an official press release on your retirement. Your reason will be that you have no more time for tennis or any desire for a career that would take you away from your husband and your adopted country."

"Do you think it matters to me?" she whispered. "Just let me alone, let me sleep."

"Your word, Asher."

She gave him a long last look before she wearily closed her eyes. "My word, Eric."

And she had kept it. She had tolerated Eric's pleasure when her father had turned away from her. She had ignored his discreet but frequent affairs. For months she had lived like a zombie, doing as she was bid. When the layers of grief began to peel away, his hold remained through guilt and threats. When she had begun to come to life again, Asher had bargained for her freedom. Nothing was more important to Eric than his reputation. She held his many women in one hand, he held the knowledge of Ty's child in the other. They'd made an uneasy agreement.

Now he was back, Asher mused. Perhaps because she was making a success of her life again. Still, she felt he would keep his silence, if only to ensure a hold over her. Once he spoke, all ties were severed. Or if she spoke…

She remembered the look on Ty's face when he had seen her with Eric. Explanations would never be accepted now. Perhaps the day would come when they fully trusted each other, when the memory of betrayal would be dimmed.

She'd been silent for some time. By the steadiness of her breathing she might have been sleeping. Ty knew she was awake and thinking. What secrets was she holding from him? he wondered. And how long would it be before the air between them was finally cleared? He wanted to demand, but her vulnerability prevented him. More than anything else, he didn't want to risk her slipping behind the wall she could so easily erect.

"Better?" he murmured.

She sighed before he felt the faint movement of her head as she nodded. There was one thing she could settle between them, one thing she could make him understand. "Ty, he means nothing to me. Do you believe that?"

"I want to."

"Believe it." Suddenly intense, she sat up and leaned against his chest. If she could give him nothing else, she could give him this. "I feel nothing for Eric, not even hate. The marriage was a mistake. From the start it was nothing more than a façade."

"Then why—"

"It's always been you," she said before she crushed her mouth to his. "Always you." She pressed her lips to his throat, passion erupting in her as swiftly as the tears. "I stopped living for so long and now…" Her mouth ran wildly over his face. "I need you now, only you."

Her mouth met his fervently, saying more than words. Her ardor touched off his own. There was no need for questions now, or for answers. She pulled the shirt from him, eager to touch. Pressing her lips to heated flesh, she heard him groan. Though her hands moved swiftly to undress him, her lips loitered, lingering to arouse. With her tongue she left a moist trail of fire.

His body was a pleasure to her—hard muscle, long bones, taut flesh. Delighting in him, she sought new secrets. If she nibbled at his waist, his breathing grew shallow, his fingers gripped her hair. If she moved her palm along his thigh, his moan vibrated with need. Giddy with power, she ran a crazed trail from stomach to chest, her lips hungry and seeking.

He struggled to pull the robe from her as she caught his earlobe between her teeth. Low, sultry laughter drove him wild. Neither heard the seam rip as he tugged the terry cloth from her. Limber and quick, she made it impossible for him to grant them both the final relief. Her lovemaking tormented and thrilled him while her agility held him off.

"Now," he demanded, grasping her hips. "Asher, for God's sake."

"No, no, no," she murmured, then cut off his oath with a

searing kiss. She found the torture exquisite. Though her own body begged for fulfillment, she wanted to prolong it. As his hands slid over her damp skin, she arched back, reveling in his touch. She belonged, and always would, to the man who could release her fires.

Neither was in control, each a slave to the other. She wanted nothing more than to be bound to him—here, in a dark room with the sound of her own breathing raging in her ears, in the sunlight with the secrets of the night still humming between them. For always.

Beneath her, his body was hot and moist and moving. The rhythm seduced her. Everything warm, everything giving, flowed through her. Thoughts vanished, memories dimmed. Now—there was only now—the all-powerful, greedy present.

This time when he gripped her hips she made no attempt to stop him. Her head fell back in complete abandonment as they joined. The moan was rich and deep, and from both of them. As one, they were catapulted up, beyond pleasure, into ecstasy.

Chapter Eight

Asher had driven in limousines all her life. As a child she'd ridden behind a chauffeur named George in a shiny maroon car with smoked glass and a built-in bar. George had remained the family driver though the cars had changed—an elegant white Rolls, a sturdy blue Mercedes.

Lady Wickerton's driver had been Peter and the car had been an old discreet gray Daimler. Peter had been as silent and as efficient as the car. Asher felt no thrill at being driven in the long black limo toward Wimbledon.

As they passed through Roehampton, she watched the scenery. Tidy, healthy trees, trimmed shrubs, orderly flowers. In a few hours, she would be in Centre Court. Aching, sweating…and winning. This was the big prize. Credibility, prestige, press. They were all at Wimbledon.

Once before she and Ty had taken the championships and led the dancing at the Wimbledon Ball—in that year of her life that had brought complete joy and complete misery. Now she would play her old foe Maria Rayski with all the verve and all the cunning she had at her disposal.

Though she'd thought her life had begun to come to order with her first win, Asher now realized she'd been wrong. The turning point was today, here in the arena that was synonymous with her profession. She would play her best here, on the surface she knew best, in the country in which she had lived like a prisoner. Perhaps true confidence would begin after this match was over.

She thought of Ty, the young boy who had once vowed to play and win. Now, in the lush interior of the limo, Asher made a similar vow. She would have a championship season. Reestablish Asher Wolfe *for* Asher Wolfe. Then she would be ready to face the woman. The woman would face the only man who mattered.

The crowds waited for her and other arriving players. The greetings were enthusiastic. Roaming spectators sipped champagne and nibbled on strawberries and cream. Signing autographs, Asher felt light, confident, ready. Nothing, she thought, could mar such a day. The Fourth of July, the brilliant sunshine, the scent of garden flowers.

She remembered other Wimbledons. So little had changed. Fans mingled with players, chatting, laughing. The atmosphere was one of an informal tea party with the promise of a spectacle. But she could feel the nerves. They were there, just under the bonhomie, in the young players, the veterans, doubles and singles finalists. Mixing among them were rock stars and celebrities, millionaires and landed gentry.

Asher saw faces from the past, players from her father's generation. For them it was a reunion, nostalgia, tradition. There were people she had entertained in Grosvenor Square. For them it was a social event. The dress was summer-garden-party chic—picture hats and pastels. Because yesterdays had to be faced, Asher greeted former acquaintances.

"Asher, how lovely to see you again. . . ." "What a sweet little outfit. . . ." "How strange it is not to see you at the club anymore. . . ." There was speculation, thinly veiled by stretched manners. She dealt with it calmly, as she had during her three years of marriage.

"Where's that old man of yours?"

Turning, Asher clasped two large hands warmly. "Stretch McBride, you haven't changed a bit."

Of course he had. When he'd first tickled Asher's chin, he'd been thirty. His face had been unlined, his hair untouched with gray. He'd won nearly every major championship there was to win twice around. Though he was still tall, and nearly as lean as he had been in his prime, the twenty years showed on his face.

"You always told a lie beautifully." Grinning, he kissed her cheek. "Where's Jim?"

"In the States," she answered, keeping her smile bright. "How have you been, Stretch?"

"Just fine. Got five grandchildren and a nice string of sporting goods stores on the East Coast." He patted her hand. "Don't tell me Jim isn't going to be here? He hasn't missed it in forty years."

It was a struggle not to show the pain, much less not to feel it. "As far as I know, he won't be. I'm awfully glad to see you again. I haven't forgotten that you taught me the dump shot."

Pleased, he laughed. "Use it on Maria today," he advised. "I love to see Americans win at Wimbledon. Tell your old man hello for me."

"Take care, Stretch." Her smile evaded the promise she couldn't give. With a parting kiss, he moved away.

Turning, Asher found herself face-to-face with Lady Daphne Evans. The striking brunette had been one of Eric's more discreet dalliances, and one of Asher's more difficult trials. Her eyes automatically cooled, though her voice was scrupulously polite.

"Daphne, you look exquisite."

"Asher." Daphne skimmed cool eyes over Asher's brief tennis dress, down long bare legs to her court shoes. "You look different. How odd to find you an athlete."

"Odd?" Asher countered. "I've always been an athlete. Tell me, how is your husband?"

The thrust was parried with a quick laugh. "Miles is in Spain on business. As it happens, Eric escorted me today."

Though her stomach churned, her face remained composed. "Eric's here?"

"Yes, of course." Meticulously Daphne adjusted the brim of her rose-pink hat. "You don't think he'd miss this Wimbledon, do you?" Long mink lashes swept down, then up again. "We're all very interested in the results. Will we see you at the ball, darling?"

"Naturally."

"Well, I must let you mingle, mustn't I? That's traditional. Best of luck." With a flash of a smile Daphne swirled her skirts and was gone.

Asher fought the nausea, but began to nudge her way through the crowd. All she wanted was the comparative peace of the A locker rooms. The day ahead promised to be enough of a fight without contending with ghosts. With a few smiles and mechanically gracious greetings, she made her way out of the main throng. A few moments to herself—that was what she needed before the stands began to fill, before her strength and abilities were put to the test.

She knew Eric well enough to be certain he had asked Daphne to seek her out. Yes, he would want to be sure she knew he was there—before the match. As she slipped into the locker room, Asher noticed her hands were shaking. She couldn't allow it. In thirty minutes she would have to be in complete control.

When she walked onto the court Asher was careful not to look into the crowd. It would be easier on her nerves if the people who watched and cheered remained anonymous. As she attempted to empty her mind of all but the first game, Asher watched Maria Rayski.

On her own side of the court, Rayski paced, gesturing occasionally to the crowd, tossing comments. Her nerves were undisguised. It was always so, Asher mused. Rayski chewed her nails, cracked her knuckles and said the first thing that came into her mind. In a wary sort of fashion Asher had always liked her. At five foot ten, she was tall for a woman and rangy, with a deadly stretch. Fatalistically Asher recalled she had a habit of badgering her opponent.

Well, she decided as she chose her game racket, Rayski's histrionics might just keep her mind off who was, and who was not, in the stands. She eyed the television camera dispassionately. With the wonder of technology, the match would be relayed to the

States with only a brief delay. Would her father even bother to watch? she wondered. Silently she walked to the baseline for the first serve.

There was no cautious testing in the first games. Rayski went straight for the jugular. Both were fast players, and while Rayski was more aggressive, Asher was a better strategist. A ball could take ungodly bounces on grass, particularly the lush grass of Wimbledon's Centre Court. To defend, to attack, required instinct and timing. It also required complete concentration.

The lead jockeyed back and forth during the first set as the players gave the fourteen thousand spectators the show they'd come to see. Over the elegant, century-old court, they sweated, gritted their teeth and scrambled, not for the enjoyment of those who paid to see, but for the game. Rayski tossed an occasional taunt over the net between rallies. Asher might have been deaf for all the response she gave. She had her rhythm—nothing was going to interfere with it. She placed her ground strokes with deadly precision, charged the net for short angling volleys. Both her form and her energy seemed at perfect peak.

Everything changed when the women took their seats for the towel-off before the third set.

Because she had forgotten about everything but the game, Asher's defenses were lowered. An inadvertent glance up in the stands had her eyes locking with Eric's. A slow, icy smile spread over his face as he lifted a hand in salute—or reminder.

What the devil's wrong with her? Ty asked himself. He shifted closer to the edge of his seat and studied Asher with narrowed eyes. She'd just dropped two games straight, the second one on a double fault. True, Rayski was playing superbly, but so had Asher—until the third set. She was playing mechanically now, as if the life had gone out of her. Too often she was missing basic shots or failing to put anything extra on a return. Rayski's serve was not her strongest weapon, yet she was repeatedly breezing service winners past Asher.

If he didn't know her better, he would have sworn Asher was tanking the match. But Asher wasn't capable of deliberately losing.

Carefully Ty watched for signs of an injury. A strained muscle or twisted ankle would explain the change in her. She gave no sign of favoring a leg. The composure on her face was as perfect as a mask. Too perfect, Ty reflected as the third game went to fifteen-love. Something was definitely wrong, but it wasn't physical. Disturbed, he quickly scanned the crowd.

There were dozens of faces he knew, some by name, some by reputation. There was an award-winning actor he'd once played a celebrity tourney with. Ty had found him an earthy man with a credible forehand. He recognized the ballet star because Asher had once dragged him to see *The Firebird.* Beside the ballerina was a country-western singer with a crossover hit. Ty passed over them, looking for an answer. He found it sitting near the Royal Box.

There was a cool, satisfied smile on Eric's face as he watched his ex-wife. Beside him, a thin, flashy woman in a rose-colored hat looked bored. Rage rose in Ty instantly. His first instinct was to yank Eric up by his five-hundred-dollar lapels and rearrange the expression on his face with his fists.

"Son of a bitch," he muttered, already rising. The hand that grasped his wrist was strong.

"Where are you going?" Madge demanded.

"To do something I should've done three years ago."

Still clinging to his arm, Madge twisted her head to follow the direction of his eyes. "Oh, boy," she said under her breath. Through her fingertips she could feel Ty's temper. Only briefly did she consider the personal satisfaction she would gain from letting Ty do what he wanted. "Hold on," she snapped between her teeth. "Listen to me. Punching him out isn't going to do anything for Asher."

"The hell it won't," he retorted. "You know why he's here."

"To upset her," Madge managed calmly enough. "Obviously he's succeeding. Go talk to her." A strong man might have cringed from the blazing look Ty turned on her. Madge merely arched a brow. "You want to start a fight, Starbuck, do it after the match. I'll referee. Right now, use your head."

His control didn't come easily. Madge watched him struggle for it, lose it, then finally win. Though his eyes were still stormy, the hand under hers relaxed. "If talking doesn't work," he said flatly, "I'm going to break him in half."

"I'll hold your coat," she promised before Ty slipped away.

Knowing he'd have only a moment, Ty decided to use words sparingly—and make them count. After losing the game without making a point, Asher slumped into her chair. She didn't see Ty waiting for her.

"What the hell's wrong with you?"

Her head jerked up at the harsh tone. "Nothing." She was tired, already defeated as she mopped at the sweat on her face.

"You're handing the match to Rayski on a platter."

"Leave me alone, Ty."

"Going to give him the satisfaction of watching you fall apart in front of fourteen thousand people, Face?" There was sarcasm without a trace of sympathy in his voice. He noted the quick, almost indiscernible flash in her eyes. He'd wanted to see it. Always, she played better if there was anger beneath the ice.

"I never thought I'd see you tank a match."

"Go to hell." Whirling, she stalked back to the baseline. Nobody, she thought as she waited for Rayski to take position, nobody accused Asher Wolfe of tanking. Rayski crouched in her pendulum receiving stance while Asher gave the ball a few testing bounces. Tossing it, she drew back her racket and lunged. The effort of the serve came out in a force of breath. The finely pulverized chalk at the baseline rose on contact. Without giving the ace a thought, Asher took her stance for the next serve.

Her anger had teeth. She could feel it gnawing at her. A photographer zoomed in on her face and captured the contradictory placid expression and frosted eyes. Temper was energy. Asher flew across the court, striking the ball as if it were the enemy. Yet her battle was sternly controlled. No one watching her would realize that she cursed Ty with each stroke. No one but Ty himself. Satisfied, he watched her turn her fury on her opponent.

Oh, she was fabulous to see, he thought. Those long, slim legs, the strong shoulders. Her form was so smooth, so precise, yet beneath was that excitement, that smoldering passion. She was as she played, he mused, and wanted her. No one but he knew just how reckless she could be, just how abandoned. The thought had desire moving through him. She was the woman all men fantasized about—part lady, part wanton. And his, Ty told himself fiercely. Only his.

After watching Asher fire a backhand volley past Rayski, he glanced up. Eric's smile was gone. As if sensing the scrutiny, the Englishman looked down. The two men studied each other as the crowd applauded Asher's game. Ty laughed, softly, insolently, then walked away.

Though the match held close to the last point, the impetus Ty had instilled in her carried Asher to the win. She was polite, even charming as she accepted the Wimbledon plate. Inside she was raging. The joy of victory couldn't penetrate the fury and resentment she was feeling. Ty had turned the tide of her emotions away from Eric and onto himself.

She wanted to shout. She smiled and raised her trophy for the crowd to see. She wanted to scream. Politely she allowed the army of cameras to snap her. Fatigue didn't touch her. The ache in her arm might not have existed.

At last freeing herself from the press and well-wishers, she simmered under the shower and changed. Determination made her remain at Wimbledon to watch Ty's match. Stubbornness made her refuse to admire his game. Eric was forgotten. Asher's only thought was to vent her fury at the first possible moment. It took five hard sets and two and a half hours before Ty could claim his own trophy.

Asher left the stadium before the cheers had died.

He knew she'd be waiting for him. Even before Ty slipped the key in the lock, he knew what to expect. He looked forward to it. His adrenaline was still flowing. Neither the shower nor the massage had taken it from him. Wimbledon always affected him this way. As long as he played, winning there would be his first goal.

Now, the demanding games behind him, the win still sweet, he felt like a knight returning home victorious from the wars. His woman waited. But she wouldn't throw herself into his arms. She was going to scratch at him. Oh, yes, he was looking forward to it.

Grinning, Ty turned the knob. He had no more than shut the door behind him than Asher stormed out of the bedroom.

"Congratulations, Face," he said amiably. "Looks like I get first dance at the ball."

"How dare you say those things to me in the middle of the match?" she demanded. Eyes glittering, she advanced on him. "How dare you accuse me of tanking?"

Ty set his bag and rackets on a chair. "What do you call what you were doing?"

"Losing."

"Quitting," he corrected her. "You might as well have put up a sign."

"I've never quit!"

He lifted a brow. "Only for three years."

"Don't you dare throw that in my face." Raising both hands, she shoved him. Instead of being offended, he laughed. It pleased him enormously that he could rattle her control.

"You did good," he reminded her. "I couldn't take a chance on your losing." He gave her cheek an affectionate pinch. "I didn't want to open the ball with Maria."

"You conceited, overconfident louse!" She shoved him again. "Gramaldi almost took you. I wish he had." She shouted the lie at him. "You could use a good kick in the ego." With the intention of storming back into the bedroom, she whirled. Catching her wrist, Ty spun her back around.

"Aren't you going to congratulate me?"

"No."

"Aw, come on, Face." He grinned appealingly. "Give us a kiss."

For an answer Asher balled her hand into a fist. Ducking the blow, Ty gripped her waist and slung her over his shoulder. "I love it when you're violent," he said huskily as she pulled his hair.

To her own surprise—and annoyance—she had to choke back a laugh. "Then you're going to get a real charge out of this," she promised, kicking wildly as he threw her on the bed. Even though her reflexes were quick, Ty had her pinned beneath him in seconds. Breathless, she struggled to bring her knee up to his weakest point.

"Not that violent." Wisely he shifted to safety.

She twisted, squirmed and struggled. "You take your hands off me."

"Soon as I'm finished," he agreed, slipping a hand under the blouse that had come loose from her waistband.

Refusing to acknowledge the sensation of pleasure, Asher glared at him. "Don't you touch me."

"I have to touch you to make love to you." His smile was reasonable and friendly. "It's the only way I know how."

I will not laugh, she ordered herself as the gurgle rose in her throat. She was angry, furious, she reminded herself.

Ty recognized the weakening and capitalized on it. "Your eyes get purple when you're mad. I like it." He kissed her firmly shut mouth. "Why don't you yell at me some more?"

"I have nothing more to say to you," Asher claimed haughtily. "Please go away."

"But we haven't made love yet." Lightly he rubbed his nose against hers.

Refusing to be charmed, she turned her head away. "We aren't going to."

"Wanna bet?" With one swift move he ripped her blouse from neck to waist.

"Ty!" Shocked, Asher gaped at him, her mouth open.

"I nearly did that when you were on Centre Court today. You should be glad I waited." Before she could react he tore her shorts into ragged pieces. Thinking he might have gone mad, Asher stayed perfectly still. "Something wrong?" he asked as his hand moved to cup her breast.

"Ty, you can't tear my clothes."

"I already did." Soft as a feather, his hand roamed down to her stomach. "Want to tear mine?"

"No." Her skin was beginning to quiver. She tried to shift away and found herself held prisoner.

"I made you angry."

Her head cleared long enough for her to glare at him. "Yes, and—"

"Angry enough to win," he murmured, trailing his lips along her throat. "And when I watched you I nearly exploded from wanting you. All that passion simmering just under the surface. And only I know what it's like when it escapes."

She gave a little moan as his fingers stroked the point of her breast but tried to cling to reality. "You had no business saying I was tanking."

"I didn't say that, I only planted the idea." When he lifted his head, the look in his eyes had her drawing in a quick breath. "Did you think I'd stand by and watch him get to you like that? No man gets to you, Asher, no man but me."

With a savage kiss he cut off all words, all thoughts.

It always surprised Asher that Ty could project such raw sexuality in black tie. Conservative, formal dress could do nothing to alter his air of primitive masculinity. The material could cover the muscles, but it couldn't disguise the strength. There had been times Asher had wondered if it was his earthiness that had drawn her to him. Glimpsing him in a room filled with elegantly attired men and women, she knew it was more than that. It was all of him, every aspect, from temper to humor, that had made her his.

The Wimbledon Ball was as traditional as the tournament. The music, the lights, the people. It was always an evening to remember for its beauty and tastefulness. Asher counted the hours until it would be over. Scolding herself, she tuned back into the conversation of her dance partner. She'd always enjoyed a party, always found pleasure in quiet well-run affairs. But now she wished she and Ty could have shared a bottle of wine in their room.

She didn't want the spotlight this evening, but candlelight. Over the heads of the other dancers her eyes met Ty's. It took only one brief glance to know that his thoughts mirrored hers. Love threatened to drown her.

"You're a lovely dancer, Miss Wolfe."

As the music ended, Asher smiled at her partner. "Thank

you." Her smile never wavered as it ran through her head that she had completely forgotten the man's name.

"I was a great fan of your father's, you know." The man cupped a hand under her elbow to lead her from the dance floor. "The Golden Boy of Tennis." With a sigh he patted Asher's hand. "Of course, I remember his early days, before you were born."

"Wimbledon has always been his favorite. Dad loved the tradition…and the pomp," Asher added with a smile.

"Seeing the second generation here is good for the soul." In a courtly gesture he lifted her hand to his lips. "My best to you, Miss Wolfe."

"Jerry, how are you?"

A stately woman in silk brocade swept up to them. Lady Mallow, Eric Wickerton's sister, was, as always, elegant. Asher's spine stiffened.

"Lucy, what a pleasure!"

She offered her fingers to be kissed, sending Asher a brief glance as she did so. "Jerry, Brian's been searching for you to say hello. He's just over there."

"Well then, if you ladies will excuse me."

Having dispatched him, Lucy turned to her former sister-in-law. "Asher, you're looking well."

"Thank you, Lucy."

She gave Asher's simple ivory sheath a brief survey, thinking that if she had worn something so basic, she would have blended in with the wallpaper. On Asher, the muted color and simple lines were stunning. Lucy gave her a candid stare. "And are you well?"

A bit surprised, Asher lifted a brow. "Yes, quite well. And you?"

"I meant that as more than small talk." Lucy's hesitation was brief, as was her glance to determine if they could be overheard. "There's something I've wanted to say to you for a long time." Stiffening, Asher waited. "I love my brother," Lucy began. "I know you didn't. I also know that throughout your marriage you did nothing to disgrace him, though he didn't return the favor."

The unexpected words had Asher staring. "Lucy—"

"Loving him doesn't blind me, Asher," she continued briskly. "My loyalty is with Eric, and always will be."

"Yes, I understand that."

Lucy studied Asher's face a moment, then she seemed to sigh. "I gave you no support when you were my brother's wife and I wanted to offer my apologies."

Touched, Asher took her hand. "There's no need. Eric and I were simply wrong for each other."

"I often wondered why you married him," Lucy mused, still searching Asher's face. "At first I thought it was the title, but that had nothing to do with it. Something seemed to change between you so soon after you were married, hardly two months." Asher's eyes clouded for only a moment under Lucy's direct gaze. "I wondered if you'd taken a lover. But it became very obvious in a short time that it was Eric, not you, who was...dallying. Just as it's become obvious that there's been only one man in your life." Her gaze shifted. Asher didn't have to follow it to know it rested on Ty.

"Knowing that hurt Eric."

"Knowing that, Eric should never have married you." Lucy sighed again, a bit indulgently. "But then, he's always wanted what belonged to someone else. I won't speak of that, but I'll tell you now what I should have told you long before—I wish you happiness."

On impulse, Asher kissed her cheek. "Thank you, Lucy."

Smiling, she glanced over at Ty again. "Your taste, Asher, has always been exquisite. I've envied it, though it's never been right for me. It's time I joined Brian."

As she turned away, Asher touched her hand. "If I wrote you, would you be uncomfortable?"

"I'd be very pleased." Lucy moved away, silks rustling.

Smiling, Asher realized she had been right. Wimbledon was her turning point. Another layer of guilt had been lifted. She was coming closer to discovering who she was, and what she needed. Feeling a hand on her arm, she turned to smile at Ty.

"Who was that?"

"An old friend." Asher lifted a hand to his cheek. "Dance with me? There's no other way I can hold you until we can be alone."

Chapter Nine

Asher knew she had made great strides when pressure from the press no longer tightened her nerves. Her habitual terror of saying the wrong thing, or saying too much, faded. She still had secrets. Before coming to Australia she'd promised herself a moratorium. Whatever decisions had to be made would wait. For the moment she wanted to concentrate on happiness. Happiness was Ty—and tennis.

There were good memories in Australia—wins, losses. Good tennis. The people were relaxed, casual. The friendliness was exactly what Asher needed after the tension of England. Aussies remembered The Face, and welcomed her. For the first time since her comeback Asher found the winning taking second place to the enjoying.

The change in her was noticeable even during the early rounds. Her smiles came more frequently. Though her play was no less intense and concentrated, the air of being driven was fading.

From the first row of the stands Ty watched her in early morning practice. He'd just completed two hours of his own. Now, his legs stretched out, he studied her from behind the protection of tinted glasses. She'd improved, he mused...not only as an athlete. He remembered how important athletic ability was to her. The fact that she was a strategist and a craftsman had never been enough. Always, she had striven to be recognized as a good athlete. And so she would be, he thought, as she raced to the net to slap a return with her two-fisted backhand. Perhaps in some ways the years of retirement had toughened her.

His face clouded a moment. Consciously he smoothed the frown away. This wasn't the time to think of that or to dwell on the questions that still plagued him. Whys—so many whys hammered at him. Yet he recognized that she was grabbing this time to be carefree. He'd give her that. He would wait. But when the season was over, he'd have his answers.

When her laughter floated to him he forgot the doubts. It was a rich, warm sound, heard all too rarely. Leaning back, Ty chugged down cold fruit juice and looked around him.

If Wimbledon was his favorite stadium, the grass of Kooyong was his favorite surface. It was as hard as a roadbed and fast. A ball bounced true here, unlike other grass courts. Even at the end of the season, when the courts were worn and soiled, the surface remained even. Even after a deluge of rain, the Australian grass was resilient. Kooyong was a treasure for the fast, for the aggressive. Ty was ready for just such a match. Through half-closed eyes he watched Asher. She was ready, too, he decided. And ever more ready to enjoy it. A smile touched his mouth. Whatever questions there were, whatever answers, nothing could harm what was between them now.

Noting the practice session was winding up, Ty jumped lightly down to the court. "How about a quick game?"

Madge shot him a look and continued to pack up her rackets. "Forget it, hotshot."

He grabbed a racket from her, bouncing a ball lightly on the strings. "Spot you two points."

With a snort Madge snatched the ball, dropping it into the can. "Take him on, Asher," she suggested. "He needs a lesson."

Catching her tongue between her teeth, Asher studied him. "Head to head," she decided.

"You serve."

Asher waited until he had taken his receiving position. Cupping two balls in her hand, she sent him a smile. "Been a while, hasn't it, Starbuck?"

"Last time we played you never got to game point." He gave Madge a wink. "Sure you don't want that handicap?"

Her ace answered for her. As pleased as he was surprised, Ty sent her a long look. Removing the tinted glasses, he tossed them to Madge. "Not bad, Face." His eyes followed the trail of the next serve. He sent it to the far corner to brush the service line. Ty liked nothing better than to watch Asher run. The range of her backhand was limited, but perfectly placed. He was on it in a flash. The last time they had played he had beaten her handily even while holding back. Now he scented challenge.

Asher lined the ball straight at him, hard and fast. Pivoting, Ty slammed it back. The ball whistled on her return. With a powerful swing Ty sent her to the baseline, then nipped her return so that the ball brushed the net and died in the forecourt.

"Fifteen-all." Ty feigned a yawn as he went back to position.

Narrowing her eyes, Asher served. The rally was a study in speed and footwork. She knew he was playing with her, moving her all over the court. Aware that she was no match for his power, she chose to catch him off guard. The ball thudded. She raced. It soared. She followed. The sounds of rackets cutting air had a steady, almost musical sound. A rhythm was set. Patiently she adhered to it until she sensed Ty relaxing. Abruptly she altered the pacing and slapped the ball past him.

"Getting crafty," he muttered.

"Getting slow, old timer," she retorted sweetly.

Ty slammed her next serve crosscourt. After the bounce, it landed somewhere in the grandstands. Under her breath Asher swore pungently.

"Did you say something?"

"Not a thing." Disgusted, Asher shook her hair back. As she readied to serve, she caught the look in Ty's eyes. They rested not on her ball or racket, but on her mouth.

All's fair, she mused with a secret smile. Slowly and deliberately she moistened her lips with the tip of her tongue. Taking a long, preliminary stretch, she served. Distracted, Ty was slow to meet the ball. Asher had little trouble blowing the return past him.

"Game point," she said softly, sending him an intimate smile. Keeping her back to him, she bent to pick up a fresh ball, taking her time about it. She could almost feel Ty's eyes run up the long length of her legs. Smoothing a hand down her hip, she walked back to the baseline. "Ready?"

He nodded, dragging his eyes away from the subtle sweep of her breasts. When his eyes met hers, he read an invitation that had his pulse racing. His concentration broken, he barely returned her serve. The rally was very short.

Victorious, Asher let out a hoot of laughter before she walked to the net. "Your game seemed to be a bit off, Starbuck."

The gibe and the laughter in her eyes had him wanting to strangle her…and devour her. "Cheat," he murmured as he walked to meet her at the net.

Asher's look was guileless and she was faintly shocked. "I have no idea what you're talking about." The words were hardly out of her mouth when she was pulled against him, her lips crushed under his. Laughter and desire seemed to bubble in her simultaneously. Without being aware of it, she dropped her racket and clung to him.

"You're lucky I don't toss you on the ground here and now," he mumbled against her mouth.

"What's lucky about that?" Enchanted, Asher strained against him. How was it possible for one kiss to make her head swim?

Ty drew back, inches only. His whole body was throbbing for her. "Don't tempt me."

"Do I?" she asked huskily.

"Damn you, Asher. You know just how much."

His voice shook, delighting her. She found she needed him to be as vulnerable as she. "I'm never sure," she whispered, dropping her head to his chest.

His heart was beating too rapidly. Ty tried to fight down the impossible surge of need. Not the time, not the place, his sanity stated. Control was necessary. "You were sure enough to use a few tricks to distract me."

Lifting her head, Asher smiled at him. "Distract you? How?"

"Took your time picking up that ball, didn't you?"

She seemed to consider a moment. "Why, I've seen Chuck do the same thing playing against you. It never seemed to make any difference." She let out a whoop of surprise as he lifted her up and over the net.

"Next time I'll be ready for you, Face." After giving her a brief, bruising kiss, he dropped her to her feet. "You could play naked and I wouldn't blink an eye."

Catching her lip between her teeth, she sent him a teasing glance. "Wanna bet?" Before he could connect his racket with her bottom, she dashed away.

The locker room wasn't empty as Asher walked in, but the crowd was thinning. With the fifth rounds completed, there were fewer contenders, and therefore fewer bodies. She was looking forward to her match that afternoon with a hot newcomer who had hopped up in the rankings from one hundred and twentieth to forty-third in one year. Asher had no intention of strolling into the finals. Even the pressure of Grand Slam potential couldn't mar her mood. If ever there was a year she could win it, Asher felt it was this one.

She greeted a towel-clad Tia Conway as the Australian emerged from the showers. Both women knew they would face each other before the tournament was over. Asher could hear a laughing argument taking place over the sound of running water. As she started to remove her warm-up jacket, she spotted Madge in a corner.

The brunette sat with her head leaning back against the wall, her eyes shut. She was pale despite her tan, and there were beads of perspiration on her brow. Asher rushed over to kneel at her feet.

"Madge."

Opening her eyes slowly, Madge sighed. "Who won?"

For a moment Asher went blank. "Oh, I did. I cheated."

"Smart girl."

"Madge, what's wrong? God, your hands are like ice."

"No, it's nothing." She let out a breath as she leaned forward.

"You're sick, let me—"

"No, I've finished being sick." After a weak smile Madge swiped the sweat from her brow. "I'll be fine in a minute."

"You look terrible. You need a doctor." Asher sprang to her feet. "I'll call someone." Before she could move, Madge had her hand.

"I've seen a doctor."

Every sort of nightmare went through Asher's head. In stark terror she stared at her friend. "Oh, God, Madge, how bad?"

"I've got seven months." As Asher swayed, Madge caught her arm tightly. "Good grief, Asher, I'm pregnant, not dying."

Stunned, Asher sank to the bench. *"Pregnant!"*

"Shh." Quickly Madge glanced around. "I'd like to keep this quiet for a while. Damn morning sickness catches me off guard at the worst times." Letting out a shaky breath, she relaxed against the wall again. "The good news is it's not supposed to last long."

"I don't—Madge, I don't know what to say."

"How about congratulations?"

Shaking her head, Asher gripped both of Madge's hands in hers. "Is this what you want?"

"Are you kidding?" On a half laugh, Madge leaned against Asher's shoulder. "I might not look too happy at the moment, but inside I'm doing cartwheels. I've never wanted anything so badly in my life." She sat silently for a moment, her hand still in Asher's. "You know, during my twenties all I could think about was being number one. It was great being there. The Wrightman Cup, Wimbledon, Dallas—all of it. I was twenty-eight when I met The Dean, and still ambitious as hell. I didn't want to get married, but I couldn't live without him. As for kids, I thought, hell, there's plenty of time for that. Later, always later. Well, I woke up one morning in the hospital with my leg screaming at me and I realized I was thirty-two years old. I'd won just about everything I thought I had to win, and yet something was missing. For the better part of my life I've floated around this old world from court to court. Team tennis, pro-am tourneys, celebrity exhibitions, you name it. Until The Dean there was nothing but tennis for me. Even after him, it was the biggest slice of the pie."

"You're a champion," Asher said softly.

"Yeah." Madge laughed again. "Yeah, by God, I am, and I like it. But you know what? When I looked at the snapshot of Ty's nephew I realized that I wanted a baby, The Dean's baby, more than I'd ever wanted a Wimbledon plate. Isn't that wild?"

She let the statement hang in silence a moment as both women absorbed it. "This is going to be my last tournament, and even while that's hurting, I keep wishing it was over so I could go home and start knitting booties."

"You don't know how to knit," Asher murmured.

"Well, The Dean can knit them then. I'll just sit around and get fat." Twisting her head to grin at Asher, Madge saw the tears. "Hey, what's this?"

"I'm happy for you," Asher muttered. She could remember her own feelings on learning of her pregnancy—the fear, the joy, the nausea and elation. She'd wanted to learn to sew. Then it had been over so quickly.

"You look overjoyed," Madge commented, brushing a tear away.

"I am really." She caught Madge to her in a viselike hug. "You'll take care of yourself, won't you? Don't overdo or take any chances?"

"Sure." Something in the tone had the seed of a thought germinating. "Asher, did you… Did something happen when you were married to Eric?"

Asher held her tighter for a moment, then released her. "Not now. Maybe someday we'll talk about it. How does The Dean feel about all this?"

Madge gave her a long, measuring look. The non-answer was answer enough, so she let it lay. "He was all set to take out a full-page ad in *World of Sports,*" she stated. "I've made him wait until I officially retire."

"There's no need to retire, Madge. You can take a year or two off, lots of women do."

"Not this one." Stretching her arms to the ceiling, Madge grinned. "I'm going out a winner, ranked fifth. When I get home, I'm going to learn how to use a vacuum cleaner."

"I'll believe that when I see it."

"You and Ty are invited to my first home-cooked dinner."

"Great." Asher kissed her cheek. "We'll bring the antacid."

"Not nice," Madge mused. "But wise. Hey, Face," she continued before Asher could rise. "I wouldn't want this to get around but—" her eyes were suddenly very young, and she looked very vulnerable "—I'm scared right out of my socks. I'll be almost thirty-four by the time this kid makes an appearance. I've never even changed a diaper."

Firmly Asher took Madge's shoulders and kissed both of her cheeks. "You're a champion, remember?"

"Yeah, but what do I know about chicken pox?" Madge demanded. "Kids get chicken pox, don't they? And braces, and corrective shoes, and—"

"And mothers who worry before there's anything to worry about," Asher finished. "You're already slipping right into the slot."

"Hey, you're right." Rather pleased with herself, Madge rose. "I'm going to be great."

"You're going to be terrific. Let's get a shower. You've got a doubles match this afternoon."

With feelings mixed and uncertain, Asher rode the elevator to her hotel room late that afternoon. She had won her round with the young upstart from Canada in straight sets. Six-two, six-love. There was little doubt that Asher had played some of the finest tennis in her career in court one. But she didn't think of that now. Her mind kept drifting back to her interlude with Madge, and from there back to her thoughts on learning of her own pregnancy.

Would Ty have wanted to take out full-page ads, or would he have cursed her? Like Eric, would he have accused her of deceit, of trickery? Now that they were being given a second chance, would he want marriage and children? What was it Jess had said that day? she wondered. *Ty will always be a gypsy, and no woman should ever expect to hold him.*

Yet Asher had expected to hold him, and, despite all her vows, was beginning to expect it again. Her love was so huge, so consuming, that when she was with him, it was simply impossible to conceive of doing without him. And perhaps because she had once, briefly, carried his child inside her, the need to do so again was overwhelming.

Could a woman tame a comet? she asked herself. Should she? For that's what he was—a star that flew, full of speed and light. He wasn't the prince at the end of the fairy tale who would calmly take up his kingdom and sit on a throne. Ty would always search for the next quest. And the next woman? Asher wondered, recalling Jess's words again.

Shaking her head, she told herself to think of today. Today they were together. Only a woman who had lived through change after change, hurt after hurt, could fully appreciate the perfection of a moment. Others might not recognize it, but Asher did. And the moment was hers.

She unlocked the door to their suite and was immediately disappointed. He wasn't there. Even had he been sleeping in the other room, she would have sensed him. The air was never still when Ty was around. Tossing her bag aside, she wandered to the window. The light was still full as the sun had only just began to set. Perhaps they would go out and explore Melbourne, find one of the tiny little clubs with loud music and laughter. She'd like to dance.

Twirling in a circle, Asher laughed. Yes, she would like to dance, to celebrate for Madge...and for herself. She was with the man she loved. A bath, she decided. A long, luxurious bath before she changed into something cool and sexy. When she opened the door to the bedroom, Asher stopped and stared in astonishment.

Balloons. Red, yellow, blue, pink and white. They floated throughout the room in a jamboree of color. Helium-filled, they rose to the ceiling, trailing long ribbons. There were dozens of them—round, oval, thin and fat. It was as if a circus had passed hurriedly through, leaving a few souvenirs. Grasping a ribbon, Asher drew one down to her while she continued to stare.

They were three layers deep, she saw in astonishment—at least a hundred of them bumping against one another. Her laughter came out in a quick burst that went on and on.

Who else would think of it? Who else would take the time? Not flowers or jewelry for Ty Starbuck. At that moment she could have floated to the ceiling to join the gift he had given her.

"Hi."

She turned to see him lounging in the doorway. In a flash Asher had launched herself into his arms, the single balloon still grasped in her hand. "Oh, you're crazy!" she cried before she found his lips with hers. With her arms wrapped around his neck, her legs around his waist, she kissed him again and again. "Absolutely insane."

"Me?" he countered. "You're the one standing here surrounded by balloons."

"It's the best surprise I've ever had."

"Better than roses in the bathtub?"

Tossing her head back, she laughed. "Even better than that."

"I thought about diamonds, but they didn't seem like as much fun." As he spoke he moved toward the bed.

"And they don't float," Asher put in, looking up at the ceiling of colorful shapes.

"Good point," Ty conceded as they fell together onto the bed. "Got any ideas how we should spend the evening?"

"One or two," Asher murmured. The balloon she held drifted up to join the others.

"Let's do both." He stopped her laugh with a soft kiss that became hungry quickly. "Oh, God, I've waited all day to be alone with you. When the season's over we'll find someplace—an island, another planet—anyplace where there's no one but us."

"Anyplace," she whispered in agreement while her hands tugged at his shirt.

Passion soared swiftly. Ty's needs doubled as he sensed hers. She was always soft, always eager for him. If the pounding of his blood would have allowed, he would have revered her. But the force of their joined desire wouldn't permit reverence. Clothes were hastily peeled away—a blouse flung aside, a shirt cast to the floor. Overhead, the balloons danced while they savored each other. The scent of victory seemed to cling to both of them, mixed with the faint fragrance of soap and shampoo from the post-game showers. Her lips tasted warm and moist, and somehow of himself as much as of her.

When there was nothing to separate them, they tangled together, their bodies hot and throbbing. With questing hands he moved over territory only more exciting in its familiarity. He could feel reason spin away into pure sensation. Soft here, firm there, her body was endless delight. The warmth of her breath along his skin could make him tremble. Her moan, as he slipped his fingers into her, made him ache. With open-mouthed kisses he trailed over her, seeking the hot heady flavor of her flesh. It seemed to melt into him, filling him to bursting.

When she arched, offering everything, Ty felt a surge of power so awesome he almost feared to take her. Too strong, he thought hazily. He was too strong and was bound to hurt her. He felt he could have lifted the world without effort. Yet she was drawing him to her with murmuring pleas.

There was no control in madness. She stole his sanity with her smooth skin and soft lips. There were no more pastel colors from frivolous balloons. Now there was gleaming silver and molten reds and pulsing blacks whirling and churning into a wild kaleidoscope that seemed to pull him into its vortex. Gasping her name, Ty thrust into her. The colors shattered, seeming to pierce his skin with a multitude of shards. And in the pain was indescribable pleasure.

When he was spent, nestled between her breasts, Asher gazed up at the darkening ceiling. How could it be, she wondered, that each time they were together it was different? Sometimes they loved in laughter, sometimes in tenderness. At other times with a smoldering passion. This time there had been a taste of madness in their loving. Did other lovers find this infinite variety, this insatiable delight in each other? Perhaps the two of them were unique. The thought was almost frightening.

"What are you thinking?" Ty asked. He knew he should shift his weight from her, but found no energy to do so.

"I was wondering if it should be so special each time I'm with you."

He laughed, kissing the side of her breast. "Of course it should, I'm a special person. Don't you read the sports section?"

She tugged his hair, but tenderly. "Don't let your press go to your head, Starbuck. You have to win a few more matches before you wrap up the Grand Slam."

He massaged the muscles of her thigh. "So do you, Face."

"I'm only thinking as far ahead as the next game," she said. She didn't want to think of Forest Hills, or the States—or the end of the season. "Madge is pregnant," she said half to herself.

"What!" Like a shot, Ty's head came up.

"Madge is pregnant," Asher repeated. "She wants to keep it quiet until the Australian Open is over."

"I'll be damned," he exclaimed. "Old Madge."

"She's only a year older than you," Asher stated defensively, causing him to laugh again.

"It's an expression, love." Absently he twined one of Asher's curls around a finger. "How does she feel about it?"

"She's thrilled—and scared." Her lashes lowered, shielding her expression a moment. "She's going to retire."

"We're going to have to throw her one hell of a party." Rolling onto his back, he drew Asher close to his side.

After a moment she moistened her lips and spoke casually. "Do you ever think about children? I mean, it would be difficult, wouldn't it, combining a family with a profession like this?"

"It's done all the time, depends on how you go about it."

"Yes, but all the traveling, the pressure."

He started to pass it off, then remembered how she had lived her childhood. Though he had never sensed any resentment in her, he wondered if she felt a family would be a hindrance to her career. Physically a baby would prevent her from playing for some time. And she'd already lost three years, he reflected with an inner sigh. Ty pushed the idea of their children out of his mind. There was time, after all.

"I imagine it's a hassle to worry about kids when you've got a tournament to think of," he said lightly. "A player's got enough trouble keeping track of his rackets."

With a murmured agreement, Asher stared into space.

In the thin light of dawn she shifted, brushing at a tickle on her arm. Something brushed over her cheek. Annoyed, Asher lifted her hand to knock it away. It came back. With a softly uttered complaint she opened her eyes.

In the gray light she could see dozens of shapes. Some hung halfway to the ceiling, others littered the bed and floor. Sleepy, she stared at them without comprehension. Irritated at having been disturbed, she knocked at the shape that rested on her hip. It floated lazily away.

Balloons, she realized. Turning her head, she saw that Ty was all but buried under them. She chuckled, muffling the sound with her hand as she sat up. He lay flat on his stomach, facedown in the pillow. She plucked a red balloon from the back of his head. He didn't budge. Leaning over, she outlined his ear with kisses. He muttered and stirred and shifted away. Asher lifted a brow. A challenge, she decided.

After brushing the hair from the nape of his neck, she began to nibble on the exposed flesh. "Ty," she whispered. "We have company."

Feeling a prickle of drowsy pleasure, Ty rolled to his side, reaching for her. Asher placed a balloon in his hand. Unfocused, his eyes opened.

"What the hell is this?"

"We're surrounded," Asher told him in a whisper. "They're everywhere."

A half dozen balloons tipped to the floor as he shifted to his back. After rubbing his face with his hands, he stared. "Good God." With that he shut his eyes again.

Not to be discouraged, Asher straddled him. "Ty, it's morning."

"Uh-uh."

"I have that talk show to do at nine."

He yawned and patted her bottom. "Good luck."

She planted a soft, nibbling kiss on his lips. "I have two hours before I have to leave."

"'S okay, you won't bother me."

Wanna bet? she asked silently. Reaching out, she trailed her fingers up his thigh. "Maybe I'll sleep a bit longer."

"Mmm-hmm."

Slowly she lay on top of him, nuzzling her lips at his throat. "I'm not bothering you, am I?"

"Hmm?"

She snuggled closer, feeling her breasts rub against his soft mat of hair. "Cold," she mumbled, and moved her thigh against his.

"Turn down the air-conditioning," Ty suggested.

Brows lowered, Asher lifted her head. Ty's eyes met hers, laughing, and not a bit sleepy. With a toss of her head Asher rolled from him and tugged on the blanket. Though her back was to him, she could all but see his grin.

"How's this?" Wrapping an arm around her waist, he fit his body to hers. She gave him a shrug as an answer. "Warmer?" he asked as he slid his hand up to cup her breast. The point was already taut, her pulse already racing. Ty moved sinuously against her.

"The air-conditioning's too high," she said plaintively. "I'm freezing."

Ty dropped a kiss at the base of her neck. "I'll get it." He rose, moving to the unit. It shut off with a dull mechanical thud. With a teasing remark on the tip of his tongue, he turned.

In the fragile morning light she lay naked in the tumbled bed, surrounded by gay balloons. Her hair rioted around a face dominated by dark, sleepy eyes. The faintest of smiles touched her lips, knowing, inviting, challenging. All thoughts of joking left him. Her skin was so smooth and touched with gold. Like a fist in the solar plexus, desire struck him and stole his breath.

As he went to her, Asher lifted her arms to welcome him.

Chapter Ten

"Asher, how does it feel being only three matches away from the Grand Slam?"

"I'm trying not to think about it."

"You've drawn Stacie Kingston in the quarter-finals. She's got an oh-for-five record against you. Does that boost your confidence?"

"Stacie's a strong player, and very tough. I'd never go into a match with her overconfident."

Her hands folded loosely, Asher sat behind the table facing the lights and reporters. The microphone in front of her picked up her calm, steady voice and carried it to the rear of the room. She wore her old team tennis jacket with loose warm-up pants and court shoes. Around her face her hair curled damply. They'd barely given her time to shower after her most recent win at Forest Hills before scheduling the impromptu press conference. The cameras were rolling, taping her every movement, recording every expression. One of the print reporters quickly scribbled down that she wore no jewelry or lipstick.

"Did you expect your comeback to be this successful?"

Asher gave a lightning-fast grin—here then gone—something she would never have done for the press even two months before. "I trained hard," she said simply.

"Do you still lift weights?"

"Every day."

"Have you changed your style this time around?"

"I think I've tightened a few things up." She relaxed, considering. Of all the people in the room, only Asher was aware that her outlook toward the press had changed. There was no tightness in her throat as she spoke. No warning signals to take care flashing in her brain. "Improved my serve particularly," she continued. "My percentage of aces and service winners is much higher than it was three or four years ago."

"How often did you play during your retirement?"

"Not often enough."

"Will your father be coaching you again?"

Her hesitation was almost too brief to be measured. "Not officially," she replied evasively.

"Have you decided to accept the offer of a layout in *Elegance* magazine?"

Asher tucked a lock of hair behind her ear. "News travels fast." Laughter scattered around the room. "I haven't really decided," she continued. "At the moment I'm more concerned with the U.S. Open."

"Who do you pick to be your opponent in the finals?"

"I'd like to get through the quarters and semis first."

"Let's say, who do you think will be your strongest competition?"

"Tia Conway," Asher answered immediately. Their duel in Kooyong was still fresh in her mind. Three exhausting sets—three tie breakers—in two grueling hours. "She's the best all-around woman player today."

"What makes you say that?"

"Tia has court sense, speed, strength and a big serve."

"Yet you've beaten her consistently this season."

"But not easily."

"What about the men's competition? Would you predict the U.S. will have two Grand Slam winners this year?"

Asher fielded the question first with a smile. "I think someone mentioned that there were still three matches to go, but I believe it's safe to say that if Starbuck continues to play as he's played all season, no one will beat him, particularly on grass, as it's his best surface."

"Is your opinion influenced by personal feelings?"

"Statistics don't have any feelings," she countered. "Personal or otherwise." Asher rose, effectively curtailing further questioning. A few more were tossed out at random, but she merely leaned toward the mike and apologized for having to end the meeting. As she started to slip through a rear door, she spotted Chuck.

"Nicely done, Face."

"And over," she breathed. "What are you doing here?"

"Keeping an eye on my best friend's lady," he said glibly as he slipped an arm around her shoulders. "Ty thought it would be less confusing if he kept out of the way during your little tête-à-tête with the members of the working press."

"For heaven's sake," Asher mumbled, "I don't need a keeper."

"Don't tell me." Chuck flashed his boy-next-door smile. "Ty had it in his head the press might badger you."

Tilting her head, Asher studied his deceptively sweet face. "And what were you going to do if they had?"

"Strong-arm 'em," he claimed while flexing his muscle. "Though I might have been tempted to let them take a few bites out of you after that comment about nobody beating Ty. Didn't you hear they were naming a racket after me?"

Asher circled his waist with her arm. "Sorry, friend, I call 'em like I see 'em."

Stopping, he put both hands on Asher's shoulders and studied her. His look remained serious even when she gave him a quizzical smile. "You know, Face, you really look good."

She laughed. "Well, thanks...I think. Did I look bad before?"

"I don't mean you look beautiful, that never changes. I mean you look happy."

Lifting a hand to the one on her shoulder, Asher squeezed. "I am happy."

"It shows. In Ty too." Briefly he hesitated, then plunged ahead. "Listen, I don't know what happened between you two before, but—"

"Chuck..." Asher shook her head to ward off questions.

"But," he continued, "I want you to know I hope you make it this time."

"Oh, Chuck." Shutting her eyes, she went into his arms. "So do I," she sighed. "So do I."

"I asked you to keep an eye on her," Ty said from behind them. "I didn't say anything about touching."

"Oh, hell." Chuck tightened his hold. "Don't be so selfish. Second-seeds need love too." Glancing down at Asher, he grinned. "Can I interest you in lobster tails and champagne?"

"Sorry." She kissed his nose. "Somebody already offered me pizza and cheap wine."

"Outclassed again." With a sigh Chuck released her. "I need somebody to hit with tomorrow," he told Ty.

"Okay."

"Six o'clock, court three."

"You buy the coffee."

"We'll flip for it," Chuck countered before he sauntered away.

Alone, Asher and Ty stood for a moment in awkward silence while an airplane droned by overhead. The awkwardness had cropped up occasionally on their return to the States. It was always brief and never commented on. In the few seconds without words, each of them admitted that full truths would soon be necessary. Neither of them knew how to approach it.

"So," Ty began as the moment passed, "how did it go?"

"Easily," Asher returned, smiling as she stood on tiptoe to kiss him. "I didn't need the bodyguard."

"I know how you feel about press conferences."

"How?"

"Oh…" He combed her hair with his fingers. "*Terrified*'s a good word."

With a laugh she held out her hand as they started to walk. "*Was* a good word," Asher corrected him. "I'm amazed I ever let it get to me. There was one problem though."

"What?"

"I was afraid I'd faint from starvation." She sent him a pitiful look from under her lashes. "Someone did mention pizza, didn't they?"

"Yeah." He grinned, catching her close. "And cheap wine."

"You really know how to treat a woman, Starbuck," Asher told him in a breathless whisper.

"We'll go Dutch," he added before he pulled her toward the car.

Twenty minutes later they sat together at a tiny round table. There was the scent of rich sauce, spice and melted candles. From the jukebox in the corner poured an endless succession of popular rock tunes at a volume just below blaring. The waitresses wore bib aprons sporting pictures of grinning pizzas. Leaning her elbows on the scarred wooden table, Asher stared soulfully into Ty's eyes.

"You know how to pick a class joint, don't you?"

"Stick with me, Face," he advised. "I've got a hamburger palace picked out for tomorrow. You get your own individual plastic packs of ketchup." Her lips curved up, making him want to taste them. Leaning forward, he did. The table tilted dangerously.

"You two ready to order?" Snapping her wad of gum, the waitress shifted her weight to one hip.

"Pizza and a bottle of Chianti," Ty told her, kissing Asher again.

"Small, medium or large?"

"Small, medium or large what?"

"Pizza," the waitress said with exaggerated patience.

"Medium ought to do it." Twisting his head, Ty sent the waitress a smile that had her pulling back her shoulders. "Thanks."

"Well, that should improve the service," Asher considered as she watched the woman saunter away.

"What's that?"

Asher studied his laughing eyes. "Never mind," she decided. "Your ego doesn't need any oiling."

Ty bent his head closer to hers as a defense against the jukebox. "So what kind of questions did they toss at you?"

"The usual. They mentioned the business from *Elegance*."

"Are you going to do it?"

She moved her shoulders. "I don't know. It might be fun. And I don't suppose it would hurt the image of women's tennis for one of the players to be in a national fashion magazine."

"It's been done before."

Asher conquered a grin and arched her brows instead. "Do you read fashion magazines, Starbuck?"

"Sure. I like to look at pretty women."

"I always thought jocks tended to favor other sorts of magazines for that."

He gave her an innocent look. "What sorts of magazines?"

Ignoring him, Asher went back to his original question. "They're playing up this Grand Slam business for all it's worth."

"Bother you?" As he laced their fingers together, he studied them. There was an almost stunning difference in size and texture. Often he'd wondered how such an elegant little hand could be so strong…and why it should fit so perfectly with his.

"A bit," Asher admitted, enjoying the rough feel of his skin against hers. "It makes it difficult to go into a match thinking of just that match. What about you? I know you're getting the same kind of pressure."

The waitress brought the wine, giving Ty a slow smile as she set down the glasses. To Asher's amusement, he returned it. He's a devil, she thought. And he knows it.

"I always look at playing a game at a time, one point at a time." He poured a generous amount of wine in both glasses. "Three matches is a hell of a lot of points."

"But you'd like to win the Grand Slam?"

Raising his glass, he grinned. "Damn right." He laughed into her eyes as he drank. "Of course, Martin's already making book on it."

"I'm surprised he's not here," Asher commented, "analyzing every volley."

"He's coming in tomorrow with the rest of the family."

Asher's fingers tightened on the stem of her glass. "The rest of the family?"

"Yeah, Mom and Jess for sure. Mac and Pete if it can be arranged." The Chianti was heavy and mellow. Ty relaxed with it. "You'll like Pete; he's a cute kid."

She mumbled something into her wine before she swallowed. Martin had been there three years ago, along with Ty's mother and sister. Both she and Ty had gone into the U.S. Open as top seeds; both had been hounded by the press. The two of them had shared meals then, too, and a bed. So much was the same—terrifyingly so. But there had been so much in between.

There'd been no small boy with Ty's coloring then. No small boy with that air of perpetual energy to remind her of what was lost. Asher felt the emptiness inside her, then the ache, as she did each time she thought of the child.

Misinterpreting her silence, Ty reached over to take her hand. "Asher, you still haven't spoken to your father?"

"What?" Disoriented, she stared at him a moment. "No, no, not since... Not since I retired."

"Why don't you call him?"

"I can't."

"That's ridiculous. He's your father."

She sighed, wishing it were so simple. "Ty, you know him. He's a very stringent man, very certain of what's right and what's wrong. When I left tennis I did more than disappoint him, I...wasted what he'd given me."

Ty answered with a short, explicit word that made her smile. "From his viewpoint that's the way it was," she went on. "As Jim Wolfe's daughter I had certain responsibilities. In marrying Eric and giving up my career I shirked them. He hasn't forgiven me."

"How do you know that?" he demanded. His voice was low under the insistent music, but rich with annoyance. "If you haven't spoken to him, how can you be sure how he feels now?"

"Ty, if his feelings had changed, wouldn't he be here?" She shrugged, wishing they could have avoided the subject for a while longer. "I thought, at first, that when I started playing again it might make the difference. It hasn't."

"But you miss him."

Even that wasn't so simple. To Ty, family meant something warm and loving and eternal. He'd never understand that Asher looked not so much now for her father's presence or even his love, but simply his forgiveness. "I'd like him to be here," she said finally. "But I understand his reasons for not coming." Her brow clouded for a moment with a realization that had just come to her. "Before, I played for him, to please him, to justify the time and effort he put into my career. Now I play for myself."

"And you play better," Ty put in. "Perhaps that's one of the reasons."

With a smile she lifted his hand to her lips. "Perhaps that's one of them."

"Here's your pizza." The waitress plopped the steaming pan between them.

They ate amid noise and their own casual chatter. Even the pressure of the upcoming matches had no effect on Asher's mood. The cheese was hot and stringy, making Ty laugh as she struggled against it. The contents of the squat bottle of Chianti lowered as they drank leisurely, content to let the meal drag on. Tennis was forgotten while they spoke of everything and nothing at all. A group of teenagers poured in, laughing and rowdy, to feed another succession of quarters into the jukebox.

Why am I so happy to be in this loud, crowded room? she wondered. The cooling pizza and lukewarm wine were as appealing as the champagne and caviar they had shared in Paris. It was Ty. The place never mattered when she was with him. Abruptly it occurred to Asher that it was herself as well. She was being herself. There weren't any guards, or the need for any. Ty was the only man she'd ever been close to who required none from her.

Her father had wanted her to be perfect—his glass princess. All through her youth she had done everything in her power to please him. With Eric, she had been expected to be the cool, well-mannered Lady Wickerton, a woman who could discuss art and politics intelligently. She was to have been like crystal, many-faceted, elegant and cold.

All Ty had ever expected her to be was Asher. He accepted her flaws, even admired them. Because he had wanted her to be herself, she'd been able to be just that. Not once in all the time she had known him had he ever demanded that she fit a pattern or requested that she conform to any standards but her own. Impulsively she reached over to take his hand, then pressed it to her cheek. There was warmth against warmth, flesh against flesh.

"What's this for?" he asked, allowing his fingers to spread.

"For not wanting glass."

His brows drew together in confusion. "Am I supposed to know what that means?"

"No." Laughing, Asher leaned closer. "Have you drunk enough wine that your resistance is down and you'll be easily seduced?"

A slow smile spread. "More than enough."

"Then come with me," Asher ordered.

It was late when Ty lay sleepless beside Asher. Curled close, her hand caught loosely in his, she slept deeply, drugged with loving and fatigue. Her scent hung in the air so that even in the dark Ty could visualize her. A small alarm clock ticked monotonously at his left, its luminous dial glowing. Twelve twenty-seven.

His mind was far too active for sleep. He sensed, as he knew Asher did, that the idyll was nearly over. They were back where they had once ended, and questions would not be put off too much longer. Impatience gnawed at him. Unlike Asher, Ty looked for the end of the season. Only then would the time be right for answers and explanations. He was not used to biding his time, and the strain was beginning to tell. Even tonight under the laughter he had understood her wordless request that he not probe.

The question of her father, Ty mused, shifting the pillow to brace his back. She was more unhappy about the estrangement than she admitted. It showed in her eyes. It was incomprehensible to him that members of a family could turn away from one another. His thoughts drifted to his mother, to Jess. There was nothing either of them could do he wouldn't forgive. He'd never be able to bear the thought of being responsible for their unhappiness. Could a father feel any different about a daughter? An only daughter, a much-loved daughter, Ty reflected.

He could remember Jim Wolfe's pride in Asher. Ty had often sat beside him during one of Asher's matches in her early days as a pro, then consistently during her last year. Even in such a private man the adoration had showed. It wasn't possible to believe it had been only for the athlete and not for the woman.

Surprisingly Jim had accepted Ty's relationship with his daughter. No, Ty corrected, approved. He'd seemed to enjoy seeing them together. Once, Ty recalled, he had gone as far as outlining his expectations to Ty of their future. At the time Ty had been both amused and annoyed at the fatherly interference. What plans he had had for a future with Asher had still been vague. Then, when they had crystalized in his mind, it had been too late. Frowning, Ty glanced down at her.

In the pale shaft of moonlight her face seemed very fragile. Her hair was a silvery, insubstantial cloud around it. A wave of longing swamped him so that he had to fight the need to wake her and satisfy himself that she was there for him. His feelings for her had always been mixed—wild desire, unbearable tenderness, traces of fear. There had been no other woman who had ever brought him such sharp and conflicting emotions. Watching her sleep, he felt the need to protect. There should be no shadow of unhappiness in her eyes when they opened.

How many obstacles would they have to overcome before they were really together? he wondered. There was one he might remove himself. Perhaps the time had come to take the first step. On impulse, Ty slipped from the bed and into the sitting room.

It took only moments by phone to travel from coast to coast. Dropping into a chair, Ty listened to the faint crackling on the wire before it began to ring.

"Wolfe residence."

In the two words, Ty recognized the trained voice of a servant. "Jim Wolfe please. It's Ty Starbuck."

"One moment please."

Ty sat back, keeping one ear trained on the adjoining bedroom. He heard two distinct clicks as one extension was lifted and the other replaced.

"Starbuck."

The quiet, cautious voice was instantly recognizable. "Jim. How are you?"

"Well." A bit surprised by the late night call, Jim Wolfe settled behind his desk. "I've been reading quite a bit about you."

"It's been a good year. You were missed at Wimbledon."

"That makes five for you there."

"And three for Asher," he returned pointedly.

There was a moment of complete silence. "Your slice volley's cleaner than it once was."

"Jim, I called to talk about Asher."

"Then we have nothing to say."

For a moment the cool, calm statement left Ty speechless. In a flood, fury took over. "Just a damn minute. I have plenty to say. Your daughter's battled her way back to the top. She's done it without you."

"I'm aware of that. Do you have a point?"

"Yes, I have a point," Ty retorted. "I've never seen anyone work as hard as she has these past few months. And it hasn't been easy, dealing with the pressure, the press, the constant questions on why her father isn't in the stands while she wins championship after championship."

"Asher knows my feelings," Jim said flatly. "They're no concern of yours."

"Whatever concerns Asher concerns me."

"So..." Jim picked up a slim gold pen from the desk and carefully examined it. "We're back to that."

"Yes, we are."

"If you've decided to resume your relationship with Asher, it's your business, Ty." He flung the pen back onto the desk. "And it's my business if I don't."

"For God's sake, Jim," Ty began heatedly, "she's your daughter. You can't turn your back on your own child."

"Like father, like daughter," Jim murmured.

"What the hell does that mean?" Frustrated, Ty rose to pace, dragging the phone with him.

"Asher wiped her child out of existence. I've done the same."

All movement stopped. Ty felt something freeze in him as his knuckles turned white on the receiver. "What child?"

"She turned her back on everything I taught her," Jim went on, not hearing Ty's harshly whispered question. "The daughter I knew couldn't have done it." The words, and the anger that accompanied them, had been held in for years. Now they came bursting out. "I tried to understand why she married that pale excuse for a man, even tried to resign myself to her throwing away her career. But some things I won't forgive. If the life she chose to live was worth the price of my grandchild, she's welcome to it."

Enraged at letting his feelings pour out so openly, Jim slammed down the receiver.

Three thousand miles away Ty stood, staring at nothing. With infinite care he placed the phone back on the table. Too many thoughts were whirling in his head, too many questions and half-answers. He had to think, to take his time. Silently he walked back into the bedroom and dressed.

He wanted to shake her awake and demand an explanation; he wanted to wait until he had a grip on himself. Torn, Ty sat on a chair and stared at the still form in the bed. Asher slept so peacefully, her quiet breathing hardly stirred the air.

A child? Asher's child? But there was no child, Ty reasoned. If Lord and Lady Wickerton had produced an offspring, there would have been some mention of it in the press. An heir was never kept secret. Dragging a hand through his hair, Ty shifted. Besides, he reasoned, if Asher had had a child, where was it? Struggling to overcome the jealousy at imagining Asher's bearing another man's child, Ty went over his conversation with Jim Wolfe again.

Asher wiped her child out of existence....

His fingers tightened on the arms of the chair as he stared at her sleeping form. Abortion? Without warning, a storm of emotion took over that he had to systematically fight back until his pulse leveled. All attempts to think of the word with an open mind were futile. He couldn't rationalize it, not when it was Asher, not when the child was part of her. Could the woman he thought he knew have made that kind of choice? For what purpose? Was it possible that the social life she had sought had been more important than...

As bitterness filled him, Ty shook his head. He wouldn't believe it of her. Controlled, yes. There were times Asher could be infuriatingly controlled. But never calculating. Jim had been talking in riddles, he decided. There'd never been a child. There couldn't have been.

He watched Asher stir. With a soft murmur she shifted toward the emptiness beside her where Ty should have been. He sensed the moment she woke.

The moonlight gleamed on her arm as she lifted it, brushing her fingers at the hair that curled around her face. She placed her hand on his pillow, as if testing it for warmth.

"Ty?"

Not trusting himself, he said nothing. If only she would go back to sleep until he had resolved his feelings. He could still taste the bitterness at the back of his throat.

But she wouldn't sleep. Although groggy, Asher sensed tension in the air. Ty's emotions were always volatile enough to be felt tangibly. *Something's wrong, something's wrong,* hammered in her brain.

"Ty?" she called again, and a hint of fear touched the word. Asher had struggled to a sitting position before she saw him. The moonlight was enough to allow her to see that his eyes were dark and fixed on her face. It was also enough to let her see that they were cold. Her pulse began to race. "Couldn't you sleep?" she asked, struggling to convince herself it was all her imagination.

"No."

Asher laced her fingers together as she swallowed. "You should have woke me."

"Why?"

"We—we could have talked."

"Could we?" Cold anger filled him. "We can talk as long as I don't ask any questions you don't want to answer."

She'd been expecting the showdown, but not like this. His resentment was already wrapping around her. Still, he had a right, and she'd put him off too long. "Ty, if it's answers you want, I'll give them to you."

"Just like that?" he snapped, rising. "Just ask and you'll answer. Nothing more to hide, Asher?"

Stung by his tone, she stared up at him. "It wasn't a matter of hiding, Ty, not really. I needed time—we needed time."

"Why was that, Asher?" he asked in a tone that was uncharacteristically cool. She felt a shudder zip down her spine. "Why was time so important?"

"There were things I wasn't sure you'd understand."

"Like the baby?"

If he had slapped her, Asher couldn't have been more stunned. Even in the moonlight he could see her face go white. Her eyes grew huge and dark and desperate. "How..." The words wouldn't form. Though they raced around in her mind, Asher seemed incapable of forcing any through her lips. How had he found out? Who had told him? How long had he known?

"Eric," she managed, though the name threatened to strangle her. "Eric told you."

Sharp disappointment cut through him. Somehow he had hoped it hadn't been true that she had conceived and rejected another man's child. "So it's true," he exclaimed. Turning from her, Ty stared through the window at the darkness. He found he couldn't be logical or objective. It was one thing to understand the concept of freedom of choice, and another to apply it to Asher.

"Ty, I..." She tried to speak. All of her worst fears were hurtling down on her. The gulf between them was already tangible and threatening to widen. If only she had been able to tell him in her own way, in her own time. "Ty, I wanted to tell you myself. There were reasons why I didn't at first, and then..." Asher shut her eyes. "Then I made excuses."

"I suppose you thought it was none of my business."

Her eyes flew open again. "How can you say that?"

"What you do with your life when you're married to one man isn't the concern of another, even when he loves you."

Simultaneous flashes of pain and joy rushed through her. "You didn't," she whispered.

"Didn't what?"

"You didn't love me."

He gave a brief laugh, but didn't turn back to her. "No, of course I didn't. That's why I couldn't stay away from you. That's why I thought of you every moment."

Asher pressed the heel of her hand between her eyes. Why now? she thought wildly. Why is it all happening now? "You never told me."

This time he turned. "Yes, I did."

Furiously she shook her head. "You never said it. Not once. Even once would have been enough."

In concentration, his brows drew together. She was right, he decided. He'd never said the words. He'd shown her in every way he knew how, but he'd never said the words. "Neither did you," he blurted, speaking his thoughts.

She let out a breath that was perilously close to a sob. "I was afraid to."

"Damn it, Asher, so was I."

For a long, tense moment they stared at each other. Had she been that blind? Had she needed words so badly that she hadn't seen what he'd been giving her? The words would never have come easily to him because they meant everything.

For Ty, a declaration of love wasn't a casual phrase but a declaration of self.

Asher swallowed a tremor, wanting her voice to be strong. "I love you, Ty. I've always loved you. And I'm still afraid." As she held out a hand he glanced down at it, but made no move to accept it. "Don't turn away from me now." She thought of the child she had lost. "Please, don't hate me for what I did."

He couldn't understand, but he could feel. It seemed love for her justified anything. Crossing to her, Ty took the offered hand and brought it to his lips. "It'll be better when we've talked this out. We need to start clean, Asher."

"Yes." She closed her hand over their joined ones. "I want that too. Oh, Ty, I'm so sorry about the baby." Her free arm wrapped around his waist as she dropped her head on his chest. The relief, she thought. The relief of at last being able to share it with him. "I couldn't tell you before, when it happened. I didn't know what to do. I didn't know how you'd feel."

"I don't know either," he answered.

"I felt so guilty." She shut her eyes tight. "When Jess showed me that picture of your nephew, I could almost see how the baby would have looked. I always knew he would have had your hair, your eyes."

"Mine?" For a moment nothing seemed to function. His mind, his heart, his lungs. Then, in a torrent, everything came together. *"Mine?"* Asher gave an involuntary cry as he crushed her fingers in his. Before she could speak he had her by the shoulders, digging into her flesh. His eyes alone brought her ice-cold terror. "The baby was mine?"

Her mouth moved to form words, but nothing came out. Confusion and fear overtook her. But he'd already known, she thought desperately. No, no, he hadn't. Eric's baby, her mind flashed. He'd thought it was Eric's baby.

"Answer me, damn you!" He was shaking her now, violently. Limp as a rag doll, Asher made no protest and sought no defense. Both would have been futile. "Was it my baby? Was it mine?"

She nodded, too numb to feel the pain.

He wanted to strike her. Looking at her face, Ty could almost feel the sensation of his hand stinging against it. And he'd want to keep striking her until rage and grief could no longer be felt. Reading his thoughts in his eyes, Asher made no move to protect herself. For an instant his fingers tightened on her arms. With a violent oath he hurled her away. Hardly daring to breathe, she lay on the bed and waited.

"You bitch. You had my child in you when you married him." He flung the words at her, struggling not to use his fists. "Did he make you get rid of it when he found out? Or did you take carc of it so you could play thc lady without encumbrances?"

She wasn't aware that her breathing was ragged, or that she was trembling. Her mind was too numb to take in more than half of his words. All she understood was the fury of his feelings. "I didn't know. I didn't know I was pregnant when I married Eric."

"You had no right to keep this from me." Towering over her, he reached down to yank her to her knees. "You had no right to make a decision like that when the child was mine!"

"Ty—"

"Shut up. Damn you!" He shoved her away, knowing neither of them was safe if they remained together. "There's nothing you can say, nothing that could make me even want to look at you again."

He strode from the room without a second glance. The sound of the slamming door echoed over and over in Asher's mind.

Chapter Eleven

Ty took the quarter-finals in straight sets. Most said he played the finest tennis in his career on that hazy September afternoon. Ty knew he wasn't playing tennis. He was waging war. He'd gone onto the court full of vengeance and fury, almost pummeling his opponent with the ball. His swing was vicious, his aim deadly.

The violence showed in his face, in the grim set of his mouth, in the eyes that were nearly black with emotion. It wasn't the winning or losing that mattered to him, but the release of the physical aspcct of the temper that he'd barely controlled the night before. When he struck, he struck brutally, always moving. The motion itself was a threat. He'd often been called a warrior, but the description had never been more true. As if scenting blood, he hounded his opponent, then ground him mercilessly into the ground.

Ty's only disappointment was that the match didn't last longer. There hadn't been enough time to sweat out all of his fury. He wondered if there would ever be enough time.

In the stands there were differing reactions as he stalked off the courts.

"Name of God, Ada, I've never seen the boy play better." Martin Derick beamed like a new father. His voice was hoarse from cheering and cigarettes. A pile of butts lay crushed at his feet. "Did you see how he massacred that Italian?"

"Yes."

"Oh-ho, two matches more and our boy's going to have a Grand Slam." Martin squeezed Ada's workworn hands between his two smooth ones. "Nothing's going to stop him now!"

In her quiet, steady way, Ada stared down at the court. She'd seen more than Ty's victory. There'd been fury in her son's eyes. Outrage, hurt. She recognized the combination too well. She'd seen it in a little boy who'd been teased because his father had deserted him. Then, he'd used his fists to compensate. Today, Ada mused, he'd used a racket. As Martin recounted every serve and smash, Ada sat silently and wondered what had put that look back in her son's eyes.

"Mom." Jess leaned close so that her voice wouldn't carry. "Something's wrong with Ty, isn't it?"

"I'd say something's very wrong with Ty."

Jess rubbed her cheek against Pete's, wishing his powdery scent would calm her. Giggling, he squirmed out of her arms and dove toward his father. "Asher wasn't in the stands today."

Ada lifted her eyes to her daughter's. Jess had mentioned, perhaps too casually, that Ty was seeing Asher Wolfe again. Ada had hardly needed the information. Once she had heard Asher was competing again, she'd known what the results would be.

The only time she had ever seen Ty truly devastated had been when Asher had married the polished British lord. His rage and threats had been expected. But they turned to a brooding that had concerned her a great deal more.

"Yes, I noticed," Ada replied. "Then, she's got a match of her own."

"On the next court, and not for a half hour." Jess cast another worried glance around at the people who filled the stands. "She should have been here."

"Since she wasn't, there must be a reason."

A fresh tremor of unease ran up Jess's back. "Mom, I've got to talk to you—alone. Can we go get a cup of coffee?"

Without question, Ada rose. "You fellas keep Pete entertained," she ordered, tousling her grandson's hair. "Jess and I'll be back in a few minutes."

"You're going to tell her?" Mac spoke softly as he touched his wife's hand.

"Yes. Yes, I need to."

Bouncing his son on his knee, he watched them melt into the crowd.

After they had settled at a table, Ada waited for her daughter to begin. She knew Jess was marking time, ordering coffee, speculating on the chances of rain. Ada let her ramble. An orderly, even-tempered woman, she had learned the best way to deal with her emotional offspring was to ride out the storm. Eventually Jess stopped stirring her coffee and lifted her eyes to her mother's.

"Mom, do you remember when we were here three years ago?"

How could she forget? Ada thought with a sigh. That was the year Ty had won the U.S. Open, then barely had time to savor it before the world had crumbled around his ears. "Yes, I remember."

"Asher left Ty and married Eric Wickerton." When Ada remained silent, Jess lifted her coffee cup and drank as if to fortify herself. "It was my fault," she blurted out.

Ada took the time to taste her own coffee, deciding it wasn't half bad for restaurant brew. "Your fault, Jess? How?"

"I went to see her." In quick jerks Jess began to shred her napkin. She'd thought it would be easier now that she had told Mac everything, but with her mother's gaze steady and patient on hers, she felt like a child again. "I went to her hotel room when I knew Ty wouldn't be there." After pressing her lips together, she let the confession come out in a burst. "I told her Ty was tired of her. I told her he—he was bored."

"I'm surprised she didn't laugh in your face," Ada commented.

Quickly Jess shook her head. "I was convincing," she went on. "Maybe because I was convinced it was the truth. And I—I was sympathetic." Remembering how well she had played the role of reluctant messenger tore at her. "Oh, God, Mom, when I look back and remember the things I told her, how I said them…" Anguished, her eyes met her mother's. "I told her Ty thought she and Eric were suited to each other. There was enough truth in that, but I turned it around to give her the impression that Ty was hoping Eric would take her off his hands. And I defended Ty, telling Asher he'd never want to hurt her, that he was really very concerned that she'd gotten in over her head. I—I made it seem as though Ty had asked my opinion on the best way to untangle himself from an affair he had no more interest in."

"Jess." Ada stopped the movement of her nervous daughter's hands with her own. "Why did you do such a thing?"

"Ty wasn't happy. I'd talked to him just the night before, and he was so down, so unsure of himself. I'd never seen Ty unsure of himself." Her fingers began to move restlessly under her mother's. "It seemed so clear to me that Asher was wrong for him, hurting him. I was convinced I had to save him from being hurt more."

Leaning back, Ada let her gaze drift. The West Side Tennis Club was respectfully dingy, very American. Perhaps that was why she'd always liked it. It was noisy. The Long Island Railroad ran alongside, competing with helicopters, planes and road traffic. Ada had never completely gotten used to the relative quiet of suburbia after a lifetime in the inner city. Now she sat back, absorbing the noise, trying to think of the right words. It occurred to her that parenting didn't stop when children became adults. Perhaps it never stopped at all.

"Ty loved Asher, Jess."

"I know." Jess stared down at the shredded paper napkin. "I didn't think he did. I thought if he'd loved her, he would have been happy. And if she had loved him, she would have... well, she would have acted like all the other women who hung around him."

"Do you think Ty would have loved her if she had been like all the other women?"

Jess flushed, amazing herself and amusing her mother. It was a bit disconcerting to think of the tiny, white-haired Ada Starbuck, mother, grandmother, knowing about passion. "It wasn't until after I met Mac that I realized love doesn't always make you smile and glow," Jess went on, keeping her eyes lowered. "There are times when I was miserable and confused over my feelings for Mac and I began to remember that last talk I had with Ty before I went to see Asher. I realized how alike Ty and I are, how the stronger our feelings are, the more moody we can become."

On a deep breath she met her mother's gaze levelly. "I tried to rationalize that Asher wouldn't have left Ty, that she wouldn't have married Eric if she had really cared. And that if he had, Ty wouldn't have let her go."

"Pride can be just as strong as love. The things you said to Asher made her feel unwanted, and betrayed, I imagine, that Ty would have spoken to you about it."

"If the situation had been reversed, I would have scratched her eyes out and told her to go to hell."

Ada's laugh was a warm, young sound. "Yes, you would. Then you'd have gone to the man you loved and used your claws on him. Asher's different."

"Yes." Miserable, Jess pushed her untouched coffee aside. "Ty always said so. Mom, when they got back together, I was so guilty and frightened. Then I was relieved. And now, I can tell something's gone wrong again." As she had as a child, Jess gave her mother a long, pleading look. "What should I do?"

Strange, Ada mused, that her children wanted to pamper her on one hand, thrusting dishwashers and fancy jewelry on her, while on the other, they still looked to her for all the answers. "You'll have to talk to both of them," Ada said briskly. "Then you'll have to back off and let the two of them work it out. You might be able to heal what you did three years ago, but you can do nothing about what's between them now."

"If they love each other—"

"You made a decision for them once," Ada pointed out. "Don't make the same mistake again."

She hadn't been able to sleep. She hadn't been able to eat. Only the promise she had made to herself never to quit again forced Asher onto the court. Purposely she remained in the dressing room until the last moment to avoid the fans who wandered the walkways and mingled with players. It would take more effort than she could have summoned to smile and make small talk.

When she came outside the humidity hit her like a fist. Shaking off the weakness, Asher went directly to her chair. She heard the applause, but didn't acknowledge it. She couldn't afford to. Even before she began, Asher knew her biggest problem would be concentration.

Her arms ached, her whole body ached and she felt bone-deep exhausted. Pain was something she could ignore once the match was under way, but she wasn't sure she could ignore the jellied weakness inside her, the feeling that someone had punched a yawning hole in the center of her life. Still wearing her warm-up jacket, she took a few experimental swings.

"Asher." Cursing the interruption, she glanced over at Chuck. Concern touched his eyes as he stepped toward her. "Hey, you don't look good. Are you sick?"

"I'm fine."

He studied the shadowed eyes and pale cheeks. "Like hell."

"If I come out on the court, I'm well enough to play," she returned, exchanging one racket for another. "I've got to warm up."

Baffled, Chuck watched her stalk onto the court. It took only a moment of study to see that she wasn't in top form. Chuck moved away to find Ty.

He was in the showers, his eyes closed under the spray. He'd been curt and brief with the press and even briefer with his colleagues. He wasn't in the mood for congratulations. Anger lay curled inside him, undiminished by the physical demands he had placed on himself. He needed more—a sparring match, a marathon run—anything to pump the poison out of his system. Though he heard Chuck call him, Ty remained silent and kept his eyes shut.

"Ty, will you listen to me? Something's wrong with Asher."

Taking his time, Ty stepped back so that the water beat on his chest. Slowly he opened his eyes. "So?"

"So?" Astonished, Chuck gaped at him. "I said something's wrong with Asher."

"I heard you."

"She looks sick," Chuck continued, certain that Ty didn't comprehend. "I just saw her. She shouldn't be playing today. She looks awful."

Ty fought the instinctive need to go to her. He could remember vividly the scene the night before. With a flick of the wrist he shut off the shower. "Asher knows what she's doing. She makes her own decisions."

Too stunned to be angry, Chuck stared at him. He'd never seen Ty look cold any more than he'd ever seen Asher look furious. Until today. "What the devil's going on here?" he demanded. "I just told you your woman's sick."

Ty felt the tightening in his belly and ignored it. "She's not my woman." Grabbing a towel, he secured it lightly around his waist.

After dragging a hand through his hair, Chuck followed Ty into the locker room. He'd known since that morning when he and Ty had practiced together that something was wrong. Accustomed to his friend's mercurial moods, he had dismissed it, assuming Ty and Asher had had a lover's quarrel. But no lover's quarrel would make Ty indifferent to Asher's health.

"Look, if you two have had a fight, that's no reason—"

"I said she's not my woman." Ty's voice was deadly calm as he pulled on jeans.

"Fine," Chuck snapped. "Then if the field's clear, I might just try my luck." He was slammed back against the lockers, feet dangling as Ty grabbed his shirt in both hands, jerking him up. Coolly, Chuck looked into the stormy eyes. "Not your woman, friend?" he said softly. "Tell that to somebody who doesn't know you."

Breathing hard, Ty struggled against the need to strike back. The hours of violent tennis hadn't drained the anger or the grief. Without a word he dropped Chuck to his feet, then snatched a shirt from his locker.

"Are you going out there?" Chuck demanded. "Somebody should stop her before she makes whatever's wrong with her worse. You know damn well she isn't going to listen to me."

"Don't push me." Ty dragged the shirt over his head before he slammed the locker door. This time Chuck kept his silence. He heard the tremor in Ty's voice and recognized that the emotion wasn't anger. Only once before had he seen his friend this torn apart. It had been Asher then, as it was obviously Asher now. With warring loyalties, he reached out.

"Okay, you want to talk about it?"

"No." Clenching his fists, Ty fought to regain his control. "No, just go on out…keep an eye on her."

She was fighting, and losing. Asher had used almost all her reserve of energy to take the first set to a tie breaker. The ultimate loss had taken its emotional toll. Kingston was a crafty enough player to sense her opponent's flagging stamina and capitalized on it. Precision was nothing without strength. Asher's strength was ebbing quickly.

The noise played havoc with her concentration. Already playing below par, she needed the sound of the ball hitting the racket. Engines drowned it out, denying her the sense of hearing. On the brittle grass the ball jumped, skidded and stopped. Top speed was necessary, and she didn't have it.

Unable to prevent himself, Ty came to the edge of the tunnel to watch. Immediately he could see that Chuck hadn't exaggerated. She was too pale, too slow. Instinctively he took a step forward. Restraining himself was more difficult than going on, but he stopped, cursing her even as he cursed himself. She'd made her own choice. She herself had cut off any right he had to influence her. From where he stood he could hear her labored breathing, see the strain she fought to keep from her face. At the twinge of fresh pain he turned away from the court.

With a blind determination that was more nerves than power, Asher had taken the second set to three-all. Her face shone with sweat. Weakened, Asher knew that she would have to find a hole in Kingston's game soon, and have the wit and stamina to exploit it. Grit was a weapon, but not weapon enough against power, precision and cunning.

At double break point Asher prepared to serve again. If she could pull this one out, she'd have a chance. If Kingston broke her serve, the match was as good as over. *Concentrate, concentrate,* she ordered herself as she gave the ball a few testing bounces. She counted each one, trying to calm herself. Ty's furious, accusing words hammered in her brain. His face, enraged and stricken, floated in front of her eyes. Tossing the ball, Asher drove at it with her racket.

"Fault."

She shut her eyes and cursed. Control, she ordered herself. If she lost control now, she lost everything. As she took an extra moment, the crowd began to hum in speculation.

"Come on, Face, let's see what you're made of!"

Gritting her teeth, Asher put everything she had left into the serve. The ace brought a roar of approval. She wasn't beaten yet.

But her next serve was soft. Slapping it back to her, Kingston incited a hard, punishing rally. Asher battled by instinct, all reserve depleted. Her eyes, her mind, were fixed on the ball and the ball only. Dodging after a slice, she skidded, barely meeting it with her racket as she stumbled. She went down to her knees, crumbling into a ball of exhaustion and pain.

Someone's hands hooked under her armpits, pulling her to her feet. Asher pushed them away blindly to stagger to her chair.

"Come on, Asher." Chuck toweled off her streaming face, talking to her as she drew in ragged, straining breaths. "Come on, babe, you're not in any shape to be out here today. I'll help you inside."

"No." She shook off his hand. "No, I won't forfeit." Rising, she dropped the towel to the ground. "I'm going to finish."

Helpless, Chuck watched her fight a losing battle.

Asher slept for almost twenty-four hours straight. Her body recharged as she lay motionless in the bed she had shared so recently with Ty. The loss of the match—and the Grand Slam—meant little. She'd finished. Her pride was whole because she had refused to give up, because she had managed to face the reporters after the match and give them a calm accounting. When they had speculated on the state of her health, she'd told them she'd been fit to play. She would give no excuses for losing. If there was blame, it lay within herself. That was the primary rule of the game.

On returning to her room, Asher only took time to strip to her underwear before falling exhausted onto the bed. Sleep came immediately. Hours later she didn't hear the door open or Ty's footsteps as he crossed to the bedroom to look at her.

Asher lay flat on her stomach across the spread—something he knew she did only when absolutely depleted. Her breathing was deep, a heavy sound of fatigue. The hands he had thrust in his pockets balled into fists.

His emotions were pulling in too many directions. She shouldn't be allowed to do this to him, he thought furiously. She shouldn't make him want to hurt and protect at the same time.

Walking to the window, he remained silent for a quarter of an hour, listening to her breathe. Before he left her, Ty drew the drapes closed so that the sunlight wouldn't disturb her.

When Asher awoke, a full day had passed. The aches made themselves known.

Keeping her mind a blank, she ran a hot bath. As the water lapped over her, she slipped into a half doze. Asher heard the knock on the door, and ignored it. The phone rang, but she didn't open her eyes.

Disturbed, Jess replaced the receiver after ten full rings. Where could Asher be? she wondered. She knew Asher was still registered at the hotel, but she hadn't answered the phone or the door in more than a day. She'd tried to tell Ty, but he simply wouldn't listen. Any more than he'd listened to her attempts at confession.

Her conscience plagued her. She hadn't tried hard enough, Jess berated herself. She'd been so afraid of losing Ty's love, she had allowed him to brush her off when she tried to talk to him. Well, no more, she determined.

Checking her watch, Jess calculated that Ty would be preparing for the day's match. She cursed, then fretted, then made herself a promise. When it was over, win or lose, she was going to corner her brother and make him listen until she'd told him everything.

Now that the vow had been made, Jess discovered that the waiting wasn't easy. In the stands she marked time. Ty played with the same fierce anger she had observed in his quarter-final match. It was just as effective.

Beneath her pride in him was the constant thought that her

brother might turn away from her after he'd heard her out. But Jess sat patiently through the match and through the press conference. She'd left it to her mother to persuade Martin to go back to the hotel instead of dragging Ty off for a replay of the match. Like a tennis groupie, Jess waited for Ty to emerge from the locker room, then pounced.

"Ty, I need to talk to you."

"I'm talked out, Jess." He patted her hand, then removed it from his arm. "I want to get out of here before the next sportswriter latches onto me."

"Fine, I'll drive. You'll listen."

"Look, Jess—"

"Now, Ty."

Annoyed, Ty stalked to the car. For the first time in his life he wished his family hadn't come. He'd managed to avoid them for the most part, using fatigue or practice as excuses. His mother knew him too well, and her silence questioned him constantly. Martin was ecstatic, wanting to analyze every volley and shower praise. And the hardest of all was watching Pete, darting here and there, babbling, laughing, reminding Ty of something that might have been.

"Look, Jess, I'm tired—"

"Just get in," she interrupted tersely. "I've already put this off for too long."

They slammed their doors simultaneously. Not a very auspicious start, she mused as she merged with traffic, but she'd never finish if she didn't begin. "Okay, I've got some things to tell you, and I'd like you to hear me out before you say anything."

"Unless I want to hitch a damn ride back, I don't have much choice, do I?"

She sent him a worried look. "Don't hate me, Ty."

"Oh, come on, Jess." Ashamed of wishing her away, he gave her hair a quick tousle. "I might be mad at being shanghaied, but I'm not going to hate you."

"Just listen," she started. Staring straight ahead, she began.

At first, Ty paid little attention. She was hopping back to the summer he had first been with Asher. He started once to interrupt, not wanting to be reminded. Jess shook her head fiercely and silenced him. With strained patience Ty sat back and watched the passing scenery.

When Jess told him that she had gone to see Asher, his brows lowered. His concentration focused. Listening to her pouring out the things she had said—*Ty's tired of you.... He doesn't know exactly how to end things without hurting you*—his rage built swiftly. Jess felt the fury swirling, and barely paused for breath.

"She seemed to have no reaction to anything I said. She was very cool, totally in control of herself. It just seemed to reinforce what I thought of her." Stopping for a light, Jess swallowed quickly. "I didn't understand how anyone could have strong feelings and not express them, not then. After I met Mac I realized..." When the light changed she gunned the motor with a jerk of her foot, then stalled the engine. On a frustrated oath she started the car again as Ty remained silent.

"When I look back on it," Jess continued after a shaky breath, "I remember how pale she got, how quiet. It wasn't indifference, but shock. She listened to everything I said, never raising her voice or shedding a tear. I must have hurt her terribly."

Her voice broke and she waited for him to speak, but there was nothing but thick, vibrant silence. "I had no right, Ty," Jess continued quickly. "I know that. I wanted—I wanted to help, to pay you back somehow for everything you'd done for me. At the time, I thought I was telling her the things you couldn't bring yourself to. I'd convinced myself… Oh, I don't know." Jess made a quick gesture with her hand before she gripped the gear shift. "Maybe I was even jealous, but I didn't think you loved her and I was so sure she didn't love you. Especially when she married so quickly."

Because tears were forming, she pulled over to the side of the road. "Ty, to tell you I'm sorry isn't enough, but I don't have anything else."

The silence in the car vibrated for the space of three heartbeats. "What made you think you could play God with my life?" Ty demanded in a sudden burst that had her jolting. "Who the hell put you in charge?"

Forcing herself to meet his eyes, Jess spoke quietly. "There's nothing you can say to me I haven't said to myself, but you're entitled."

"Do you have any idea what you did to my life?"

She shuddered involuntarily. "Yes."

"I was going to ask Asher to marry me that night, the night I got back and found you in our room. The night you told me she'd gone off with Wickerton."

"Oh, God, Ty." Choking back a sob, Jess laid her head on the steering wheel. "I never thought…I never realized she meant that much to you."

"She was everything I wanted, don't you understand? Everything! I was half crazy because I wasn't sure she'd say yes." He drummed his fist against the dash. "And, God, I'm still not sure. I'll never be sure." The anguish in his voice made Jess straighten.

"Ty, if you'd go see her. If you'd—"

"No." He thought again of the child. His child. "There are other reasons now."

"I'll go," Jess began. "I can—"

"No!" The word whipped out at her, causing Jess to swallow the rest of the sentence. "Stay away from her."

"All right," she agreed unsteadily. "If that's the way you want it."

"That's the way I want it."

"You still love her," Jess asked.

Ty turned his head so that his eyes met his sister's. "Yes, I love her. That isn't always enough, Jess. I don't think I'd ever be able to forget…"

"Forget?" she prompted when he trailed off. "Forget what?"

"Something she took from me…" Angry energy built up again, grinding at his nerves. "I've got to walk."

"Ty." Jess stopped him with a tentative hand on the arm as he jerked open the door of the car. "Do you want me to go away—back to California? I can make up an excuse, even leave Pete and Mac here for the rest of the tournament. I won't stay for the finals if it upsets you."

"Do what you want," he told her shortly. He started to slam

the door of the car when he caught the look in her eyes. He'd protected her all of his life, too long to change now. Love was rooted in him. "It's history, Jess," he said in calmer tones. "Past history. Forget it."

Turning, Ty walked away, hoping he'd be able to believe his own words.

Chapter Twelve

Asher sat on the bed to watch the men's singles championship. The television commentary barely penetrated as she judged and dissected each stroke and volley for herself. She couldn't go to the stadium, but nothing would prevent her from watching Ty compete.

On the close-ups, she studied his face carefully. Yes, some strain showed, she noted, but his concentration was complete. His energy was as volatile as ever, perhaps more so. For that she could be grateful.

Each time they replayed a shot in slow motion, Asher could fully appreciate the beauty of his form. Muscles rippled as he stretched; feet left the turf in a leap for more power. He was a raw athlete with anger simmering just under the discipline. The graphite racket was no more than an extension of the arm that was whipping the ball harder and harder. As always, his hair flew around the sweatband, dramatic and unruly. His eyes were dark with a rage barely contained. Was it the game that drove him? she wondered. The insatiable thirst to win? Or were there other emotions pushing him this time?

If there were, it was easy to see that they added to the impetus. He was an explosion heating up, a storm rumbling just overhead. Asher knew him well enough to recognize that his control balanced on a very thin edge, but it made his game all the more exciting.

His topspin drove to Chuck's backhand and was returned, power for power. A slice, a lob, an overhead. Turned the wrong way, Chuck pivoted, sprinted, but had no chance to return. The call was late, judging Ty's ball long.

His head whipped around to the judge, his eyes deadly. Asher shuddered when the camera zoomed in so that the undisguised fury seemed aimed directly at her. For a moment they seemed to stare into each other's eyes. Disgust warred with temper before he turned to resume his receiving stance. Crouched like a cat, his eyes intense, he waited. Asher let out an unsteady breath.

Ty was judging the bounce with uncanny accuracy. If it threatened to die, he was under it. When it chose to soar, he got behind it. With unrelenting challenge he charged the net. He baited Chuck, dared him, and, time after time, outwitted him. His game was all aggression and power—Starbuck at his best, she thought with undiminished pride. He could demoralize even a seasoned pro like Chuck with a lightning-fast return that lifted chalk from the service line. With each swing she could hear the grunt of exertion and the swish of air. How she wanted to be there.

He wouldn't want her. She wouldn't soon forget that look of rage and disgust he had turned on her—too much like the one his video image had projected. A man like Starbuck had no ambivalent emotions. It was love or hate; she'd felt them both.

She'd been cut out of his life. She had to accept that. She had to…quit? Asher asked herself. Suddenly her chin rose. Was that what she was doing again? She looked back at the screen as the camera zoomed in on Ty's face. His eyes were opaque and dangerous before he went into a full stretch for his serve. The force of her feelings attacked her. She loved and wanted and needed.

No, damn it! Rising, Asher cursed him. No, if she was going to lose, she was going down fighting, just as she had on the courts. He wouldn't brush her out of his life so easily this time. Briefly she'd forgotten that she no longer aimed her actions at pleasing those around her. Perhaps he didn't want to see her, but that was just too bad. He would see her…and he would listen.

Just as she snapped off the set, a knock sounded on her door. Battling impatience, Asher went to answer. Her expression changed from grim determination to wonder.

"Dad!"

"Asher." Jim met her stunned expression with an unsmiling nod. "May I come in?"

He hadn't changed, she thought wildly. He hadn't changed at all. He was still tall and tanned and silvery-blond. He was still her father. Her eyes filled with love and tears. "Oh, Dad, I'm so glad to see you." Grasping his hand, she drew him into the room. Then the awkwardness set in. "Sit down, please." While gesturing to a chair, Asher sought something to fill the gap. "Shall I order up something to drink? Some coffee?"

"No." He sat as she suggested and looked at his daughter. She was thinner, he noted. And nervous, as nervous as he was himself. Since Ty's phone call, he'd done little but think of her. "Asher," he began, then sighed. "Please sit down." He waited until she settled across from him. "I want to tell you I'm proud of the way you've played this season."

His voice was stiff, but she expected little else. "Thank you."

"I'm most proud of the last match you played."

Asher gave him a small smile. How typical that it was tennis he spoke of first. "I lost."

"You played," he countered. "Right down to the last point, you played. I wonder how many people who watched knew that you were ill."

"I wasn't ill," Asher corrected him automatically. "If I came on court—"

"Then you were fit," he finished, before he shook his head. "I drummed that into you well, didn't I?"

"A matter of pride and sportsmanship," she said quietly, giving him back the words he had given her again and again during her training.

Jim lapsed into silence, frowning at the elegant hands that lay folded in her lap. She'd always been his princess, he thought, his beautiful, golden princess. He'd wanted to give her the world, and he'd wanted her to deserve it.

"I didn't intend to come here to see you."

If the statement hurt, she gave no sign. "What changed your mind?"

"A couple of things, most particularly, your last match."

Rising, Asher walked to the window. "So, I had to lose to have you speak to me again." The words came easily, as did the light trace of bitterness. Though love had remained constant, she found no need to give him unvarnished adulation any longer. "All those years I needed you so badly, I waited, hoping you'd forgive me."

"It was a hard thing to forgive, Asher."

He rose, too, realizing his daughter had grown stronger. He wasn't sure how to approach the woman she had become.

"It was a hard thing to accept," she countered in the calm voice he remembered. "That my father looked at me as athlete first and child second."

"That's not true."

"Isn't it?" Turning, she fixed him with a level stare. "You turned your back on me because I gave up my career. Not once when I was suffering did you hold out a hand to me. I had no one to go to but you, and because you said no, I had no one at all."

"I tried to deal with it. I tried to accept your decision to marry that man, though you knew how I felt about him." The unexpected guilt angered him and chilled his voice. "I tried to understand how you could give up what you were to play at being something else."

"I had no choice," she began furiously.

"No choice?" His derision was sharp as a blade. "You made your own decision, Asher—your career for a title—just as you made it about the child. My grandchild."

"Please." She lifted both hands to her temples as she turned away. "Please don't. Have you any idea how much and how often I've paid for that moment of carelessness?"

"Carelessness?" Stunned into disbelief, Jim stared at the back of her head. "You call the conception of a child carelessness?"

"No, *no!*" Her voice trembled as it rose. "The loss. If I hadn't let myself get upset, if I had looked where I was going, I never would have fallen. I never would have lost Ty's child."

"What!" As the pain slammed into his stomach, Jim sank into the chair. "Fallen? Ty's child? *Ty's?*" He ran a hand over his eyes as he tried to sort it out. Suddenly he felt old and frail and frightened. "Asher, are you telling me you miscarried Ty's child?"

"Yes." Wearily she turned back to face him. "I wrote you, I told you."

"If you wrote, I never received the letter." Shaken, Jim held out a hand, waiting until she grasped it. "Asher, Eric told me you aborted his child." For an instant, the words, their meaning, failed to penetrate. Her look was blank and vulnerable enough to make him feel every year of his age. "A calculated abortion of your husband's child," he said deliberately. When she swayed he gripped her other hand. "He told me you'd done so without his knowledge or permission. He seemed devastated. I believed him, Asher." As she went limp, he drew her down to her knees in front of him. "I believed him."

"Oh, God." Her eyes were huge and dark with shock.

Her father's fingers trembled in hers. "He phoned me from London. He sounded half mad—I thought with grief. He said that you hadn't told him until after it was done. That you had told him you wanted no children to interfere with the life you intended to build as Lady Wickerton."

Too numb for anger, Asher shook her head. "I didn't know even Eric could be so vindictive, so cruel."

It all began to make horrid sense. Her letters to her father hadn't been answered. Eric had seen that they were never mailed. Then, when she had phoned him, Jim had been cold and brief. He'd told her that he could never resolve himself to her choice. Asher had assumed he meant her rejection of her career.

"He wanted me to pay," she explained as she dropped her head on her father's lap. "He never wanted me to stop paying."

Gently Jim cupped her face in his hands. "Tell me everything. I'll listen, as I should have a long time ago."

She started with Jess, leaving nothing out including her final stormy estrangement from Ty. Jim's mouth tightened at her recounting of the accident and the hospital scene with Eric. Listening, he cursed himself for being a fool.

"And now, Ty..." As realization struck her, she paled. "Ty thinks—Eric must have told him I'd had an abortion."

"No, I told him."

"You?" Confused, Asher pressed her fingers to the headache in her temple. "But how—"

"He called me a few nights ago. He wanted to convince me to see you. I told him enough to make him believe the lie just as I'd believed it."

"That night when I woke up," Asher remembered. "Oh, my God, when he realized it had been his baby... The things he was saying! I couldn't think at the time." She shut her eyes. "No wonder he hates me."

Color flooded back into her face. "I have to tell him the truth and make him believe it." Scrambling up, she dashed for the door. "I'll go to the club. I have to make him listen. I have to make him understand."

"The match must be nearly over." Jim rose on unsteady legs. His daughter had been through hell, and he had done nothing but add to it. "You'll never catch him there."

Frustrated, Asher looked at her watch. "I don't know where he's staying." Releasing the doorknob, she went to the phone. "I'll just have to find out."

"Asher..." Awkward, unsure, Jim held out his hand. "Forgive me."

Asher stared into his face as she replaced the receiver. Ignoring the hand, she went into his arms.

It was nearly midnight when Ty reached the door of his room. For the past two hours he'd been drinking steadily. Celebrating. It wasn't every day you won the Grand Slam, he reminded himself as he searched for his keys. And it wasn't every day a man had a half dozen women offering to share their beds with him. He gave a snort of laughter as he slid the key into the lock. And why the hell hadn't he taken one of them up on it?

None of them was Asher. He shook away the thought as he struggled to make the doorknob function. No, he simply hadn't wanted a woman, Ty told himself. It was because he was tired and had had too much to drink. Asher was yesterday.

The hotel room was dark as he stumbled inside. If he was right about nothing else, he was right about having too much to drink. Through glass after glass Ty had told himself the liquor was for celebrating, not for forgetting. The kid from the Chicago slum had made it to the top, in spades.

The hell with it, he decided, tossing his keys into the room.

With a thud they landed on the carpet. Swaying a bit, he stripped off his shirt and threw it in the same direction. Now if he could just find his way to the bed without turning on a light, he'd sleep. Tonight he'd sleep—with enough liquor in his system to anesthetize him. There'd be no dreams of soft skin or dark blue eyes tonight.

As he fumbled toward the bedroom, a light switched on, blinding him. With a pungent curse Ty covered his eyes, balancing himself with one hand on the wall.

"Turn that damn thing off," he muttered.

"Well, the victor returns triumphant."

The quiet voice had him lowering the hand from his eyes. Asher sat primly in a chair, looking unruffled, soft and utterly tempting. Ty felt desire work its way through the alcohol.

"What the hell are you doing here?"

"And very drunk," she said as if he hadn't spoken. Rising, she went to him. "I suppose you deserve it after the way you played today. Should I add my congratulations to the host of others?"

"Get out." He pushed away from the wall. "I don't want you."

"I'll order up some coffee," she said calmly. "We'll talk."

"I said get out!" Catching her wrist, he whirled her around. "Before I lose my temper and hurt you."

Though her pulse jumped under his fingers, she stood firm. "I'll leave after we talk."

"Do you know what I want to do to you?" he demanded, shoving her back against the wall. "Do you know that I want to beat you senseless?"

"Yes." She didn't cringe as his fury raged down on her. "Ty, if you'll listen—"

"I don't want to listen to you." The image of her lying exhausted on the bed raced through his mind. "Get out while I can still stop myself from hurting you."

"I can't." She lifted a hand to his cheek. "Ty—"

Her words were cut off as he pressed her back into the wall. For an instant she thought he would strike her, then his mouth came down on hers, bruising, savage. He forced her lips apart, thrusting his tongue deep as she struggled. His teeth ground against hers as though to punish them both. There was the faint taste of liquor, reminding her he had drink as well as anger in his system. When she tried to turn her head, he caught her face in his hand—not gently, in the touch she remembered, but viselike.

He could smell her—the soft talc, the lightly sexy perfume. And the fear. She made a small, pleading sound before she stopped fighting him. Without being aware of what he did, he lightened the grip to a caress. His lips gentled on hers, tasting, savoring. Mumbling her name, he trailed kisses over her skin until he felt the essence of her flowing back into him. God, how he'd missed her.

"I can't do without you," he whispered. "I can't." He sank to the floor, drawing her down with him.

He was lost in her—the feel, the taste, the fragrance. His mind was too full of Asher to allow him to think. Sensation ruled him, trembling along his skin to follow the path of her fingers. It was as if she sought to soothe and arouse him at once. He was helpless to resist her—or his need for her. As if in a trance, he took his lips over her, missing nothing as his hunger seemed insatiable. Her quickening breaths were like music, setting his rhythm.

The air grew steamier as his hands homed in on secrets that made her moan. Her body shuddered into life. No longer gentle, but demanding, she tangled her fingers in his hair and guided him to sweet spaces he'd neglected. Then ever greedy, ever giving, she drew him back to her mouth. Her tongue toyed with his lips, then slid inside to drink up all the flavors. His head swimming, he answered the kiss.

The need for her was unreasonable, but Ty was beyond reason. Without her there'd been an emptiness that even his fury couldn't fill. Now the void was closing. She was in his blood, in his bone, so essential a part of him he had been able to find no place of separation. Now there was no will to do so.

Under him, she was moving, inviting, entreating. He whispered a denial against her mouth, but his pounding blood took control. He was inside her without being aware of it. Then all sensations spiraled together in an intensity that made him cry out. And it was her name he spoke, in both ecstasy and in despair.

Drained, Ty rolled from her to stare at the ceiling. How could he have let that happen? he demanded. How could he have felt such love, found such pleasure in a woman he had vowed to amputate from his life? He wondered now if he'd ever find the strength to stay away from her. Life with her, and life without her, would be two kinds of hell.

"Ty." Reaching over, Asher touched his shoulder.

"Don't." Without looking at her he rose. "Get dressed, for God's sake," he muttered as he tugged on his own jeans with trembling hands. Who had used whom? he wondered. "Do you have a car?"

Sitting up, Asher pushed her hair out of her face. Hair, she remembered, that only moments before he had been kissing. "No."

"I'll call you a cab."

"That won't be necessary." In silence she began to dress. "I realize you're sorry that this happened."

"I'm damned if I'll apologize," he snapped.

"I wasn't asking you to," she told him quietly. "I was going to say that I'm not sorry. I love you, and making love with you is only one way to show it." She managed, after three attempts, to button her blouse. When she looked up, he was at the window, his back to her. "Ty, I came here to tell you some things you must know. When I'm finished, I'll go and give you time to think about them."

"Can't you understand I don't want to think anymore?"

"It's the last thing I'll ask of you."

"All right." In a gesture of fatigue she rarely saw in him, he rubbed both hands over his face. The liquor had burned out of his system—by the anger or the passion, he wasn't sure. But he was cold sober. "Maybe I should tell you first that what Jess said to you three years ago was her own fabrication. I didn't know anything about it until the other day when she told me what she'd done. In her own way, she was trying to protect me."

"I don't understand what you're talking about."

Turning, he gave her a grim smile. "Did you really think I was tired of you? Looking for a way out? Wondering how I could ditch you without raising too much fuss or interfering with my career?"

Asher opened her mouth to speak, then shut it again. How strange that the words still hurt and made her defensive.

"Obviously you did."

"And if I did?" she countered. "Everything she said fit. You'd never made a commitment to me. There'd never been any talk about the future."

"On either side," he reminded her.

Asher pushed away the logic. "If you'd once told me—"

"Or perhaps you were uncertain enough of your own feelings that when Jess dumped that on you, you ran right to Wickerton. Even though you were carrying my baby."

"I didn't know I was pregnant when I married Eric." She saw him shrug her words away. In fury she grabbed both of his arms. "I tell you I didn't know! Perhaps if I had known before I would have simply gone away. I don't know what I would have done. I was already terrified you were growing tired of me before Jess confirmed it."

"And where the hell did you get a stupid idea like that?"

"You'd been so moody, so withdrawn. Everything she said made sense."

"If I was moody and withdrawn, it was because I was trying to work out the best way to ask Asher Wolfe, Miss Society Tennis, to marry Starbuck, from the wrong side of the tracks."

Asher took an uncertain step toward him. "You would have married me?"

"I still have the ring I bought you," he answered.

"A ring?" she repeated stupidly. "You'd bought me a ring?" For some inexplicable reason the thought of it stunned her more than anything else.

"I'd planned to try a very conventional proposal. And if that didn't work, maybe a kidnapping."

She tried to laugh because tears were entirely too close. "It would have worked."

"If you'd told me you were pregnant—"

"Ty, I didn't know! Damn it!" She pounded once against his chest. "Do you think I would have married Eric if I had known? It was weeks afterward that I found out."

"Why the hell didn't you tell me then?"

"Do you think I wanted to get you back that way?" The old pride lifted her chin. "And I was married to another man. I'd made him a promise."

"A promise that meant more than the life of the child we'd made together," he retorted bitterly. "A promise that let you walk into one of those antiseptic clinics and destroy something innocent and beautiful. And mine."

The image was too ugly, the truth too painful. Flying at him, Asher struck him again and again until he pinned her hands behind her back. *"And mine!"* she shouted at him. "And mine, or doesn't my part matter?"

"You didn't want it." His fingers closed like steel as she tried to pull away. "But you didn't have the decency to ask me if I did. Couldn't you bear the thought of carrying part of me inside you for nine months?"

“Don’t ask me what I could bear.” She wasn’t pale now, but vivid with fury. “I didn’t have an abortion,” she spat at him. “I miscarried. I miscarried and nearly died in the process. Would you feel better if I had? God knows I tried to.”

“Miscarried?” His grip shifted from her wrists to her shoulders. “What are you talking about?”

“Eric hated me too!” she shouted. “When I learned I was pregnant and told him, all he could say was that I’d deceived him. I’d tried to trick him into claiming the baby after you’d refused me. Nothing I said got through to him. We argued and argued. We were near the steps and he was shouting. All I wanted to do was get away.” Her hands flew up to cover her face as she remembered again, all too clearly. “I didn’t look, I only ran. Then I was falling. I tried to stop, but my head hit the railing, I think. Then I don’t remember anything until I woke up and the baby was gone.”

Somehow he could see it as vividly as though it were being played on film in front of his eyes. “Oh, God, Asher.” When he tried to take her in his arms, she pulled away.

“I wanted you, but I knew you’d never forgive me. It didn’t seem to matter anymore, so I did what Eric wanted.” To force back the tears, she pressed her fingers to her eyes. “I didn’t want you to know, I couldn’t have stood it if you had known when you didn’t want me.” Lowering her hands, she looked at him, dry-eyed. “I paid for losing your baby, Ty. For three years I did without everything that mattered to me, and I grieved alone. I can’t mourn any longer.”

“No.” Going to the window, he flung it up as if he needed air. There was no breeze, nothing to relieve the burning that he felt. “You’ve had years to deal with it. I’ve had days.” And she’d had no one, he thought. Years with no one. Ty took several long breaths. "How badly were you hurt?"

Puzzled by the question, she shook her head. "What?"

"Were you badly hurt?" The question was rough and turbulent. When she remained silent he turned. "When you fell, how bad was it?"

"I—I lost the baby."

"I asked about you."

She stared without comprehension. No one had asked her that, not even her father. Looking into Ty's ravaged face, she could only shake her head again.

"Damn it, Asher, did you have a concussion, did you break any bones? You said you almost died."

"The baby died," she repeated numbly.

Crossing to her, he grabbed her shoulders. *"You!"* he shouted. "Don't you know that you're the most important thing to me? We can have a dozen babies if you want. I need to know what happened to you."

"I don't remember very much. I was sedated. There were transfusions..." The full impact of his words penetrated slowly. The anguish in his eyes was for her. "Ty." Burying her face against his chest, she clung. "All that's over."

"I should have been with you." He drew her closer. "We should have gone through that together."

"Just tell me you love me. Say the words."

"You know that I do." He cupped her chin to force her head back. "I love you." He saw the first tear fall and kissed it away. "Don't," he pleaded. "No more tears, Face. No more grieving."

She held him close again until the fullness left her chest. "No more grieving," she repeated, and lifted her face.

He touched it gently, fingertips only. "I hurt you."

"We let other people hurt us," she contradicted. "Never again."

"How could we be stupid enough to almost lose it all twice?" he wondered aloud. "No more secrets, Asher."

She shook her head. "No more secrets. A third chance, Ty?"

"I work best under pressure." He brushed his lips over her temple. "Double break point, Face, I'm on a winning streak."

"You should be celebrating."

"I did my share."

"Not with me." She gave him a light kiss full of promise. "We could go to my place. Pick up a bottle of champagne on the way."

"We could stay here," he countered. "And worry about the champagne tomorrow."

"It is tomorrow," she reminded him.

"Then we've got all day." He began to pull her toward the bedroom.

"Wait a minute." Snatching her hand away, she stepped back. "I'd like to hear that conventional proposal now."

"Come on, Asher." He made another grab for her hand, but she eluded him.

"I mean it."

Flustered, he stuck his hands into his pockets. "You know I want you to marry me."

"That's not a conventional proposal." She folded her arms and waited. "Well," she began when he remained silent, "should I write you a cheat sheet? You say something like, Asher—"

"I know what I'm supposed to say," he muttered. "I'd rather try the kidnapping."

Laughing, she walked over and twined her arms around his neck. "Ask me," she whispered, letting her lips hover an inch from his.

"Will you marry me, Asher?" The lips held tantalizingly near his curved, but she remained silent. His eyes dropped to them, lingered, then rose to hers. "Well?"

"I'm thinking it over," she told him. "I was hoping for something a bit more flowery, maybe some poetry or—" The wind was knocked out of her as he hefted her over his shoulder. "Yes, that's good too," she decided. "I should be able to let you know in a few days."

From the height he dropped her, she bounced twice before she settled on the bed.

"Or sooner," she decided as he began unbuttoning her blouse.

"Shut up."

She cocked a brow. "Don't you want to hear my answer?"

"We'll get the license tomorrow."

"I haven't said—"

"And the blood tests."

"I haven't agreed—"

His mouth silenced her in a long, lingering kiss as his body fit unerringly to hers.

"Of course," Asher sighed, "I could probably be persuaded."

* * * * *

A Will and a Way

For my family members, who, fortunately,
aren't as odd as the relatives in this book.

Chapter One

One hundred fifty million dollars was nothing to sneeze at. No one in the vast, echoing library of Jolley's Folley would have dared. Except Pandora. She did so with more enthusiasm than delicacy into a tattered tissue. After blowing her nose, she sat back, wishing the antihistamine she had taken would live up to its promise of fast relief. She wished she'd never caught the wretched cold in the first place. More, she wished she were anywhere else in the world.

Surrounding her were dozens of books she'd read and hundreds more she'd never given a thought to, though she'd spent hours and hours in the library. The scent of the leather-bound volumes mixed with the lighter, homier scent of dust. Pandora preferred either to the strangling fragrance of lilies that filled three stocky vases.

In one corner of the room was a marble-and-ivory chess set, where she'd lost a great many highly disputed matches. Uncle Jolley, bless his round, innocent face and pudgy fingers, had been a compulsive and skilled cheat. Pandora had never taken a loss in stride. Maybe that's why he'd so loved to beat her, by fair means or foul.

Through the three arching windows the light shone dull and a little gloomy. It suited her mood and, she thought, the proceedings. Uncle Jolley had loved to set scenes.

When she loved—and she felt this emotion for a select few who'd touched her life—she put everything she had into it. She'd been born with boundless energy. She'd developed iron-jawed stubbornness. She'd loved Uncle Jolley in her uninhibited, expansive fashion, acknowledging then accepting all of his oddites. He might have been ninety-three, but he'd never been dull or fussy.

A month before his death, they'd gone fishing—poaching actually—in the lake that was owned and stocked by his neighbor. When they'd caught more than they could eat, they'd sent a half-dozen trout back to the owner, cleaned and chilled.

She was going to miss Uncle Jolley with his round cherub's face, high, melodious voice and wicked humors. From his ten-foot, extravagantly framed portrait, he looked down at her with the same little smirk he'd worn whether he'd been making a million-dollar merger or handing an unsuspecting vice-president a drink in a dribble glass. She missed him already. No one else in her far-flung, contrasting family understood and accepted her with the same ease. It had been one more reason she'd adored him.

Miserable with grief, aggravated by a head cold, Pandora listened to Edmund Fitzhugh drone on, and on, with the preliminary technicalities of Uncle Jolley's will. Maximillian Jolley McVie had never been one for brevity. He'd always said if you were going to do something, do it until the steam ran out. His last will and testament bore his style.

Not bothering to hide her disinterest in the proceedings, Pandora took a comprehensive survey of the other occupants of the library.

To have called them mourners would have been just the sort of bad joke Jolley would have appreciated.

There was Jolley's only surviving son, Uncle Carlson, and his wife. What was her name? Lona—Mona? Did it matter? Pandora saw them sitting stiff backed and alert in matching shades of black. They made her think of crows on a telephone wire just waiting for something to fall at their feet.

Cousin Ginger—sweet and pretty and harmless, if rather vacuous. Her hair was Jean Harlow blond this month. Good old Cousin Biff was there in his black Brooks Brothers suit. He sat back, one leg crossed over the other as if he were watching a polo match. Pandora was certain he wasn't missing a word. His wife—was it Laurie?—had a prim, respectful look on her face. From experience, Pandora knew she wouldn't utter a word unless it were to echo Biff. Uncle Jolley had called her a silly, boring fool. Hating to be cynical, Pandora had to agree.

There was Uncle Monroe looking plump and successful and smoking a big cigar despite the fact that his sister, Patience, waved a little white handkerchief in front of her nose. Probably because of it, Pandora corrected. Uncle Monroe liked nothing better than to make his ineffectual sister uncomfortable.

Cousin Hank looked macho and muscular, but hardly more than his tough athletic wife, Meg. They'd hiked the Appalachian

Trail on their honeymoon. Uncle Jolley had wondered if they stretched and limbered up before lovemaking.

The thought caused Pandora to giggle. She stifled it half-heartedly with the tissue just before her gaze wandered over to cousin Michael. Or was it second cousin Michael? She'd never been able to get the technical business straight. It seemed a bit foolish when you weren't talking blood relation anyway. His mother had been Uncle Jolley's niece by Jolley's son's second marriage. It was a complicated state of affairs, Pandora thought. But then Michael Donahue was a complicated man.

They'd never gotten along, though she knew Uncle Jolley had favored him. As far as Pandora was concerned, anyone who made his living writing a silly television series that kept people glued to a box rather than doing something worthwhile was a materialistic parasite. She had a momentary flash of pleasure as she remembered telling him just that.

Then, of course, there were the women. When a man dated centerfolds and showgirls it was obvious he wasn't interested in intellectual stimulation. Pandora smiled as she recalled stating her view quite clearly the last time Michael had visited Jolley's Folley. Uncle Jolley had nearly fallen off his chair laughing.

Then her smile faded. Uncle Jolley was gone. And if she was honest, which she was often, she'd admit that of all the people in the room at that moment, Michael Donahue had cared for and enjoyed the old man more than anyone but herself.

You'd hardly know that to look at him now, she mused. He looked disinterested and slightly arrogant. She noticed the set, grim line around his lips. Pandora had always considered

Donahue's mouth his best feature, though he rarely smiled at her unless it was to bare his teeth and snarl.

Uncle Jolley had liked his looks, and had told Pandora so in his early stages of matchmaking. A hobby she'd made sure he'd given up quickly. Well, he hadn't given it up precisely, but she'd ignored it all the same.

Being rather short and round himself, perhaps Jolley had appreciated Donahue's long lean frame, and the narrow intense face. Pandora might have liked it herself, except that Michael's eyes were often distant and detached.

At the moment he looked like one of the heroes in the action series he wrote—leaning negligently against the wall and looking just a bit out of place in the tidy suit and tie. His dark hair was casual and not altogether neat, as though he hadn't thought to comb it into place after riding with the top down. He looked bored and ready for action. Any action.

It was too bad, Pandora thought, that they didn't get along better. She'd have liked to have reminisced with someone about Uncle Jolley, someone who appreciated his whimsies as she had.

There was no use thinking along those lines. If they'd elected to sit together, they'd have been picking little pieces out of each other by now. Uncle Jolley, smirking down from his portrait, knew it very well.

With a half sigh she blew her nose again and tried to listen to Fitzhugh. There was something about a bequest to whales. Or maybe it was whalers.

Another hour of this, Michael thought, and he'd be ready to

chew raw meat. If he heard one more *whereas*... On a long breath, Michael drew himself in. He was here for the duration because he'd loved the crazy old man. If the last thing he could do for Jolley was to stand in a room with a group of human vultures and listen to long rambling legalese, then he'd do it. Once it was over, he'd pour himself a long shot of brandy and toast the old man in private. Jolley had had a fondness for brandy.

When Michael had been young and full of imagination and his parents hadn't understood, Uncle Jolley had listened to him ramble, encouraged him to dream. Invariably on a visit to the Folley, his uncle had demanded a story then had settled himself back, bright-eyed and eager, while Michael wove on. Michael hadn't forgotten.

When he'd received his first Emmy for *Logan's Run*, Michael had flown from L.A. to the Catskills and had given the statuette to his uncle. The Emmy was still in the old man's bedroom, even if the old man wasn't.

Michael listened to the dry impersonal attorney's voice and wished for a cigarette. He'd only given them up two days before. Two days, four hours and thirty-five minutes. He'd have welcomed the raw meat.

He felt stifled in the room with all these people. Every one of them had thought old Jolley was half-mad and a bit of a nuisance. The one hundred fifty-million-dollar estate was different. Stocks and bonds were extremely sane. Michael had seen several assessing glances roaming over the library furniture. Big, ornate Georgian might not suit some of the streamlined life-styles, but it would liquidate into very tidy cash. The old man, Michael knew, had loved every clunky chair and oversize table in the house.

He doubted if any of them had been to the big echoing house in the past ten years. Except for Pandora, he admitted grudgingly. She might be an annoyance, but she'd adored Jolley.

At the moment she looked miserable. Michael didn't believe he'd ever seen her look unhappy before—furious, disdainful, infuriating, but never unhappy. If he hadn't known better, he'd have gone to sit beside her, offer some comfort, hold her hand. She'd probably chomp it off at the wrist.

Still, her shockingly blue eyes were red and puffy. Almost as red as her hair, he mused, as his gaze skimmed over the wild curly mane that tumbled, with little attention to discipline or style, around her shoulders. She was so pale that the sprinkling of freckles over her nose stood out. Normally her ivory-toned skin had a hint of rose in it—health or temperament, he'd never been sure.

Sitting among her solemn, black-clad family, she stood out like a parrot among crows. She'd worn a vivid blue dress. Michael approved of it, though he'd never say so to Pandora. She didn't need black and crepe and lilies to mourn. That he understood, if he didn't understand her.

She annoyed him, periodically, with her views on his life-style and career. When they clashed, it didn't take long for him to hurl criticism back at her. After all, she was a bright, talented woman who was content to play around making outrageous jewelry for boutiques rather than taking advantage of her Master's degree in education.

She called him materialistic, he called her idealistic. She labeled him a chauvinist, he labeled her a pseudo-intellectual. Jolley had sat with his hands folded and chuckled every time they argued. Now that he was gone, Michael mused, there wouldn't be an opportunity for any more battles. Oddly enough, he found it another reason to miss his uncle.

The truth was, he'd never felt any strong family ties to anyone but Jolley. Michael didn't think of his parents very often. His father was somewhere in Europe with his fourth wife, and his mother had settled placidly into Palm Springs society with husband number three. They'd never understood their son who'd opted to work for a living in something as bourgeois as television.

But Jolley had understood and appreciated. More, much more important to Michael, he'd enjoyed Michael's work.

A grin spread over his face when he heard Fitzhugh drone out the bequest for whales. It was so typically Jolley. Several impatient relations hissed through their teeth. A hundred fifty thousand dollars had just spun out of their reach. Michael glanced up at the larger-than-life-size portrait of his uncle. You always said you'd have the last word, you old fool. The only trouble is you're not here to laugh about it.

"To my son, Carlson…" All the quiet muttering and whispers died as Fitzhugh cleared his throat. Without much interest Pandora watched her relatives come to attention. The charities and servants had their bequests. Now it was time for the big guns. Fitzhugh glanced up briefly before he continued. "Whose—aaah—mediocrity was always a mystery to me, I leave my entire collection of magic tricks in hopes he can develop a sense of the ridiculous."

Pandora choked into her tissue and watched her uncle turn beet red. First point Uncle Jolley, she thought and prepared to enjoy herself. Maybe he'd left the whole business to the A.S.P.C.A.

"To my grandson, Bradley, and my granddaughter by marriage, Lorraine, I leave my very best wishes. They need nothing more."

Pandora swallowed and blinked back tears at the reference to her parents. She'd call them in Zanzibar that evening. They would appreciate the sentiment even as she did.

"To my nephew Monroe who has the first dollar he ever made, I leave the last dollar I made, frame included. To my niece, Patience, I leave my cottage in Key West without much hope she'll have the gumption to use it."

Monroe chomped on his cigar while Patience looked horrified.

"To my grand-nephew, Biff, I leave my collection of matches, with the hopes that he will, at last, set the world on fire. To my pretty grand-niece, Ginger, who likes equally pretty things, I leave the sterling silver mirror purported to have been owned by Marie Antoinette. To my grand-nephew, Hank, I leave the sum of 3528. Enough, I believe, for a lifetime supply of wheat germ."

The grumbles that had begun with the first bequest continued and grew. Anger hovered on the edge of outrage. Jolley would have liked nothing better. Pandora made the mistake of glancing over at Michael. He didn't seem so distant and detached now, but full of admiration. When their gazes met, the giggle she'd been holding back spilled out. It earned her several glares.

Carlson rose, giving new meaning to the phrase controlled outrage. "Mr. Fitzhugh, my father's will is nothing more than a mockery. It's quite obvious that he wasn't in his right mind when he made it, nor do I have any doubt that a court will overturn it."

"Mr. McVie." Again Fitzhugh cleared his throat. The sun began to push its way through the clouds but no one seemed to notice. "I understand perfectly your sentiments in this matter. However, my client was perfectly well and lucid when this will was drawn. He may have worded it against my advice, but it is legal and binding. You are, of course, free to consult with your own counsel. Meanwhile, there's more to be read."

"Hogwash." Monroe puffed on his cigar and glared at everyone. "Hogwash," he repeated while Patience patted his arm and chirped ineffectually.

"Uncle Jolley liked hogwash," Pandora said as she balled her tissue. She was ready to face them down, almost hoped she'd have to. It would take her mind off her grief. "If he wanted to leave his money to the Society for the Prevention of Stupidity, it was his right."

"Easily said, my dear." Biff polished his nails on his lapel. The gold band of his watch caught a bit of the sun and gleamed. "Perhaps the old lunatic left you a ball of twine so you can string more beads."

"You haven't got the matches yet, old boy." Michael spoke

lazily from his corner, but every eye turned his way. "Careful what you light."

"Let him read, why don't you?" Ginger piped up, quite pleased with her bequest. Marie Antoinette, she mused. Just imagine.

"The last two bequests are joint," Fitzhugh began before there could be another interruption. "And, a bit unorthodox."

"The entire document's unorthodox," Carlson tossed out, then harrumphed. Several heads nodded in agreement.

Pandora remembered why she always avoided family gatherings. They bored her to death. Quite deliberately, she waved a hand in front of her mouth and yawned. "Could we have the rest, Mr. Fitzhugh, before my family embarrasses themselves any further?"

She thought, but couldn't be sure, that she saw a quick light of approval in the fusty attorney's eyes. "Mr. McVie wrote this portion in his own words." He paused a moment, either for effect or courage. "To Pandora McVie and Michael Donahue," Fitzhugh read. "The two members of my family who have given me the most pleasure with their outlook on life, their enjoyment of an old man and old jokes, I leave the rest of my estate, in entirety, all accounts, all business interests, all stocks, bonds and trusts, all real and personal property, with all affection. Share and share alike."

Pandora didn't hear the half-dozen objections that sprang out. She rose, stunned and infuriated. "I can't take his money." Towering over the family who sat around her, she strode straight up to Fitzhugh. The lawyer, who'd anticipated attacks from other areas, braced for the unexpected. "I wouldn't know what to do with it. It'd just clutter up my life." She waved a hand at the papers on the desk as if they were a minor annoyance. "He should've asked me first."

"Miss McVie…"

Before the lawyer could speak again, she whirled on Michael. "You can have it all. You'd know what to do with it, after all. Buy a hotel in New York, a condo in L.A., a club in Chicago and a plane to fly you back and forth, I don't care."

Deadly calm, Michael slipped his hands in his pockets. "I appreciate the offer, cousin. Before you pull the trigger, why don't we wait until Mr. Fitzhugh finishes before you embarrass yourself any further?"

She stared at him a moment, nearly nose to nose with him in heels. Then, because she'd been taught to do so at an early age, she took a deep breath and waited for her temper to ebb. "I don't want his money."

"You've made your point." He lifted a brow in the cynical, half-amused way that always infuriated her. "You're fascinating the relatives by the little show you're putting on."

Nothing could have made her find control quicker. She angled her chin at him, hissed once, then subsided. "All right then." She turned and stood her ground. "I apologize for the interruption. Please finish reading, Mr. Fitzhugh."

The lawyer gave himself a moment by taking off his glasses and polishing them on a big white handkerchief. He'd known when Jolley had made the will the day would come when he'd be forced to face an enraged family. He'd argued with his client

about it, cajoled, reasoned, pointed out the absurdities. Then he'd drawn up the will and closed the loopholes.

"I leave all of this," he continued, "the money, which is a small thing, the stocks and bonds, which are necessary but boring, the business interests, which are interesting weights around the neck. And my home and all in it, which is everything important to me, the memories made there, to Pandora and Michael because they understood and cared. I leave this to them, though it may annoy them, because there is no one else in my family I can leave what is important to me. What was mine is Pandora and Michael's now, because I know they'll keep me alive. I ask only one thing of each of them in return."

Michael's grip relaxed, and he nearly smiled again. "Here comes the kicker," he murmured.

"Beginning no more than a week after the reading of this document, Pandora and Michael will move into my home in the Catskills, known as Jolley's Folley. They will live there together for a period of six months, neither one spending more than two nights in succession under another roof. After this six-month period, the estate reverts to them, entirely and without encumbrance, share and share alike.

"If one does not agree with this provision, or breaks the terms of this provision within the six-month period, the estate, in its entirety will be given over to all my surviving heirs and the Institute for the Study of Carnivorous Plants in joint shares.

"You have my blessing, children. Don't let an old, dead man down."

For a full thirty seconds there was silence. Taking advantage of it, Fitzhugh began straightening his papers.

"The old bastard," Michael murmured. Pandora would've taken offense if she hadn't agreed so completely. Because he judged the temperature in the room to be on the rise, Michael pulled Pandora out, down the hall and into one of the funny little parlors that could be found throughout the house. Just before he closed the door, the first explosion in the library erupted.

Pandora drew out a fresh tissue, sneezed into it, then plopped down on the arm of a chair. She was too flabbergasted and worn-out to be amused. "Well, what now?"

Michael reached for a cigarette before he remembered he'd quit. "Now we have to make a couple of decisions."

Pandora gave him one of the long lingering stares she'd learned made most men stutter. Michael merely sat across from her and stared back. "I meant what I said. I don't want his money. By the time it's divided up and the taxes dealt with, it's close to fifty million apiece. Fifty million," she repeated, rolling her eyes. "It's ridiculous."

"Jolley always thought so," Michael said, and watched the grief come and go in her eyes.

"He only had it to play with. The trouble was, every time he played, he made more." Unable to sit, Pandora paced to the window. "Michael, I'd suffocate with that much money."

"Cash isn't as heavy as you think."

With something close to a sneer, she turned and sat on the window ledge. "You don't object to fifty million or so after taxes I take it."

He'd have loved to have wiped that look off her face. "I haven't your fine disregard for money, Pandora, probably because I was raised with the illusion of it rather than the reality."

She shrugged, knowing his parents existed, and always had, mainly on credit and connections. "So, take it all then."

Michael picked up a little blue glass egg and tossed it from palm to palm. It was cool and smooth and worth several thousand. "That's not what Jolley wanted."

With a sniff, she snatched the egg from his hand. "He wanted us to get married and live happily ever after. I'd like to humor him...." She tossed the egg back again. "But I'm not that much of a martyr. Besides, aren't you engaged to some little blond dancer?"

He set the egg down before he could heave it at her. "For someone who turns their pampered nose up at television, you don't have the same intellectual snobbery about gossip rags."

"I *adore* gossip," Pandora said with such magnificent exaggeration Michael laughed.

"All right, Pandora, let's put down the swords a minute." He tucked his thumbs in his pockets and rocked back on his heels. Maybe they could, if they concentrated, talk civilly with each other for a few minutes. "I'm not engaged to anyone, but marriage wasn't a term of the will in any case. All we have to do is live together for six months under the same roof."

As she studied him a sense of disappointment ran through her. Perhaps they'd never gotten along, but she'd respected him if for nothing more than what she'd seen as his pure affection for Uncle Jolley. "So, you really want the money?"

He took two furious steps forward before he caught himself. Pandora never flinched. "Think whatever you like." He said it softly, as though it didn't matter. Oddly enough, it made her shudder. "You don't want the money, fine. Put that aside a moment. Are you going to stand by and watch this house go to the clan out there or a bunch of scientists studying Venus's-flytraps? Jolley loved this place and everything in it. I always thought you did, too."

"I do." The others would sell it, she admitted. There wasn't one person in the library who wouldn't put the house on the market and run with the cash. It would be lost to her. All the foolish, ostentatious rooms, the ridiculous archways. Jolley might be gone, but he'd left the house like a dangling carrot. And he still held the stick.

"He's trying to run our lives still."

Michael lifted a brow. "Surprised?"

With a half laugh, Pandora glanced over. "No."

Slowly she walked around the room while the sun shot through the diamond panes of glass and lit her hair. Michael watched her with a sense of detached admiration. She'd look magnificent on the screen. He'd always thought so. Her coloring, her posture. Her arrogance. The five or ten pounds the camera would add couldn't hurt that too angular, bean-pole body, either. And the fire-engine-red hair would make a statement on the screen while it was simply outrageous in reality. He'd often wondered why she didn't do something to tone it down.

At the moment he wasn't interested in any of that—just in what was in her brain. He didn't give a damn about the money, but he wasn't going to sit idly by and watch everything Jolley had had and built go to the vultures. If he had to play rough with Pandora, he would. He might even enjoy it.

Millions. Pandora cringed at the outrageousness of it. That much money could be nothing but a headache, she was certain. Stocks, bonds, accountants, trusts, tax shelters. She preferred a simpler kind of living. Though no one would call her apartment in Manhattan primitive.

She'd never had to worry about money and that was just the way she liked it. Above or below a certain income level, there were nothing but worries. But if you found a nice, comfortable plateau, you could just cruise. She'd nearly found it.

It was true enough that a share of this would help her tremendously professionally. With a buffer sturdy enough, she could have the artistic freedom she wanted and continue the life-style that now caused a bit of a strain on her bank account. Her work was artistic and critically acclaimed but reviews didn't pay the rent. Outside of Manhattan, her work was usually considered too unconventional. The fact that she often had to create more mainstream designs to keep her head above water grated constantly. With fifty or sixty thousand to back her, she could…

Furious with herself, she blocked it off. She was thinking like Michael, she decided. She'd rather die. He'd sold out, turned whatever talent he had to the main chance, just as he was ready to turn these circumstances to his own financial advantage. She would think of other areas. She would think first of Jolley.

As she saw it, the entire scheme was a maze of problems. How like her uncle. Now, like a chess match, she'd have to consider her moves.

She'd never lived with a man. Purposely. Pandora liked running by her own clock. It wasn't so much that she minded sharing *things*, she minded sharing space. If she agreed, that would be the first concession.

Then there was the fact that Michael was attractive, attractive enough to be unsettling if he hadn't been so annoying. Annoying and easily annoyed, she recalled with a flash of amusement. She knew what buttons to push. Hadn't she always prided herself on the fact that she could handle him? It wasn't always easy; he was too sharp. But that made their altercations interesting. Still, they'd never been together for more than a week at a time.

But there was one clear, inarguable fact. She'd loved her uncle. How could she live with herself if she denied him a last wish? Or a last joke.

Six months. Stopping, she studied Michael as he studied her. Six months could be a very long time, especially when you weren't pleased with what you were doing. There was only one way to speed things up. She'd enjoy herself.

"Tell me, cousin, how can we live under the same roof for six months without coming to blows?"

"We can't."

He'd answered without a second's hesitation, so she laughed again. "I suppose I'd be bored if we did. I can tidy up loose ends and move in in three days. Four at the most."

"That's fine." When his shoulders relaxed, he realized he'd

been tensed for her refusal. At the moment he didn't want to question why it mattered so much. Instead he held out a hand. "Deal."

Pandora inclined her head just before her palm met his. "Deal," she agreed, surprised that his hand was hard and a bit callused. She'd expected it to be rather soft and limp. After all, all he did was type. Perhaps the next six months would have some surprises.

"Shall we go tell the others?"

"They'll want to murder us."

Her smile came slowly, subtly shifting the angles of her face. It was, Michael thought, at once wicked and alluring. "I know. Try not to gloat."

When they stepped out, several griping relatives had spilled out into the hallway. They did what they did best together. They argued.

"You'd blow your share on barbells and carrot juice," Biff said spitefully to Hank. "At least I know what to do with money."

"Lose it on horses," Monroe said, and blew out a stream of choking cigar smoke. "Invest. Tax deferred."

"You could use yours to take a course in how to speak in complete sentences." Carlson stepped out of the smoke and straightened his tie. "I'm the old man's only living son. It's up to me to prove he was incompetent."

"Uncle Jolley had more competence than the lot of you put together." Feeling equal parts frustration and disgust, Pandora stepped forward. "He gave you each exactly what he wanted you to have."

Biff drew out a flat gold cigarette case as he glanced over at his cousin. "It appears our Pandora's changed her mind about the money. Well, you worked for it, didn't you, darling?"

Michael put his hand on Pandora's shoulder and squeezed lightly before she could spring. "You'd like to keep your profile, wouldn't you, cousin?"

"It appears writing for television's given you a taste for violence." Biff lit his cigarette and smiled. If he'd thought he could get in a blow below the belt… "I think I'll decline a brawl," he decided.

"Well, I think it's fair." Hank's wife came forward, stretching out her hand. She gave both Pandora and Michael a hearty shake. "You should put a gym in this place. Build yourself up a little. Come on, Hank."

Silent, and his shoulders straining the material of his suit, Hank followed her out.

"Nothing but muscles between the head," Carlson mumbled. "Come, Mona." He strode ahead of his wife, pausing long enough to level a glare at Pandora and Michael. The inevitable line ran though Michael's mind before Carlson opened his mouth and echoed it. "You haven't heard the last of this."

Pandora gave him her sweetest smile. "Have a nice trip home, Uncle Carlson."

"Probate," Monroe said with a grunt, and waddled his way out behind them.

Patience fluttered her hands. "Key West, for heaven's sake. I've never been south of Palm Beach. My, oh my."

"Oh, Michael." Fluttering her lashes, Ginger placed a hand on his arm. "When do you think I might have my mirror?"

He glanced down into her perfectly lovely, heart-shaped face. Her eyes were as pure a blue as tropical waters. He thanked God Jolley hadn't asked that he spend six months with Cousin Ginger. "I'm sure Mr. Fitzhugh will have it shipped to you as soon as possible."

"Come along, Ginger, we'll give you a ride to the airport." Biff pulled Ginger's hand through his arm, patted it and smiled down at Pandora. "I'd be worried if I didn't know you better. You won't last six days with Michael much less six months. Beastly temper," he said confidentially to Michael. "The two of you'll murder each other before a week's out."

"Don't spend the old man's money yet," Michael warned. "We'll make the six months if for no other reason than to spite you." He smiled when he said it, a chummy, well-meaning smile that took the arrogance from Biff's face.

"We'll see who wins the game." Straight backed, Biff turned toward the door. His wife walked out behind him without having said a word since she'd walked in.

"Biff," Ginger began as they walked out. "What are you going to do with all those matches?"

"Burn his bridges, I hope," Pandora muttered. "Well, Michael, though I can't say there was a lot of love before, there's nearly none lost now."

"Are you worried about alienating them?"

With a shrug of her shoulders, she walked toward a bowl of roses, then gave him a considering look. "Well, I've never had any trouble alienating you. Why is that, do you suppose?"

"Jolley always said we were too much alike."

"Really?" Haughty, she lifted a brow. "I find myself disagreeing with him again. You and I, Michael Donahue, have almost nothing in common."

"If that's so we have six months to prove it." On impulse he moved closer and put a finger under her chin. "You know, darling, you might've been stuck with Biff."

"I'd've given the place to the plants first."

He grinned. "I'm flattered."

"Don't be." But she didn't move away from him. Not yet. It was an interesting feeling to be this close without snarling. "The only difference is you don't bore me."

"That's enough," he said with a hint of a smile. "I'm easily flattered." Intrigued, he flicked a finger down her cheek. It was still pale, but her eyes were direct and steady. "No, we won't bore each other Pandora. In six months we might experience a lot of things, but boredom won't be one of them."

It might be an interesting feeling, she discovered, but it wasn't quite a safe one. It was best to remember that he didn't find her appealing as a woman but would, for the sake of his own ego, string her along if she permitted it. "I don't flatter easily. I haven't decided exactly what your reasons are for going through with this farce, but I'm doing it only for Uncle Jolley. I can set up my equipment here quite easily."

"And I can write here quite easily."

Pandora plucked a rose from the bowl. "If you can call those implausible scripts writing."

"The same way you call the bangles you string together art."

Color came back to her cheeks and that pleased him. "You

wouldn't know art if it reached up and bit you on the nose. My jewelry expresses emotion."

His smile showed pleasant interest. "How much is lust going for these days?"

"I would have guessed you'd be very familiar with the cost." Pandora fumbled for a tissue, sneezed into it, then shut her bag with a click. "Most of the women you date have price tags."

It amused him, and it showed. "I thought we were talking about work."

"My profession is a time-honored one, while yours—yours stops for commercial breaks. And furthermore—"

"I beg your pardon."

Fitzhugh paused at the doorway of the library. He wanted nothing more than to be shed of the McVie clan and have a quiet, soothing drink. "Am I to assume that you've both decided to accept the terms of the will?"

Six months, she thought. It was going to be a long, long winter.

Six months, he thought. He was going to have the first daffodil he found in April bronzed.

"You can start counting the days at the end of the week," he told Fitzhugh. "Agreed, cousin?"

Pandora set her chin. "Agreed."

Chapter Two

It was a pleasant trip from Manhattan along the Hudson River toward the Catskills. Pandora had always enjoyed it. The drive gave her time to clear her mind and relax. But then, she'd always taken it at her own whim, her own pace, her own convenience. Pandora made it a habit to do everything just that way. This time, however, there was more involved than her own wants and wishes. Uncle Jolley had boxed her in.

He'd known she'd have to go along with the terms of the will. Not for the money. He'd been too smart to think she could be lured into such a ridiculous scheme with money. But the house, her ties to it, her need for the continuity of family. That's what he'd hooked her with.

Now she had to leave Manhattan behind for six months. Oh, she'd run into the city for a few hours here and there, but it was hardly the same as living in the center of things. She'd always liked that—being in the center, surrounded by movement, being able to watch and become involved whenever she liked. Just as she'd always liked long weekends in the solitude of Jolley's Folley.

She'd been raised that way, to enjoy and make the most of whatever environment she was in. Her parents were gypsies. Wealth had meant they'd traveled first class instead of in covered wagons. If there'd been campfires, there had also been a servant to gather kindling, but the spirit was the same.

Before she'd been fifteen, Pandora had been to more than thirty countries. She'd eaten sushi in Tokyo, roamed the moors in Cornwall, bargained in Turkish markets. A succession of tutors had traveled with them so that by her calculations, she'd spent just under two years in a classroom environment before college.

The exotic, vagabond childhood had given her a taste for variety—in people, in foods, in styles. And oddly enough the exposure to widely diverse cultures and mores had formed in her an unshakable desire for a home and a sense of belonging.

Though her parents liked to meander through countries, recording everything with pen and film, Pandora had missed a central point. Where was home? This year in Mexico, next year in Athens. Her parents made a name for themselves with their books and articles on the unusual, but Pandora wanted roots. She'd discovered she'd have to find them for herself.

She'd chosen New York, and in her way, Uncle Jolley.

Now, because her uncle and his home had become her central point, she was agreeing to spend six months living with a man she could hardly tolerate so that she could inherit a fortune she didn't want or need. Life, she'd discovered long ago, never moved in straight lines.

Jolley McVie's ultimate joke, she thought as she turned up the long drive toward his Folley. Well, he could throw them together, but he couldn't make them stick.

Still, she'd have felt better if she'd been sure of Michael. Was it the lure of the millions of dollars, or an affection for an old man that would bring him to the Catskills? She knew his *Logan's Run* was in its very successful fourth year, and that he'd had other lucrative ventures in television. But money was a seduction itself. After all, her Uncle Carlson had more than he could ever spend, yet he was already taking the steps for a probate of the will.

That didn't worry her. Uncle Jolley had believed in hiring the best. If Fitzhugh had drawn up the will, it was air-tight. What worried her was Michael Donahue.

Because of the trap she'd fallen into, she'd found herself thinking of him a great deal too much over the past couple of days. Ally or enemy, she wasn't sure. Either way, she was going to have to live with him. Or around him. She hoped the house was big enough.

By the time she arrived, she was worn-out from the drive and the lingering head cold. Though her equipment and supplies had been shipped the day before, she still had three cases in the car. Deciding to take one at a time, Pandora popped the trunk, then simply looked at Jolley's Folley.

He'd built it when he'd been forty, so the house was already over a half century old. It went in all directions at once, as if he'd never been able to decide where he wanted to start and where he wanted to finish. The truth about Jolley, she admitted, was that he'd never wanted to finish. The project, the game, the puzzle, was always more interesting to him before the last pieces were in place.

Without the wings, it might have been a rather somber and sedate late-nineteenth-century mansion. With them, it was a mass of walls and corners, heights and widths. There was no symmetry, yet to Pandora it had always seemed as sturdy as the rock it had been built on.

Some of the windows were long, some were wide, some of them were leaded and some sheer. Jolley had made up his mind then changed it again as he'd gone along.

The stone had come from one of his quarries, the wood from one of his lumberyards. When he'd decided to build a house, he'd started his own construction firm. McVie Construction, Incorporated was one of the five biggest companies in the country.

It struck her suddenly that she owned half of Jolley's share in the company and her mind spun at how many others. She had interests in baby oil, steel mills, rocket engines and cake mix. Pandora lifted the case and set her teeth. What on earth had she let herself in for?

From the upstairs window, Michael watched her. The jacket she wore was big and baggy with three vivid colors, blue, yellow and pink patched in. The wind caught at her slacks and rippled them from thigh to ankle. She wasn't looking teary-eyed and pale this time, but grim and resigned. So much the better. He'd been tempted to comfort her during their uncle's funeral. Only the knowledge that too much sympathy for a woman like Pandora was fatal had prevented him.

He'd known her since childhood and had considered her a spoiled brat from the word go. Though she'd often been off for months at a time on one of her parents' journalistic safaris, they'd seen enough of each other to feed a mutual dislike. Only the fact that she had cared for Jolley had given Michael some tolerance for her. And the fact, he was forced to admit, that she had more honesty and humanity in her than any of their other relations.

There had been a time, he recalled, a brief time, during late adolescence that he'd felt a certain…stirring for her. A purely shallow and physical teenage hunger, Michael assured himself. She'd always had an intriguing face; it could be unrelentingly plain one moment and striking the next, and when she'd hit her teens…well, that had been a natural enough reaction. And it had passed without incident. He now preferred a woman with more subtlety, more gloss and femininity—and shorter fangs.

Whatever he preferred, Michael left the arranging of his own office to wander downstairs.

"Charles, did my shipment come?" Pandora pulled off her leather driving gloves and dropped them on a little round table in the hall. Since Charles was there, the ancient butler who had served her uncle since before she was born, she felt a certain pleasure in coming.

"Everything arrived this morning, miss." The old man would have taken her suitcase if she hadn't waved him away.

"No, don't fuss with that. Where did you have them put everything?"

"In the garden shed in the east yard, as you instructed."

She gave him a smile and a peck on the cheek, both of which

pleased him. His square bulldog's face grew slightly pink. "I knew I could count on you. I didn't tell you before how happy I was that you and Sweeney are staying. The place wouldn't be the same without you serving tea and Sweeney baking cakes."

Charles managed to pull his back a bit straighter. "We wouldn't think about going anywhere else, miss. The master would have wanted us to stay."

But made it possible for them to go, Pandora mused. Leaving each of them three thousand dollars for every year of service. Charles had been with Jolley since the house was built, and Sweeney had come some ten years later. The bequest would have been more than enough for each to retire on. Pandora smiled. Some weren't made for retirement.

"Charles, I'd love some tea," she began, knowing if she didn't distract him, he'd insist on carrying her bags up the long staircase.

"In the drawing room, miss?"

"Perfect. And if Sweeney has any of those little cakes…"

"She's been baking all morning." With only the slightest of creaks, he made his way toward the kitchen.

Pandora thought of rich icing loaded with sugar. "I wonder how much weight a person can gain in six months."

"A steady diet of Sweeney's cakes wouldn't hurt you," Michael said from above her head. "Men are generally more attracted to flesh than bone."

Pandora spun around, then found herself in the awkward position of having to arch her neck back to see Michael at the top of the stairs. "I don't center my life around attracting men."

"I'd be the last one to argue with that."

He looked quite comfortable, she thought, feeling the first stirrings of resentment. And negligently, arrogantly attractive. From several feet above her head, he leaned against a post and looked down on her as though he was the master. She'd soon put an end to that. Uncle Jolley's will had been very clear. Share and share alike.

"Since you're already here and settled in, you can come help me with the rest of my bags."

He didn't budge. "I always thought the one point we were in perfect agreement on was feminism."

Pandora paused at the door to toss a look over her shoulder. "Social and political views aside, if you don't help me up with them before Charles comes back, he'll insist on doing it himself. He's too old to do it and too proud to be told he can't." She walked back out and wasn't surprised when she heard his footsteps on the gravel behind her.

She took a deep breath of crisp autumn air. All in all, it was a lovely day. "Drive up early?"

"Actually, I drove up late last night."

Pandora turned at the open trunk of her car. "So eager to start the game, Michael?"

If he hadn't been determined to start off peacefully, he'd have found fault with the tone of her voice, with the look in her eyes. Instead he let it pass. "I wanted to get my office set up today. I was just finishing it when you drove in."

"Work, work, work," she said with a long sigh. "You must put in slavish hours to come up with an hour of chase scenes and steam a week."

Peace wasn't all that important. As she reached for a suitcase, he closed a hand over her wrist. Later he'd think about how slim it was, how soft. Now he could only think how much he wished she were a man. Then he could've belted her. "The amount of work I do and what I produce is of absolutely no concern to you."

It occurred to Pandora, oddly, she thought, just how much she enjoyed seeing him on the edge of temper. All of her other relatives were so bland, so outwardly civilized. Michael had always been a contrast, and therefore of more interest. Smiling, she allowed her wrist to stay limp.

"Did I indicate that it was? Nothing, I promise you, could be further from the truth. Shall we get these in and have that tea? It's a bit chilly."

He'd always admired, grudgingly, how smoothly she could slip into the lady-of-the-manor routine. As a writer who wrote for actors and for viewers, he appreciated natural talent. He also knew how to set a scene to his best advantage. "Tea's a perfect idea." He hauled one case out and left the second for her. "We'll establish some guidelines."

"Will we?" Pandora pulled out the case, then let the trunk shut quietly. Without another word, she started back toward the house, holding the front door open for him, then breezing by the suitcase she'd left in the main hall. Because she knew Michael was fond of Charles, she hadn't a doubt he'd pick it up and follow.

The room she always took was on the second floor in the east wing. Jolley had let her decorate it herself, and she'd chosen white on white with a few startling splashes of color. Chartreuse and blazing blue in throw pillows, a long horizontal oil painting, jarring in its colors of sunset, a crimson waist-high urn stuffed with ostrich plumes.

Pandora set her case by the bed, noted with satisfaction that a fire had been laid in the small marble fireplace, then tossed her jacket over a chair.

"I always feel like I'm walking into *Better Homes*," he commented as he let her cases drop.

Pandora glanced down at them briefly, then at him. "I'm sure you're more at home in your own room. It's more—*Field and Stream*. I expect tea's ready."

He gave her a long, steady survey. Her jacket had concealed the trim cashmere sweater tucked into the narrow waist of her slacks. It reminded Michael quite forcibly just what had begun to attract him all those teenage years ago. For the second time he found himself wishing she were a man.

Though they walked abreast down the stairs, they didn't speak. In the drawing room, amid the Mideast opulence Jolley had chosen there, Charles was setting up the tea service.

"Oh, you lit the fire. How lovely." Pandora walked over and began warming her hands. She wanted a moment, just a moment, because for an instant in her room she thought she'd seen something in Michael's eyes. And she thought she'd felt the same something in response. "I'll pour, Charles. I'm sure Michael and I won't need another thing until dinner."

Casually she glanced around the room, at the flowing drapes, the curvy brocade sofas, the plump pillows and brass urns. "You know, this has always been one of my favorite rooms." Going to the tea set, she began to fill cups. "I was only twelve when we visited Turkey, but this room always makes me remember it vividly. Right down to the smells in the markets. Sugar?"

"No." He took the cup from her, plopped a generous slice of cake on a dish, then chose a seat. He preferred the little parlor next door with its tidy English country air. This was the beginning, he thought, with the old butler and plump cook as witnesses. Six months from today, they'd all sign a document swearing that the terms of the will had been adhered to and that would be that. It was the time in between that concerned him.

"Rule number one," Michael began without preamble. "We're both in the east wing because it makes it easier for Charles and Sweeney. But—" he paused, hoping to emphasize his point "—both of us will, at all times, respect the other's area."

"By all means." Pandora crossed her legs and sipped her tea.

"Again, because of the staff, it seems fair that we eat at the same time. Therefore, in the interest of survival, we'll keep the conversations away from professional matters."

Pandora smiled at him and nibbled on cake. "Oh yes, let's do keep things personal."

"You're a nasty little package—"

"See, we're off to a perfect start. Rule number two. Neither of us, no matter how bored or restless, will disturb the other during his or her set working hours. I generally work between ten and one, then again between three and six."

"Rule number three. If one of us is entertaining, the other will make him or herself scarce."

Pandora's eyes narrowed, only for a moment. "Oh, and I so

wanted to meet your dancer. Rule number four. The first floor is neutral ground and to be shared equally unless specific prior arrangements are made and agreed upon." She tapped her finger against the arm of the chair. "If we both play fair, we should manage."

"I don't have any trouble playing fair. As I recall, you're the one who cheats."

Her voice became very cool, her tone very rounded. "I don't know what you're talking about."

"Canasta, poker, gin."

"That's absurd and you have absolutely no proof." Rising, she helped herself to another cup of tea. "Besides, cards are entirely different." Warmed by the fire, soothed by the tea, she smiled at him. As Michael recalled, that particular smile was lethal. And stunning. "Are you still holding a grudge over that five hundred I won from you?"

"I wouldn't if you'd won it fairly."

"I won it," she countered. "That's what counts. If I cheated and you didn't catch me, then it follows that I cheated well enough for it to be legal."

"You always had a crooked sense of logic." He rose as well and came close. She had to admire the way he moved. It wasn't quite a swagger because he didn't put the effort into it. But it was very close. "If we play again, whatever we play, you won't cheat me."

Confident, she smiled at him. "Michael, we've known each other too long for you to intimidate me." She reached a hand up to pat his cheek and found her wrist captured a second time.

And a second time she saw and felt that same dangerous something she'd experienced upstairs.

There was no Uncle Jolley as a buffer between them now. Perhaps they'd both just begun to realize it. Whatever was between them that made them snarl and snap would have a long, cold winter to surface.

Perhaps neither one of them wanted to face it, but both were too stubborn to back down.

"Perhaps we're just beginning to know each other," Michael murmured.

She believed it. And didn't like it. He wasn't a posturing fool like Biff nor a harmless hulk like Hank. He might be a cousin by marriage only, but the blood between them had always run hot. There was violence in him. It showed sometimes in a look in his eyes, in the way he held himself. As though he wouldn't ward off a blow but counter it. Pandora recognized it because there was violence in her, as well. Perhaps that was why she always felt compelled to shoot darts at him, just to see how many he could boomerang back at her.

They stood as they were a moment, gauging each other, reassessing. The wise thing to do was for each to acknowledge a hit and step aside. Pandora threw up her chin. Michael set for the volley. "We'll go to the mat another time, Michael. At the moment, I'm a bit tired from the drive. If you'll excuse me?"

"Rule number five," he said without releasing her. "If one of us takes potshots at the other, they'll damn well pay the consequences." When he freed her arm, he went back for his cup. "See you at dinner, cousin."

* * *

Pandora awoke just past dawn fully awake, rested and bursting with energy. Whether it had been the air in the mountains or the six hours of deep sleep, she was ready and eager to work. Breakfast could wait, she decided as she showered and dressed. She was going out to the garden shed, organizing her equipment and diving in.

The house was perfectly quiet and still dim as she made her way downstairs. The servants would sleep another hour or two, she thought as she stuck her head in the pantry and chose a muffin. As she recalled, Michael might sleep until noon.

They had made it through dinner without incident. Perhaps they'd been polite to each other because of Charles and Sweeney or perhaps because both of them had been too tired to snipe. Pandora wasn't sure herself.

They'd dined under the cheerful lights of the big chandelier and had talked, when they'd talked, about the weather and the food.

By nine they'd gone their separate ways. Pandora to read until her eyes closed and Michael to work. Or so he'd said.

Outside the air was chill enough to cause Pandora's skin to prickle. She hunched up the collar of her jacket and started across the lawn. It crunched underfoot with the early thin frost. She liked it—the absolute solitude, the lightness of the air, the incredible smell of mountain and river.

In Tibet she'd once come close to frostbite because she hadn't been able to resist the snow and the swoop of rock. She didn't find this slice of the Catskills any less fascinating. The winter was best, she'd always thought, when the snow skimmed the top of your boots and your voice came out in puffs of smoke.

Winter in the mountains was a time for the basics. Heat, food, work. There were times Pandora wanted only the basics. There were times in New York she'd argue for hours over unions, politics, civil rights because the fact was, she loved an argument. She wanted the stimulation of an opposing view over broad issues or niggling ones. She wanted the challenge, the heat and the exercise for her brain. But…

There were times she wanted nothing more than a quiet sunrise over frost-crisped ground and the promise of a warm drink by a hot fire. And there were times, though she'd rarely admit it even to herself, that she wanted a shoulder to lay her head against and a hand to hold. She'd been raised to see independence as a duty, not a choice. Her parents had the most balanced of relationships, equal to equal. Pandora saw them as something rare in a world where the scales tipped this way or that too often. At age eighteen, Pandora had decided she'd never settle for less than a full partnership. At age twenty, she decided marriage wasn't for her. Instead she put all her passion, her energy and imagination into her work.

Straight-line dedication had paid off. She was successful, even prominent, and creatively she was fulfilled. It was more than many people ever achieved.

Now she pulled open the door of the utility shed. It was a big square building, as wide as the average barn, with hardwood floors and paneled walls. Uncle Jolley hadn't believed in the primitive. Hitting the switch, she flooded the building with light.

As per her instructions, the crates and boxes she'd shipped had been stacked along one wall. The shelves where Uncle Jolley had kept his gardening tools during his brief, torrid gardening stage had been packed away. The plumbing was good, with a full-size stainless-steel sink and a small but more than adequate bath with shower enclosed in the rear. She counted five workbenches. The light and ventilation were excellent.

It wouldn't take her long, Pandora figured, to turn the shed into an organized, productive workroom.

It took three hours.

Along one shelf were boxes of beads in various sizes—jet, amethyst, gold, polished wood, coral, ivory. She had trays of stones, precious and semiprecious, square cut, brilliants, teardrops and chips. In New York, they were kept in a safe. Here, she never considered it. She had gold, silver, bronze, copper. There were solid and hollow drills, hammers, tongs, pliers, nippers, files and clamps. One might have thought she did carpentry. Then there were scribes and drawplates, bottles of chemicals, and miles of string and fiber cord.

The money she'd invested in these materials had cost her every penny of an inheritance from her grandmother, and a good chunk of savings she'd earned as an apprentice. It had been worth it. Pandora picked up a file and tapped it against her palm. Well worth it.

She could forge gold and silver, cast alloys and string impossibly complex designs with the use of a few beads or shells. Metals could be worked into thin, threadlike strands or built into big bold chunks. Pandora could do as she chose, with tools that had hardly changed from those used by artists two centuries earlier.

It was and always had been, both the sense of continuity and the endless variety that appealed to her. She never made two identical pieces. That, to her, would have been manufacturing rather than creating. At times, her pieces were elegantly simple, classic in design. Those pieces sold well and allowed her a bit of artistic freedom. At other times, they were bold and brash and exaggerated. Mood guided Pandora, not trends. Rarely, very rarely, she would agree to create a piece along specified lines. If the lines, or the client, interested her.

She turned down a president because she'd found his ideas too pedestrian but had made a ring at a new father's request because his idea had been unique. Pandora had been told that the new mother had never taken the braided gold links off. Three links, one for each of the triplets she'd given birth to.

At the moment, Pandora had just completed drafting the design for a three-tiered necklace commissioned to her by the husband of a popular singer. Emerald. That was her name and the only requirement given to Pandora. The man wanted lots of them. And he'd pay, Pandora mused, for the dozen she'd chosen just before leaving New York. They were square, three karats apiece and of the sharp, sharp green that emeralds are valued for.

This was, she knew, her big chance, professionally and, most importantly, artistically. If the necklace was a success, there'd not only be reviews for her scrapbook, but acceptance. She'd be freer to do more of what she wanted without compromise.

The trick would be to fashion the chain so that it held like steel and looked like a cobweb. The stones would hang from each tier as if they'd dripped there.

For the next two hours, she worked in gold.

Between the two heaters at each end of the shed and the flame from her tools, the air became sultry. Sweat rolled down under her sweater, but she didn't mind. In fact, she barely noticed as the gold became pliable. Again and again, she drew the wire through the drawplate, smoothing out the kinks and subtly, slowly, changing the shape and size. When the wire looked like angel hair she began working it with her fingers, twisting and braiding until she matched the design in her head and on her drawing paper.

It would be simple—elegantly, richly simple. The emeralds would bring their own flash when she attached them.

Time passed. After careful, meticulous use of drawplate, flame and her own hands, the first thin, gold tier formed.

She'd just begun to stretch out the muscles in her back when the door of the shed opened and cool air poured in. Her face glowing with sweat and concentration, she glared at Michael.

"Just what the hell do you think you're doing?"

"Following orders." He had his hands stuffed in his jacket pockets for warmth, but hadn't buttoned the front. Nor, she noticed, had he bothered to shave. "This place smells like an oven."

"I'm working." She lifted the hem of the big apron she wore and wiped at her brow. It was being interrupted that annoyed her, Pandora told herself. Not the fact that he'd walked in on her when she looked like a steelworker. "Remember rule number three?"

"Tell that to Sweeney." Leaving the door ajar, he wandered in. "She said it was bad enough that you skipped breakfast, but you're not getting away with missing lunch." Curious, he poked his finger into a tray that held brilliant colored stones. "I have orders to bring you back."

"I'm not ready."

He picked up a tiny sapphire and held it to the light. "I had to stop her from tramping out here herself. If I go back alone, she's going to come for you. Her arthritis is acting up again."

Pandora swore under her breath. "Put that down," she ordered, then yanked the apron off.

"Some of this stuff looks real," he commented. Though he put the sapphire back, he picked up a round, winking diamond.

"Some of this stuff is real." Pandora crouched to turn the first heater down.

The diamond was in his hand as he scowled down at her head. "Why in hell do you have it sitting out like candy? It should be locked up."

Pandora adjusted the second heater. "Why?"

"Don't be any more foolish than necessary. Someone could steal it."

"Someone?" Straightening, Pandora smiled at him. "There aren't many someones around. I don't think Charles and Sweeney are a problem, but maybe I should worry about you."

He cursed her and dropped the diamond back. "They're your little bag of tricks, cousin, but if I had several thousand dollars sitting around that could slip into a pocket, I'd be more careful."

Though under most circumstances she fully agreed, Pandora

merely picked up her jacket. After all, they weren't in Manhattan but miles away from anyone or anything. If she locked everything up, she'd just have to unlock it again every time she wanted to work. "Just one of the differences between you and me, Michael. I suppose it's because you write about so many dirty deeds."

"I also write about human nature." He picked up the sketch of the emerald necklace she had drawn. It had the sense of scale that would have pleased an architect and the flare and flow that would appeal to an artist. "If you're so into making bangles and baubles, why aren't you wearing any?"

"They get in the way when I'm working. If you write about human nature, how come the bad guy gets caught every week?"

"Because I'm writing for people, and people need heroes."

Pandora opened her mouth to argue, then found she agreed with the essence of the statement. "Hmm," was all she said as she turned out the lights and went out ahead of him.

"At least lock the door," Michael told her.

"I haven't a key."

"Then we'll get one."

"*We* don't need one."

He shut the door with a snap. "*You* do."

Pandora only shrugged as she started across the lawn. "Michael, have I mentioned that you've been more crabby than usual?"

He pulled a piece of hard candy out of his pocket and popped it into his mouth. "Quit smoking."

The candy was lemon. She caught just a whiff. "So I noticed. How long?"

He scowled at some leaves that skimmed across the lawn. They were brown and dry and seemed to have a life of their own. "Couple weeks. I'm going crazy."

She laughed sympathetically before she tucked her arm into his. "You'll live, darling. The first month's the toughest."

Now he scowled at her. "How would you know? You never smoked."

"The first month of anything's the toughest. You just have to keep your mind occupied. Exercise. We'll jog after lunch."

"We?"

"And we can play canasta after dinner."

He gave a quick snort but brushed the hair back from her cheek. "You'll cheat."

"See, your mind's already occupied." With a laugh, she turned her face up to his. He looked a bit surly, but on him, oddly, it was attractive. Placid, good-natured good looks had always bored her. "It won't hurt you to give up one of your vices, Michael. You have so many."

"I like my vices," he grumbled, then turned his head to look down at her. She was giving him her easy, friendly smile, one she sent his way rarely. It always made him forget just how much trouble she caused him. It made him forget he wasn't attracted to dramatically bohemian women with wild red hair and sharp bones. "A woman who looks like you should have several of her own."

Her mouth was solemn, her eyes wicked. "I'm much too busy. Vices take up a great deal of time."

"When Pandora opened the box, vices popped out."

She stopped at the back stoop. "Among other miseries. I suppose that's why I'm careful about opening boxes."

Michael ran a finger down her cheek. It was the sort of gesture he realized could easily become a habit. She was right, his mind was occupied. "You have to lift off the lid sooner or later."

She didn't move back, though she'd felt the little tingle of tension, of attraction, of need. Pandora didn't believe in moving back, but in plowing through. "Some things are better off locked up."

He nodded. He didn't want to release what was in their private box any more than she did. "Some locks aren't as strong as they need to be."

They were standing close, the wind whistling lightly between them. Pandora felt the sun on her back and the chill on her face. If she took a step nearer, there'd be heat. That she'd never doubted and had always avoided. He'd use whatever was available to him, she reminded herself. At the moment, it just happened to be her. She let her breath come calmly and easily before she reached for the doorknob.

"We'd better not keep Sweeney waiting."

Chapter Three

The streets are almost deserted. A car turns a corner and disappears. It's drizzling. Neon flashes off puddles. It's garish rather than festive. There's a gray, miserable feel to this part of the city. Alleyways, cheap clubs, dented cars. The small, neatly dressed blonde walks quickly. She's nervous, out of her element, but not lost. Close-up on the envelope in her hands. It's damp from the rain. Her fingers open and close on it. Tires squeal off screen and she jolts. The blue lights of the club blink off and on in her face as she stands outside. Hesitates. Shifts the envelope from hand to hand. She goes in. Slow pan of the street. Three shots and freeze.

Three knocks sounded at the door of Michael's office. Before he could answer, Pandora swirled in. "Happy anniversary, darling."

Michael looked up from his typewriter. He'd been up most of the night working the story line out in his mind. It was nine in the morning, and he'd only had one cup of coffee to prime him for the day. Coffee and cigarettes together were too precious a memory. The scene that had just jelled in his mind dissolved.

"What the hell are you talking about?" He reached his hand into a bowl of peanuts and discovered he'd already eaten all but two.

"Two full weeks without any broken bones." Pandora swooped over to him, clucked her tongue at the disorder, then chose the arm of a chair. It was virtually the only free space. She brushed at the dust on the edge of the table beside her and left a smear. "And they said it wouldn't last."

She looked fresh with her wild mane of red pulled back from her face, comfortable in sweater and slacks that were too big for her. Michael felt like he'd just crawled out of a cave. His sweatshirt had ripped at the shoulder seam two years before, but he still favored it. A few weeks before, he'd helped paint a friend's apartment. The paint smears on his jeans showed her preference for baby pink. His eyes felt as though he'd slept facedown in the sand.

Pandora smiled at him like some bright, enthusiastic kindergarten teacher. She had a fresh, clean, almost woodsy scent. "We have a rule about respecting the other's work space," he reminded her.

"Oh, don't be cranky." It was said with the same positive smile. "Besides, you never gave me any schedule. From what I've noticed in the past couple of weeks, this is early for you."

"I'm just starting the treatment for a new episode."

"Really?" Pandora walked over and leaned over his shoulder. "Hmm," she said, though she wondered who had shot whom. "Well, I don't suppose that'll take long."

"Why don't you go play with your beads?"

"Now you're being rude when I came up here to invite you to go with me into town." After brushing off the sleeve of her sweater, she sat on the edge of the desk. She didn't know exactly why she was so determined to be friendly. Maybe it was because the emerald necklace was nearly finished and was exceeding even her standards. Maybe it was because in the past two weeks she'd found a certain enjoyment in Michael's company. Mild enjoyment, Pandora reminded herself. Nothing to shout about.

Suspicious, Michael narrowed his eyes. "What for?"

"I'm going in for some supplies Sweeney needs." She found the turtle shell that was his lampshade intriguing, and ran her fingers over it. "I thought you might like to get out for a while."

He would. It had been two weeks since he'd seen anything but the house and grounds. He glanced back at the page in his typewriter. "How long will you be?"

"Oh, two, three hours I suppose." She moved her shoulders. "It's an hour's round trip to begin with."

He was tempted. Free time and a change of scene. But the half-blank sheet remained in his typewriter. "Can't. I have to get this fleshed out."

"All right." Pandora rose from the desk a bit surprised by the degree of disappointment she felt. Silly, she thought. She loved to drive alone with the radio blaring. "Don't strain your fingers."

He started to growl something at her back, then because his bowl of nuts was empty, thought better of it. "Pandora, how about picking me up a couple pounds of pistachios?"

As she stopped at the door, she lifted a brow. "Pistachios?"

"Real ones. No red dye." He ran a hand over the bristle on his chin and wished for a pack of cigarettes. One cigarette. One long deep drag.

She glanced at the empty bowl and nearly smiled. The way he was nibbling, he'd lose that lean, rangy look quickly. "I suppose I could."

"And a copy of the *New York Times*."

Her brow rose. "Would you like to make me a list?"

"Be a sport, will you? Next time Sweeney needs supplies, I'll go in."

She thought about it a moment. "Very well then, nuts and news."

"And some pencils," he called out.

She slammed the door smartly.

Nearly two hours passed before Michael decided he deserved another cup of coffee. The story line was bumping along just as he'd planned, full of twists and turns. The fans of *Logan's Run* expected the gritty with occasional bursts of color and magic. That's just the way it was panning out.

Critics of the medium aside, Michael enjoyed writing for the small screen. He liked knowing his stories would reach literally millions of people every week and that for an hour, they could involve themselves with the character he had created.

The truth was, Michael liked Logan—the reluctant but steady heroism, the humor and the flaws. He'd made Logan human and fallible and reluctant because Michael had always imagined the best heroes were just that.

The ratings and the mail proved he was on target. His writing for Logan had won him critical acclaim and awards, just as the one-act play he'd written had won him critical acclaim and awards. But the play had reached a few thousand at best, the bulk of whom had been NewYorkers. *Logan's Run* reached the family of four in Des Moines, the steelworkers in Chicago and the college crowd in Boston. Every week.

He didn't see television as the vast wasteland but as the magic box. Michael figured everyone was entitled to a bit of magic.

Michael switched off the typewriter so that the humming died. For a moment he sat in silence. He'd known he could work at the Folley. He'd done so before, but never long-term. What he hadn't known was that he'd work so well, so quickly or be so content. The truth was, he'd never expected to get along half so well with Pandora. Not that it was any picnic, Michael mused, absently running the stub of a pencil between his fingers.

They fought, certainly, but at least they weren't taking chunks out of each other. Or not very big ones. All in all he enjoyed the evenings when they played cards if for no other reason than the challenge of trying to catch her cheating. So far he hadn't.

Also true was the odd attraction he felt for her. That hadn't been in the script. So far he'd been able to ignore, control or smother it. But there were times... There were times, Michael thought as he rose and stretched, when he'd like to close her smart-tongued mouth in a more satisfactory way. Just to see what it'd be like, he told himself. Curiosity about people was part of his makeup. He'd be interested to see how Pandora would react if he hauled her against him and kissed her until she went limp.

He let out a quick laugh as he wandered to the window. Limp? Pandora? Women like her never went soft. He might satisfy his curiosity, but he'd get a fist in the gut for his trouble. Even that might be worth it....

She wasn't unmoved. He'd been sure of that since the first day they'd walked back together from her workshop. He'd seen it in her face, heard it, however briefly in her voice. They'd both been circling around it for two weeks. Or twenty years, Michael speculated.

He'd never felt about another woman exactly the way he felt about Pandora McVie. Uncomfortable, challenged, infuriated. The truth was that he was almost always at ease around women. He liked them—their femininity, their peculiar strengths and weaknesses, their style. Perhaps that was the reason for his success in relationships, though he'd carefully kept them short-term.

If he romanced a woman, it was because he was interested in her, not simply in the end result. True enough he was interested in Pandora, but he'd never considered romancing her. It surprised him that he'd caught himself once or twice considering seducing her.

Seducing, of course, was an entirely different matter than romancing. But all in all, he didn't know if attempting a casual seduction of Pandora would be worth the risk.

If he offered her a candlelight dinner or a walk in the moonlight—or a mad night of passion—she'd come back with a sarcastic remark. Which would, inevitably, trigger some caustic rebuttal from him. The merry-go-round would begin again.

In any case, it wasn't romance he wanted with Pandora. It was simply curiosity. In certain instances, it was best to remember what had happened to the intrepid cat. But as he thought of her, his gaze was drawn toward her workshop.

They weren't so very different really, Michael mused. Pandora could insist from dawn to dusk that they had nothing in common, but Jolley had been closer to the mark. They were both quick-tempered, opinionated and passionately protective of their professions. He closed himself up for hours at a time with a typewriter. She closed herself up with tools and torches. The end result of both of their work was entertainment. And after all, that was…

His thoughts broke off as he saw the shed door open. Odd, he hadn't thought she was back yet. His rooms were on the opposite end of the house from the garage, so he wouldn't have heard her car, but he thought she'd drop off what she'd picked up for him.

He started to shrug and turn away when he saw the figure emerge from the shed. It was bundled deep in a coat and hat, but he knew immediately it wasn't Pandora. She moved fluidly, unselfconsciously. This person walked with speed and wariness. Wariness, he thought again, that was evident in the way the head swiveled back and forth before the door was closed again. Without stopping to think, Michael dashed out of the room and down the stairs.

He nearly rammed into Charles at the bottom. "Pandora back?" he demanded.

"No, sir." Relieved that he hadn't been plowed down, Charles rested a hand on the rail. "She said she might stay in town and do some shopping. We shouldn't worry if—"

But Michael was already halfway down the hall.

With a sigh for the agility he hadn't had in thirty years, Charles creaked his way into the drawing room to lay a fire.

The wind hit Michael the moment he stepped outside, reminding him he hadn't stopped for a coat. As he began to race toward the shed, his face chilled and his muscles warmed. There was no one in sight on the grounds. Not surprising, he mused as he slowed his pace just a bit. The woods were close at the edge, and there were a half a dozen easy paths through them.

Some kid poking around? he wondered. Pandora would be lucky if he hadn't pocketed half her pretty stones. It would serve her right.

But he changed his mind the minute he stood in the doorway of her workshop.

Boxes were turned over so that gems and stones and beads were scattered everywhere. Balls of string and twine had been unraveled and twisted and knotted from wall to wall. He had to push some out of his way to step inside. What was usually almost pristine in its order was utter chaos. Gold and silver wire had been bent and snapped, tools lay where they'd been carelessly tossed to the floor.

Michael bent down and picked up an emerald. It glinted sharp and green in his palm. If it had been a thief, he decided, it had been a clumsy and shortsighted one.

"Oh, God!" Pandora dropped her purse with a thud and stared.

When Michael turned, he saw her standing in the doorway,

ice pale and rigid. He swore, wishing he'd had a moment to prepare her. "Take it easy," he began as he reached for her arm.

She shoved him aside forcibly and fought her way into the shed. Beads rolled and bounced at her feet. For a moment there was pure shock, disbelief. Then came a white wall of fury. "How could you?" When she turned back to him she was no longer pale. Her color was vivid, her eyes as sharp as the emerald he still held.

Because he was off guard, she nearly landed the first blow. The air whistled by his face as her fist passed. He caught her arms before she tried again. "Just a minute," he began, but she threw herself bodily into him and knocked them both against the wall. Whatever had been left on the shelves shuddered or fell off. It took several moments, and a few bruises on both ends, before he managed to pin her arms back and hold her still.

"Stop it." He pressed her back until she glared up at him, dry-eyed and furious. "You've a right to be upset, but putting a hole in me won't accomplish anything."

"I knew you could be low," she said between her teeth. "But I'd never have believed you could do something so filthy."

"Believe whatever the hell you want," he began, but he felt her body shudder as she fought for control. "Pandora," and his voice softened. "I didn't do this. Look at me," he demanded with a little shake. "Why would I?"

Because she wanted to cry, her voice, her eyes were hard. "You tell me."

Patience wasn't one of his strong points, but he tried again.

"Pandora, listen to me. Try for common sense a minute and just listen. I got here a few minutes before you. I saw someone coming out of the shed from my window and came down. When I got here, this is what I found."

She was going to disgrace herself. She felt the tears backing up and hated them. It was better to hate him. "Let go of me."

Perhaps he could handle her anger better than her despair. Cautiously Michael released her arms and stepped back. "It hasn't been more than ten minutes since I saw someone coming out of here. I figured they cut through the woods."

She tried to think, tried to clear the fury out of her head. "You can go," she said with deadly calm. "I have to clean up and take inventory."

Something hot backed up in his throat at the casual dismissal. Remembering his own reaction when he'd opened the shed door, he swallowed it. "I'll call the police if you like, but I don't know if anything was stolen." He opened his palm and showed her the emerald. "I can't imagine any thief leaving stones like this behind."

Pandora snatched it out of his hand. When her fingers closed over it, she felt the slight prick of the hoop she'd fastened onto it only the day before. The emerald seemed to grow out of the braided wire.

Her heart was thudding against her ribs as she walked to her worktable. There was what was left of the necklace she'd been fashioning for two weeks. The deceptively delicate tiers were in pieces, the emeralds that had hung gracefully from them, scattered. Her own nippers had been used to destroy it. She gathered up the pieces in her hands and fought back the urge to scream.

"It was this, wasn't it?" Michael picked up the sketch from the floor. It was stunning on paper—at once fanciful and bold. He supposed what she had drawn had some claim to art. He imagined how he'd feel if someone took scissors to one of his scripts. "You'd nearly finished."

Pandora dropped the pieces back on the table. "Leave me alone." She crouched and began to gather up stones and beads.

"Pandora." When she ignored him, Michael grabbed her by the shoulders and shook. "Dammit, Pandora, I want to help."

She sent him a long, cold look. "You've done enough, Michael. Now leave me alone."

"All right, fine." He released her and stormed out. Anger and frustration carried him halfway across the lawn. Michael stopped, swore and wished bitterly for a cigarette. She had no right to accuse him. Worse, she had no right to make him feel responsible. The guilt he was experiencing was nearly as strong as it would have been if he'd actually vandalized her shop. Hands in his pockets, he stood staring back at the shed and cursing her.

She really thought he'd done that to her. That he was capable of such meaningless, bitter destruction. He'd tried to talk to her, soothe her. Every offer of help had been thrown back at him. Just like her, he thought with his teeth gritted. She deserved to be left alone.

He nearly started back to the house again when he remembered just how shocked and ill she'd looked in the doorway of the shed. Calling himself a fool, he went back.

When he opened the door of the shed again, the chaos was just as it had been. Sitting in the middle of it on the floor by her workbench was Pandora. She was weeping quietly.

He felt the initial male panic at being confronted with feminine tears and surprise that they came from Pandora who never shed them. Yet he felt sympathy for someone who'd been dealt a bull's-eye blow. Without saying a word, he went to her and slipped his arms around her.

She stiffened, but he'd expected it. "I told you to go away."

"Yeah. Why should I listen to you?" He stroked her hair.

She wanted to crawl into his lap and weep for hours. "I don't want you here."

"I know. Just pretend I'm someone else." He drew her against his chest.

"I'm only crying because I'm angry." With a sniff, she turned her face into his shirt.

"Sure." He kissed the top of her head. "Go ahead and be angry for a while. I'm used to it."

She told herself it was because she was weakened by shock and grief, but she relaxed against him. The tears came in floods. When she cried, she cried wholeheartedly. When she was finished, she was done.

Tears dry, she sat cushioned against him. Secure. She wouldn't question it now. Along with the anger came a sense of shame she was unaccustomed to. She'd been filthy to him. But he'd come back and held her. Who'd have expected him to be patient, or caring? Or strong enough to make her accept both. Pandora let out a long breath and kept her eyes shut for just a moment. He smelled of soap and nothing else.

"I'm sorry, Michael."

She was soft. Hadn't he just told himself she wouldn't be? He let his cheek brush against her hair. "Okay."

"No, I mean it." When she turned her head her lips skimmed across his cheek. It surprised them both. That kind of contact was for friends—or lovers. "I couldn't think after I walked in here. I—" She broke off a moment, fascinated by his eyes. Wasn't it strange how small the world could become if you looked into someone's eyes? Why hadn't she ever noticed that before? "I need to sort all this out."

"Yeah." He ran a fingertip down her cheek. She was soft. Softer than he'd let himself believe. "We both do."

It was so easy to settle herself in the crook of his arm. "I can't think."

"No?" Her lips were only an inch from his—too close to ignore, too far to taste. "Let's both not think for a minute."

When he touched his mouth to hers, she didn't draw away but accepted, experimented with the same sense of curiosity that moved through him. It wasn't an explosion or a shock, but a test for both of them. One they'd both known would come sooner or later.

She tasted warm, and her sweetness had a bite. He'd known her so long, shouldn't he have known that? Her body felt primed to move, to act, to race. Soft, yes, she was soft, but not pliant. Perhaps he'd have found pliancy too easy. When he slipped his tongue into her mouth hers met it teasingly, playfully. His stomach knotted. She made him want more, much more of that unapologetically earthy scent, the taut body. His fingers tangled in her hair and tightened.

He was as mysterious and bold as she'd always thought he would be. His hands were firm, his mouth giving. Sometimes she'd wondered what it would be like to meet him on these terms. But she'd always closed her mind before any of the answers could slip through. Michael Donahue was dangerous simply because he was Michael Donahue. By turns he'd attracted and alienated her since they'd been children. It was more than any other man had been able to do for more than a week.

Now, as her mouth explored his, she began to understand why. He was different, for her. She didn't feel altogether safe in his arms, and not completely in control. Pandora had always made certain she was both those things when it came to a man. The scrape of his unshaved cheek didn't annoy her as she'd thought it would. It aroused. The discomfort of the hard floor seemed suitable, as was the quick rush of cold air through the still-open door.

She felt quietly and completely at home. Then the quick nip of his teeth against her lip made her feel as though she'd just stepped on uncharted land. New territory was what she'd been raised on, and yet, in all her experience, she'd never explored anything so unique, so exotic or so comfortable.

She wanted to go on and knew she had to stop.

Together they drew away.

"Well." She scrambled for composure as she folded her hands in her lap. Be casual, she ordered herself while her pulse thudded at her wrists. Be careless. She couldn't afford to say anything that might make him laugh at her. "That's been coming for a while, I suppose."

He felt as though he'd just slid down a roller coaster without a cart. "I suppose." He studied her a moment, curious and a bit unnerved. When he saw her fingers twist together he felt a small sense of satisfaction. "It wasn't altogether what I'd expected."

"Things rarely are." Too many surprises for one day, Pandora decided, and rose unsteadily to her feet. She made the mistake of looking around and nearly sunk to the floor again.

"Pandora—"

"No, don't worry." She shook her head as he rose. "I'm not going to fall apart again." Concentrating on breathing evenly, she took one long look at her workshop. "It looks like you were right about the locks. I suppose I should be grateful you haven't said I told you so."

"Maybe I would if it applied." Michael picked up the emeralds scattered on her table. "I'm no expert, cousin, but I'd say these are worth a few thousand."

"So?" She frowned as her train of thought began to march with his. "No thief would've left them behind." Reaching down, she picked up a handful of stones. Among them were two top-grade diamonds. "Or these."

As was his habit, he began to put the steps together in a sort of mental scenario. Action and reaction, motive and result. "I'd wager once you've inventoried, you won't be missing anything. Whoever did this didn't want to risk more than breaking and entering and vandalism."

With a huff, she sat down on her table. "You think it was one of the family."

"'They said it wouldn't last,'" he quoted, and stuck his hands in his pockets. "You may've had something there, Pandora. Something neither of us considered when we were setting out the guidelines. None of them believed we'd be able to get through six months together. The fact is, we've gotten through the first two weeks without a hitch. It could make one of them nervous enough to want to throw in a complication. What was your first reaction when you saw all this?"

She dragged her hand through her hair. "That you'd done it for spite. Exactly what our kith and kin would expect me to think. Dammit, I hate to be predictable."

"You outsmarted them once your mind cleared."

She sent him a quick look, not certain if she should thank him or apologize again. It was best to do neither. "Biff," Pandora decided with relish. "This sort of low-minded trick would be just up his alley."

"I'd only vote for Biff if you find a few rocks missing." Michael rocked back on his heels. "He'd never be able to resist picking up a few glitters that could be liquidated into nice clean cash."

"True enough." Uncle Carlson—no, it seemed a bit crude for his style. Ginger would've been too fascinated with the sparkles to have done any more than fondle. Pulling a hand through her hair, she tried to picture one of her bland, civilized relations wielding a pair of nippers. "Well, I don't suppose it matters a great deal which one of them did it. They've put me two weeks behind on my commission." Again she picked up pieces of thin gold. "It'll never be quite the same," she murmured. "Nothing is when it's done over."

"Sometimes it's better."

With a shake of her head, she walked over to a heater. If he gave her any more sympathy now, she wouldn't be able to trust herself. "One way or the other I've got to get started. Tell Sweeney I won't make it in for lunch."

"I'll help you clean this up."

"No." She turned back when he started to frown. "No, really, Michael, I appreciate it. I need to be busy. And alone."

He didn't like it, but understood. "All right. I'll see you at dinner."

"Michael…" He paused at the doorway and looked back. Amid the confusion she looked strong and vivid. He nearly closed the door and went back to her. "Maybe Uncle Jolley was right."

"About what?"

"You may have one or two redeeming qualities."

He smiled at her then, quick and dashing. "Uncle Jolley was always right, cousin. That's why he's still pulling the strings."

Pandora waited until the door shut again. Pulling the strings he was, she mused. "But you're not playing matchmaker with my life," she mumbled. "I'm staying free, single and unattached. Just get that through your head."

She wasn't superstitious, but Pandora almost thought she heard her uncle's high, cackling laugh. She rolled up her sleeves and got to work.

Chapter Four

Because after a long, tedious inventory Pandora discovered nothing missing, she vetoed Michael's notion of calling in the police. If something had been stolen, she'd have seen the call as a logical step. As it was, she decided the police would poke and prod around and lecture on the lack of locks. If the vandal had been one of the family—and she had to agree with Michael's conclusion there—a noisy, official investigation would give the break-in too much importance and undoubtedly too much publicity.

Yes, the press would have a field day. Pandora had already imagined the headlines. "Family vs. family in the battle of eccentric's will." There was, under her independent and straightforward nature, a prim part of her that felt family business was private business.

If one or more of the members of the family were keeping an eye on Jolley's Folley and the goings-on there, Pandora wanted them to think that she'd brushed off the vandalism as petty and foolish. As a matter of pride, she didn't want anyone to believe she'd been dealt a stunning blow. As a matter of practicality, she didn't want anyone to know that she had her eyes open. She was determined to find out who had broken into her shop and how they'd managed to pick such a perfect time for it.

Michael hadn't insisted on calling the police because his thoughts had run along the same lines as Pandora's. He'd managed, through a lot of maneuvering and silence, to keep his career totally separate from his family. In his business, he was known as Michael Donahue, award-winning writer, not Michael Donahue, relative of Jolley McVie, multimillionaire. He wanted to keep it that way.

Stubbornly, each had refused to tell the other of their reasons or their plans for some personal detective work. It wasn't so much a matter of trust, but more the fact that neither of them felt the other could do the job competently. So instead, they kept the conversation light through one of Sweeney's four-star meals and let the vandalism rest. More important, they carefully avoided any reference that might trigger some remark about what had happened on a more personal level in Pandora's workshop.

After two glasses of wine and a generous portion of chicken fricassee, Pandora felt more optimistic. It would have been much worse if any of her stock or tools had been taken. That would have meant a trip into Manhattan and days, perhaps weeks of delay. As it was, the worst crime that she could see was the fact that she'd been spied on. Surely that was the only explanation for the break-in coinciding so perfectly with her trip to town. And that would be her first order of business.

"I wonder," Pandora began, probing lightly, "if the Saundersons are in residence for the winter."

"The neighbors with the pond." Michael had thought of the Saunderson place himself. There were certain points on that property where, with a good set of binoculars, someone could watch the Folley easily. "They spend a lot of time in Europe, don't they?"

"Hmm." Pandora toyed with her chicken. "He's in hotels, you know. They tend to pop off here or there for weeks at a time."

"Do they ever rent the place out?"

"Oh, not that I know of. I'm under the impression that they leave a skeleton staff there even when they fly off. Now that I think of it, they were home a few months ago." The memory made her smile. "Uncle Jolley and I went fishing and Saunderson nearly caught us. If we hadn't scrambled back to the cabin—" She broke off as the thought formed.

"Cabin." Michael picked up where she'd left off. "That old two-room wreck Jolley was going to use as a hunting lodge during his eat-off-the-land stage? I'd forgotten all about it."

Pandora shrugged as though it meant nothing while her mind raced ahead. "He ended up eating more beans than game. In any case, we caught a bundle of trout, ate like pigs and sent the rest along to Saunderson. He never sent a thank-you note."

"Poor manners."

"Well, I've heard his grandmother was a barmaid in Chelsea. More wine?"

"No, thanks." He thought it best to keep a clear head if he

was going to carry out the plans that were just beginning to form. "Help yourself."

Pandora set the bottle down and sent him a sweet smile. "No, I'm fine. Just a bit tired really."

"You're entitled." It would clear his path beautifully if he could ship her off to bed early. "What you need is a good night's sleep."

"I'm sure you're right." Both of them were too involved with their own moves to notice how excruciatingly polite the conversation had become. "I'll just skip coffee tonight and go have a bath." She feigned a little yawn. "What about you? Planning to work late?"

"No—no, I think I'll get a fresh start in the morning."

"Well then." Pandora rose, still smiling. She'd give it an hour, she calculated, then she'd be out and gone. "I'm going up. Good night, Michael."

"Good night." Once the light in her room was off, he decided, he'd be on his way.

Pandora sat in her darkened room for exactly fifteen minutes and just listened. All she had to do was get outside without being spotted. The rest would be easy. Opening her door a crack, she held her breath, waited and listened a little longer. Not a sound. It was now or never, she decided and bundled into her coat. Into the deep pockets, she shoved a flashlight, two books of matches and a small can of hair spray. As good as mace, Pandora figured, if you ran into something unfriendly. She crept out into the hall and started slowly down the stairs, her back to the wall.

An adventure, she thought, feeling the familiar pulse of excitement and anxiety. She hadn't had one since Uncle Jolley died. As she let herself out one of the side doors, she thought how much he'd have enjoyed this one. The moon was only a sliver, but the sky was full of stars. The few clouds that spread over them were hardly more than transparent wisps. And the air—she took a deep breath—was cool and crisp as an apple. With a quick glance over her shoulder at Michael's window, she started toward the woods.

The starlight couldn't help her there. Though the trees were bare, the branches were thick enough to block out big chunks of sky. She dug out her flashlight and, turning it side to side, found the edges of the path. She didn't hurry. If she rushed, the adventure would be over too soon. She walked slowly, listened and imagined.

There were sounds—the breeze blew through pine needles and scattered the dry leaves. Now and again there was a skuddle in the woods to the right or left. A fox, a raccoon, a bear not quite settled down to hibernate? Pandora liked not being quite certain. If you walked through the woods alone, in the dark, and didn't have some sense of wonder, it was hardly worth the trip.

She liked the smells—pine, earth, the hint of frost that would settle on the ground before morning. She liked the sense of being alone, and more, of having something up ahead that warranted her attention.

The path forked, and she swung to the left. The cabin wasn't much farther. She stopped once, certain she'd heard something move up ahead that was too big to be considered a fox. For a moment she had a few uncomfortable thoughts about bears and bobcats. It was one thing to speculate and another to have to deal with them. Then there was nothing. Shaking her head, Pandora went on.

What would she do if she got to the cabin, and it wasn't dusty and deserted? What would she do if she actually found one of her dear, devoted relatives had set up housekeeping? Uncle Carlson reading the *Wall Street Journal* by the fire? Aunt Patience fussing around the rocky wooden table with a dust cloth? The thought was almost laughable. Almost, until Pandora remembered her workshop.

Drawing her brows together, she walked forward. If someone was there, they were going to answer to her. In moments, the shadow of the cabin loomed up before her. It looked as it was supposed to look, desolate, deserted, eerie. She kept her flashlight low as she crept toward the porch, then nearly let out a scream when her own weight caused the narrow wooden stair to creak. She held a hand to her heart until it no longer felt as though it would break her ribs. Then slowly, quietly, stealthily, she reached for the doorknob and twisted it.

The door moaned itself open. Wincing at the sound, Pandora counted off ten seconds before she took the next step. With a quick sweep of her light, she stepped in.

When the arm came around her neck, she dropped the flashlight with a clatter. It rolled over the floor, sending an erratic beam over the log walls and brick fireplace. Even as she drew the breath to scream, she reached in her pocket for the hair spray. After she was whirled around, she found herself face-to-face with Michael. His fist was poised inches from her face, her can inches from his. Both of them stood just as they were.

"Dammit!" Michael dropped his arm. "What are you doing here?"

"What are you doing here?" she tossed back. "And what do you mean by grabbing me that way? You may've broken my flashlight."

"I almost broke your nose."

Pandora shook back her hair and walked over to retrieve her light. She didn't want him to see her hands tremble. "Well, I certainly think you should find out who someone is before you throw a headlock on them."

"You followed me."

She sent him a cool, amused look. It helped to be able to do so when her stomach was still quaking. "Don't flatter yourself. I simply wanted to see if something was going on out here, and I didn't want you to interfere."

"Interfere." He shone his own light directly in her face so that she had to throw up a hand in defense. "And what the hell were you going to do if something was going on? Overpower them?"

She thought of how easily he'd taken her by surprise. It only made her lift her chin higher. "I can take care of myself."

"Sure." He glanced down at the can she still held. "What have you got there?"

Having forgotten it, Pandora looked down herself, then had to stifle a chuckle. Oh, how Uncle Jolley would've appreciated the absurdity. "Hair spray," she said very precisely. "Right between the eyes."

He swore, then laughed. He couldn't have written a scene so implausible. "I guess I should be glad you didn't get a shot off at me."

"I look before I pounce." Pandora dropped the can back into her pocket. "Well, since we're here, we might as well look around."

"I was doing just that when I heard your catlike approach." She wrinkled her nose at him, but he ignored her. "It looks like someone's been making themselves at home." To prove his point, Michael shone his light at the fireplace. Half-burnt logs still smoldered.

"Well, well." With her own light, Pandora began to walk around the cabin. The last time she'd been there, the chair with the broken rung had been by the window. Jolley had sat there himself, keeping a lookout for Saunderson while she'd opened a tin of sardines to ward off starvation. Now the chair was pulled up near the fire. "A vagrant, perhaps."

Watching her, Michael nodded. "Perhaps."

"But not likely. Suppose they'll be back?"

"Hard to say." The casual glance showed nothing out of place. The cabin was neat and tidy. Too tidy. The floor and table surfaces should have had a film of dust. Everything had been wiped clean. "It could be they've done all the damage they intend to do."

Disgruntled, Pandora plopped down on the bunk and dropped her chin in her hands. "I'd hoped to catch them."

"And what? Zap them with environmentally safe hair spray?"

She glared up at him. "I suppose you had a better plan."

"I think I might've made them a bit more uncomfortable."

"Black eyes and broken noses." She made an impatient sound. "Really, Michael, you should try to get your mind out of your fists."

"I suppose you just wanted to talk reasonably with whichever member of our cozy family played search and destroy with your workshop."

She started to snap, caught herself, then smiled. It was the slow, wicked smile Michael could never help admiring. "No," she admitted. "Reason wasn't high on my list. Still, it appears we've both missed our chance for brute force. Well, you write the detective stories—so to speak—shouldn't we look for clues?"

His lips curved in something close to a sneer. "I didn't think to bring my magnifying glass."

"You can almost be amusing when you put your mind to it." Rising, Pandora began to shine her light here and there. "They might've dropped something."

"A name tag?"

"Something," she muttered, and dropped to her knees to look under the bunk. "Aha!" Hunkering down, she grabbed at something.

"What is it?" Michael was beside her before she'd straightened up.

"A shoe." Feeling foolish and sentimental, she held it in both hands. "It's nothing. It was Uncle Jolley's."

Because she looked lost, and more vulnerable than he'd expected, Michael offered the only comfort he knew. "I miss him, too."

She sat a moment, the worn sneaker in her lap. "You know, sometimes it's as though I can almost feel him. As though he's around the next corner, in the next room, waiting to pop up and laugh at the incredible joke he's played."

With a quick laugh, Michael rubbed a hand over her back. "I know what you mean."

Pandora looked at him, steady, measuring. "Maybe you do," she murmured. Briskly she set the sneaker on the bunk and rose. "I'll have a look in the cupboards."

"Let me know if you find any cookies." He met the look she tossed over her shoulder with a shrug. "In the early stages of nonsmoking, you need a lot of oral satisfaction."

"You ought to try chewing gum." Pandora opened a cupboard and shone her light over jars and cans. There was peanut butter, chunky, and caviar, Russian. Two of Jolley's favorite snacks. She passed over taco sauce and jumbo fruit cocktail, remembering that her ninety-three-year-old uncle had had the appetite of a teenager. Then reaching in, she plucked out a can and held it up.

"Aha!"

"Again?"

"Tuna fish," Pandora announced waving the can at Michael. "It's a can of tuna."

"Right you are. Any mayo to go with it?"

"Don't be dense, Michael. Uncle Jolley hated tuna."

Michael started to say something sarcastic, then stopped. "He did, didn't he?" he said slowly. "And he never kept anything around he didn't like."

"Exactly."

"Congratulations, Sherlock. Now which of the suspects has an affection for canned fish?"

"You're just jealous because I found a clue and you didn't."

"It's only a clue," Michael pointed out, a little annoyed at being outdone by an amateur, "if you can do something with it."

He'd never give her credit, she thought, for anything, not her craft, her intelligence and never her womanhood. There was an edge to her voice when she spoke again. "If you're so pessimistic, why did you come out here?"

"I was hoping to find someone." Restless, Michael moved his light from wall to wall. "As it is all we've done is prove someone was here and gone."

Pandora dropped the can of tuna in disgust. "A waste of time."

"You shouldn't've followed me out."

"I didn't follow you out." She shone her light back at him. He looked too male, too dangerous in the shadows. She wished, only briefly, that she had the spectacular build and stunning style that would bring him whimpering to his knees. Their breath came in clouds and merged together. "For all I know, you followed me."

"Oh, I see. That's why I was here first."

"Beside the point. If you'd planned to come out here tonight, why didn't you tell me?"

He came closer. But if he came too close to her, he discovered, he began to feel something, something like an itch along the skin. Try to scratch it, he reminded himself, and she'd rub you raw in seconds. "For the same reason you didn't tell me. I don't trust you, cousin. You don't trust me."

"At least we can agree on something." She started to brush by him and found her arm captured. In one icy movement, she tilted her head down to look at his hand, then up to look at his face. "That's a habit you should try to break, Michael."

"They say when you break one habit, you pick up another."

The ice in Pandora's voice never changed, but her blood was warming. "Do they?"

"You're easier to touch than I'd once thought, Pandora."

"Don't be too sure, Michael." She took a step back, not in retreat, she told herself. It was a purely offensive move. Still, he moved with her.

"Some women have trouble dealing with physical attraction."

The temper that flared in her eyes appealed to him as much as the passion he'd seen there briefly that afternoon. "Your ego's showing again. This dominant routine might work very well with your centerfolds, but—"

"You've always had an odd fascination with my sex life." Michael grinned at her, pleased to see frustration flit over her face.

"The same kind of educated fascination one has with the sex lives of lower mammals." It infuriated her that her heart was racing. And not from anger. She was too honest to pretend it was anger. She'd come looking for an adventure, and she'd found one. "It's getting late," she said, using the tone of a parochial schoolteacher to a disruptive student. "You'll have to excuse me."

"I've never asked about your sex life." When she took

another step away, he boxed her neatly into a corner. Pandora's hand slipped into her pocket and rested on the can of hair spray. "Let me guess. You prefer a man with a string of initials after his name who philosophizes about sex more than he acts on it."

"Why you pompous, arrogant—"

Michael shut her mouth the way he'd once fantasized. With his own.

The kiss was no test this time, but torrid, hot, edging toward desperate. Whatever she might feel, she'd dissect later. Now she'd accept the experience. His mouth was warm, firm, and he used it with the same cocky male confidence that would have infuriated her at any other time. Now she met it with her own.

He was strong, insistent. For the first time Pandora felt herself body to body with a man who wouldn't treat her delicately. He demanded, expected and gave a completely uninhibited physicality. Pandora didn't have to think her way through the kiss. She didn't have to think at all.

He'd expected her to rear back and take a swing at him. Her instant and full response left him reeling. Later Michael would recall that nothing as basic and simple as a kiss had made his head spin for years.

She packed a punch, but she did it with soft lips. If she knew just how quickly she'd knocked him out, would she gloat? He wouldn't think of it now. He wouldn't think of anything now. Without a moment's hesitation, he buried his consciousness in her and let the senses rule.

The cabin was cold and dark without even a single stream of

moonlight for romance. It smelled of dying smoke and settling dust. The wind had kicked up enough to moan grumpily at the windows. Neither of them noticed. Even when they broke apart, neither of them noticed.

He wasn't steady. That was something else he'd think about later. At least he had the satisfaction of seeing she wasn't steady, either. She looked as he felt, stunned, off balance and unable to set for the next blow. Needing some equilibrium, he grinned at her.

"You were saying?"

She wanted to slug him. She wanted to kiss him again until he didn't have the strength to grin. He'd expect her to fall at his feet as other women probably did. He'd expect her to sigh and smile and surrender so he'd have one more victory. Instead she snapped, "Idiot."

"I love it when you're succinct."

"Rule number six," Pandora stated, aiming a killing look. "No physical contact."

"No physical contact," Michael agreed as she stomped toward the doorway, "unless both parties enjoy it."

She slammed the door and left him grinning.

When two people are totally involved in their own projects, they can live under the same roof for days at a time and rarely see each other. Especially if the roof is enormous and the people very stubborn. Pandora and Michael brushed together at meals and otherwise left each other alone. This wasn't out of any sense of politeness or consideration. It was simply because each of them was too busy to heckle the other.

Separately, however, each felt a smug satisfaction when the first month passed. One down, five to go.

When they were into their second month, Michael drove into New York for a day to handle a problem with a script that had to be dealt with personally. He left, cross as a bear and muttering about imbeciles. Pandora prepared to enjoy herself tremendously in his absence. She wouldn't have to keep up her guard or share the Folley for hours. She could do anything she wanted without worrying about anyone coming to look over her shoulder or make a caustic remark. It would be wonderful.

She ended up picking at her dinner, then watching for his car through the heavy brocade drapes. Not because she missed *him*, she assured herself. It was just that she'd become used to having someone in the house.

Wasn't that one of the reasons she'd never lived with anyone before? She wanted to avoid any sense of dependence. And dependence, she decided, was natural when you shared the same space—even when it was with a two-legged snake.

So she waited, and she watched. Long after Charles and Sweeney had gone to bed, she continued to wait and watch. She wasn't concerned, and certainly not lonely. Only restless. She told herself she didn't go to bed herself because she wasn't tired. Wandering the first floor, she walked into Jolley's den. Game room would have been a more appropriate name. The decor was a cross between video arcade and disco lounge with its state-of-the-art components and low, curved-back sofas.

She turned on the huge, fifty-four-inch television, then left it on the first show that appeared. She wasn't going to *watch* it. She just wanted the company.

There were two pinball tables where she passed nearly an hour trying to beat the high scores Jolley had left behind. Another legacy. Then there was an arcade-size video game that simulated an attack on the planet Zarbo. Under her haphazard defense system, the planet blew up three times before she moved on. There was computerized chess, but she thought her mind too sluggish to take it on. In the end she stretched out on the six-foot sofa in front of the television. Just to rest, not to watch.

Within moments, she was hooked on the late-night syndication of a cop show. Squealing tires and blasting bullets. Head pillowed on her arms, one leg thrown over the top of the sofa, she relaxed and let herself be entertained.

When Michael came to the doorway, she didn't notice him. He'd had a grueling day and had hit some nasty traffic on the drive back. The fact was he'd considered staying in the city overnight—the sensible thing to do. He'd found himself making a dozen weak excuses why he had to go back instead of accepting the invitation of the assistant producer—a tidily built brunette with big brown eyes.

He'd intended to crawl upstairs, fall into his bed and sleep until noon, but he'd seen the lights and heard the racket. Now, here was Pandora, self-proclaimed critic of the small screen, sprawled on a sofa watching reruns at one in the morning. She looked suspiciously as though she were enjoying herself.

Not a bad show, Michael mused, recognizing the series. In

fact, he'd written a couple of scripts for it in his early days. The central character had a sly sort of wit and a fumbling manner that caused the perpetrator to spill out enough information for an arrest by the end of the show.

Michael watched Pandora as she shifted comfortably on the couch. He waited until the commercial break. "Well, how the mighty have fallen."

She nearly did, rolling quickly to look back toward the doorway. She sat up, scowled and searched her mind for a plausible excuse. "I couldn't sleep," she told him, which was true enough. She wouldn't add it was because he hadn't been home. "I suppose television is made for the insomniac. Valium for the mind."

He was tired, bone tired, but he realized how glad he was she'd had a comeback. He came over, plopped down beside her and propped his feet on a coffee table made out of a fat log. "Who done it?" he asked, and sighed. It was good to be home.

"The greedy business partner." She was too pleased to have him back to be embarrassed. "There's really very little challenge in figuring out the answers."

"This show wasn't based on the premise of figuring out who did the crime, but in how the hero maneuvers them into betraying themselves."

She pretended she wasn't interested, but shifted so that she could still see the screen. "So, how did things go in New York?"

"They went." Michael pried off one shoe with the toe of the other. "After several hours of hair tearing and blame casting, the script's intact."

He looked tired. Really tired, she realized, and unbent enough to take off his other shoe. He merely let out a quick grunt of appreciation. "I don't understand why people would get all worked up about one silly hour a week."

He opened one eye to stare at her. "It's the American way."

"What's there to get so excited about? You have a crime, the good guys chase the bad guys and catch them before the final credits. Seems simple enough."

"I can't thank you enough for clearing that up. I'll point it out at the next production meeting."

"Really, Michael, it seems to me things should run fairly smoothly, especially since you've been on the air with this thing for years."

"Know anything about ego and paranoia?"

She smiled a little. "I've heard of them."

"Well, multiply that with artistic temperament, the ratings race and an escalating budget. Don't forget to drop in a good dose of network executives. Things haven't run smoothly for four years. If *Logan* goes another four, it still won't run smoothly. That's show biz."

Pandora moved her shoulders. "It seems a foolish way to make a living."

"Ain't it just," Michael agreed, and fell sound asleep.

She let him doze for the next twenty minutes while she watched the sly, fumbling cop tighten the ropes on the greedy business partner. Satisfied that justice had been done, Pandora rose to switch off the set and dim the lights.

She could leave him here, she considered as she watched

Michael sleep. He looked comfortable enough at the moment. She thought about it as she walked over to brush his hair from his forehead. But he'd probably wake up with a stiff neck and a nasty disposition. Better get him upstairs into bed, she decided, and shook his shoulder.

"Michael."

"Mmm?"

"Let's go to bed."

"Thought you'd never ask," he mumbled, and reached half-heartedly for her.

Amused, she shook him harder. "Never let your reach exceed your grasp. Come on, cousin, I'll help you upstairs."

"The director's a posturing idiot," he grumbled as she dragged him to his feet.

"I'm sure he is. Now, see if you can put one foot in front of the other. That's the way. Here we go." With an arm around his waist, she began to lead him from the room.

"He kept screwing around with my script."

"Of all the nerve. Here come the steps."

"Said he wanted more emotional impact in the second act. Bleaches his hair," Michael muttered as she half pulled him up the steps. "Lot he knows about emotional impact."

"Obviously a mental midget." Breathlessly she steered him toward his room. He was heavier than he looked. "Here we are now, home again." With a little strategy and a final burst of will, she shoved him onto the bed. "There now, isn't that cozy?" Leaving him fully dressed, she spread an afghan over him.

"Aren't you going to take my pants off?"

She patted his head. "Not a chance."

"Spoilsport."

"If I helped you undress this late at night, I'd probably have nightmares."

"You know you're crazy about me." The bed felt like heaven. He could've burrowed in it for a week.

"You're getting delirious, Michael. I'll have Charles bring you some warm tea and honey in the morning."

"Not if you want to live." He roused himself to open his eyes and smile at her. "Why don't you crawl in beside me? With a little encouragement, I could show you the time of your life."

Pandora leaned closer, closer, until her mouth was inches from his. Their breath mixed quickly, intimately. She hovered there a moment while her hair fell forward and brushed his cheek. "In a pig's eye," she whispered.

Michael shrugged, yawned and rolled over. "'Kay."

In the dark, Pandora stood for a moment with her hands on her hips. At least he could've acted insulted. Chin up, she walked out—making sure she slammed the door at her back.

Chapter Five

Tier by painstaking tier, Pandora had completed the emerald necklace. When it was finished, she was pleased to judge it perfect. This judgment pleased her particularly because she was her own toughest critic. Pandora didn't feel emotionally attached or creatively satisfied by every piece she made. With the necklace, she felt both. She examined it under a magnifying glass, held it up in harsh light, went over the filigree inch by inch and found no flaws. Out of her own imagination she'd conceived it, then with her own skill created it. With a kind of regret, she boxed the necklace in a bed of cotton. It wasn't hers any longer.

With the necklace done, she looked around her workshop without inspiration. She'd put so much into that one piece, all her concentration, her emotion, her skill. She hadn't made a single plan for the next project. Restless, wanting to work, she picked up her pad and began to sketch.

Earrings perhaps, she mused. Something bold and chunky and ornate. She wanted a change after the fine, elegant work she'd devoted so much time to. Circles and triangles, she thought. Something geometric and blatantly modern. Nothing romantic like the necklace.

Romantic, she mused, and sketched strong, definite lines. She'd been working with a romantic piece; perhaps that's why she'd nearly made a fool of herself with Michael. Her emotions were involved with her work, and her work had been light and feminine and romantic. It made sense, she decided, satisfied. Now, she'd work with something strong and brash and arrogant. That should solve the problem.

There shouldn't be a problem in the first place. Teeth gritted, she flipped a page and started over. Her feelings for Michael had always been very definite. Intolerance. If you were intolerant of someone, it went against the grain to be attracted to him.

It wasn't real attraction in any case. It was more some sort of twisted...curiosity. Yes, curiosity. The word satisfied her completely. She'd been curious, naturally enough, to touch on the sexuality of a man she'd known since childhood. Curious, again naturally, to find out what it was about Michael Donahue that attracted all those poster girls. She'd found out.

So he had a way of making a woman feel utterly a woman, utterly involved, utterly willing. It wasn't something that had happened to her before nor something she'd looked for. As Pandora saw it, it was a kind of skill. She decided he'd certainly honed it as meticulously as any craftsman. Though she found it difficult to fault him for that, *she* wasn't about to fall in with the horde. If he knew, if he even suspected, that she'd had the same reaction to him that she imagined dozens of other women had, he'd gloat for a month. If he guessed that from time to time she'd wished—just for a moment—that he'd think of her the way he thought of those dozens of other women, he'd gloat for twice as long. She wouldn't give him the pleasure.

Individuality was part of her makeup. She didn't want to be one of his women, even if she could. Now that her curiosity had been satisfied, they'd get through the next five months without any more...complications.

Just because she'd found him marginally acceptable as a human being, almost tolerable as a companion wouldn't get in the way. It would, if anything, make the winter pass a bit easier.

And when she caught herself putting the finishing touches on a sketch of Michael's face, she was appalled. The lines were true enough, though rough. She'd had no trouble capturing the arrogance around the eyes or the sensitivity around the mouth. Odd, she realized; she'd sketched him to look intelligent. She ripped the sheet from her pad, crumpled it up in a ball and tossed it into the trash. Her mind had wandered, that was all. Pandora picked up her pencil again, put it down, then dug the sketch out again. Art was art, after all, she told herself as she smoothed out Michael's face.

He wasn't having a great deal of success with his own work. Michael sat at his desk and typed like a maniac for five minutes. Then he stared into space for fifteen. It wasn't like him. When he worked, he worked steadily, competently, smoothly until the scene was set.

Leaning back in his chair, he picked up a pencil and ran his fingers from end to end. Whatever the statistics said, he should never have given up smoking. That's what had him so edgy. Restless, he pushed away from the desk and wandered over to the window. He stared down at Pandora's workshop. It looked cheerful under a light layer of snow that was hardly more than a dusting. The windows were blank.

That's what had him so edgy.

She wasn't what he'd expected. She was softer, sweeter. Warmer. She was fun to talk to, whether she was arguing and snipping and keeping you on the edge of temper, or whether she was being easy and companionable. There wasn't an overflow of small talk with Pandora. There weren't any trite conversations. She kept your mind working, even if it was in defense of her next barb.

It wasn't easy to admit that he actually enjoyed her company. But the weeks they'd been together at the Folley had gone quickly. No, it wasn't easy to admit he liked being with her, but he'd turned down an interesting invitation from his assistant producer because… Because, Michael admitted on a long breath, he hadn't wanted to spend the night with one woman when he'd known his thoughts would have been on another.

Just how was he going to handle this unwanted and unexpected attraction to a woman who'd rather put on the gloves and go a few rounds than walk in the moonlight?

Romantic women had always appealed to him because he was, unashamedly, a romantic himself. He enjoyed candlelight, quiet music, long, lonely walks. Michael courted women in old-fashioned ways because he felt comfortable with old-fashioned ways. It didn't interfere with the fact that he was, and had been since college, a staunch feminist. Romance and sociopolitical views were worlds apart. He had no trouble balancing equal pay for equal work against offering a woman a carriage ride through the park.

And he knew if he sent Pandora a dozen white roses, she'd complain about the thorns.

He wanted her. Michael was too much a creature of the senses to pretend otherwise. When he wanted something, he worked toward it in one of two ways. First, he planned out the best approach, then took the steps one at a time, maneuvering subtly. If that didn't work, he tossed out subtlety and went after it with both hands. He'd had just as much success the first way as the second.

As he saw it, Pandora wouldn't respond to patience and posies. She wouldn't go for being swept off her feet, either. With Pandora, he might just have to toss his two usual approaches and come up with a whole new third.

An interesting challenge, Michael decided with a slow smile. He liked nothing better than arranging and rearranging plot lines and shifting angles. And hadn't he always thought Pandora would make a fascinating character? So, he'd work it like a screenplay.

Hero and heroine living as housemates, he began. Attracted to each other but reluctant. Hero is intelligent, charming. Has tremendous willpower. Hadn't he given up smoking—five weeks, three days and fourteen hours ago? Heroine is stubborn and opinionated, often mistakes arrogance for independence.

Hero gradually cracks through her brittle shield to their mutual satisfaction.

Michael leaned back in his chair and grinned. He might just make it a play. A great deal of the action would be ad-lib, of course, but he had the general theme. Satisfied, and looking forward to the opening scene, Michael went back to work with a vengeance.

Two hours breezed by with Michael working steadily. He answered the knock at his door with a grunt.

"I beg your pardon, Mr. Donahue." Charles, slightly out of breath from the climb up the stairs, stood in the doorway.

Michael gave another grunt and finished typing the paragraph. "Yes, Charles?"

"Telegram for you, sir."

"Telegram?" Scowling, he swiveled around in the chair. If there was a problem in New York—as there was at least once a week—the phone was the quickest way to solve it. "Thanks." He took the telegram, but only flapped it against his palm. "Pandora still out in her shop?"

"Yes, sir." Grateful for the chance to rest, Charles expanded a bit. "Sweeney is a bit upset that Miss McVie missed lunch. She intends to serve dinner in an hour. I hope that suits your schedule."

Michael knew better than to make waves where Sweeney was concerned. "I'll be down."

"Thank you, sir, and if I may say, I enjoy your television show tremendously. This week's episode was particularly exciting."

"I appreciate that, Charles."

"It was Mr. McVie's habit to watch it every week in my company. He never missed an episode."

"There probably wouldn't have been a *Logan's Run* without Jolley," Michael mused. "I miss him."

"We all do. The house seems so quiet. But I—" Charles reddened a bit at the thought of overstepping his bounds.

"Go ahead, Charles."

"I'd like you to know that both Sweeney and I are pleased to remain in your service, yours and Miss McVie's. We were glad when Mr. McVie left you thc housc. The others..." He straightened his back and plunged on. "They wouldn't have been suitable, sir. Sweeney and I had both discussed resigning if Mr. McVie had chosen to leave the Folley to one of his other heirs." Charles folded his bony hands. "Will there be anything else before dinner, sir?"

"No, Charles. Thank you."

Telegram in hand, Michael leaned back as Charles went out. The old butler had known him since childhood. Michael could remember distinctly when Charles had stopped calling him Master Donahue. He'd been sixteen and visiting the Folley during the summer months. Charles had called him Mr. Donahue and Michael had felt as though he'd just stepped from childhood, over adolescence and into adulthood.

Strange how much of his life had been involved with the Folley and the people who were a part of it. Charles had served him his first whisky—with dignity if not approval on his eighteenth birthday. Years before that, Sweeney had given him his first ear boxing. His parents had never bothered to swat him and his tutors wouldn't have dared. Michael still remembered that after the sting had eased, he'd felt like part of a family.

Pandora had been both bane and fantasy during his adolescence. Apparently that hadn't changed as much as Michael had thought. And Jolley. Jolley had been father, grandfather, friend, son and brother.

Jolley had been Jolley, and Michael had spoken no less than the truth when he'd told Charles he missed the old man. In some part of himself, he always would. Thinking of other things, Michael tore open the telegram.

Your mother gravely ill. Doctors not hopeful. Make arrangements to fly to Palm Springs immediately. L. J. KEYSER.

Michael stared at the telegram for nearly a minute. It wasn't possible; his mother was never ill. She considered it something of a social flaw. He felt a moment's disbelief, a moment's shock. He was reaching for the phone before either had worn off.

When Pandora walked by his room fifteen minutes later, she saw him tossing clothes into a bag. She lifted a brow, leaned against the jamb and cleared her throat. "Going somewhere?"

"Palm Springs." He tossed in his shaving kit.

"Really?" Now she folded her arms. "Looking for a sunnier climate?"

"It's my mother. Her husband sent me a telegram."

Instantly she dropped her cool, sarcastic pose and came into the room. "Is she ill?"

"The telegram didn't say much, but it doesn't sound good."

"Oh, Michael, I'm sorry. Can I do anything? Call the airport?"

"I've already done it. I've got a flight in a couple of hours. They're routing me through half a dozen cities, but it was the best I could do."

Feeling helpless, she watched him zip up his bag. "I'll drive you to the airport if you like."

"No, thanks anyway." He dragged a hand through his hair as he turned to face her. The concern was there, though he realized she'd only met his mother once, ten, perhaps fifteen years before. The concern was for him and unexpectedly solid. "Pandora, it's going to take me half the night to get to the coast. And then I don't know—" He broke off, not able to imagine his mother seriously ill. "I might not be able to make it back in time—not in forty-eight hours."

She shook her head. "I don't want you to think about it. I'll call Fitzhugh and explain. Maybe he'll be able to do something. After all, it's an emergency. If he can't, he can't."

He was taking a step that could pull millions of dollars out from under her. Millions of dollars and the home she loved. Torn, Michael went to her and rested his hands on her shoulders. She was so slender. He'd forgotten just how fragile a strong woman could be. "I'm sorry, Pandora. If there was any other way..."

"Michael, I told you I didn't want the money. I meant it."

He studied her a moment. Yes, the strength was there, the stubbornness and the basic goodness he often overlooked. "I believe you did," he murmured.

"As for the rest, well, we'll see. Now go ahead before you

miss your plane." She waited until he'd grabbed his bag then walked with him to the hall. "Call me if you get the chance and let me know how your mother is."

He nodded, started for the stairs, then stopped. Setting his bag down, he came back and pulled her against him. The kiss was hard and long, with hints of a fire barely banked. He drew her away just as abruptly. "See you."

"Yeah." Pandora swallowed. "See you."

She stood where she was until she heard the front door slam.

She had a long time to think about the kiss, through a solitary dinner, during the hours when she tried to read by the cheery fire in the parlor. It seemed to Pandora that there'd been more passion concentrated in that brief contact than she'd experienced in any of her carefully structured relationships. Was it because she'd always been able to restrict passion to her temper, or her work?

It might have been because she'd been sympathetic, and Michael had been distraught. Emotions had a way of feeding emotions. But for the second time she found herself alone in the house, and to her astonishment, lonely. It was foolish because the fire was bright, the book entertaining and the brandy she sipped warming.

But lonely she was. After little more than a month, she'd come to depend on Michael's company. Even to look forward to it, as strange as that may have been. She liked sitting across from him at meals, arguing with him. She especially liked watching the way he fought, exploding when she poked pins in his work. Perverse? she wondered with a sigh. Perhaps she was, but life was so boring without a bit of friction. No one seemed to provide it more satisfactorily than Michael Donahue.

She wondered when she'd see him again. And she wondered if now they'd have to forgo spending the winter together. If the terms of the will were broken, there would be no reason for them to stay on together. In fact, they'd have no right to stay at the Folley at all. They'd both go back to New York where, due to separate life-styles, they never saw one another. Not until now, when it was a possibility, did Pandora fully realize how much she didn't want it to happen.

She didn't want to lose the Folley. There were so many memories, so many important ones. Wouldn't they begin to fade if she couldn't walk into a room and bring them back? She didn't want to lose Michael. His companionship, she amended quickly. It was more satisfying than she'd imagined to have someone near who could meet you head to head. If she lost that daily challenge, life would be terribly flat. Since it was Michael who was adding that certain spark to the days, it was only natural to want him around. Wasn't it?

With a sigh, Pandora shut the book and decided an early night would be more productive than idle speculation. Just as she reached over to shut out the lamp, it went out on its own. She was left with the glow of the fire.

Odd, she thought and reached for the switch. After turning it back and forth, she rose, blaming a defective bulb. But when she walked into the hall she found it in darkness. The light she'd left burning was out, along with the one always left on at the top of the stairs. Again Pandora reached for a switch and again she found it useless.

Power failure, she decided but found herself hesitating in the dark. There was no storm. Electricity at the Folley went out regularly during snow and thunderstorms, but the back-up generator took over within minutes. Pandora waited, but the house remained dark. It occurred to her as she stood there hoping for the best, that she'd never really considered how dark dark could be. She was already making her way back into the parlor for a candle when the rest occurred to her. The house was heated with electricity, as well. If she didn't see about the power soon, the house was going to be very cold as well as very dark before too long. With two people in their seventies in the house, she couldn't let it go.

Annoyed, she found three candles in a silver holder and lit them. It wasn't any use disturbing Charles's sleep and dragging him down to the basement. It was probably only a faulty fuse or two. Holding the candles ahead of her, Pandora wound her way through the curving halls to the cellar door.

She wasn't bothered about going down into the cellar in the dark. So she told herself as she stood with her hand on the knob. It was, after all, just another room. And one, if memory served, which was full of the remains of several of Uncle Jolley's rejected hobbies. The fuse box was down there. She'd seen it when she'd helped her uncle cart down several boxes of photographic equipment after he'd decided to give up the idea of becoming a portrait photographer. She'd go down, check for faulty fuses and replace them. After the lights and heat were taken care of, she'd have a hot bath and go to bed.

But she drew in a deep breath before she opened the door.

The stairs creaked. It was to be expected. And they were steep and narrow as stairs were in any self-respecting cellar. The light from her candles set the shadows dancing over the crates and boxes her uncle had stored there. She'd have to see if she could talk Michael into helping her sort through them. On some bright afternoon. She was humming nervously to herself before she reached the bottom stair.

Pandora held the candles high and scanned the floor as far as the light circled. She knew mice had an affection for dark, dank cellars and she had no affection for them. When nothing rushed across the floor, she skirted around two six-foot crates and headed for the fuse box. There was the motorized exercise bike that Uncle Jolley had decided took the fun out of staying fit. There was a floor-to-ceiling shelf of old bottles. He'd once been fascinated by a ten-dollar bottle cutter. And there, she saw with a sigh of relief, was the fuse box. Setting the candles on a stack of boxes, she opened the big metal door and stared inside. There wasn't a single fuse in place.

"What the hell's this?" she muttered. Then as she shifted to look closer, her foot sent something rattling over the concrete floor. Jolting, she stifled a scream and the urge to run. Holding her breath, she waited in the silence. When she thought she could manage it, she picked up the candles again and crouched. Scattered at her feet were a dozen fuses. She picked one up and let it lay in her palm. The cellar might have its quota of mice, but they weren't handy enough to empty a fuse box.

She felt a little shudder, which she ignored as she began to gather up the fuses. Tricks, she told herself. Just silly tricks. Annoying, but not as destructive as the one played in her workshop. It wasn't even a very clever trick, she decided, as it was as simple to put fuses back as it had been to take them out.

Working quickly, and trying not to look over her shoulder, Pandora put the fuses back in place. Whoever had managed to get into the basement and play games had wasted her time, nothing more.

Finished, she went over to the stairs, and though she hated herself, ran up them. But her sigh of relief was premature. The door she'd carefully left open was closed tightly. For a few moments she simply refused to believe it. She twisted the knob, pushed, shoved and twisted again. Then she forgot everything but the fear of being closed in a dark place. Pandora beat on the door, shouted, pleaded, then collapsed half sobbing on the top step. No one would hear her. Charles and Sweeney were on the other side of the house.

For five minutes she gave in to fear and self-pity. She was alone, all alone, locked in a dark cellar where no one would hear her until morning. It was already cold and getting colder. By morning. . .her candles would go out by then, and she'd have no light at all. That was the worst, the very worst, to have no light.

Light, she thought, and called herself an idiot as she wiped away tears. Hadn't she just fixed the lights? Scrambling up, Pandora hit the switch at the top of the stairs. Nothing happened. Holding back a scream, she held the candles up. The socket over the stairs was empty.

So, they'd thought to take out the bulbs. It had been a clever trick after all. She swallowed fresh panic and tried to think. They wanted her to be incoherent, and she refused to give them the satisfaction. When she found out which one of her loving family was playing nasty games…

That was for later, Pandora told herself. Now she was going to find a way out. She was shivering, but she told herself it was anger. There were times it paid to lie to yourself. Holding the candles aloft, she forced herself to go down the steps again when cowering at the top seemed so much easier.

The cellar was twice the size of her apartment in New York, open and barnlike without any of the ornate decorating Uncle Jolley had been prone to. It was just dark and slightly damp with concrete floors and stone walls that echoed. She wouldn't think about spiders or things that scurried into corners right now. Slowly, trying to keep calm, she searched for an exit.

There were no doors, but then she was standing several feet underground. Like a tomb. That particular thought didn't soothe her nerves so she concentrated on other things. She'd only been down in the cellar a handful of times and hadn't given a great deal of thought to the setup. Now she had to think about it—and pretend her palms weren't clammy.

She eased by a pile of boxes as high as her shoulders, then let out a scream when she ran into a maze of cobwebs. More disgusted than frightened, she brushed and dragged at them. It didn't sit well with her to make a fool out of herself, even if no one was around to see it. Someone was going to pay, she told herself as she fought her way clear.

Then she saw the window, four feet above her head and tiny.

Though it was hardly the size of a transom, Pandora nearly collapsed in relief. After setting the candles on a shelf, she began dragging boxes over. Her muscles strained and her back protested, but she hauled and stacked against the wall. The first splinter had her swearing. After the third, she stopped counting. Out of breath, streaming with sweat, she leaned against her makeshift ladder. Now all she had to do was climb it. With the candles in one hand, she used the other to haul herself up. The light shivered and swayed. The boxes groaned and teetered a bit. The thought passed through her mind that if she fell, she could lie there on the frigid concrete with broken bones until morning. She pulled herself high and refused to think at all.

When she reached the window, she found the little latch rusted and stubborn. Swearing, praying, she balanced the candles on the box under her and used both hands. She felt the latch give, then stick again. If she'd only thought to find a tool before she'd climbed up. She considered climbing back down and finding one, then made the mistake of looking behind her. The stack of boxes looked even more rickety from up there.

Turning back to the window, she tugged with all the strength she had. The latch gave with a grind of metal against metal, the boxes swayed from the movement. She saw her candles start to tip and grabbed for them. Out of reach, they slid from the box and clattered to the concrete, their tiny flames extinguished as they hit the ground. She almost followed them, but managed to fight for balance. Pandora found herself perched nine feet off the floor in pitch-darkness.

She wouldn't fall, she promised herself as she gripped the

little window ledge with both hands. Using her touch to guide her, she pulled the window out and open, then began to ease herself through. The first blast of cold air made her almost giddy. After she'd pushed her shoulders through she gave herself a moment to breathe and adjust to the lesser dark of starlight. From somewhere to the west, she heard a hardy night bird call twice and fall silent. She'd never heard anything more beautiful.

Grabbing the base of a rhododendron, she pulled herself through to the waist. When she heard the crash of boxes behind her, she laid her cheek against the cold grass. Inch by inch, she wiggled her way out, ignoring the occasional rip and scratch. At last, she was flat on her back, looking up at the stars. Cold, bruised and exhausted, she lay there, just breathing. When she was able, Pandora dragged herself up and walked around to the east terrace doors.

She wanted revenge, but first, she wanted a bath.

After three layovers and two plane changes, Michael arrived in Palm Springs. Nothing, as far as he could see, had changed. He never came to the exclusive little community but that he came reluctantly. Now, thinking of his mother lying ill, he was swamped with guilt.

He rarely saw her. True, she was no more interested in seeing him than he was her. Yet, she was still his mother. They had been on a different wavelength since the day he'd been born, but she'd taken care of him. At least, she'd hired people to take care of him. Affection, Michael realized, didn't have to enter into a child's feelings for his parent. The bond was there whether or not understanding followed it.

With no more than a flight bag, he bypassed the crowd at baggage claim and hailed a cab. After giving his mother's address, he sat back and checked his watch, subtracting time zones. Even with the hours he'd gained, it was probably past visiting hours. He'd get around that, but first he had to know what hospital his mother was in. If he'd been thinking straight, he would have called ahead and checked.

If his mother's husband wasn't in, one of the servants could tell him. It might not be as bad as the telegram made it sound. After all his mother was still young. Then it struck Michael that he didn't have the vaguest idea how old his mother was. He doubted his father knew, and certainly not her current husband. At another time, it might have struck him as funny.

Impatient, he watched as the cab glided by the gates and pillars of the elite. His career had caused him to stay in California for extended lengths of time, but he preferred L.A. to Palm Springs. There, at least, was some action, some movement, some edge. But he liked New York best of all; the pace matched his own and the streets were tougher.

He thought of Pandora. Both of them lived in New York, but they never saw each other unless it was miles north of the city at the Folley. The city could swallow you. Or hide you. It was another aspect Michael appreciated.

Didn't he often use it to hide—from his stifling upbringing, from his recurring lack of faith in the human race? It was at the Folley that he felt the easiest, but it was in New York that he felt

the safest. He could be anonymous there if he chose to be. There were times he wanted nothing more. He wrote about heroes and justice, sometimes rough but always human. He wrote, in his own fashion, about basic values and simple rights.

He'd been raised with the illusions and hypocrisy of wealth and with values that were just as unstable. He'd broken away from that, started on his own. New York had helped make it possible because in the city backgrounds were easily erased. So easily erased, Michael mused, that he rarely thought of his.

The cab cruised up the long semicircle of macadam, under the swaying palms, toward the towering white house where his mother had chosen to live. Michael remembered there was a lily pond in the back with goldfish the size of groupers. His mother refused to call them carp.

"Wait," he told the driver, then dashed up two levels of stairs to the door. The butler who answered was new. It was his mother's habit to change the staff regularly, before, as she put it, they got too familiar. "I'm Michael Donahue, Mrs. Keyser's son."

The butler glanced over his shoulder at the waiting cab, then back at Michael's disheveled sweater and unshaven face. "Good evening, sir. Are you expected?"

"Where's my mother? I want to go to the hospital directly."

"Your mother isn't in this evening, Mr. Donahue. If you'll wait, I'll see if Mr. Keyser's available."

Intolerant, as always, of cardboard manners, he stepped inside. "I know she's not in. I want to go see her tonight. What's the name of the hospital?"

The butler gave a polite nod. "What hospital, Mr. Donahue?"

"Jackson, where did that cab come from?" Wrapped in a deep-rose smoking jacket, Lawrence Keyser strolled downstairs. He had a thick cigar between the fingers of one hand and a snifter of brandy in the other.

"Well, Lawrence," Michael began over a wave of fury. "You look comfortable. Where's my mother?"

"Well, well, it's—ah, it's Matthew."

"It's Michael."

"Michael, of course. Jackson, pay off Mr. ah, Mr. Donavan's cab."

"No, thanks, Jackson." Michael held up a hand. Another time, he'd have been amused at his stepfather's groping for his name. "I'll use it to get to the hospital. Wouldn't want to put you out."

"No trouble at all, not at all." Big, round and only partially balding, Keyser gave Michael a friendly grin. "Veronica will be pleased to see you, though we didn't know you were coming. How long are you in town?"

"As long as I'm needed. I left the minute I got the telegram. You didn't mention the name of the hospital. Since you're home and relaxing," he said with only the slightest trace of venom, "should I assume that my mother's condition's improved?"

"Condition?" Keyser gave a jovial laugh. "Well now, I don't know how she'd take to that term, but you can ask her yourself."

"I intend to. Where is she?"

"Playing bridge at the Bradleys'. She'll be coming along in about an hour. How about a brandy?"

"Playing bridge!" Michael stepped forward and grabbed his surprised stepfather by the lapels. "What the hell do you mean she's playing bridge?"

"Can't stomach the game myself," Keyser began warily. "But Veronica's fond of it."

It came to Michael, clear as a bell. "You didn't send me a telegram about Mother?"

"A telegram?" Keyser patted Michael's arm, and hoped Jackson stayed close. "No need to send you a telegram about a bridge game, boy."

"Mother's not ill?"

"Strong as a horse, though I wouldn't let her hear me say so just that way."

Michael swore and whirled around. "Someone's going to pay," he muttered.

"Where are you going?"

"Back to New York," Michael tossed over his shoulder as he ran down the steps.

Relieved, Keyser opted against the usual protests about his departure. "Is there a message for your mother?"

"Yeah." Michael stopped with a hand on the door of the cab. "Yeah, tell her I'm glad she's well. And I hope she wins—in spades." Michael slammed the door shut behind him.

Keyser waited until the cab shot out of sight. "Odd boy," Keyser grumbled to his butler. "Writes for television."

Chapter Six

Pandora, sleeping soundly, was awakened at seven in the morning when Michael dropped on her bed. The mattress bounced. He snuggled his head into the pillow beside her and shut his eyes.

"Sonofabitch," he grumbled.

Pandora sat up, remembered she was naked and grabbed for the sheets. "Michael! You're supposed to be in California. What are you doing in my bed?"

"Getting horizontal for the first time in twenty-four hours."

"Well, do that in your own bed," she ordered, then saw the lines of strain and fatigue. "Your mother." Pandora grabbed for his hand. "Oh, Michael, is your mother—"

"Playing bridge." He rubbed his free hand over his face. Even to him it felt rough and seedy. "I bounced across country, once in a tuna can with propellers, to find out she was sipping sherry and trumping her partner's ace."

"She's better then?"

"She was always better. The telegram was a hoax." He yawned, stretched and settled. "God, what a night."

"You mean..." Pandora tugged on the sheets and glowered. "Well, the rats."

"Yeah. I plotted out several forms of revenge when I was laid over in Cleveland. Maybe our friend who stomped through your workshop figured it was my turn. Now we each owe them one."

"I owe 'em two." Pandora leaned back against the headboard with the sheets tucked under her arms. Her hair fell luxuriously over her naked shoulders. "Last night while you were off on your wild-goose chase, I was locked in the cellar."

Michael's attention shot away from the thin sheet that barely covered her. "Locked in? How?"

Crossing one ankle over the other, Pandora told him what happened from the time the lights went out.

"Climbed up on boxes? To that little window? It's nearly ten feet."

"Yes, I believe I noticed that at the time."

Michael scowled at her. The anger he'd felt at being treated to a sleepless night doubled. He could picture her groping her way around in the dank cellar all too well. Worse, he could see her very clearly climbing on shaky boxes and crates. "You could've broken your neck."

"I didn't. What I did do was rip my favorite pair of slacks, scratch both knees and bruise my shoulder."

Michael managed to hold back his fury. He'd let it go, he

promised himself, when the time was right. "It could've been worse," he said lightly, and thought of what he'd do to whoever had locked her in.

"It was worse," Pandora tossed back, insulted. "While you were sipping Scotch at thirty thousand feet, I was locked in a cold, damp cellar with mice and spiders."

"We might reconsider calling the police."

"And do what with them? We can't prove anything. We don't even know whom we can't prove anything against."

"New rule," Michael decided. "We stick together. Neither of us leaves the house overnight without the other. At least until we find out which of our devoted relations is playing games."

Pandora started to protest, then remembered how frightened she'd been, and before the cellar, before the fear, how lonely. "Agreed. Now..." With one hand hanging onto the sheet, she shifted toward him. "I vote for Uncle Carlson on this one. After all, he knows the house better than any of the others. He lived here."

"It's as good a guess as any. But it's only a guess." Michael stared up at the ceiling. "I want to know. Biff stayed here for six weeks one summer when we were kids."

"That's right." Pandora frowned at the ceiling herself. The mirror across the room reflected them lying companionably, hip to hip. "I'd forgotten about that. He hated it."

"He's never had a sense of humor."

"True enough. As I recall he certainly didn't like you."

"Probably because I gave him a black eye."

Pandora's brow lifted. "You would." Then, because the image

of Biff with a shiner wasn't so unappealing, she added: "Why did you? You never said."

"Remember the frogs in your dresser?"

Pandora sniffed and smoothed at the sheets. "I certainly do. It was quite immature of you."

"Not me. Biff."

"Biff?" Astonished, she turned toward him again. "You mean that little creep put the frogs in my underwear?" The next thought came, surprisingly pleasing. "And you punched him for it?"

"It wasn't hard."

"Why didn't you deny it when I accused you?"

"It was more satisfying to punch Biff. In any case, he knows the house well enough. And I imagine if we checked up, we'd find most of our happy clan has stayed here, at least for a few days at a time. Finding a fuse box in the cellar doesn't take a lot of cunning. Think it through, Pandora. There are six of them, seven with the charity added on. Split a hundred fifty million seven ways and you end up with plenty of motive. Every one of them has a reason for wanting us to break the terms of the will. None of them, as far as I'm concerned, is above adding a little pressure to help us along."

"Another reason the money never appealed to me," she mused. "They haven't done anything but vandalize and annoy, but, dammit, Michael, I want to pay them back."

"The ultimate payback comes in just under five months." Without thinking about it, Michael put his arm around her shoulders. Without thinking about it, Pandora settled against him. A light fragrance clung to her skin. "Can't you see

Carlson's face when the will holds up and he gets nothing but a magic wand and a trick hat?"

His shoulder felt more solid than she'd imagined. "And Biff with three cartons of matchbooks." Comfortable, she chuckled. "Uncle Jolley's still having the last laugh."

"We'll have it with him in a few months."

"It's a date. And you've got your shoes on my sheets."

"Sorry." With two economical movements, he pried them off.

"That's not exactly what I meant. Don't you want to wander off to your own room now?"

"Not particularly. Your bed's nicer than mine. Do you always sleep naked?"

"No."

"My luck must be turning then." He shifted to press his lips to a bruise on her shoulder. "Hurt?"

She shrugged and prayed it came off as negligent. "A little."

"Poor little Pandora. And to think I always thought you were tough-skinned."

"I am—"

"Soft," he interrupted, and skimmed his fingers down her arm. "Very soft. Any more bruises?" He brushed his lips over the curve of her neck. They both felt her quick, involuntary shudder.

"Not so you'd notice."

"I'm very observant." He rolled, smoothly, so that his body pressed more intimately into hers as he looked down on her. He was tired. Yes, he was tired and more than a little punchy with jet lag, but he hadn't forgotten he wanted her. Even if he had, the way her body yielded, the way her face looked rosy and soft with sleep, would've jogged his memory. "Why don't I look for myself?" He ran his fingers down to where the sheet lay, neat, prim and arousing, at her breast.

She sucked in her breath, incredibly moved by his lightest touch. She couldn't let it show…could she? She couldn't reach out for something that was only an illusion. He wasn't stable. He wasn't real. He was with her now because she was here and no one else was. Why was it becoming so hard to remember that?

His face was close, filling her vision. She saw the little things she'd tried not to notice over the years. The way a thin ring of gray outlined his irises, the straight, almost aristocratic line of his nose that had remained miraculously unbroken through countless fistfights. The soft, sculpted, somehow poetic shape of his mouth. A mouth, she remembered, that was hot and strong and inventive when pressed against hers.

"Michael…" The fact that she hesitated, then fumbled before she reached down to take his hand both pleased and unnerved him. She wasn't as cool and self-contained as she'd always appeared. And because she wasn't, he could slip his way under her skin. But he might not slip out again so easily.

Be practical, she told herself. Be realistic. "Michael, we have almost five months more to get through."

"Good point." He needed the warmth. He needed the woman. Maybe it was time to risk the consequences. He lowered his head and nibbled at her mouth. "Why waste it?"

She let herself enjoy him. For just a moment, she promised

herself. For only a moment. He was warm and his hands were easy. The night had been long and cold and frightening. No matter how much she hated to admit it, she'd needed him. Now, with the sun pouring through the tiny square panes in the windows, falling bright and hard on the bed, she had him. Close, secure, comforting.

Her lips opened against his.

He'd had no plan when he'd come into her room. He'd simply been drawn to her; he'd wanted to lie beside her and talk to her. Passion hadn't guided him. Desire hadn't pushed him. There'd only been the basic need to be home, to be home with her. When she'd snuggled against him, hair tousled, eyes heavy, it had been so natural that the longing had snuck up on him. He wanted nothing more than to stay where he was, wrapped around her, slowly heating.

And for her, passion didn't bubble wildly, but easily, like a brew that had been left to simmer through the day while spices were added. One sample, then another, and the taste changed, enriched, deepened. With Michael, there the flavors were only hinted at, an aroma to draw in and savor. She could have gone on, and on, hour after hour, until what they made between them was perfected. She wanted to give in to the need, the beginnings of greed. If she did, everything would change. It was a change she couldn't predict, couldn't see clearly, could only anticipate. So she resisted him and herself and what could happen between them.

"Michael…" But she let her fingers linger in his hair for just a minute more. "This isn't smart."

He kissed her eyes closed. It was something no one had done before. "It's the smartest thing either of us has done in years."

She wanted to agree, felt herself on the edge of agreeing. "Michael, things are complicated enough. If we were lovers and things went wrong, how could we manage to go on here together? We've made a commitment to Uncle Jolley."

"The will doesn't have a damn thing to do with you and me in this bed."

How could she have forgotten just how intense he could look when he was bent on something? How was it she'd never noticed how attractive it made him? She'd have to make a stand now or go under. "The will has everything to do with you and me in this house. If we go to bed together and our relationship changes, then we'll have to deal with all the problems and complications that go with it."

"Name some."

"Don't be amusing, Michael."

"Giving you a laugh wasn't my intention." He liked the way she looked against the pillow—hair spread out like wildfire, cheeks a bit flushed, her mouth on the edge of forming a pout. Strange he'd never pictured her this way before. It didn't take any thought to know he'd picture her like this again and again. "I want you, Pandora. There's nothing amusing about it."

No, that wasn't something she could laugh or shrug off, not when the words brushed over her skin and made her muscles limp. He didn't mean it. He couldn't mean it. But she wanted to believe it. If she couldn't laugh it off, she had to throw up a guard and block it. "Becoming lovers is something that takes a lot of thought. If we're going to discuss it—"

"I don't want to discuss it." He pressed his lips against hers until he felt her body soften. "We're not making a corporate merger, Pandora, we're making love."

"That's just it." She fought back an avalanche of longing. Be practical. It was her cardinal rule. "We're business partners. Worse, we're family business partners, at least for the next few months. If we change that now it could—"

"If," he interrupted. "It could. Do you always need guarantees?"

Her brows drew together as annoyance competed with desire. "It's a matter of common sense to look at all the angles."

"I suppose you have any prospective lover fill out an application form."

Her voice chilled. It was, in a distorted way, close to the truth. "Don't be crude, Michael."

Pushed to the limit, he glared down at her. "I'd rather be crude than have your brand of common sense."

"You've never had any brand of common sense," she tossed back. "Why else would every busty little blonde you've winked at be public knowledge? You don't even have the decency to be discreet."

"So that's it." Shifting, Michael drew her into a sitting position. There was no soft yielding now. She faced him with fire in her eyes. "Don't forget the brunettes and the redheads."

She hadn't. She promised herself she wouldn't. "I don't want to discuss it."

"You brought it up, and we'll finish it. I've gone to bed with women. So put me in irons. I've even enjoyed it."

She tossed her hair behind her shoulder. "I'm sure you have."

"And I haven't had a debate with every one of them beforehand. Some women prefer romance and mutual enjoyment."

"Romance?" Her brows shot up under her tousled hair. "I've always had another word for it."

"You wouldn't recognize romance if it dropped on your head. Do you consider it discreet to take lovers and pretend you don't? To pledge undying fidelity to one person while you're looking for another? What you want to call discretion, I call hypocrisy. I'm not ashamed of any of the women I've known, in bed or out."

"I'm not interested in what you are or aren't ashamed of. I'm not going to be your next mutual enjoyment. Keep your passion for your dancers and starlets and chorus girls."

"You're as big a snob as the rest of them."

That hit home and had her shoulders stiffening. "That's not true. I've simply no intention of joining a crowd."

"You flatter me, cousin."

"There's another word for that, too."

"Think about this." He gave her a shake, harder than he'd intended. "I've never made love with a woman I didn't care for and respect." Before he cut loose and did more than shake her, he got up and walked to the door while she sat in the middle of the bed clutching sheets and looking furious.

"It appears you give respect easily."

He turned back to study her. "No," he said slowly. "But I don't make people jump through hoops for it."

* * *

A cold war might not be as stimulating as an active battle, but with the right participants, it could be equally destructive. For days Pandora and Michael circled around each other. If one made a sarcastic comment, the other reached into the stockpile and used equal sarcasm. Neither drew out the red flag for full-scale attack, instead they picked and prodded at each other while the servants rolled their eyes and waited for bloodshed.

"Foolishness," Sweeney declared as she rolled out the crust for two apple pies. "Plain foolishness." She was a sturdy, red-faced woman, as round as Charles was thin. In her pragmatic, no-nonsense way, she'd married and buried two husbands, then made her way in the world by cooking for others. Her kitchen was always neat and tidy, all the while smelling of the sinfully rich food she prepared. "Spoiled children," she told Charles. "That's what they are. Spoiled children need the back of the hand."

"They've over four months to go." Charles sat gloomily at the kitchen table, hunched over a cup of tea. "They'll never make it."

"Hah!" Sweeney slammed the rolling pin onto a fresh ball of dough. "They'll make it. Too stubborn not to. But it's not enough."

"The master wanted them to have the house. As long as they do, we won't lose it."

"What'll we be doing in this big empty house when both of them go back to the city? How often will either of them be visiting with the master gone?" Sweeney turned the crust into a pan and trimmed it expertly. "The master wanted them to have the house, true enough. And he wanted them to have each other. The house needs a family. It's up to us to see it gets one."

"You didn't hear them over breakfast." Charles sipped his tea and watched Sweeney pour a moist apple mixture into the crust.

"That has nothing to do with it. *I've* seen the way they look at each other when they think the other one's not noticing. All they need's a push."

With quick, economic movements, she filled the second crust. "We're going to give 'em one."

Charles stretched out his legs. "We're too old to push young people."

Sweeney gave a quick grunt as she turned. Her hands were thick, and she set them on her hips. "Being old's the whole trick. You've been feeling poorly lately."

"No, to tell you the truth, I've been feeling much better this week."

"You've been feeling poorly," Sweeney repeated, scowling at him. "Now here's our Pandora coming in for lunch. Just follow my lead. Look a little peaked."

Snow had come during the night, big fat flakes that piled on the ground and hung in the pines. As she walked, Pandora kicked it up, pleased with herself. Her work couldn't have been going better. The earrings she'd finally fashioned had been unique, so unique, she'd designed a necklace to complement them. It was chunky and oversize with geometric shapes of copper and gold. Not every woman could wear it, but the one who could wouldn't go unnoticed.

It was, to Pandora, a statement of the strong, disciplined woman. She was just as pleased with the shoulder-brushing earrings she was making with jet and silver beads. They had been painstakingly strung together and when finished would be elegantly flirtatious. Another aspect of woman. If her pace kept steady, she'd have a solid inventory to ship off to the boutique she supplied. In time for the Christmas rush, she reminded herself smugly.

When she opened the kitchen door, she was ravenously hungry and in the best of moods.

"...if you're feeling better in a day or two," Sweeney said briskly, then turned as if surprised to see Pandora inside. "Oh, time must've got away from me. Lunch already and I'm just finishing up the pies."

"Apple pies?" Grinning, Pandora moved closer. But Sweeney saw with satisfaction that Pandora was already studying Charles. "Any filling left?" she began, and started to dip her fingers into the bowl. Sweeney smacked them smartly.

"You've been working with those hands. Wash them up in the sink, and you'll have your lunch as soon as I can manage it."

Obediently, Pandora turned on a rush of water. Under the noise, she murmured to Sweeney. "Is Charles not feeling well?"

"Bursitis is acting up. Cold weather's a problem. Just being old's a problem in itself." She pushed a hand at the small of her back as though she had a pain. "Guess we're both slowing down a bit. Aches and pains," Sweeney sighed and cast a sidelong look at Pandora. "Just part of being old."

"Nonsense." Concerned, Pandora scrubbed her hands harder. She told herself she should have been keeping a closer eye on Charles. "You just try to do too much."

"With the holidays coming..." Sweeney trailed off and made a business out of arranging a top crust. "Well, decorating the house is a lot of work, but it's its own reward. Charles and I'll deal with the boxes in the attic this afternoon."

"Don't be silly." Pandora shut off the water and reached for a towel. "I'll bring the decorations down."

"No, now, missy, there're too many boxes and most of them are too heavy for a little girl like you. That's for us to see to. Isn't that right, Charles?"

Thinking of climbing the attic stairs a half-dozen times, Charles started to sigh. A look from Sweeney stopped him. "Don't worry, Miss McVie, Sweeney and I will see to it."

"You certainly will not." Pandora hung the towel back on the hook. "Michael and I will bring everything down this afternoon, and that's that. Now I'll go tell him to come to lunch."

Sweeney waited until the door swung shut behind Pandora before she grinned.

Upstairs, Pandora knocked twice on Michael's office door, then walked in. He kept on typing. Putting her pride on hold, Pandora walked over to his desk and folded her arms. "I need to talk to you."

"Come back later. I'm busy."

Abuse rose up in her throat. Remembering Sweeney's tired voice, she swallowed it. "It's important." She ground her teeth on the word, but said it. "Please."

Surprised, Michael stopped typing in midword. "What? Has one of the family been playing games again?"

"No, it's not that. Michael, we have to decorate the house for Christmas."

He stared at her a moment, swore and turned back to his machine. "I've got a twelve-year-old boy kidnapped and being held for a million-dollar ransom. That's important."

"Michael, will you put away fantasyland for a moment? This is real."

"So's this. Just ask my producer."

"Michael!" Before he could stop her, Pandora pulled the sheet from the typewriter. He was halfway out of his chair to retaliate. "It's Sweeney and Charles."

It stopped him, though he snatched the paper back from her. "What about them?"

"Charles's bursitis is acting up again, and I'm sure Sweeney's not feeling well. She sounded, well, old."

"She is old." But Michael tossed the paper on the desk. "Think we should call in a doctor?"

"No, they'd be furious." She swung around his desk, trying to pretend she wasn't reading part of his script. "I'd rather just keep an eye on them for a few days and make sure they don't overdo. That's where the Christmas decorations come in."

"I figured you'd get to them. Look, if you want to deck the halls, go ahead. I haven't got time to fool with it today."

"Neither do I." She folded her arms in a manner that amused him. "Sweeney and Charles have it in their heads that it has to be done. Unless we want them dragging up and down the attic stairs, we have to take care of it."

"Christmas is three weeks away."

"I know the date." Frustrated, she strode to the window then back. "They're old and they're set on it. You know Uncle Jolley would've had them up the day after Thanksgiving. It's traditional."

"All right, all right." Trapped, Michael rose. "Let's get started."

"Right after lunch." Satisfied she'd gotten her way, Pandora swept out.

Forty-five minutes later, she and Michael were pushing open the attic door. The attic was, in Jolley's tradition, big enough to house a family of five. "Oh, I'd forgotten what a marvelous place this is." Forgetting herself, Pandora grabbed Michael's hand and pulled him in. "Look at this table, isn't it horrible?"

It was. Old and ornate with curlicues and cupids, it had been shoved into a corner to hold other paraphernalia Jolley had discarded. "And the bird cage out of Popsicle sticks. Uncle Jolley said it took him six months to finish it, then he didn't have the heart to put a bird inside."

"Lucky for the bird," Michael muttered, but found himself, as always, drawn to the dusty charm of the place. "Spats," he said, and lifted a pair from a box. "Can't you see him in them?"

"And this hat." Pandora found a huge circular straw with a garden of flowers along the brim. "Aunt Katie's. I've always wished I'd met her. My father said she was just as much fun as Uncle Jolley."

Michael watched Pandora tip the brim over her eyes. "If that was her hat, I believe it. How about this?" He found a black derby and tilted it rakishly.

"It's you," Pandora told him with her first easy laugh in days. "All you need's a high white collar and a walking stick. Look."

She pulled him in front of a tall cheval mirror that needed re-silvering. Together, they studied themselves.

"An elegant pair," Michael decided, though his sweater bagged over his hips, and she already had dust on her nose. "All you need is one of those slim little skirts that sweep the floor and a lace blouse with padded shoulders."

"And a cameo on a ribbon," she added as she tried to visualize herself. "No, I probably would've worn bloomers and picketed for women's rights."

"The hat still suits you." He turned to adjust it just a bit. "Especially with your hair long and loose. I've always liked it long, though you looked appealingly lost and big-eyed when you had it all chopped short."

"I was fifteen."

"And you'd just come back from the Canary Islands with the longest, brownest legs I'd ever seen in my life. I nearly ate my saucer when you walked into the parlor."

"You were in college and had some cheerleader hanging on your arm."

Michael grinned. "You had better legs."

Pandora pretended little interest. She remembered the visit perfectly, but was surprised, and pleased, that he did. "I'm surprised you noticed or remembered."

"I told you I was observant."

She acknowledged the thrust with a slight nod. There were times when it was best to pad quietly over dangerous ground. "We'd better start digging out the decorations. Sweeney said the boxes were back along the left and clearly marked." Without waiting for agreement, she turned and began to look. "Oh good grief." She stopped again when she saw the stacks of boxes, twenty, perhaps twenty-five of them. Michael stood at her shoulder and stuck his hands in his pockets.

"Think we can hire some teamsters?"

Pandora blew out a breath. "Roll up your sleeves."

On some trips, they could pile two or three boxes apiece and maneuver downstairs. On others, it took both of them to haul one. Somewhere along the way they'd stopped arguing. It was just too much effort.

Grimy and sweaty, they dropped the last boxes in the parlor. Ignoring the dust on her slacks, Pandora collapsed in the nearest chair. "Won't it be great fun hauling them all up again after New Year's?"

"Couldn't we've settled on a plastic Santa?"

"It'll be worth it." Drumming up the energy, she knelt on the floor and opened the first box. "Let's get started."

Once they did, they went at it with a vengeance. Boxes were opened, garland strewed and bulbs tested. They squabbled good-naturedly about what looked best where and the proper way to drape lights at the windows. When the parlor, the main hall and the staircase were finished, Pandora stood at the front door and took a long look.

The garland was white and silver, twisting and twining down the banister. There were bright red bells, lush green ribbon and tiny lights just waiting for evening.

"It looks good," she decided. "Really good. Of course, Sweeney and Charles will want to decorate the servants' quarters and that entire box goes into the dining room, but it's a wonderful start."

"Start?" Michael sat on the stairs. "We're not entering a contest, cousin."

"These things have to be done right. I wonder if my parents will make it home for Christmas. Well..." She brushed that off. They always considered wherever they were home. "I'd say we're ready for the tree. Let's go find one."

"You want to drive into town now?"

"Of course not." Pandora was already pulling coats out of the hall closet. "We'll go right out in the woods and dig one up."

"We?"

"Certainly. I hate it when people cut trees down and then toss them aside after the new year. The woods are loaded with nice little pines. We'll dig one up, then replant it after the holidays."

"How handy are you with a shovel?"

"Don't be a spoilsport." Pandora tossed his coat to him, then pulled on her own. "Besides, it'll be nice to spend some time outside after being in that stuffy attic. We can have some hot buttered rum when we're finished."

"Heavy on the rum."

They stopped at the toolshed for a shovel. Michael picked two and handed one to Pandora. She took it without a blink, then together they walked through the ankle-high snow to the woods. The air had a bite and the scent of pine was somehow stronger in the snow.

"I love it when it's like this." Pandora balanced the shovel on her shoulder and plowed through the woods. "It's so quiet, so—separated. You know, sometimes I think I'd rather live here and visit the city than the other way around."

He'd had the same thought, but was surprised to hear it from her. "I always thought you liked the bright lights and confusion."

"I do. But I like this, too. How about this one?" She paused in front of a spruce. "No, the trunk's too crooked." She walked on. "Besides, I wonder if it wouldn't be more exciting to go into the city for a week now and again and know you had someplace like this to come back to. I seem to work better here. Here's one."

"Too tall. We're better off digging up a young one. Wouldn't it put a crimp in your social life?"

"What?" She studied the tree in question and was forced to agree with him. "Oh. My social life isn't a priority, my work is. In any case, I could entertain here."

He had a picture of her spending long, cozy weekends with flamboyant, artsy types who read Keats aloud. "You don't have to come all the way to the Catskills to play house."

Pandora merely lifted a brow. "No, I don't. This one looks good." She stopped again and took a long study of a four-and-a-half-foot spruce. Behind her, Michael worked hard to keep his mouth shut. "It's just the right size for the parlor."

"Fine." Michael stuck his shovel into the ground. "Put your back into it."

As he bent over to dig, Pandora scooped up a shovelful of snow and tossed it into his face. "Oh, sorry." She smiled and batted her eyes. "Looks like my aim's off." Digging with more effort, she began to hum.

He let it go, probably because he appreciated the move and wished he'd thought of it himself. Within fifteen minutes, they had the hole dug.

"There now." Only a little out of breath, Pandora leaned on her shovel. "The satisfaction of a job well done."

"We only have to carry it back to the house, set it up and...damn, we need something to wrap the roots and dirt in. There was burlap in the shed."

They eyed each other blandly.

"All right," he said after a moment. "I'll go get it, then you have to sweep up the needles and dirt we trail on the floor."

"Deal."

Content, Pandora turned away to watch a cardinal when a snowball slapped into the back of her head. "Sorry." Michael gave her a companionable smile. "Aim must be off." He whistled as he walked back to the shed.

Pandora waited until he was out of sight, then smiling smugly, knelt down to ball snow. By the time he got back, she calculated, she could have an arsenal at hand. He wouldn't have a chance. She took her time, forming and smoothing each ball into a sophisticated weapon. Secure in her advantage, she nearly fell on her face when she heard a sound behind her. She had the ball in her hand and was already set to throw as she whirled. No one was there. Narrowing her eyes, she waited. Hadn't she seen a movement back in the trees? It would be just like him to skirt around and try to sneak up on her. She saw the cardinal fly up again as if startled and heard the quiet plop of snow hitting snow as it was shaken from branches.

"All right, Michael, don't be a coward." She picked up a ball in her left hand, prepared to bombard.

"Guarding your flank?" Michael asked so that this time when she whirled back around, she slid onto her bottom. He grinned at her and dropped the burlap sack in her lap.

"But weren't you..." She trailed off and looked behind her again. How could he be here if he was there? "Did you circle around?"

"No, but from the looks of that mound of balls, I should've. Want to play war?"

"It's just a defense system," she began, then looked over her shoulder again. "I thought I heard you. I would've sworn there was someone just beyond the trees there."

"I went straight to the shed and back." He looked beyond her. "You saw something out there?"

"Michael, if you're playing tricks—"

"No." He cut her off and reached down to pull her to her feet. "No tricks. Let's have a look."

She moved her shoulders but didn't remove her hand from his as they walked deeper into the trees. "Maybe I was a bit jumpy."

"Or expecting me to be sneaky?"

"That, too. It was probably just a rabbit."

"A rabbit with big feet," he murmured as he looked down at the tracks. They were clear enough in the snow, tracks leading to and away from the spot ten yards behind where they'd dug up the tree. "Rabbits don't wear boots."

"So, we still have company. I was beginning to think they'd given the whole business up." She kept her voice light, but felt the uneasiness of anyone who'd been watched. "Maybe it's time we talked to Fitzhugh, Michael."

"Maybe, in the meantime—" The sound of an engine cut him off. He was off in a sprint with Pandora at his heels. After a five-minute dash, they came, clammy and out of breath, to what was hardly more than a logging trail. Tire tracks had churned up the snow and blackened it. "A Jeep, I'd guess." Swearing, Michael stuck his hands in his pockets. If he'd started out right away, he might have caught someone or at least have caught a glimpse of someone.

Pandora let out an annoyed breath. Racing after someone was one thing, being outmaneuvered another. "Whoever it is is only wasting his time."

"I don't like being spied on." He wanted physical contact. Longed for it. Frustrated, he stared at the tracks that led back to the main road. "I'm not playing cat and mouse for the next four months."

"What are we going to do?"

His smile spread as he looked at the tracks. "We'll spread the word through Fitzhugh that we've been bothered by trespassers. Being as there's any number of valuables on the premises, we've decided to haul out one of Jolley's old .30-.30's."

"Michael! They may be a nuisance, but they're still family." Unsure, she studied him. "You wouldn't really shoot at anyone."

"I'd rather shoot at family than strangers," he countered, then shrugged. "They're also fond of their own skin. I can't think of one of them who wouldn't hesitate to play around if they thought they might be picking buckshot out of embarrassing places."

"I don't like it. Guns, even the threat of guns, are trouble."

"Got a better idea?"

"Let's buy a dog. A really big, mean dog."

"Great, then we can let him loose and have him sink his teeth into one of our favorite relatives. They'd like that a lot better than buckshot."

"He doesn't have to be that mean."

"We'll compromise and do both."

"Michael—"

"Let's call Fitzhugh."

"And take his advice?" Pandora demanded.

"Sure…if I like it."

Pandora started to object, then laughed. It was all as silly as a plot of one of his shows. "Sounds reasonable," she decided, then tucked her arm through his. "Let's get the tree inside first."

Chapter Seven

"I know it's Christmas Eve, Darla." Michael picked up his coffee cup, found it empty and lifted the pot from his hot plate. Dregs. He bit off a sigh. The trouble with the Folley was that you had to hike a half a mile to the kitchen whenever the pot ran dry. "I know it'll be a great party, but I can't get away."

That wasn't precisely true, Michael mused as he listened to Darla's rambles about a celebration in Manhattan. *Everyone*, according to her estimate, was going to be there. That meant a loud, elbow-to-elbow party with plenty of booze. He could have taken a day and driven into the city to raise a glass or two with friends. He was well ahead of schedule. So far ahead, he could have taken off a week and not felt the strain. The precise truth was, he didn't want to get away.

"I appreciate that...you'll just have to tell everyone Merry Christmas for me. No, I like living in the country, Darla. Weird? Yeah, maybe." He had to laugh. Darla was a top-notch dancer and a barrel of laughs, but she didn't believe life went on outside of the island of Manhattan. "New Year's if I can manage it. Okay, babe. Yeah, yeah, *ciao*."

More than a little relieved, Michael hung up. Darla was a lot of fun, but he wasn't used to being clung to by a woman, especially one he'd only dated casually. The truth was, she was just as attracted to the influence he had with certain casting agents as she was interested in him. He didn't hold it against her. She had ambition and talent, a combination that could work in the tough-edged business of entertaining if a dash of luck was added. After the holidays he'd make a few calls and see what he could do.

From the doorway, Pandora watched as Michael ran a hand along the back of his neck. Darla, she repeated silently. She imagined the women his taste leaned toward had names like Darla, or Robin and Candy. Sleek, smooth, sophisticated and preferably empty-headed.

"Popularity's such a strain, isn't it, darling?"

Michael turned in his chair to give her a long, narrowed look. "Eavesdropping's so rude, isn't it, darling?"

She shrugged but didn't come in. "If you'd wanted privacy, you should've closed your door."

"Around here you have to nail it shut for privacy."

One brow raised, head slightly inclined, Pandora looked as aloof as royalty. "Your phone conversations have absolutely no interest for me. I only came up as a favor to Charles. You've a package downstairs."

"Thanks." He didn't bother to hide amusement at her tone. If he knew Pandora, and he did, she'd listened to every word. "I thought these were your sacred working hours."

"Some of us schedule our work well enough that we can take some time off during the holidays. No, no, let's not bicker," she decided abruptly before he could retaliate. "It is nearly Christmas after all, and we've had three weeks of peace from our familial practical jokers. Truce," Pandora offered with a smile Michael wasn't sure he should trust. "Or a moratorium if you prefer."

"Why?"

"Let's just say I'm a sucker for holly and ivy. Besides, I'm relieved we didn't have to buy a big drooling dog or a supply of buckshot."

"For now." Not completely satisfied, Michael tipped back in his chair. "Fitzhugh's notion of notifying the local police of trespassers and spreading the rumor of an official investigation might be working temporarily. Or maybe our friends and family are just taking a holiday break themselves. Either way I'm not ready to relax."

"You'd rather break someone's nose than solve things peaceably," Pandora began, then waved a hand. "Never mind. I, for one, am going to enjoy the holidays and not give any of our dear family a thought." She paused a moment, toying with her braided chain of gold and amethyst. "I suppose Darla was disappointed."

Michael watched the way the stones caught the thin winter light and made sparks from it. "She'll pull through."

Pandora twisted the chain one way, twisted it back, then let it go. It was the sort of nervous gesture Michael hadn't expected from her. "Michael, you know you don't have to stay. I really will be fine if you want to run into New York for the holiday."

"Rule number six," he reminded her. "We stick together,

and you've turned down a half-dozen invitations for the holidays yourself."

"My choice." She reached for the chain again, then dropped her hands. "I don't want you to feel obligated—"

"My choice," he interrupted. "Or have you suddenly decided I'm chivalrous and unselfish?"

"Certainly not," she tossed back, but smiled. "I prefer thinking you're just too lazy to make the trip."

He shook his head, but his lips curved in response. "I'm sure you would."

She hesitated in the doorway until he lifted a brow in question. "Michael, would you become totally obnoxious if I told you I'm glad you're staying?"

He studied her as she stood, looking slim and neat in the doorway, her hair a riotous contrast to the trim sweater and stovepipe pants. "I might."

"Then I won't tell you." Without another word, she slipped out of the doorway and disappeared.

Contrary woman, Michael thought. He was close to being crazy about her. And crazy was the perfect word. She baited him or, he admitted, he baited her at every possible opportunity. He could imagine no two people less inclined to peaceful coexistence, much less harmony. And yet…and yet he was close to being crazy about her. Knowing better than to try to go back to work, he rose and followed her downstairs.

He found her in the parlor, rearranging packages under the tree. "How many have you shaken?"

"All of them," she said easily. But she didn't turn because he might have seen how pleased she was he'd come downstairs with her. "I don't want to show any preference. Thing is," she added, poking at an elegantly wrapped box, "I seem to have missed my present from you."

Michael gave her a bland smile. "Who says I got you anything?"

"You would have been terribly rude and insensitive otherwise."

"Yep. In any case, you seem to've done well enough." He crouched down to study the stacks of boxes under the tree. "Who's Boris?" Idly he picked up a small silver box with flowing white ribbon.

"A Russian cellist who defected. He admires my…gold links."

"I bet. And Roger?"

"Roger Madison."

His mouth dropped open, but only for a moment. "The Yankee shortstop who batted .304 last year?"

"That's right. You may've noticed the silver band he wears on his right wrist. I made that for him last March. He seems to think it straightened out his bat or something." She lifted the blue-and-gold box and shook it gently. "He tends to be very generous."

"I see." Michael took a comprehensive study of the boxes. "There don't seem to be a great many packages here for you from women."

"Really?" Pandora took a scan herself. "It appears you make up for that with your pile. Chi-Chi?" she asked as she picked up a box with a big pink bow.

"She's a marine biologist," Michael said with his tongue in his cheek.

"Fascinating. And I imagine Magda's a librarian."

"Corporate attorney," he said blandly.

"Hmm. Well, whoever sent this one's obviously shy." She picked up a magnum of champagne with a glittering red ribbon. The tag read "Happy Holidays, Michael," and nothing more.

Michael scanned the label with approval. "Some people don't want to advertise their generosity."

"How about you?" She tilted her head. "After all, it is a magnum. Are you going to share?"

"With whom?"

"I should've known you'd be greedy." She picked up a box with her name on it. "Just for that I'm eating this entire box of imported chocolates myself."

Michael eyed the box. "How do you know they're chocolates?"

She only smiled. "Henri always gives me chocolate."

"Imported?"

"Swiss."

Michael put out a hand. "Share and share alike."

Pandora accepted it. "I'll chill the wine."

Hours later when there was starlight on the snow and a fire in the hearth, Pandora lit the tree. Like Michael, she didn't miss any of the crowded, frenzied parties in the city. She was where she wanted to be. It had taken Pandora only a matter of weeks to discover she wasn't as attached to the rush of the city as she'd once thought. The Folley was home. Hadn't it always been? No, she no longer thought of going back to Manhattan in the spring. But what would it be like to live in the Folley alone?

Michael wouldn't stay. True, he'd own half of the Folley in a few months, but his life—including his active social life—was in the city. He wouldn't stay, she thought again, and found herself annoyed with her own sense of regret. Why should he stay? she asked herself as she wandered over to poke at the already crackling fire. How could he stay? They couldn't go on living together indefinitely. Sooner or later she'd have to approach him about her decision to remain there. To do so, she'd have to explain herself. It wouldn't be easy.

Still, she was grateful to Jolley for doing something she'd once resented. Boxing her in. She may have been forced into dealing with Michael on a day-to-day level, but in the few months she'd done so, her life had had more energy and interest than in the many months before. It was that, Pandora told herself, that she hated to give up.

She'd dealt with her attraction to him semisuccessfully. The fact was, he was no more her type than she was his. She jammed hard at a log. From all the many reports, Michael preferred a more flamboyant, exotic sort of woman. Actresses, dancers, models. And he preferred them in droves. She, on the other hand, looked for more intellectual men. The men she spent time with could discuss obscure French novelists and appreciate small, esoteric plays. Most of them wouldn't have known if *Logan's Run* was a television show or a restaurant in SoHo.

The fact that she had a sort of primitive desire for Michael was only a tempest in a teapot. Pandora smiled as she replaced the poker. She couldn't deny she enjoyed a tempest now and again.

When a small one erupted behind her, Pandora turned in disbelief. A little white dog with oversize feet scrambled into the room, slid on the Aubusson carpet and rammed smartly into a table. Barking madly, it rolled over twice, righted itself, then dashed at Pandora to leap halfheartedly and loll its tongue. Entertained, Pandora crouched down and was rewarded when the puppy sprang onto her lap and licked her face.

"Where'd you come from?" Laughing, and defending herself as best she could, Pandora found the card attached to the red bow around the puppy's neck. It read:

> My name is Bruno. I'm a mean, ugly dog looking for a lady to defend.

"Bruno, huh?" Laughing again, Pandora stroked his unfortunately long ears. "How mean are you?" she asked as he contented himself with licking her chin.

"He especially likes to attack discontented relatives," Michael announced as he wheeled in a tray carrying an ice bucket and champagne. "He's been trained to go after anyone wearing a Brooks Brothers suit."

"We might add Italian loafers."

"That's next."

Moved, incredibly moved, she concentrated on the puppy. She hadn't the least idea how to thank Michael without making a fool of herself. "He isn't really ugly," she murmured.

"They promised me he would be."

"They?" She buried her face in the puppy's fur a moment. "Where did you get him?"

"Pound." Watching her, Michael ripped the foil from the champagne. "When we went into town for supplies last week and I deserted you in the supermarket."

"And I thought you'd gone off somewhere to buy pornographic magazines."

"My reputation precedes me," he said half to himself. "In any case, I went to the pound and walked through the kennels. Bruno bit another dog on the—on a sensitive area in order to get to the bars first. Then he grinned at me with absolutely no dignity. I knew he was the one."

The cork came out with a bang and champagne sprayed up and dripped onto the floor. Bruno scrambled out of Pandora's lap and greedily licked it up. "Perhaps his manners are lacking a bit," Pandora observed. "But his taste is first class." She rose, but waited until Michael had poured two glasses. "It was a lovely thing to do, dammit."

He grinned and handed her a glass. "You're welcome."

"It's easier for me when you're rude and intolerable."

"I do the best I can." He touched his glass to hers.

"When you're sweet, it's harder for me to stop myself from doing something foolish."

He started to lift his glass, then stopped. "Such as?"

"Such as." Pandora set down her champagne, then took Michael's and set it on the table as well. Watching him, only him, she put her arms around his neck. Very slowly—unwise acts done slowly often take on a wisdom of their own—she touched her mouth to his.

It was, as she'd known it would be, warm and waiting. His hands came to her shoulders, holding her without pressure. Perhaps they'd both come to understand that pressure would never hold her. When she softened, when she gave, she gave through her own volition, not through seduction, not through demand. So it was Pandora who moved closer, Pandora who pressed body to body, offering hints of intimacy with no submission.

It wasn't submission he wanted. It wasn't submission he looked for, though it was often given to him. He didn't look for matching strength, but strength that meshed. In Pandora, where he'd never thought to search for it, he found it. Her scent twisted around him, heightening emotions her taste had just begun to stir. Under his hands, her body was firm with the underlying softness women could exploit or be exploited by. He thought she'd do neither, but would simply be. By being alone, she drew him in.

She didn't resist his touch, not when his hands slipped down to her hips or skimmed up again. It seemed he'd done so before, though only in dreams she'd refused to acknowledge. If this was the time for acceptance, she'd accept. If this was the time for pleasure, she'd take it. If she found both with him, she wouldn't refuse. Even questions could come later. Maybe tonight was a night without questions.

She drew back, but only to smile at him. "You know, I don't think of you as a cousin when I'm kissing you."

"Really?" He nipped at her lips. She had an incredibly alluring mouth—full and pouty. "What do you think of me as?"

She cocked a brow. His arms surrounded her, but didn't imprison. Pandora knew she'd have to analyze the difference later. "I haven't figured that out yet."

"Then maybe we should keep working it out." He started to pull her back, but she resisted.

"Since you've broken tradition to give me my Christmas present a few hours early, I'll do the same." Going to the tree, Pandora reached down and found the square, flat box. "Happy Christmas, Michael."

He sat down on the arm of a chair to open it while Pandora picked up her glass of champagne. She sipped, watching a bit nervously for his reaction. It was only a token after all, she told herself, as she played with the stem of her glass. When he ripped off the paper then said nothing, she shrugged. "It's not as inventive as a guard dog."

Michael stared down at the pencil sketch of their uncle without any idea what to say. The frame she'd made herself, he knew. It was silver and busily ornate in a style Jolley would have appreciated. But it was the sketch that held him silent. She'd drawn Jolley as Michael remembered him best, standing, a bit bent forward from the waist as though he were ready to pop off on a new tangent. What thin hair he'd had left was mussed. His cheeks were stretched out in a big, wide-open grin. It had been drawn with love, talent and humor, three qualities Jolley had possessed and admired. When Michael looked up, Pandora was still twisting the stem of the glass in her hands.

Why she's nervous, he realized. He'd never expected her to be anything but arrogantly confident about her work. About herself. The secrets he was uncovering were just as unnerving to him as they were to her. A man tended to get pulled into a woman who had soft spots in unexpected places. If he was pulled in, how would he work his way out again? But she was waiting, twisting the stem of her glass in her hand.

"Pandora. No one's ever given me anything that's meant more."

The line between her brows smoothed out as her smile bloomed. The ridiculous sense of pleasure was difficult to mask. "Really?"

He held a hand out to her. "Really." He glanced down at the sketch again and smiled. "It looks just like him."

"It looks like I remember him." She let her fingers link with Michael's. Pandora could tell herself it was Jolley who drew them together, and nothing else. She could nearly believe it. "I thought you might remember him that way, too. The frame's a bit gaudy."

"And suitable." He studied it with more care. The silver shone dully, set off with the deep curls and lines she'd etched. It could, he realized, be put in an antique shop and pass for an heirloom. "I didn't know you did this sort of thing."

"Now and again. The boutique carries a few of them."

"Doesn't fit in the same category as bangles and beads," he mused.

"Doesn't it?" Her chin tilted. "I thought about making you a big gold collar with rhinestones just to annoy you."

"It would have."

"Maybe next year then. Or perhaps I'll make one for Bruno." She glanced around. "Where'd he go?"

"He's probably behind the tree gnawing on presents. During his brief stay in the garage, he ate a pair of golf shoes."

"We'll put a stop to that," Pandora declared, and went to find him.

"You know, Pandora, I'd no idea you could draw like this." Michael settled against the back of the chair to study the sketch again. "Why aren't you painting?"

"Why aren't you writing the Great American Novel?"

"Because I enjoy what I'm doing."

"Exactly." Finding no sign of the puppy around the tree, Pandora began to search under the furniture. "Though certainly a number of painters have toyed with jewelry design successfully enough—Dali for one—I feel...Michael!"

He set his untouched champagne back down and hurried over to where she knelt by a divan. "What is it?" he demanded, then saw for himself. Eyes closed, breathing fast and heavy, the puppy lay half under the divan. Even as Pandora reached for him, Bruno whimpered and struggled to stand.

"Oh, Michael, he's sick. We should get him to a vet."

"It'll be midnight before we get to town. We won't find a vet at midnight on Christmas Eve." Gently Michael laid a hand on Bruno's belly and heard him moan. "Maybe I can get someone on the phone."

"Do you think it's something he ate?"

"Sweeney's been supervising his feeding like a new mother."

On cue Bruno struggled and shuddered and relieved himself of what offended his stomach. Exhausted from the effort, he lay back and dozed fitfully. "Something he drank," Michael murmured.

Pampering and soothing, Pandora stroked the dog. "That little bit of champagne shouldn't have made him ill." Because the dog was already resting easier, she relaxed a bit. "Charles isn't going to be pleased Bruno cast up his accounts on the carpet. Maybe I should—" She broke off as Michael grabbed her arm.

"How much champagne did you drink?"

"Only a sip. Why—" She broke off again to stare. "The champagne. You think something's wrong with it?"

"I think I'm an idiot for not suspecting an anonymous present." He grabbed her by the chin. "Only a sip. You're sure? How do you feel?"

Her skin had gone cold, but she answered calmly enough. "I'm fine. Look at my glass, it's still full." She turned her head to look at it herself. "You—you think it was poisoned?"

"We'll find out."

Logic seeped through, making her shake her head. "But, Michael, the wine was corked. How could it have been tampered with?"

"The first season on *Logan* I used a device like this." He thought back, remembering how he'd tested the theory by adding food coloring to a bottle of Dom Perignon. "The killer poisoned champagne by shooting cyanide through the cork with a hypodermic."

"Fiction," Pandora claimed, and fought a shiver. "That's just fiction."

"Until we find out differently, we're going to treat it as fact. The rest of the bottle's going into New York to Sanfield Labs for testing."

Shaky, Pandora swallowed. "For testing," she said on an unsteady breath. "All right, I suppose we'll both be easier when we're sure. Do you know someone who works there?"

"We own Sanfield." He looked down at the sleeping puppy. "Or we will own it in a matter of months. That's just one of the reasons someone might've sent us some doctored champagne."

"Michael, if it was poisoned..." She tried to imagine it and found it nearly impossible. "If it was poisoned," she repeated, "this wouldn't just be a game anymore."

He thought of what might have happened if they hadn't been distracted from the wine. "No, it wouldn't be a game."

"It doesn't make any sense." Uneasy and fighting to calm herself, Pandora rose. "Vandalism I can see, petty annoyances I can understand, but I just can't attribute something like this to one of the family. We're probably overreacting. Bruno's had too much excitement. He could very well have picked up something in the pound."

"I had him sent to the vet for his shots before he was delivered here yesterday." Michael's voice was calm, but his eyes were hot. "He was healthy, Pandora, until he lapped up some spilled champagne."

One look at him told her rationalizing was useless. "All right. The wine should be tested in any case so we can stop speculating. We can't do anything about it until day after tomorrow. In the meantime, I don't want to dwell on it."

"Pulling the blinds down, Pandora?"

"No." She picked up Bruno, who whimpered and burrowed into her breast. "But until it's proven, I don't want to consider that a member of my family tried to kill me. I'll fix him something warm to drink, then I'm going to take him upstairs. I'll keep an eye on him tonight."

"All right." Fighting a combination of frustration and fury, Michael stood by the fire.

Long after midnight when he couldn't sleep, couldn't work, Michael looked in on her. She'd left a light burning low across the room so that the white spreads and covers took on a rosy hue. Outside snow was falling again in big, festive flakes. Michael could see her, curled in the wide bed, the blankets up to her chin. The fire was nearly out. On the rug in front of it, the puppy snored. She'd put a mohair throw over him and had set a shallow bowl filled with what looked like tea nearby. Michael crouched beside the dog.

"Poor fella," he murmured. As he stroked, Bruno stirred, whimpered, then settled again.

"I think he's better."

Glancing over, Michael saw the light reflected in Pandora's eyes. Her hair was tousled, her skin pale and soft. Her shoulders, gently sloped, rose just above the covers pooled around her. She looked beautiful, desirable, arousing. He told himself he was mad. Pandora didn't fit into his carefully detailed notion of beauty. Michael looked back at the dog.

"Just needs to sleep it off. You could use another log on this fire." Needing to keep busy, Michael dug in the woodbox, then added a log to the coals.

"Thanks. Can't sleep?"

"No."

"Me, either." They sat in silence a moment, Pandora in the big bed, Michael on the hearth rug. The fire crackled greedily at the fresh log and flickered light and shadow. At length, she drew her knees up to her chest. "Michael, I'm frightened."

It wasn't an easy admission. He knew it cost her to tell him. He stirred at the fire a moment, then spoke lightly as he replaced the screen. "We can leave. We can drive into New York tomorrow and stay there. Forget this whole business and enjoy the holidays."

She didn't speak for a minute, but she watched him carefully. His face was turned away toward the fire so that she had to judge his feelings by the way he held himself. "Is that what you want to do?"

He thought of Jolley, then he thought of Pandora. Every muscle in his body tightened. "Sure." He tossed it off like a shrug. "I've got to think about myself." He said it as if to remind himself it had once been true.

"For someone who earns his living by making up stories, you're a lousy liar." She waited until he turned to face her. "You don't want to go back. What you want is to gather all our relatives together and beat them up."

"Can you see me pounding Aunt Patience?"

"With a few exceptions," Pandora temporized. "But the last thing you want is to give up."

"All right, that's me." He rose and, hands in pockets, paced back and forth in front of the fire. He could smell the wood-smoke mixed with some light scent from one of the bottles on Pandora's dresser. "What about you? You didn't want to hassle with this whole business from the beginning. I talked you into it. I feel responsible."

For the first time in hours she felt her humor return. "I hate to dent your ego, Michael, but you didn't talk me into anything. No one does. And I'm completely responsible for myself. I don't want to quit," she added before he could speak. "I said I didn't want the money, and that was true. I also said I didn't need it, and that's not precisely true. Over and above that, there's pride. I'm frightened, yes, but I don't want to quit. Oh, stop pacing around and come sit down." The order was cross and impatient, nearly making him smile. He came over and sat on the bed.

"Better?"

She gave him a long, steady look that had the hint of a smile fading. "Yes. Michael, I've been lying here for hours thinking this thing through. I've realized a few things. You called me a snob once, and perhaps you were right in a way. I've never thought much about money. Never allowed myself to. When Uncle Jolley cut everyone out, I thought of it as a cross between a joke and a slap on the wrist. I figured they'd grumble and complain certainly, but that was all." She lifted her hand palm up. "It was only money, and every one of them has their own."

"Ever heard of greed or the lust for power?"

"That's just it, I didn't think. How much do I know about any of those people? They bore or annoy me from time to time, but I've never thought about them as individuals." Now she ran the hand through her hair so that the blankets fell to her waist. "Ginger must be about the same age as I am, and I can't think of two things we have in common. I'd probably pass Biff's wife on the street without recognizing her."

"I have a hard time remembering her name," Michael put in, and earned a sigh from Pandora.

"That's my point. We don't really know them. The family, in a group, is a kind of parlor joke. Separately, who are they and what are they capable of? I've just begun to consider it. It's not a joke, Michael."

"No, it's not."

"I want to fight back, but I don't know how."

"The surest way is by staying. And maybe," he added, and took her hand. It was cool and soft. "Add a little psychological warfare."

"Such as?"

"What if we sent each one of our relatives a nice bottle of champagne?"

Her smile came slowly. "A magnum."

"Naturally. It'd be interesting to see what sort of reaction we get."

"It would be a nasty gesture, wouldn't it?"

"Uh-hmm."

"Maybe I haven't given your creative brain enough credit." She fell silent as he wound her hair around his finger. "I suppose we should get some sleep."

"I suppose." But his fingers skimmed down her shoulders.

"I'm not very tired."

"We could play canasta."

"We could." But she made no move to stop him when he nudged the thin straps of her chemise from her shoulders. "There's always cribbage."

"That, too."

"Or…" It was her decision, they both understood that. "We might finish playing out the hand we started downstairs earlier."

He lifted her hand and pressed his lips to the palm. "Always best to finish what you start before going on. As I recall, we were…here." He lowered his mouth to hers. Slowly, on a sigh, she wound her arms around his neck.

"That seems about right."

Holding fast, they sunk into the bed together.

Perhaps it was because they knew each other well. Perhaps it was because they'd already waited a lifetime, but each moved slowly. Desire, for the moment, was comfortable, easy to satisfy with a touch, a taste. Passion curled inside him then unwound with a sigh. There was inch after inch of her to explore with his fingertips, with his lips. He'd waited too long, wanted too long, to miss any part of what they could give to each other.

She was more generous than he'd imagined, less inhibited, more open. She didn't ask to be coaxed, she didn't pretend to need persuasion. She ran her hands over him with equal curiosity. Her mouth took from him and gave again. When his lips parted from hers, her eyes were on him, clouded with desire, dark with amusement of a shared joke. They were together,

Michael thought as he buried his face in her hair. About to become lovers. The joke was on both of them.

Her hands were steady when she pulled his sweatshirt over his head, steady still as she ran them over his chest. Her pulse wasn't. She'd avoided this, refused this. Now she was accepting it though she knew there would be consequences she couldn't anticipate.

The fire crackled steadily. The soft light glowed. Consequences were for more practical times.

Her skin slid over his with each movement. Each movement enticed. With his heartbeat beginning to hammer in his head, he journeyed lower. With openmouthed kisses he learned her body in a way he'd only been able to imagine. Her scent was everywhere, subtle at the curve of her waist, stronger at the gentle underside of her breasts. He drew it in and let it swim in his head.

He felt the instant her lazy enjoyment darkened with power. When her breath caught on a moan, he took her deeper. They reached a point where he no longer knew what they did to each other, only that strength met need and need became desperation.

His skin was damp. She tasted the moistness of it and craved more. So this was passion. This was the trembling, churning hunger men and women longed for. She'd never wanted it. That's what she told herself as her body shuddered. Pleasure and pain mixed, needs and fears tangled. Her mind was as swamped with sensations as her flesh—heat and light, ecstasy and terror. The vulnerability overwhelmed her though her body arched taut and her hands clung. No one had ever brushed back her defenses so effortlessly and taken. Taken and taken.

Breathless and desperate, she dragged his mouth back to hers. They rolled over the bed, rough, racing. Neither had had enough. While she tugged and pulled at his jeans, Michael drove her higher. He'd wanted the madness, for himself and for her. Now he felt the wild strength pouring out of her. No thought here, no logic. He rolled on top of her again, reveling in her frantic breathing.

She curled around him, legs and arms. When he plunged into her, they watched the astonishment on each other's faces. Not like this—it had never been like this. They'd come home. But home, each discovered, wasn't always a peaceful place.

There was silence, stunned, awkward silence. They lay tangled in the covers as the log Michael had set to fire broke apart and showered sparks against the screen. They knew each other well, too well to speak of what had happened just yet. So they lay in silence as their skin cooled and their pulses leveled. Michael shifted to pull the spread up over them both.

"Merry Christmas," he murmured.

With a sound that was both sigh and laugh, Pandora settled beside him.

Chapter Eight

They left the Folley in the hard morning light the day after Christmas. Sun glared off snow, melting it at the edges and forming icicles down branches and eaves. It was a postcard with biting wind.

After a short tussle they'd agreed that Pandora would drive into the city and Michael would drive back. He pushed his seat back to the limit and managed to stretch out his legs. She maneuvered carefully down the slushy mountain road that led from the Folley. They didn't speak until she'd reached clear highway.

"What if they don't let us in?"

"Why shouldn't they?" Preferring driving to sitting, Michael shifted in his seat. For the first time he was impatient with the miles of road between the Folley and New York.

"Isn't that like counting your chickens?" Pandora turned the heat down a notch and loosened the buttons of her coat. "We don't own the place yet."

"Just a technicality."

"Always cocky."

"You always look at the negative angles."

"Someone has to."

"Look..." He started to toss back something critical, then noticed how tightly she gripped the wheel. All nerves, he mused. Though the scenery was a print by Currier and Ives, it wasn't entirely possible to pretend they were off on a holiday jaunt. He was running on nerves himself, and they didn't all have to do with doctored champagne. How would he have guessed he'd wake up beside her in the cool light of dawn and feel so involved? So responsible. So hungry.

He took a deep breath and watched the scenery for another moment. "Look," he began again in a lighter tone. "We may not own the lab or anything else at the moment, but we're still Jolley's family. Why should a lab technician refuse to do a little analysis?"

"I suppose we'll find out when we get there." She drove another ten miles in silence. "Michael, what difference is an analysis going to make?"

"I have this odd sort of curiosity. I like to know if someone's tried to poison me."

"So we'll know if, and we'll know why. We still won't know who."

"That's the next step." He glanced over. "We can invite them all to Folley for New Year's and take turns grilling them."

"Now you're making fun of me."

"No, actually, I'd thought of it. I just figure the time's not quite right." He waited a few minutes. In thin leather gloves, her fingers curled and uncurled on the wheel. "Pandora, why don't you tell me what's really bothering you?"

"Nothing is." Everything was. She hadn't been able to think straight for twenty-four hours.

"Nothing?"

"Nothing other than wondering if someone wants to kill me." She tossed it off arrogantly. "Isn't that enough?"

He heard the edge under the sarcasm. "Is that why you hid in your room all day yesterday."

"I wasn't hiding." She had enough pride to sound brittle. "I was tending to Bruno. And I was tired."

"You hardly ate any of that enormous goose Sweeney slaved over."

"I'm not terribly fond of goose."

"I've had Christmas dinner with you before," he corrected. "You eat like a horse."

"How gallant of you to point it out." For no particular reason, she switched lanes, pumped the gas and passed another car. "Let's just say I wasn't in the mood."

"How did you manage to talk yourself into disliking what happened between us so quickly?" It hurt. He felt the hurt, but it didn't mean he had to let it show. His voice, as hers had been, was cool and hard.

"I haven't. That's absurd." Dislike? She hadn't been able to think of anything else, feel anything else. It scared her to death. "We slept together." She managed to toss it off with a shrug. "I suppose we both knew we would sooner or later."

He'd told himself precisely the same thing. He'd lost count of the number of times. He'd yet to figure out when he'd stopped believing. For himself. "And that's it?"

The question was deadly calm, but she was too preoccupied with her own nerves to notice. "What else?" She had to stop dwelling on a moment of impulse. Didn't she? She couldn't go on letting her common sense be overrun by an attraction that would lead nowhere. Could she? "Michael, there's no use blowing what happened out of proportion."

"Just what is that proportion?"

The car felt stuffy and close. Pandora switched off the heat and concentrated on the road. "We're two adults," she began, but had to swallow twice.

"And?"

"Dammit, Michael, I don't have to spell it out."

"Yes, you do."

"We're two adults," she said again, but with temper replacing nerves. "We have normal adult needs. We slept together and satisfied them."

"How practical."

"I am practical." Abruptly, and very badly, she wanted to weep. "Much too practical to weave fantasies about a man who likes his women in six packs. Too practical," she went on, voice rising, "to picture myself emotionally involved with a man I spent one night with. And too practical to romanticize what was no more than an exchange of normal and basic lust."

"Pull over."

"I will not."

"Pull over to the shoulder, Pandora, or I'll do it for you."

She gritted her teeth and debated calling his bluff. There was just enough traffic on the road to force her hand. With only a slight squeal of tires, Pandora pulled off to the side of the road. Michael turned off the key then grabbed her by the lapels and pulled her half into his seat. Before she could struggle away, he closed his mouth over hers.

Heat, anger, passion. They seemed to twist together into one emotion. He held her there as cars whizzed by, shaking the windows. She infuriated him, she aroused him, she hurt him. In Michael's opinion, it was too much for one man to take from one woman. As abruptly as he'd grabbed her, he released her.

"Make something practical out of that," he challenged.

Breathless, Pandora struggled back into her own seat. In a furious gesture, she turned the key, gunning the motor. "Idiot."

"Yeah." He sat back as she pulled back onto the highway. "We finally agree on something."

It was a long ride into the city. Longer still when you sat in a car in tense silence. Once they entered Manhattan, Pandora was forced to follow Michael's directions to the lab.

"How do you know where it is?" she demanded after they left the car in a parking garage. The sidewalk was mobbed with people hurrying to exchange what had been brightly boxed and wrapped the day before. As they walked, Pandora held her coat closed against the wind.

"I looked the address up in Jolley's files yesterday." Michael walked the half block hatless, his coat flapping open, clutching the box with the champagne under one arm. He wasn't immune to the cold but found it a relief after the hot tension of the drive.

With a brisk gesture to Pandora, he pushed through revolving doors and entered the lobby of a steel-and-glass building. “He owned the whole place.”

Pandora looked across the marble floor. It sloped upward and widened into a crowded, bustling area with men and women carrying briefcases. “This whole place?”

“All seventy-two floors.”

It hit her again just how complicated the estate was. How many companies operated in the building? How many people worked there? How could she possibly crowd her life with this kind of responsibility? If she could get her hands on Uncle Jolley—Pandora broke off, almost amused. How he must be enjoying this, she thought.

“What am I supposed to do with seventy-two floors in midtown?”

“There are plenty of people to do it for you.” Michael gave their names to the guard at the elevators. With no delay, they were riding to the fortieth floor.

“So there are people to do it for us. Who keeps track of them?”

“Accountants, lawyers, managers. It’s a matter of hiring people to look after people you hire.”

“That certainly clears that up.”

“If you’re worried, think about Jolley. Having a fortune didn’t seem to keep him from enjoying himself. For the most part, he looked at the whole business as a kind of hobby.”

Pandora watched the numbers above the door. “A hobby.”

“Everyone should have a hobby.”

“Tennis is a hobby,” she muttered.

"The trick is to keep the ball moving. Jolley tossed it in our court, Pandora."

She folded her arms. "I'm not ready to be grateful for that."

"Look at it this way then." He put a hand on her shoulder and squeezed lightly. "You don't have to know how to build a car to own one. You just have to drive steady and follow the signs. If Jolley didn't think we could follow the signs, he wouldn't have given us the keys."

It helped to look at it that way. Still it was odd to consider she was riding on an elevator she would own when the six months were up. "Do we know whom to go to?" Pandora glanced at the box Michael held, which contained the bottle of champagne.

"A man named Silas Lockworth seems to be in charge."

"You did your homework."

"Let's hope it pays off."

When the elevator stopped, they walked into the reception area for Sanfield Laboratories. The carpet was pale rose, the walls lacquered in cream. Two huge split-leaf philodendrons flanked the wide glass doors that slid open at their approach. A woman behind a gleaming desk folded her hands and smiled.

"Good morning. May I help you?"

Michael glanced at the computer terminal resting on an extension of her desk. Top of the line. "We'd like to see Mr. Lockworth."

"Mr. Lockworth's in a meeting. If I could have your names, perhaps his assistant can help you."

"I'm Michael Donahue. This is Pandora McVie."

"McVie?"

Pandora saw the receptionist's eyebrows raise. "Yes, Maximillian McVie was our uncle."

Already polite and efficient, the receptionist became gracious. "I'm sure Mr. Lockworth would have greeted you himself if we'd known you were coming. Please have a seat. I'll ring through."

It took under five minutes.

The man who strode out into reception didn't look like Pandora's conception of a technician or scientist. He was six-three, lean as a gymnast with blond hair brushed back from a tanned, lantern-jawed face. He looked, Pandora thought, more like a man who'd be at home on the range than in a lab with test tubes.

"Ms. McVie." He walked with an easy rolling gait, hand outstretched. "Mr. Donahue. I'm Silas Lockworth. Your uncle was a good friend."

"Thank you." Michael accepted the handshake. "I apologize for dropping in unannounced."

"No need for that." Lockworth's smile seemed to mean it. "We never knew when Jolley was going to drop in on us. Let's go back to my office."

He led them down the corridor. Lockworth's office was the next surprise. It was plush enough, with curvy chairs and clever lithographs, to make you think of a corporate executive. The desk was piled high with enough files and papers to make you think of a harried clerk. It carried the scent from the dozens of leather-bound books on a floor-to-ceiling shelf. Built into one wall was a round aquarium teeming with exotic fish.

"Would you like coffee? I can guarantee it's hot and strong."

"No." Pandora was already twisting her gloves in her hands. "Thank you. We don't want to take too much of your time."

"It's my pleasure," Lockworth assured her. "Jolley certainly spoke often of both of you," Lockworth went on as he gestured to chairs. "There was never a doubt you were his favorites."

"And he was ours," Pandora returned.

"Still you didn't come to pass the time." Lockworth leaned back on his desk. "What can I do for you?"

"We have something we'd like analyzed," Michael began. "Quickly and quietly."

"I see." Silas stopped there, brow raised. Lockworth was a man who picked up impressions of people right away. In Pandora he saw nerves under a sheen of politeness. In Michael he saw violence, not so much buried as thinly coated. He thought he detected a bond between them though they hadn't so much as looked at each other since entering the room.

Lockworth could have refused. His staff was slimmed down during the holidays, and work was backlogged. He was under no obligation to either of them yet. But he never forgot his obligation to Jolley McVie. "We'll try to accommodate you."

In silence, Michael opened the box and drew out the bottle of champagne. "We need a report on the contents of this bottle. A confidential report. Today."

Lockworth took it and examined the label. His lips curved slightly. "Seventy-two. A good year. Were you thinking of starting a vineyard?"

"We need to know what's in there other than champagne."

Rather than showing surprise, Lockworth leaned back on the desk again. "You've reason to think there is?"

Michael met the look. "We wouldn't be here otherwise."

Lockworth only inclined his head. "All right. I'll run it through the lab myself."

With a quick scowl for Michael's manners, Pandora rose and offered her hand. "We appreciate the trouble, Mr. Lockworth. I'm sure you have a great many other things to do, but the results are important to Michael and me."

"No problem." He decided he'd find out why it was important after he'd analyzed the wine. "There's a coffee shop for the staff. I'll show you where it is. You can wait for me there."

"There was absolutely no reason to be rude." Pandora settled herself at a table and looked at a surprisingly varied menu.

"I wasn't rude."

"Of course you were. Mr. Lockworth was going out of his way to be friendly, and you had a chip on your shoulder. I think I'm going to have the shrimp salad."

"I don't have a chip on my shoulder. I was being cautious. Or maybe you think we should spill everything to a total stranger."

Pandora folded her hands and smiled at the waitress. "I'd like the shrimp salad and coffee."

"Two coffees," Michael muttered. "And the turkey platter."

"I've no intention of spilling, as you put it, everything to a total stranger." Pandora picked up her napkin. "However, if we weren't going to trust Lockworth, we'd have been better off to buy a chemistry set and try to handle it ourselves."

"Drink your coffee," Michael muttered, and picked up his own the moment the waitress served it.

Pandora frowned as she added cream. "How long do you think it'll take?"

"I don't know. I'm not a scientist."

"He didn't look like one, either, did he?"

"Bronc rider." Michael sipped his black coffee and found it as strong as Lockworth had promised.

"What?"

"Looks like a bronc rider. I wonder if Carlson or any of the others have any interest in this building."

Pandora set her coffee down before she tasted it. "I hadn't thought of that."

"As I remember, Jolley turned over Tristar Corporation to Monroe about twenty-five years ago. I remember my parents talking about it."

"Tristar. Which one is that?"

"Plastics. I know he gave little pieces of the pie out here and there. He told me once he wanted to give all his relatives a chance before he crossed them off the list."

After a moment's thought, she shrugged and picked up her coffee again. "Well, if he did give a few shares of Sanfield to one of them, what difference does it make?"

"I don't know how much we should trust Lockworth."

"You'd have felt better if he'd been bald and short with Coke-bottle glasses and a faint German accent."

"Maybe."

"See?" Pandora smiled. "You're just jealous because he has great shoulders." She fluttered her lashes. "Here's your turkey."

They ate slowly, drank more coffee, then passed more time with pie. After an hour and a half, both of them were restless and edgy. When Lockworth came in, Pandora forgot to be nervous about the results.

"Thank God, here he comes."

After maneuvering around chairs and employees on lunch break, Lockworth set a computer printout on the table and handed the box back to Michael. "I thought you'd want a copy." He took a seat and signaled for coffee. "Though it's technical."

Pandora frowned down at the long, chemical terms printed out on the paper. It meant little more than nothing to her, but she doubted trichloroethanol or any of the other multisyllabic words belonged in French champagne. "What does it mean?"

"I wondered that myself." Lockworth reached in his pocket and drew out a pack of cigarettes. Michael looked at it for a moment with longing. "I wondered why anyone would put rose dust in vintage champagne."

"Rose dust?" Michael repeated. "Pesticide. So it was poisoned."

"Technically, yes. Though there wasn't enough in the wine to do any more than make you miserably ill for a day or two. I take it neither one of you had any?"

"No." Pandora looked up from the report. "My puppy did," she explained. "When we opened the bottle, some spilled and he lapped it up. Before we'd gotten around to drinking it, he was ill."

"Luckily for you, though I find it curious that you'd jumped to the conclusion that the champagne had been poisoned because a puppy was sick."

"Luckily for us, we did." Michael folded the report and slipped it into his pocket.

"You'll have to pardon my cousin," Pandora said. "He has no manners. We appreciate you taking time out to do this for us, Mr. Lockworth. I'm afraid it isn't possible to fully explain ourselves at this point, but I can tell you that we had good reason to suspect the wine."

Lockworth nodded. As a scientist he knew how to theorize. "If you find you need a more comprehensive report, let me know. Jolley was an important person in my life. We'll call it a favor to him."

As he rose, Michael stood with him. "I'll apologize for myself this time." He held out a hand.

"I'd be a bit edgy myself if someone gave me pesticide disguised as Moët et Chandon. Let me know if I can do anything else."

"Well," Pandora began when they were alone. "What next?"

"A little trip to the liquor store. We've some presents to buy."

They sent, first-class, a bottle of the same to each of Jolley's erstwhile heirs. Michael signed the cards simply, "One good turn deserves another." After it was done and they walked outside in the frigid wind, Pandora huffed and pulled on her gloves.

"An expensive gesture."

"Look at it as an investment," Michael suggested.

It wasn't the money, she thought, but the sudden futility she felt. "What good will it do really?"

"Several bottles'll be wondered over, then appreciated. But one," Michael said with relish. "One makes a statement, even a threat."

"An empty threat," Pandora returned. "It's not as if we'll be there when everyone gets one to gauge reactions."

"You're thinking like an amateur."

Michael was halfway across the street when Pandora grabbed his arm. "Just what does that mean?"

"When an amateur plays a practical joke, he thinks he has to be in on the kill."

Ignoring the people who brushed by them, Pandora held her ground. "Since when is pesticide poisoning a practical joke?"

"Revenge follows the same principle."

"Oh, I see. And you're an expert."

The light changed. Cars started for them, horns blaring. Gritting his teeth, Michael grabbed her arm and pulled her to the curb. "Maybe I am. It's enough for me to know someone's going to look at the bottle and be very nervous. Someone's going to look at it and know we intend to give as good as we get. Your trouble is you don't like to let your emotions loose long enough to appreciate revenge."

"Leave my emotions alone."

"That's the plan," he said evenly, and started walking again.

In three strides she'd caught up with him. Her face was pink from the wind, the anger in her voice came out in thin wisps.

"You're not annoyed with Lockworth or about the champagne or over differing views on revenge. You're mad because I defined our relationship in practical terms."

He stared at her as her phrasing worked on both his temper and his humor. "Okay," he declared, turning to walk on. Patience straining, he turned back when Pandora grabbed his arm. "You want to hash this out right here?"

"I won't let you make me feel inadequate just because I broke things off before you had a chance to."

"Before I had a chance to?" He took her by the coat. With the added height from the heels on her boots, she looked straight into his eyes. Another time, another place, he might have considered her magnificent. "I barely had the chance to recover from what happened before you were shoving me out. I wanted you. Dammit, I still want you. God knows why."

"Well, I want you, too, and I don't like it, either."

"Looks like that puts us in the same fix, doesn't it?"

"So what're we going to do about it?"

He looked at her and saw the anger. But he looked closely enough to see confusion, as well. One of them had to make the first move. He decided it was going to be him. Taking her hand, he dragged her across the street.

"Where are we going?"

"The Plaza."

"The Plaza Hotel? Why?"

"We're going to get a room, put the chain on the door and make love for the next twenty-four hours. After that, we'll decide how we want to handle it."

There were times, Pandora decided, when it was best to go along for the ride. "We don't have any luggage."

"Yeah. My reputation's about to be shattered."

She made a sound that might have been a laugh. When they walked into the elegant lobby, the heat warmed her skin and stirred up her nerves. It was all impulse, she told herself. She knew better than to make any important decision on impulse. He could change everything. That was something she hadn't wanted to admit but had known for years. When she started to draw away, his hand locked on her arm.

"Coward," he murmured. He couldn't have said anything more perfectly designed to make her march forward.

"Good afternoon." Michael smiled at the desk clerk. Pandora wondered briefly if the smile would have been so charming if the clerk had been a man. "Checking in."

"You have a reservation?"

"Donahue. Michael Donahue."

The clerk punched some buttons and stared at her computer screen. "I'm afraid I don't show anything under Donahue for the twenty-sixth."

"Katie," Michael said on a breath of impatience. He sent Pandora a long suffering look. "I should never have trusted her to handle this."

Catching the drift, Pandora patted his hand. "You're going to have to let her go, Michael. I know she's worked for your family for forty years, but when a person gets into their seventies..." She trailed off and let Michael take the ball.

"We'll decide when we get home." He turned back to the

desk clerk. "Apparently there's been a mix-up between my secretary and the hotel. We'll only be in town overnight. Is anything available?"

The clerk went back to her buttons. Most people in her experience raised the roof when there was a mix-up in reservations. Michael's quiet request touched her sympathies. "You understand there's a problem because of the holiday." She punched more buttons, wanting to help. "We do have a suite available."

"Fine." Michael took the registration form and filled it out. With the key in his hand, he sent the clerk another smile. "I appreciate the trouble." Noting the bellhop hovering at his elbow, he handed him a bill. "We'll handle it, thanks."

The clerk looked at the twenty in his palm and the lack of luggage. "Yes, sir!"

"He thinks we're having an illicit affair," Pandora murmured as they stepped onto the elevator.

"We are." Before the doors had closed again, Michael grabbed her to him and locked her in a kiss that lasted twelve floors. "We don't know each other," he told her as they stepped into the hallway. "We've just met. We don't have mutual childhood memories or share the same family." He put the key in the lock. "We don't give a damn what the other does for a living nor do we have any long-standing opinions about each other."

"Is that supposed to simplify things?"

Michael drew her inside. "Let's find out."

He didn't give her a chance to wonder, a chance to debate. The moment the door was shut behind them, he had her in his arms. He took questions away. He took choice away. For once, she wanted him to. In a fury of passions, of hungers, of cravings, they came together. Each fought to draw more, still more out of the other, to touch faster, to possess more quickly. They forgot what they knew, what they thought and reveled in what they felt.

Coats, still chill from the wind, were pushed to the floor. Sweaters and shirts followed. Hardly more than a foot inside the door, they slid to the carpet.

"Damn winter," Michael muttered as he fought with her boots.

Laughing, Pandora struggled with his, then moaned when he pressed his lips to her breast.

It was a race, part warring, part loving. Neither gave the other respite. When their clothes were shed, they sprinted ahead, hands reaching, lips arousing. There was none of the dreamy déjà vu they'd experienced the first time. This was new. The fingers tracing her skin had never been felt before. The lips, hot and searing, had never been tasted. Fresh, erotically fresh, their mouths met and clung.

Her heart had never beat so fast. She was sure of it. Her body had never ached and pulsed so desperately. She'd never wanted it to. Now she wanted more, everything. Him. She rolled so that she could press quick, hungry kisses over his face, his neck, his chest. Everywhere.

His mind was teeming with her, with every part of her that he could touch or taste or smell. She was wild in a way he'd never imagined. She was demanding in a way any man would desire. His body seemed to fascinate her, every curve, every angle. She exploited it until he was half mad, then he groped for her.

She'd never known a man could give so much. Racked with sensations, she arched under him. Hot and ready, she offered. But he was far from through. The taste of her thighs was subtle, luring him toward the heat. He found her, drove her and kept her helplessly trapped in passion. Helplessly. The sensation shivered over her. She'd never known what it had meant to be truly vulnerable to another. He could have taken anything from her then, asked anything and she couldn't have refused. But he didn't ask, he gave.

She crested wave after wave. Between heights and depths she pinwheeled, delighting in the spin. On the rug with the afternoon light streaming through the windows, she was locked in blinding darkness without any wish to see. *Make me feel,* her mind seemed to shout. More. Again. Still.

And he was inside her, joined, melded. She found there was more. Impossibly more.

They stayed where they were, sprawled on scattered clothes. Gradually Pandora found her mind swimming back to reality. She could see the pastel walls, the sunlight. She could smell the body heat that was a mix of hers and his. She could feel Michael's hair brushing over her cheek, the beat of his heart, still fast, against her breast.

It happened so fast, she thought. Or had it taken hours? All she was certain of was that she'd never experienced anything like it. Never permitted herself to, she amended. Strange things could happen to a woman who lifted the lid from her passion. Other things could sneak in before the top closed again. Things like affection, understanding. Even love.

She caught herself stroking Michael's hair and let her hand fall to the carpet. She couldn't let love in, not even briefly. Love took as well as gave. That she'd always known. And it didn't always give and take in equal shares. Michael wasn't a man a woman could love practically, and certainly not wisely. That she understood. He wouldn't follow the rules.

She'd be his lover, but she wouldn't love him. Though there would be no pretending they could live with each other for the next three months platonically, she wouldn't risk her heart. For an instant Pandora thought she felt it break, just a little. Foolishness, she told herself. Her heart was strong and unimpaired. What she and Michael had together was a very basic, very uncomplicated arrangement. Arrangement, she thought, sounded so much more practical than romance.

But her sigh was quiet, and a little wistful.

"Figure it all out?" He shifted a little as he spoke, just enough so that he could brush his lips down her throat.

"What do you mean?"

"Have you figured out the guidelines for our relationship?" Lifting his head, he looked down at her. He wasn't smiling, but Pandora thought he was amused.

"I don't know what you're talking about."

"I can almost hear the wheels turning. Pandora, I can see just what's going on in your head."

Annoyed that he probably could, she lifted a brow. "I thought we'd just met."

"I'm psychic. You're thinking...." He trailed off to nibble at her lips. "That there should be a way to keep our...relationship on a practical level. You're wondering how you'll keep an emotional distance when we're sleeping together. You've decided that there'll be absolutely no romantic overtones to any arrangement between us."

"All right." He made her feel foolish. Then he ran a hand over her hip and made her tremble. "Since you're so smart, you'll see that I've only been using common sense."

"I like it better when your skin gets hot, and you haven't any sense at all. But—" he kissed her before she could answer "—we can't stay in bed all the time. I don't believe in practical affairs, Pandora. I don't believe in emotional distance between lovers."

"You've had a great deal of experience there."

"That's right." He sat up, drawing her with him. "And I'll tell you this. You can wall up your emotions all you want. You can call whatever we have here by any practical term you can dream up. You can turn up your nose at candlelight dinners and quiet music. It's not going to make any difference." He gathered her hair in his hand and pulled her head back. "I'm going to get to you, cousin. I'm going to get to you until you can't think of anything, anyone but me. If you wake up in the middle of the night and I'm not there, you'll wish I were. And when I touch you, any time I touch you, you're going to want me."

She had to fight the shudder. She knew, as well as she'd ever known anything, that he was right. And she knew, perhaps they both did, that she'd fight it right down to the end. "You're arrogant, egocentric and simpleminded."

"True enough. And you're stubborn, willful and perverse. The only thing we can be sure of at this point is that one of us is going to win."

Sitting on the pile of discarded clothes, they studied each other. "Another game?" Pandora murmured.

"Maybe. Maybe it's the only game." With that, he stood and lifted her into his arms.

"Michael, I don't need to be carried."

"Yes, you do."

He walked across the suite toward the bedroom. Pandora started to struggle, then subsided. Maybe just this once, she decided, and relaxed in his arms.

Chapter Nine

January was a month of freezing wind, pelting snow and gray skies. Each day was as bitterly cold as the last, with tomorrow waiting frigidly in the wings. It was a month of frozen pipes, burst pipes, overworked furnaces and stalled engines. Pandora loved it. The frost built up on the windows of her shop, and the inside temperature always remained cool even with the heaters turned up. She worked until her fingers were numb and enjoyed every moment.

Throughout the month, the road to the Folley was often inaccessible. Pandora didn't mind not being able to get out. It meant no one could get in. The pantry and freezer were stocked, and there was over a cord of wood stacked beside the kitchen door. The way she looked at it, they had everything they needed. The days were short and productive, the nights long and relaxing. Since the incident of the champagne, it had been a quiet, uneventful winter.

Uneventful, Pandora mused, wasn't precisely the right term.

With quick, careful strokes, she filed the edges of a thick copper bracelet. It certainly wasn't as though nothing had happened. There'd been no trouble from outside sources, but… Trouble, as she'd always known, was definitely one of Michael Donahue's greatest talents.

Just what was he trying to pull by leaving a bunch of violets on her pillow? She was certain a magic wand would have been needed to produce the little purple flowers in January. When she'd questioned him about them, he'd simply smiled and told her violets didn't have thorns. What kind of an answer was that? Pandora wondered, and examined the clasp of the bracelet through a magnifying glass. She was satisfied with the way she'd designed it to blend with the design.

Then, there'd been the time she'd come out of the bath to find the bedroom lit with a dozen candles. When she'd asked if there'd been a power failure, Michael had just laughed and pulled her into bed.

He did things like reaching for her hand at dinner and whispering in her ear just before dawn. Once he'd joined her in the shower uninvited and silenced her protests by washing every inch of her body himself. She'd been right. Michael Donahue didn't follow the rules. He'd been right. He was getting to her.

Pandora removed the bracelet from the vise, then absently began to polish it. She'd made a half a dozen others in the last two weeks. Big chunky bracelets, some had gaudy stones, some had ornate engraving. They suited her mood—daring, opinionated and a bit silly. She'd learned to trust her instincts, and her instincts told her they'd sell faster than she could possibly make them—and be copied just as quickly.

She didn't mind the imitations. After all, there was only one of each type that was truly a Pandora McVie. Copies would be recognized as copies because they lacked that something special, that individuality of the genuine.

Pleased, she turned the bracelet over in her hand. No one would mistake any of her work for an imitation. She might often use glass instead of precious or semiprecious stones because glass expressed her mood at the time. But each piece she created carried her mark, her opinion and her honesty. She never gave a thought to the price of a piece when she crafted it or its market value. She created what she needed to create first, then after it was done, her practical side calculated the profit margin. Her art varied from piece to piece, but it never lied.

Looking down at the bracelet, Pandora sighed. No, her art never lied, but did she? Could she be certain her emotions were as genuine as the jewelry she made? A feeling could be imitated. An emotion could be fraudulent. How many times in the past few weeks had she pretended? Not pretended to feel, Pandora thought, but pretended not to feel. She was a woman who'd always prided herself on her honesty. Truth and independence went hand in hand with Pandora's set of values. But she'd lied—over and over again—to herself, the worst form of deception.

It was time to stop, Pandora told herself. Time to face the truth of her feelings if only in the privacy of her own heart and mind.

How long had she been in love with Michael? She had to stand

and move around the shop as the question formed in her mind. Weeks? Months? Years? It wasn't something she could answer because she would never be sure. But she was certain of the emotion. She loved. Pandora understood it because she loved only a few people, and when she did, she loved boundlessly. Perhaps that was the biggest problem. Wasn't it a sort of suicide to love Michael boundlessly?

Better to face it, she told herself. No problem resolved itself without being faced first and examined second. However much a fool it made her, she loved Michael. Pandora rubbed at the steam on the windows and looked out at the snow. Strange, she'd really believed once she accepted it she'd feel better. She didn't.

What options did she have? She could tell him. And have him gloat, Pandora thought with a scowl. He would, too, before he trotted off to his next conquest. *She* certainly wasn't fool enough to think he'd be interested in a long-term relationship. Of course, she wasn't interested in one either, Pandora told herself as she began to noisily pack her tools.

Another option was to cut and run. What the relatives hadn't been able to accomplish with their malice and mischief, her own heart would succeed in doing. She could get in the car, drive to the airport and fly to anywhere. Escape was the honest word. Then, she'd not only be a coward, she'd be a traitor. No, she wouldn't let Uncle Jolley down; she wouldn't run. That left her, as Pandora saw it, with one option.

She'd go on as she was. She'd stay with Michael, sleep with Michael, share with Michael—share with him everything but what was in her heart. She'd take the two months they had left together and prepare herself to walk away with no regrets.

He'd gotten to her, Pandora admitted. Gotten to her in places no other man had touched. She loved him for it. She hated him for it. With her mood as turbulent as her thoughts, she locked the shop and stomped across the lawn.

"Here she comes now." With a new plan ready to spring, Sweeney turned away from the kitchen window and signaled to Charles.

"It's never going to work."

"Of course it is. We're going to push those children together for their own good. Any two people who spat as much as they do should be married."

"We're interfering where it's not our place."

"What malarkey!" Sweeney took her seat at the kitchen table. "Whose place is it to interfere if not ours, I'd like to know? Who'll be knocking around this big empty house if they go back to the city if not us? Now pick up that cloth and fan me. Stoop over a bit and look feeble."

"I am feeble," Charles muttered, but picked up the cloth.

When Pandora walked into the kitchen she saw Sweeney sprawled back in a chair, eyes closed, with Charles standing over her waving a dishcloth at her face.

"God, what's wrong? Charles, did she faint?" Before he could answer, Pandora had dashed across the room. "Call Michael," she ordered. "Call Michael quickly." She brushed Charles away and crouched. "Sweeney, it's Pandora. Are you in pain?"

Barely suppressing a sigh of satisfaction, Sweeney let her

eyes flutter open and hoped she looked pale. "Oh, missy, don't you worry now. Just one of my spells is all. Now and then my heart starts to flutter so that I feel it's coming right out of my head."

"I'm going to call the doctor." Pandora had taken only one step when her hand was caught in a surprisingly strong grip.

"No need for that." Sweeney made her voice thin and weary. "Saw him just a few months past and he told me I'd have to expect one of these now and again."

"I don't believe that," Pandora said fiercely. "You're just plain working too hard, and it's going to stop."

A little trickle of guilt worked its way in as Sweeney saw the concern. "Now, now, don't fret."

"What is it?" Michael swung through the kitchen door. "Sweeney?" He knelt down beside her and took her other hand.

"Now look at all this commotion." Mentally she leaped up and kicked her heels. "It's nothing but one of my little spells. The doctor said I'd have to watch for them. Just a nuisance, that's all." She looked hard at Charles when he came in. Eventually shc looked hard enough so that he remembered his cue.

"And you know what he said."

"Now, Charles—"

"You're to have two or three days of bed rest."

Pleased that he'd remembered his lines, Sweeney pretended to huff. "Pack of nonsense. I'll be right as rain in a few minutes. I've dinner to cook."

"You won't be cooking anything." In a way Sweeney considered properly masterful, Michael picked her up. "Into bed with you."

"Just who'll take care of things?" Sweeney demanded. "I'll not have Charles spreading his germs around my kitchen."

Michael was nearly out of the room with Sweeney before Charles remembered the next step. He coughed into his hand, looked apologetic and coughed again.

"Listen to that!" Pleased, Sweeney let her head rest against Michael's shoulder. "I won't go to bed and let him infect my kitchen."

"How long have you had that cough?" Pandora demanded. When Charles began to mutter, she stood up. "That's enough. Both of you into bed. Michael and I will take care of everything." Taking Charles's arm, she began to lead him into the servant's wing. "Into bed and no nonsense. I'll make both of you some tea. Michael, see that Charles gets settled, I'll look after Sweeney."

Within a half hour, Sweeney had them both where she wanted them. Together.

"Well, they're all settled in and there's no fever." Satisfied, Pandora poured herself a cup of tea. "I suppose all they need is a few days' rest and some pampering. Tea?"

He made a face at the idea and switched on the coffee. "Since the days of house calls are over, I'd think they'd be better off here in bed than being dragged into town. We can take turns keeping an eye on them."

"Mmm-hmm." Pandora opened the refrigerator and studied. "What about meals? Can you cook?"

"Sure." Michael rattled cups in the cupboard. "Badly, but I can cook. Meat loaf's my specialty." When this was met with no enthusiasm, he turned his head. "Do you?"

"Cook?" Pandora lifted a plastic lid hopefully. "I can broil a steak and scramble eggs. Anything else is chancy."

"Life's nothing without a risk." Michael joined her in her rummage through the refrigerator. "Here's almost half an apple cobbler."

"That's hardly a meal."

"It'll do for me." He took it out and went for a spoon. Pandora watched as he sat down at the table and dug in. "Want some?"

She started to refuse on principle, then decided not to cut off her nose. Going to the cupboard, she found a bowl. "What about the bedridden?" she asked as she scooped out cobbler.

"Soup," Michael said between bites. "Nothing better than hot soup. Though I'd let them rest awhile first."

With a nod of agreement, she sat across from him. "Michael…" She trailed off as she played with her cobbler. The steam from her tea rose up between them. She'd been thinking about how to broach the subject for days. It seemed the time had come. "I've been thinking. In two months, the will should be final. When Fitzhugh wrote us last week, he said Uncle Carlson's lawyers were advising him to drop the probate."

"So?"

"The house, along with everything else, will be half yours, half mine."

"That's right."

She took a bite of cobbler, then set down her spoon. "What're you smiling at?"

"You're nice to look at. I find it relaxing to sit here alone in the kitchen, in the quiet, and look at you."

It was that sort of thing, just that sort of thing, that left her light-headed and foolish. She stared at him a moment, then dropped her gaze to her bowl. "I wish you wouldn't say things like that."

"No, you don't. So you've been thinking," he prompted.

"Yes." She gave herself a moment, carefully spooning out another bite of cobbler. "We'll have the house between us, but we won't be living here together any longer. Sweeney and Charles will be here alone. I've worried about that for a while. Now, after this, I'm more concerned than ever. They can't stay here alone."

"No, I think you're right. Ideas?"

"I mentioned before that I was considering moving here on a semipermanent basis." She found she had no appetite after all and switched back to her tea. "I think I'm going to make it permanent all around."

He heard a trace of nervousness in her voice. "Because of Charles and Sweeney?"

"Only partly." She drank more tea, set the cup down and toyed with her cobbler again. She wasn't accustomed to discussing her decisions with anyone. Though she found it difficult, Pandora had already resolved that she had an obligation to do so. More, she'd realized she needed to talk to him, to be, as she couldn't be on other levels, honest. "I always felt the Folley was home, but I didn't realize just how much of a home. I need it, for myself. You see, I never had one." She lifted her gaze and met his. "Only here."

To say her words surprised him was to say too little. All his life he'd seen her as the pampered pet, the golden girl with every advantage. "But your parents—"

"Are wonderful," Pandora said quickly. "I adore them. There's nothing about them I'd change. But..." How could she explain? How could she not? "We never had a kitchen like this—a place you could come back to day after day and know it'd be the same. Even if you changed the wallpaper and the paint, it would be the same. It sounds silly." She shifted restlessly. "You wouldn't understand."

"Maybe I would." He caught her hand before she could rise. "Maybe I'd like to."

"I want a home," she said simply. "The Folley's been that to me. I want to stay here after the term's up."

He kept her hand in his, palm to palm. "Why are you telling me this, Pandora?"

Reasons. Too many reasons. She chose the only one she could give him safely. "In two months, the house belongs to you as much as to me. According to the terms of the will—"

He swore and released her hand. Rising, he stuck his hands in his back pockets and strode to the window. He'd thought for a moment, just for a moment, she'd been ready to give him more. By God, he'd waited long enough for only a few drops more. There'd been something in her voice, something soft and giving. Perhaps he'd just imagined it because he'd wanted to hear it. Terms of the will, he thought. It was so like her to see nothing else.

"What do you want, my permission?"

Disturbed, Pandora stayed at the table. "I suppose I wanted you to understand and agree."

"Fine."

"You needn't be so curt about it. After all, you haven't any plans to use the house on a regular basis."

"I haven't made any plans," he murmured. "Perhaps it's time I did."

"I didn't mean to annoy you."

He turned slowly, then just as slowly smiled. "No, I'm sure you didn't. There's never any doubt when you annoy me intentionally."

There was something wrong here, something she couldn't quite pinpoint. So she groped. "Would you mind so much if I were to live here?"

It surprised him when she rose to come to him, offering a hand. She didn't make such gestures often or casually. "No, why should it?"

"It would be half yours."

"We could draw a line down the middle."

"That might be awkward. I could buy you out."

"No."

He said it so fiercely, her brows shot up. "It was only an offer."

"Forget it." He turned to look for soup.

Pandora stood back a moment, watching his back, the tension in the muscles. "Michael…" With a sigh, she wrapped her arms around his waist. She felt him stiffen, but didn't realize it was from surprise. "I seem to be saying all the wrong things. Maybe I have an easier time when we snap at each other than when I try to be considerate."

"Maybe we both do." He turned to frame her face with his hands. For a moment they looked like friends, like lovers. "Pandora…." Could he tell her he found it impossible to think about leaving her or her leaving him? Would she understand if he told her he wanted to go on living with her, being with her? How could she possibly take in the fact that he'd been in love with her for years when he was just becoming able to accept it himself? Instead he kissed her forehead. "Let's make soup."

They couldn't work together without friction, but they discovered over the next few days that they could work together. They cooked meals, washed up, dusted furniture while the servants stayed in bed or sat, bundled up, on sofas drinking tea. True, there were times when Sweeney itched to get up and be about her business, or when Charles suffered pangs of conscience, but they were convinced they were doing their duty. Both servants felt justified when they heard laughter drift through the house.

Michael wasn't sure there had been another time in his life when he'd been so content. He was, in essence, playing house, something he'd never had the time or inclination for. He would write for hours, closed off in his office, wrapped up in plots and characters and what-ifs. Then he could break away and reality was the scent of cooking or furniture polish. He had a home, a woman, and was determined to keep them.

Late in the afternoon, he always laid a fire in the parlor. After dinner they had coffee there, sometimes quietly, sometimes during a hard-fought game of rummy. It seemed ordinary, Michael admitted. It was ordinary, unless you added Pandora. He was just setting fire to the kindling when Bruno raced into the room and upset a table. Knickknacks went flying.

"We're going to have to send you to charm school," Michael declared as he rose to deal with the rubble. Though it had been just over a month, Bruno had nearly doubled in size already. He was, without a doubt, going to grow into his paws. After righting the table, he saw the dog wiggling its way under a sofa. "What've you got there?"

Besides being large, Bruno had already earned a reputation as a clever thief. Just the day before, they'd lost a slab of pork chops. "All right, you devil, if that's tonight's chicken, you're going into solitary confinement in the garage." Getting down on all fours, Michael looked under the couch. It wasn't chicken the dog was gnawing noisily on, but Michael's shoe.

"Damn!" Michael made a grab but the dog backed out of reach and kept on chewing. "That shoe's worth five times what you are, you overgrown mutt. Give it here." Flattening, Michael scooted halfway under the sofa. Bruno merely dragged the shoe away again, enjoying the game.

"Oh, how sweet." Pandora walked into the parlor and eyed Michael from the waist down. He did, she decided, indeed have some redeeming qualities. "Are you playing with the dog, Michael, or dusting under the sofa?"

"I'm going to make a rug out of him."

"Dear, dear, we sound a little cross this evening. Bruno, here baby." Carrying the shoe like a trophy, Bruno squirmed out from under the couch and pranced over to her. "Is this what you were after?" Pandora held up the shoe while petting Bruno with her other hand. "How clever of you to teach Bruno to fetch."

Michael pulled himself up, then yanked the shoe out of her

hand. It was unfortunately wet and covered with teeth marks. "That's the second shoe he's ruined. And he didn't even have the courtesy to take both from one pair."

She looked down at what had been creamy Italian leather. "You never wear anything but tennis shoes or boots anyway."

Michael slapped the shoe against his palm. Bruno, tongue lolling, grinned up at him. "Obedience school."

"Oh, Michael, we can't send our child away." She patted his cheek. "It's just a phase."

"This phase has cost me two pairs of shoes, my dinner and we never did find that sweater he dragged off."

"You shouldn't drop your clothes on the floor," Pandora said easily. "And that sweater was already ratty. I'm sure Bruno thought it was a rag."

"He never chews up anything of yours."

Pandora smiled. "No, he doesn't, does he?"

Michael gave her a long look. "Just what're you so happy about?"

"I had a phone call this afternoon."

Michael saw the excitement in her eyes and decided the issue of the shoe could wait. "And?"

"From Jacob Morison."

"The producer?"

"*The* producer," Pandora repeated. She'd promised herself she wouldn't overreact, but the excitement threatened to burst inside her. "He's going to be filming a new movie. Jessica Wainwright's starring."

Jessica Wainwright, Michael mused. Grande dame of the

theater and the screen. Eccentric and brilliant, her career had spanned two generations. "She's retired. Wainwright hasn't made a film in five years."

"She's making this one. Billy Mitchell's directing."

Michael tilted his head in consideration as he studied Pandora's face. It made him think of the cat and the canary. "Sounds like they're pulling out all the stops."

"She plays a half-mad reclusive countess who's dragged back to reality by a visit from her granddaughter. Cass Barkley's on the point of signing for the part of the granddaughter."

"Oscar material. Now, are you going to tell me why Morison called you?"

"Wainwright's an admirer of my work. She wants me to design all her jewelry for the movie. All!" After an attempt to sound businesslike, Pandora laughed and did a quick spin. "Morison said the only way he could talk her out of retirement was to promise her the best. She wants me."

Michael grabbed her close and spun her around. Bruno raced around the room barking and shaking tables. "We'll celebrate," he decided. "Champagne with our fried chicken."

Pandora held on tight. "I feel like an idiot."

"Why?"

"I've always thought I was, well, beyond star adoration. I'm a professional." Bubbling with excitement, she clung to Michael. "While I was talking to Morison I told myself it was a great career opportunity, a wonderful chance to express myself in a large way. Then I hung up and all I could think was Jessica Wainwright! A Morison production! I felt as silly as any bubble-headed fan."

"Proves you're not half the snob you think you are." Michael cut off her retort with a kiss. "I'm proud of you," he murmured.

That threw her off. All of her pleasure in the assignment was dwarfed by that one sentence. No one but Jolley had ever been proud of her. Her parents loved her, patted her head and told her to do what she wanted. Pride was a valued addition to affection. "Really?"

Surprised, Michael drew her back and kissed her again. "Of course I am."

"But you've never thought much of my work."

"No, that's not true. I've never understood why people feel the need to deck themselves out in bangles, or why you seemed content to design on such a small scale. But as far as your work goes I'm not blind, Pandora. Some of it's beautiful, some of it's extraordinary and some of it's incomprehensible. But it's all imaginative and expertly crafted."

"Well." She let out a long breath. "This is a red-letter day. I always thought you felt I was playing with beads because I didn't want to face a real job. You even said so once."

He grinned. "Only because it made you furious. You're spectacular to look at when you're furious."

She thought about it a moment, then let out a sigh. "I suppose this is the best time to tell you."

He tensed, but forced his voice to come calmly. "To tell me what?"

"I watch the Emmy Awards every time you're nominated."

Tension flowed out in a laugh. There'd been guilt in every syllable. "What?"

"Every time," Pandora repeated, amazed that her cheeks were warm. "It made me feel good to watch you win. And..." She paused to clear her throat. "I've watched a few episodes of *Logan's Run*."

Michael wondered if she realized she sounded as though she was confessing a major social flaw. "Why?"

"Uncle Jolley was always going on about it; I'd even hear it discussed at parties. So I thought I'd see for myself. Naturally, it was just a matter of intellectual curiosity."

"Naturally. And?"

She moved her shoulders. "Of its kind—"

He stopped that line of response by twisting her ear. "Some people only tell the truth under duress."

"All right." Half laughing, she reached to free herself. "It's good!" she shouted when he held on. "I liked it."

"Why?"

"Michael, that hurts!"

"We have ways of making you talk."

"I liked it because the characters are genuine, the plots are intelligent. And—" she had to swallow hard on this one "—it has style."

When he let go of her ear to kiss her soundly, she gave him a halfhearted shove. "If you repeat that to anyone, I'll deny it."

"It'll be our little secret." He kissed her again, not so playfully.

Pandora was almost becoming used to the sensation of having her muscles loosen and feeling as if her bones were dissolving. She moved closer, delighting in the feeling of having her body mold against his. When his heart thudded, she felt the pulse inside herself. When his tiny moan escaped, she tasted it on her tongue. When the need leaped forward, she saw it in his eyes.

She pressed her mouth to his again and let her own hunger rule. There would be consequences. Hadn't she already accepted it? There would be pain. She was already braced for it. She couldn't stop what would happen in the weeks ahead, but she could direct what would happen tonight and perhaps tomorrow. It had to be enough. Everything she felt, wanted, feared, went into the kiss.

It left him reeling. She was often passionate, wildly so. She was often demanding, erotically so. But he'd never felt such pure emotion from her. There was a softness under the strength, a request under the urgency. He drew her closer, more gently than was his habit, and let her take what she wanted.

Her head tilted back, inviting, luring. His grip tightened. His fingers wound into her hair and were lost in the richness of it. He felt the need catapult through his body so that he was tense against her sudden, unexpected yielding. She never submitted, and until that moment he hadn't known how stirring it could be to have her do so. Without a thought to time and place, they lowered to the sofa.

Because she was pliant, he was tender. Because he was gentle, she was patient. In a way they'd never experienced, they made love without rush, without fire, without the whirlwind. Thoroughly, they gave to each other. A touch, a taste, a murmured request, a whispered answer. The fire sizzled gently behind them as night fell outside the windows. Fingers brushed, lips skimmed so that they learned the power of quiet arousal. Though they'd been lovers for weeks, they brought love to passion for the first time.

The room was quiet, the light dim. If she'd never looked for romance, it found her there, wrapped easily in Michael's arms. Closer they came, but comfortably. Deeper they dived, but lazily. As they came together, Pandora felt her firm line of independence crack to let him in. But the weakness she'd expected didn't follow. Only contentment.

It was contentment that followed her into that quick and final burst of pleasure.

They were still wrapped together, half dozing, when the phone rang. With a murmur of complaint, Michael reached over his head to the table and lifted the receiver.

"Hello."

"Michael Donahue, please."

"Yeah, this is Michael."

"Michael, it's Penny."

He rubbed a hand over his eyes as he tried to put a face with the name. Penny—the little blonde in the apartment next to his. Wanted to be a model. He remembered vaguely leaving her the number of the Folley in case something important was delivered to his apartment. "Hi." He watched Pandora's eyes flutter open.

"Michael, I hate to do this, but I had to call. I've already phoned the police. They're on their way."

"Police?" He struggled into a half-sitting position. "What's going on?"

"You've been robbed."

"What?" He sat bolt upright, nearly dumping Pandora on the floor. "When?"

"I'm not sure. I got home a few minutes ago and noticed your door wasn't closed all the way. I thought maybe you'd come back so I knocked. Anyway, I pushed the door open a bit. The place was turned upside down. I came right over here and called the cops. They asked me to contact you and told me not to go back over."

"Thanks." Dozens of questions ran through his mind but there was no one to answer them. "Look, I'll try to come in tonight."

"Okay. Hey, Michael, I'm really sorry."

"Yeah. I'll see you."

"Michael?" Pandora grabbed his hand as soon as he hung up the receiver.

"Somebody broke into my apartment."

"Oh no." She'd known the peace couldn't last. "Do you think it was—"

"I don't know." He dragged a hand through his hair. "Maybe. Or maybe it was someone who noticed no one had been home for a while."

She felt the anger in him but knew she couldn't soothe it. "You've got to go."

Nodding, he took her hand. "Come with me."

"Michael, one of us has to be here with Sweeney and Charles."

"I'm not leaving you alone."

"You have to go," she repeated. "If it was one of the family, maybe you can find something to prove it. In any case, you have to see to this. I'll be fine."

"Just like the last time I was away."

Pandora lifted a brow. "I'm not incompetent, Michael."

"But you'll be alone."

"I have Bruno. Don't give me that look," she ordered. "He may not be ferocious, but he certainly knows how to bark. I'll lock every door and window."

He shook his head. "Not good enough."

"All right, we'll call the local police. They have Fitzhugh's report about trespassers. We'll explain that I'm going to be alone for the night and ask them to keep an eye on the place."

"Better." But he rose to pace. "If this is a setup…"

"Then we're prepared for it this time."

Michael hesitated, thought it through, then nodded. "I'll call the police."

Chapter Ten

The moment Michael left, Pandora turned the heavy bolt on the main door. Though it had taken them the better part of an hour, she was grateful he'd insisted on checking all the doors and windows with her. The house, with Pandora safely in it, was locked up tight.

It was entirely too quiet.

In defense, Pandora went to the kitchen and began rattling pots and pans. She had to be alone, but she didn't have to be idle. She wanted to be with Michael, to stand by him when he faced the break-in of his apartment. Was it as frustrating for him to go on alone, she wondered, as it was for her to stay behind? It couldn't be helped. There were two old people in the house who couldn't be left. And they needed to eat.

The chicken was to have been a joint effort and a respite from the haphazard meals they'd managed to date. Michael had claimed to know at least the basics of deep frying. While he'd volunteered to deal with the chicken, she'd been assigned to try her hand at mashing potatoes. She'd thought competition if nothing else would have improved the end result.

Pandora resigned herself to a solo and decided the effort of cooking would keep her mind off fresh trouble. Needing company, she switched on the tuner on the kitchen wall unit and fiddled with the dial until she found a country-music station. Dolly Parton bubbled out brightly. Satisfied, she pulled one of Sweeney's cookbooks from the shelf and began to search the index. Fried chicken went on picnics, she mused. How much trouble could it be?

She had two counters crowded and splattered, and flour up to her wrists when the phone rang. Using a dishcloth, Pandora plucked the receiver from the kitchen extension. Her foot was tapping to a catchy rendition of "On the Road Again."

"Hello."

"Pandora McVie?"

Her mind on more immediate matters, Pandora stretched the cord to the counter and picked up a drumstick. "Yes."

"Listen carefully."

"Can you speak up?" Tongue caught between her teeth, Pandora dipped the drumstick in her flour mixture. "I can't hear you very well."

"I have to warn you and there's not much time. You're in danger. You're not safe in that house, not alone."

The cookbook slid to the floor and landed on her foot. "What? Who is this?"

"Just listen. You're alone because it was arranged. Someone's going to try to break in tonight."

"Someone?" She shifted the phone and listened hard. It wasn't malice she detected, but nervousness. Whoever was on the other end was as shaky as she was. She was certain—almost certain—it was a man's voice. "If you're trying to frighten me—"

"I'm trying to warn you. When I found out..." Already low and indistinct, the voice became hesitant. "You shouldn't have sent the champagne. I don't like what's going on, but it won't stop. No one was going to be hurt, do you understand? But I'm afraid of what might happen next."

Pandora felt fear curl in her stomach. Outside the kitchen windows it was dark, pitch-dark. She was alone in the house with two old, sick servants. "If you're afraid, tell me who you are. Help me stop what's going on."

"I'm already risking everything by warning you. You don't understand. Get out, just get out of the house."

It was a ploy, she told herself. A ploy to make her leave. Pandora straightened her shoulders, but her gaze shifted from blank window to blank window. "I'm not going anywhere. If you want to help, tell me who I should be afraid of."

"Just get out," the voice repeated before the line went dead.

Pandora stood holding the silent receiver. The oil in the fryer had begun to sizzle, competing with the radio. Watching the windows, listening, she hung up the phone. It was a trick, she told herself. It was only a trick to get her out of the house in hopes she'd be frightened enough to stay out. She wouldn't be shooed away by a quivering voice on the telephone.

Besides, Michael had already called the police. They knew

she was alone in the house. At the first sign of trouble, she only had to pick up the phone.

Her hands weren't completely steady, but she went back to cooking with a vengeance. She slipped coated chicken into the fryer, tested the potatoes she had cooking, then decided a little glass of wine while she worked was an excellent idea. She was pouring it when Bruno raced into the room to run around her feet.

"Bruno." Pandora crouched and gathered the dog close. He felt warm, solid. "I'm glad you're here," she murmured. But for a moment, she allowed herself to wish desperately for Michael.

Bruno licked her face, made a couple of clumsy leaps toward the counter, then dashed to the door. Jumping up against it, he began to bark.

"Now?" Pandora demanded. "I don't suppose you could wait until morning."

Bruno raced back to Pandora, circled her then raced back to the door. When he'd gone through the routine three times, she relented. The phone call had been no more than a trick, a clumsy one at that. Besides, she told herself as she turned the lock, it wouldn't hurt to open the door and take a good look outside.

The moment she opened it, Bruno jumped out and tumbled into the snow. He began to sniff busily while Pandora stood shivering in the opening and straining her eyes against the dark. Music and the smells of cooking poured out behind her.

There was nothing. She hugged herself against the cold and decided she hadn't expected to see anything. The snow was settled, the stars bright and the woods quiet. It was as it should have been; a very ordinary evening in the country. She took a deep breath of winter air and started to call the dog back. They saw the movement at the edge of the woods at the same time.

Just a shadow, it seemed to separate slowly from a tree and take on its own shape. A human shape. Before Pandora could react, Bruno began to bark and plow through the snow.

"No, Bruno! Come back." Without giving herself a chance to think, Pandora grabbed the old pea coat that hung beside the door and threw it on. As an afterthought, she reached for a cast-iron skillet before bolting through the door after her dog. "Bruno!"

He was already at the edge of the woods and hot on the trail. Picking up confidence as she went, Pandora raced in pursuit. Whoever had been watching the house had run at the sight of the clumsy, overgrown puppy. She'd found she was susceptible to fear, but she refused to be frightened by a coward. With as much enthusiasm as Bruno, Pandora sprinted into the woods. Out of breath and feeling indestructible, she paused long enough to look around and listen. For a moment there was nothing, then off to the right, she heard barking and thrashing.

"Get 'em, Bruno!" she shouted, and headed toward the chaos. Excited by the chase, she called encouragement to the dog, changing direction when she heard his answering bark. As she ran, snow dropped from the branches to slide cold and wet down the back of her neck. The barking grew wilder, and in her rush, Pandora fell headlong over a downed tree. Spitting out snow and swearing, she struggled to her knees. Bruno bounded out of the woods and sent her sprawling again.

"Not me." Flat on her back, Pandora shoved at the dog. "Dammit, Bruno, if you don't—" She broke off when the dog stiffened and began to growl. Sprawled on the snow, Pandora looked up and saw the shadow move through the trees. She forgot she was too proud to fear a coward.

Though her hands were numb from cold, she gripped the handle of the skillet and, standing, inched her way along toward the nearest tree. Struggling to keep her breathing quiet, she braced herself for attack and defense. Relative or stranger, she'd hold her own. But her knees were shaking. Bruno tensed and hurled himself forward. The moment he did, Pandora lifted the skillet high and prepared to swing.

"What the hell's going on?"

"Michael!" The skillet landed in the snow with a plop as she followed Bruno's lead and hurled herself forward. Giddy with relief, she plastered kisses over Michael's face. "Oh, Michael, I'm so glad it's you."

"Yeah. You sure looked pleased when you were hefting that skillet. Run out of hair spray?"

"It was handy." Abruptly she drew back and glared at him. "Dammit, Michael, you scared me to death. You're supposed to be halfway to New York, not skulking around the woods."

"And you're supposed to be locked in the house."

"I would've been if you hadn't been skulking in the woods. Why?"

In an offhanded gesture, he brushed snow from her face. "I got ten miles away, and I couldn't get rid of this bad feeling. It was too pat. I decided to stop at a gas station and phone my neighbor."

"But your apartment."

"I talked to the police, gave them a list of my valuables. We'll both run into New York in a day or two." Snow was scattered through her hair and matted to her coat. He thought of what might have happened and resisted the urge to shake her. "I couldn't leave you alone."

"I'm going to start believing you're chivalrous after all." She kissed him. "That explains why you're not in New York, but what were you doing in the woods?"

"Just a hunch." He bent to retrieve the frying pan. A good whack with that, he discovered, and he'd have been down for the count.

"The next time you have a hunch, don't stand at the edge of the woods and stare at the house."

"I wasn't." Michael took her arm and headed back toward the house. He wanted her inside again, behind locked doors.

"I saw you."

"I don't know who you saw." Disgusted, Michael looked back at the dog. "But if you hadn't let the dog out we'd both know. I decided to check around outside before coming in, and I saw footprints. I followed them around, then cut into the woods." He glanced over his shoulder, still tight with tension. "I was just coming up behind whoever made them when Bruno tried his attack. I started chasing." He swore and slapped a palm against the skillet. "I was gaining when this hound ran between my legs and sent me face first into the snow. About that time, you started yelling at the dog. Whoever I was chasing had enough time to disappear."

Pandora swore and kicked at the snow. "If you'd let me know what was going on, we could've worked together."

"I didn't know what was going on until it was already happening. In any case, the deal was you'd stay inside with the doors locked."

"The dog had to go out," Pandora muttered. "And I had this phone call." She looked back over her shoulder and sighed. "Someone called to warn me."

"Who?"

"I don't know. I thought it was a man's voice, but—I'm just not sure."

Michael's hand tightened on her arm. "Did he threaten you?"

"No, no it wasn't like a threat. Whoever it was certainly seemed to know what's been going on and isn't happy about it. That much was clear. He—she said someone was going to try to break into the Folley, and I should get out."

"And, of course, you handled that by running into the woods with a skillet. Pandora." This time he did shake her. "Why didn't you call the police?"

"Because I thought it was another trick and it made me mad." She sent Michael a stubborn look. "Yes, it frightened me at first, then it just plain made me mad. I don't like intimidation. When I looked out and saw someone near the woods, I only wanted to fight back."

"Admirable," he said but took her shoulders. "Stupid."

"You were doing the same thing."

"It's not the same thing. You've got brains, you've got style. I'll even give you guts. But, cousin, you're not a heavyweight.

What if you'd caught up with whoever was out there and they wanted to play rough?"

"I can play rough, too," Pandora muttered.

"Fine." With a quick move, he hooked a foot behind hers and sent her bottom first into the snow. She didn't have the opportunity to complain before he was standing over her, gesturing with the skillet. Bruno decided it was a game and leaped on top of her. "I might've come back tomorrow and found you half-buried in the snow." Before she could speak, he hauled her to her feet again. "I'm not risking that."

"You caught me off balance," she began.

"Shut up." He had her by the shoulders again, and this time his grip wasn't gentle. "You're too important, Pandora, I'm through taking chances. We're going inside and calling the cops. We're going to tell them everything."

"What can they do?"

"We'll find out."

She let out a long breath, then leaned against him. The chase might have been exciting, but her knees had yet to stop shaking. "Okay, maybe you're right. We're no farther along now than when we started."

"Calling the police isn't giving up, it's just changing the odds. I might not have come back here tonight, Pandora. The dog may not have frightened anyone off. You'd have been alone." He took both her hands, pressing them to his lips and warming them. "I'm not going to let anything happen to you."

Confused by the sense of pleasure his words gave her, she tried to draw her hands away. "I can take care of myself, Michael."

He smiled but didn't let go. "Maybe. But you're not going to have the chance to find out. Let's go home. I'm hungry."

"Typical," she began, needing to lighten the mood. "You'd think of your stomach—oh my God, the chicken!" Breaking away, Pandora loped toward the house.

"I'm not that hungry." Michael sprinted after her. The relief came again when he scooped her up into his arms. When he'd heard her shout in the woods, had realized she was outside and vulnerable, his blood had simply stopped flowing. "In fact," he said as he scooped her up, "I can think of more pressing matters than eating."

"Michael." She struggled, but laughed. "If you don't put me down, there won't be a kitchen to eat in."

"We'll eat somewhere else."

"I left the pan on. There's probably nothing left of the chicken but charred bones."

"There's always soup." With that, he pushed open the kitchen door.

Rather than a smoky, splattered mess, they found a platter piled high with crisp, brown chicken. Sweeney had wiped up the spills, and had the pans soaking in the sink.

"Sweeney." From her perch in Michael's arms, Pandora surveyed the room. "What are you doing out of bed?"

"My job," she said briskly, but gave them a quick sidelong look. As far as she was concerned, her plans were working perfectly. She imagined Pandora and Michael had decided to take a little air while dinner was cooking, and, as young people would, had forgotten the time.

"You're supposed to be in bed," Pandora reminded her.

"Posh. I've been in bed long enough." And the days of little or no activity had nearly bored her to tears. It was worth it, however, to see Pandora snug in Michael's arms. "Feeling fit as a fiddle now, I promise you. Wash up for dinner."

Michael and Pandora each took separate and careful studies. Sweeney's cheeks were pink and round, her eyes bright. She bustled from counter to counter in her old businesslike fashion. "We still want you to take it easy," Michael decided. "No heavy work."

"That's right. Michael and I'll take care of the washing up." She saw him scowl, just a little, and patted his shoulder. "We like to do it."

At Michael and Pandora's insistence, all four ate in the kitchen. Charles, sitting next to Sweeney, was left uncertain how much he should cough and settled on a middle road, clearing his throat every so often. In an unspoken agreement, Pandora and Michael decided to keep the matter of trespassers to themselves. Both of them felt the announcement that someone was watching the house would be too upsetting for the two old people while they were recuperating.

On the surface, dinner was an easy meal, but Pandora kept wondering how soon they could nudge the servants along to bed and contact the police. More than once, Pandora caught Sweeney looking from her to Michael with a smug smile. Sweet old lady, Pandora mused, innocently believing the cook to be pleased to have her kitchen back. It made Pandora only more determined to protect her and Charles from any unpleasantness. She concentrated on cleaning up and packing them off to bed, and it was nearly nine before she was able to meet Michael in the parlor.

"Settled?"

She heard the familiar restlessness in his voice and merely nodded, pouring a brandy. "It's a bit like cajoling children, but I managed to find a Cary Grant movie that interested them." She sipped the brandy, waiting for her muscles to relax with it. "I'd rather be watching it myself."

"Another time." Michael took a sip from her snifter. "I've called the police. They'll be here shortly."

She took the glass back. "It still bothers me to take the business to outsiders. After all, anything beyond simple trespass is speculation."

"We'll let the police speculate."

She managed to smile. "Your Logan always handles things on his own."

"Someone told me once that that was just fiction." He poured himself a brandy and toasted her. "I discovered I don't like having you in the middle of a story line."

The brandy and firelight gave the evening an illusion of normalcy. Pandora took his statement with a shrug. "You seem to have developed a protect-the-woman syndrome, Michael. It's not like you."

"Maybe not." He tossed back a gulp. "It's different when it's my woman."

She turned, brow lifted. It was ridiculous to feel pleasure at such a foolish and possessive term. "Yours?"

"Mine." He cupped the back of her neck with his hand. "Got a problem with that?"

Her heart beat steadily in her throat until she managed to swallow. Maybe he meant it—now. In a few months when he was back moving in his own world, with his own people, she'd be no more than his somewhat annoying cousin. But for now, just for now, maybe he meant it. "I'm not sure."

"Give it some thought," he advised before he lowered his mouth to hers. "We'll come back to it."

He left her flustered and went to answer the door.

When he returned, Pandora was sitting calmly enough in a high-backed chair near the fire. "Lieutenant Randall, Pandora McVie."

"How d'you do?" The lieutenant pulled off a wool muffler and stuck it in his coat pocket. He looked, Pandora thought, like someone's grandfather. Comfy, round and balding. "Miserable night," he announced, and situated himself near the fire.

"Would you like some coffee, Lieutenant?"

Randall gave Pandora a grateful look. "Love it."

"Please, have a seat. I'll be back in a minute."

She took her time heating coffee and arranging cups and saucers on a tray. Not putting off, Pandora insisted, just preparing. She'd never had occasion to talk to a policeman on any subject more complex than a parking ticket. She'd come out on the short end on that one. Now, she was about to discuss her family and her relationship with Michael.

Her relationship with Michael, she thought again as she fussed with the sugar bowl. That's what really had her hiding in the kitchen. She hadn't yet been able to dull the feeling that had raced through her when he'd called her his woman. Adolescent, Pandora told herself. It was absolutely absurd to feel giddy and self-satisfied and unnerved because a man had looked at her with passion in his eyes.

But they'd been Michael's eyes.

She found linen napkins and folded them into triangles. She didn't want to be anyone's woman but her own. It had been the strain and excitement of the evening that had made her react like a sixteen-year-old being offered a school ring. She was an adult; she was self-sustaining. She was in love. Talk yourself out of that one, Pandora challenged herself. Taking a long breath, she hefted the tray and went back to the parlor.

"Gentlemen." Pandora set the tray on a low table and stuck on a smile. "Cream and sugar, Lieutenant?"

"Thanks. A healthy dose of both." He set a dog-eared notepad on his knee when Pandora handed him a cup. "Mr. Donahue's been filling me in. Seems you've had a few annoyances."

She smiled at the term. Like his looks, his voice was comfortable. "A few."

"I'm not going to lecture." But he gave them both a stern look. "Still, you should've notified the police after the first incident. Vandalism's a crime."

"We'd hoped by ignoring it, it would discourage repetition." Pandora lifted her cup. "We were wrong."

"I'll need to take the champagne with me." Again, he sent them a look of disapproval. "Even though you've had it analyzed, we'll want to run it through our own lab."

"I'll get it for you." Michael rose and left them alone.

"Miss McVie, from what your cousin tells me, the terms of Mr. McVie's will were a bit unconventional."

"A bit."

"He also tells me he talked you into agreeing to them."

"That's Michael's fantasy, Lieutenant." She sipped her coffee. "I'm doing exactly what I chose to do."

Randall nodded and noted. "You agree with Mr. Donahue's idea that these incidents are connected and one of your relatives is responsible."

"I can't think of any reason to disagree."

"Do you have any reason to suspect one more than another?"

Pandora thought it through as she'd thought it through before. "No. You see, we're not at all a close family. The truth is I don't know any of them very well."

"Except Mr. Donahue."

"That's right. Michael and I often visited our uncle, and we ran into each other here at the Folley." Whether we wanted to or not, she added to herself in her own private joke. "None of the others came by very often."

"The champagne, Lieutenant." Michael brought in the box. "And the report from Sanfield Laboratories."

Randall skimmed the printout, then tucked the sheet into the box. "Your uncle's attorney..." He referred quickly to his notes. "Fitzhugh reported trespassing several weeks ago. We've had a squad car cruise the area, but at this point you might agree to having a man patrol the grounds once a day."

"I'd prefer it," Michael told him.

"I'll contact Fitzhugh." Seeing his cup was empty, Pandora took it and filled it again. "I'll also need a list of the relatives named in the will."

Pandora frowned over her rim. Between her and Michael, they tried to fill in the lieutenant, as best as they could. When they had finished, Pandora sent Randall an apologetic look. "I told you we aren't close."

"I'll get the lawyer to fill in the details." Randall rose and tried not to think about the cold drive back to town. "We'll keep the inquiries as quiet as possible. If anything else happens, call me. One of my men will be around to look things over."

"Thank you, Lieutenant." Michael helped the pudgy man on with his coat.

Randall took another look around the room. "Ever think of installing a security system?"

"No."

"Think again," he advised, and made his way out.

"We've just been scolded," Pandora murmured.

Michael wondered if *Logan's Run* had room for a cranky, well-padded cop. "Seems that way."

"You know, Michael, I have two schools of thought on bringing in the police."

"Which are?"

"It's either going to calm things down or stir things up."

"You pay your money and take your choice."

She gave him a knowing look. "You're counting on the second."

"I came close tonight." He bypassed the coffee and poured another brandy. "I nearly had my hands on something. Someone." When he looked at her, the faint amusement in his eyes had faded. The recklessness was back. "I like my fights in the open, face-to-face."

"It's better if we look at it as a chess game rather than a boxing match." She came close to wrap her arms around him and press her cheek to his shoulder. It was the kind of gesture he didn't think he'd ever get used to from her. As he rested his head on her hair, he realized that the fact that he wouldn't only added to the sweetness of the feeling. When had he stopped remembering that she didn't fit into his long-established picture of the ideal woman? Her hair was too red, her body too thin, her tongue too sharp. Michael nuzzled against her and found they fit very well.

"I've never had the patience for chess."

"Then we'll just leave it to the police." She held him tighter. The need to protect rose as sharply as the desire to be protected. "I've been thinking about what might have happened out there tonight. I don't want you hurt, Michael."

With two fingers under her chin, he lifted it. "Why not?"

"Because..." She looked into his eyes and felt her heart melt. But she wouldn't be a fool; she wouldn't risk her pride. "Because then I'd have to do the dishes by myself."

He smiled. No, he didn't have a great deal of patience, but he could call on it when circumstances warranted. He brushed a kiss on either side of her mouth. Sooner or later, he'd have more out of her. Then he'd just have to decide what to do with it. "Any other reason?"

Absorbing the sensations, Pandora searched her mind for

another easy answer. "If you were hurt, you couldn't work. I'd have to live with your foul temper."

"I thought you were already living with it."

"I've seen it fouler."

He kissed her eyes closed in his slow, sensuous way. "Try one more time."

"I care." She opened her eyes, and her look was tense and defiant. "Got a problem with that?"

"No." His kiss wasn't gentle this time, it wasn't patient. He had her caught close and reeling within moments. If there was tension in her still, he couldn't feel it. "The only problem's been dragging it out of you."

"You're family after all—"

With a laugh, he nipped the lobe of her ear. "Don't try to back out."

Indignant, she stiffened. "I never back out."

"Unless you can rationalize it. Just remember this." He had her molded against him again. "The family connection's distant." Their lips met, urgently, then parted. "This connection isn't."

"I don't know what you want from me," she whispered.

"You're usually so quick."

"Don't joke, Michael."

"It's no joke." He drew her away, holding her by the shoulders. Briefly, firmly, he ran his hands down to her elbows, then back. "No, I'm not going to spell it out for you, Pandora. I'm not going to make it easy on you. You have to be willing to admit we both want the same thing. And you will."

"Arrogant," she warned.

"Confident," he corrected. He had to be, or he'd be on his knees begging. There'd come a time, he'd promised himself, when she'd drop the last of her restrictions. "I want you."

A tremor skipped up her spine. "I know."

"Yeah." He linked his fingers with hers. "I think you do."

Chapter Eleven

Winter raged its way through February. There came a point when Pandora had to shovel her way from the house to her workshop. She found herself grateful for the physical labor. Winter was a long quiet time that provided too many hours to think.

In using this time, Pandora came to several uncomfortable realizations. Her life, as she'd known it, as she'd guided it, would never be the same. As far as her art was concerned, she felt the months of concentrated effort with dashes of excitement had only improved her crafting. In truth, she often used her jewelry to take her mind off what was happening to and around her. When that didn't work, she used what was happening to and around her in her work.

The sudden blunt understanding that her health, even her life, had been endangered made her take a step away from her usual practical outlook. It caused her to appreciate little things she'd always taken for granted. Waking up in a warm bed, watching snow fall while a fire crackled beside her. She'd learned that every second in life was vital.

Already she was considering taking a day to drive back to New York and pack what was important to her. More than packing, it would be a time of decision making. What she kept, what she didn't, would in some ways reflect the changes she'd accepted in herself.

Both the lease on her apartment and the lease on the shop over the boutique were coming up for renewal. She'd let them lapse. Rather than living alone, she'd have the company and the responsibility of her uncle's old servants. Though she'd once been determined to be responsible only to herself and her art, Pandora made the choice without a qualm. Though she had lived in the city, in the rush, in the crowds, she'd isolated herself. No more.

Through it all wove Michael.

In a few short weeks, what they had now would be over. The long winter they'd shared would be something to think of during other winters. As she prepared for a new and different life, Pandora promised herself she'd have no regrets. But she couldn't stop herself from having wishes. Things were already changing.

The police had come, and with their arrival had been more questions. Everything in her shop had to be locked up tightly after dark, and there were no more solitary walks in the woods after a snowfall. It had become a nightly ritual to go through the Folley and check doors and windows that had once been casually ignored. Often when she walked back to the house from her shop, she'd see Michael watching from the window of his room.

It should have given her a warm, comfortable feeling, but she knew he was waiting for something else to happen. She knew, as she knew him, that he wanted it. Inactivity was sitting uneasily on him.

Since they'd driven into New York to deal with the break-in at his apartment, he'd been distant, with a restlessness roiling underneath. Though they both understood the wisdom of having the grounds patrolled, she thought they felt intruded upon.

They had no sense of satisfaction from the police investigation. Each one of their relatives had alibis for one or more of the incidents. So far the investigation seemed to have twin results. Since the police had been called in, nothing else had happened. There'd been no anonymous phone calls, no shadows in the woods, no bogus telegrams. It had, as Pandora had also predicted, stirred things up. She'd dealt with an irate phone call from Carlson who insisted they were using the investigation in an attempt to undermine his case against the will.

On the heels of that had come a disjointed letter from Ginger who'd had the idea that the Folley was haunted. Michael had had a two-minute phone conversation with Morgan who'd muttered about private family business, overreacting and hogwash. Biff, in his usual style, had wired a short message:

Cops and robbers? Looks like you two are playing games with each other.

From Hank they heard nothing.

The police lab had confirmed the private analysis of the

champagne; Randall was plodding through the investigation in his precise, quiet way. Michael and Pandora were exactly where they'd been weeks before: waiting.

He didn't know how she could stand it. As Michael made his way down the narrow path Pandora had shoveled, he wondered how she could remain so calm when he was ready to chew glass. It had only taken him a few days of hanging in limbo to realize it was worse when nothing happened. Waiting for someone else to make the next move was the most racking kind of torture. Until he was sure Pandora was safe, he couldn't relax. Until he had his hands around someone's throat, he wouldn't be satisfied. He was caught in a trap of inactivity that was slowly driving him mad. Pausing just outside her shop, he glanced around.

The house looked big and foolish with icicles hanging and dripping from eaves, gutters and shutters. It belonged in a book, he thought, some moody, misty gothic. A fairy tale—the grim sort. Perhaps one day he'd weave a story around it himself, but for now, it was just home.

With his hands in his pockets he watched smoke puff out of chimneys. Foolish it might be, but he'd always loved it. The longer he lived in it, the surer he was that he was meant to. He was far from certain how Pandora would take his decision to remain after the term was over.

His last script for the season was done. It was the only episode to be filmed before the show wrapped until fall. He could, as he often did, take a few weeks in the early spring and find a hot, noisy beach. He could fish, relax and enjoy watching women in undersize bikinis. Michael knew he wasn't going anywhere.

For the past few days, he'd been toying with a screenplay for a feature film. He'd given it some thought before, but somehow something had always interfered. He could write it here, he knew. He could perfect it here with Pandora wielding her art nearby, criticizing his work so that he was only more determined to make it better. But he was waiting. Waiting for something else to happen, waiting to find who it was who'd used fear and intimidation to try to drive them out. And most of all, he was waiting for Pandora. Until she gave him her complete trust, willingly, until she gave him her heart unrestrictedly, he had to go on waiting.

His hands curled into fists and released. He wanted action.

He tried the door and satisfied himself that she'd kept her word and locked it from the inside. "Pandora?" He knocked with the side of his fist. She opened the door with a drill in her hand. After giving her flushed face and tousled hair a quick look, Michael lifted his hands, palms out. "I'm unarmed."

"And I'm busy." But her lips curved. There was a light of pleasure in her eyes. He found it easy to notice such small things.

"I know, I've invaded scheduled working hours, but I have a valid excuse."

"You're letting in the cold," she complained. Once, she might have shut the door in his face without a second thought. This time she shut it behind him.

"Not a hell of a lot warmer in here."

"It's fine when I'm working. Which I am."

"Blame Sweeney. She's sending me in for supplies, and she insisted I take you." He sent Pandora a bland look. "'That girl holes herself up in that shed too much. Needs some sun.'"

"I get plenty of sun," Pandora countered. Still, the idea of a drive into town appealed. It wouldn't hurt to talk to the jeweler in the little shopping center. She was beginning to think her work should spread out a bit, beyond the big cities. "I suppose we should humor her, but I want to finish up here first."

"I'm in no hurry."

"Good. Half an hour then." She went to exchange the drill for a jeweler's torch. Because she didn't hear the door open or shut, she turned and saw Michael examining her rolling mill. "Michael," she said with more than a trace of exasperation.

"Go ahead, take your time."

"Don't you have anything to do?"

"Not a thing," he said cheerfully.

"Not one car chase to write?"

"No. Besides, I've never seen you work."

"Audiences make me cranky."

"Broaden your horizons, love. Pretend I'm an apprentice."

"I'm not sure they can get that broad."

Undaunted, he pointed to her worktable. "What is that thing?"

"This thing," she began tightly, "is a pendant. A waterfall effect made with brass wire and some scraps of silver I had left over from a bracelet."

"No waste," he murmured. "Practical as ever. So what's the next step?"

With a long breath, she decided it would be simpler to play along than to throw him out. "I've just finished adjusting the curves of the wires. I've used different thicknesses and lengths to give it a free-flowing effect. The silver scraps I've cut and filed into elongated teardrops. Now I solder them onto the ends of the wires."

She applied the flux, shifting a bit so that he could watch. After she'd put a square of solder beside each wire, she used the torch to apply heat until the solder melted. Patient, competent, she repeated the procedure until all twelve teardrops were attached.

"Looks easy enough," he mused.

"A child of five could do it."

He heard the sarcasm and laughed as he took her hands. "You want flattery? A few minutes ago I saw a pile of metal. Now I see an intriguing ornament. Ornate and exotic."

"It's supposed to be exotic," Pandora replied. "Jessica Wainwright will wear it in the film. It's to have been a gift from an old lover. The countess claims he was a Turkish prince."

Michael studied the necklace again. "Very appropriate."

"It'll droop down from brass and silver wires twisted together. The lowest teardrop should hang nearly to her waist." Pleased, but knowing better than to touch the metal before the solder cooled, Pandora held up her sketch. "Ms. Wainwright was very specific. She wants nothing ordinary, nothing even classic. Everything she wears should add to the character's mystique."

She set the sketch down and tidied her tools. She'd solder on the hoop and fashion the neck wire when they returned from town. Then if there was time, she'd begin the next project. The gold-plated peacock pin with its three-inch filigree tail would take her the better part of two weeks.

"This thing has potential as a murder weapon," Michael mused, picking up a burnisher to examine the curved, steel tip.

"I beg your pardon?"

He liked the way she said it, so that even with her back turned she was looking down her nose. "For a story line."

"Leave my tools out of your stories." Pandora took the burnisher from him and packed it away. "Going to buy me lunch in town?" She stripped off her apron then grabbed her coat.

"I was going to ask you the same thing."

"I asked first." She locked the shop and welcomed the cold. "The snow's beginning to melt."

"In a few weeks, the five dozen bulbs Jolley planted during his gardening stage will be starting to bloom."

"Daffodils," she murmured. It didn't seem possible when you felt the air, saw the mounds of snow, but spring was closing in. "The winter hasn't seemed so long."

"No, it hasn't." He slipped an arm around her shoulders. "I never expected six months to go so quickly. I figured one of us would've attempted murder by this time."

With a laugh, Pandora matched her step to his. "We've still got a month to go."

"Now we have to behave ourselves," he reminded her. "Lieutenant Randall has his eye on us."

"I guess we blew our chance." She turned to wind her arms around his neck. "There have been times I've wanted to hit you with a blunt instrument."

"Feeling's mutual," he told her as he lowered his mouth. Her lips were cool and curved.

At the side window, Sweeney drew back the drape. "Look at this!" Cackling, she gestured to Charles. "I told you it would work. In a few more weeks, I'll be putting bells on a wedding cake."

As Charles joined Sweeney at the window, Pandora scooped a hand into the snow and tossed it in Michael's face. "Don't count your chickens," he muttered.

In a desperate move to avoid retaliation, Pandora raced to the garage. She ducked seconds before snow splattered against the door. "Your aim's still off, cousin." Hefting the door, she sprinted inside and jumped into his car. Smug, she settled into the seat. He wouldn't, she was sure, mar his spotless interior with a snowball. Michael opened the door, slid in beside her and dumped snow over her head. She was still squealing when he turned the key.

"I'm better at close range."

Pandora sputtered as she wiped at the snow. Because she'd appreciated the move, it was difficult to sound indignant. "One would have thought that a man who drives an ostentatious car would be more particular with it."

"It's only ostentatious if you buy it for status purposes."

"And, of course, you didn't."

"I bought it because it gets terrific gas mileage." When she snorted, he turned to grin at her. "And because it looks great wrapped around redheads."

"And blondes and brunettes."

"Redheads," he corrected, twining her hair around his finger. "I've developed a preference."

It shouldn't have made her smile, but it did. She was still smiling when they started down the long, curvy road. "We can't complain about the road crews," she said idly. "Except for those two weeks last month, the roads've been fairly clear." She glanced toward the mounds of snow the plows had pushed to the side of the road.

"Too bad they won't do the driveway."

"You know you loved riding that little tractor. Uncle Jolley always said it made him feel tough and macho."

"So much so he'd race it like a madman over the yard."

As they came to a curve, Michael eased on the brake and downshifted. Pandora leaned forward and fiddled with the stereo. "Most people have equipment like this in their den."

"I don't have a den."

"You don't have a stereo to put in one, either," she remembered. "Or a television."

He shrugged, but mentally listed what he'd lost from his apartment. "Insurance'll cover it."

"The police are handling that as though it were a normal break-in." She switched channels. "It might've been."

"Or it might've been a smoke screen. I wish we—" He broke off as they approached another curve. He'd pressed the brake again, but this time, the pedal had gone uselessly to the floor.

"Michael, if you're trying to impress me with your skill as a driver, it's not working." Instinctively Pandora grabbed the door handle as the car careered down the curve.

Whipping the steering wheel with one hand, Michael yanked on the emergency brake. The car continued to barrel down. He gripped the wheel in both hands and fought the next curve. "No brakes." As he told her, Michael glanced down to see the speedometer hover at seventy.

Pandora's knuckles turned white on the handle. "We won't make it to the bottom without them."

He never considered lying. "No." Tires squealed as he rounded the next curve. Gravel spit under the wheels as the car went wide. There was the scrape and scream of metal as the fender kissed the guardrail.

She looked at the winding road spinning in front of her. Her vision blurred then cleared. The sign before the S-turn cautioned for a safe speed of thirty. Michael took it at seventy-five. Pandora shut her eyes. When she opened them and saw the snowbank dead ahead, she screamed. With seconds to spare, Michael yanked the car around. Snow flew skyward as the car skidded along the bank.

Eyes intense, Michael stared at the road ahead and struggled to anticipate each curve. Sweat beaded on his forehead. He knew the road, that's what terrified him. In less than three miles, the already sharp incline steepened. At high speed, the car would ram straight through the guardrail and crash on the cliffs below. The game Jolley had begun would end violently.

Michael tasted his own fear, then swallowed it. "There's only one chance; we've got to turn off on the lane leading into the old inn. It's coming up after that curve." He couldn't take his eyes from the road to look at her. His fingers dug into the wheel. "Hang on."

She was going to die. Her mind was numb from the thought of it. She heard the tires scream as Michael dragged at the wheel. The car tilted, nearly going over. She saw trees rush by as the car slid on the slippery edge of the lane. Almost, for an instant, the rubber seemed to grip the gravel beneath. But the turn was too sharp, the speed too fast. Out of control, the car spiraled toward the trees.

"I love you," she whispered, and grabbed for him before the world went black.

He came to slowly. He hurt, and for a time didn't understand why. There was noise. Eventually he turned his head toward it. When he opened his eyes, Michael saw a boy with wide eyes and black hair gawking through the window.

"Mister, hey, mister. You okay?"

Dazed, Michael pushed open the door. "Get help," he managed, fighting against blacking out again. He took deep gulps of air to clear his head as the boy dashed off through the woods. "Pandora." Fear broke through the fog. In seconds, he was leaning over her.

His fingers shook as he reached for the pulse of her neck, but he found it. Blood from a cut on her forehead ran down her face and onto his hands. With his fingers pressed against the wound, he fumbled in the glove compartment for the first-aid kit. He'd stopped the bleeding and was checking her for broken bones when she moaned. He had to stop himself from dragging her against him and holding on.

"Take it easy," he murmured when she began to stir. "Don't move around." When she opened her eyes, he saw they were glazed and unfocused. "You're all right." Gently he cupped her face in his hands and continued to reassure her. Her eyes focused gradually. As they did, she reached for his hand.

"The brakes...."

"Yeah." He rested his cheek against hers a moment. "It was a hell of a trip, but it looks like we made it."

Confused, she looked around. The car was stopped, leaning drunkenly against a tree. It had been the deep, slushy snow that had slowed them down enough to prevent the crash from being fatal. "We—you're all right?" The tears started when she reached out and took his face in her hands as he had with hers. "You're all right."

"Terrific." His wrist throbbed like a jackhammer and his head ached unbelievably, but he was alive. When she started to move, he held her still. "No, don't move around. I don't know how badly you're hurt. There was a kid. He's gone for help."

"It's just my head." She started to take his hand, and saw the blood. "Oh God, you're bleeding. Where?" Before she could begin her frantic search, he gripped her hands together.

"It's not me. It's you. Your head's cut. You probably have a concussion."

Shaky, she lifted her hand and touched the bandage. The wound beneath it hurt, but she drew on that. If she hurt, she was alive. "I thought I was dead." She closed her eyes but tears slipped through the lashes. "I thought we were both dead."

"We're both fine." They heard the siren wail up the mountain road. He was silent until she opened her eyes again. "You know what happened?"

Her head ached badly, but it was clear. "Attempted murder."

He nodded, not turning when the ambulance pulled into the slushy lane. "I'm through waiting, Pandora. I'm through waiting all around."

Lieutenant Randall found Michael in the emergency-room lounge. He unwrapped his muffler, unbuttoned his coat and sat down on the hard wooden bench. "Looks like you've had some trouble."

"Big time."

Randall nodded toward the Ace bandage on Michael's wrist. "Bad?"

"Just a sprain. Few cuts and bruises and a hell of a headache. Last time I saw it, my car looked something like an accordion."

"We're taking it in. Anything we should look for?"

"Brake lines. It seemed I didn't have any when I started the trip down the mountain."

"When's the last time you used your car?" Randall had his notepad in hand.

"Ten days, two weeks." Wearily, Michael rubbed a temple. "I drove into New York to talk to police about the robbery in my apartment."

"Where do you keep your car?"

"In the garage."

"Locked?"

"The garage?" Michael kept his eye on the hallway where Pandora had been wheeled away. "No. My uncle had installed one of those remote control devices a few years back. Never worked unless you turned on the television. Anyway, he took it out again and never replaced the lock. Pandora's car's in there," he remembered suddenly. "If—"

"We'll check it out," Randall said easily. "Miss McVie was with you?"

"Yeah, she's with a doctor." For the first time in weeks, Michael found himself craving a cigarette. "Her head was cut." He looked down at his hands and remembered her blood on them. "I'm going to find out who did this, Lieutenant, and then I'm going to—"

"Don't say anything to me I might have to use later," Randall warned. There were some people who threatened as a means to let off steam or relieve tension. Randall didn't think Michael Donahue was one of them. "Let me do my job, Mr. Donahue."

Michael gave him a long, steady look. "Someone's been playing games, deadly ones, with someone very important to me. If you were in my place, would you twiddle your thumbs and wait?"

Randall smiled, just a little. "You know, Donahue, I never miss your show. Great entertainment. Some of this business sounds just like one of your shows."

"Like one of my shows," Michael repeated slowly.

"Problem is, things don't work the same way out here in the world as they do on television. But it sure is a pleasure to watch. Here comes your lady."

Michael sprang up and headed for her.

"I'm fine," she told him before he could ask.

"Not entirely." Behind her a young, white coated doctor stood impatiently. "Miss McVie has a concussion."

"He put a few stitches in my head and wants to hold me prisoner." She gave the doctor a sweet smile and linked arms with Michael. "Let's go home."

"Just a minute." Keeping her beside him, Michael turned to the doctor. "You want her in the hospital?"

"Michael—"

"Shut up."

"Anyone suffering from a concussion should be routinely checked. Miss McVie would be wise to remain overnight with professional care."

"I'm not staying in the hospital because I have a bump on the head. Good afternoon, Lieutenant."

"Miss McVie."

Lifting her chin, she looked back at the doctor. "Now, Doctor…"

"Barnhouse."

"Dr. Barnhouse," she began. "I will take your advice to a point. I'll rest, avoid stress. At the first sign of nausea or dizziness, I'll be on your doorstep. I can assure you, now that you've convinced Michael I'm an invalid, I'll be properly smothered and hovered over. You'll have to be satisfied with that."

Far from satisfied, the doctor directed himself to Michael. "I can't force her to stay, of course."

Michael lifted a brow. "If you think I can, you've got a lot to learn about women."

Resigned, Barnhouse turned back to Pandora. "I want to see you in a week, sooner if any of the symptoms we discussed show up. You're to rest for twenty-four hours. That means horizontally."

"Yes, Doctor." She offered a hand, which he took grudgingly. "You were very gentle. Thank you."

His lips twitched. "A week," he repeated and strode back down the hall.

"If I didn't know better," Michael mused, "I'd say he wanted to keep you here just to look at you."

"Of course. I look stunning with blood running down my face and a hole in my head."

"I thought so." He kissed her cheek, but used the gesture to get a closer look at her wound. The stitches were small and neat, disappearing into her hairline. After counting six of them, his determination iced. "Come on, we'll go home so I can start pampering you."

"I'll take you myself." Randall gestured toward the door. "I might as well look around a bit while I'm there."

Sweeney clucked like a mother hen and had Pandora bundled into bed five minutes after she'd walked in the door. If she'd had the strength, Pandora would have argued for form's sake. Instead she let herself be tucked under a comforter, fed soup and sweet tea, and fussed over. Though the doctor had assured her it was perfectly safe to sleep, she thought of the old wives' tale and struggled to stay awake. Armed with a sketch pad and pencil, she whiled away the time designing. But when she began to tire of that, she began to think.

Murder. It would have been nothing less than murder. Murder for gain, she mused, an impossible thing for her to understand. She'd told herself before that her life was threatened, but somehow it had seemed remote. She had only to touch her own forehead now to prove just how direct it had become.

An uncle, a cousin, an aunt? Which one wanted Jolley's fortune so badly to murder for it? Not for the first time, Pandora wished she knew them better, understood them better. She realized she'd simply followed Jolley's lead and dismissed them as boring.

And that was true enough, Pandora assured herself. She'd been to a party or two with all of them. Monroe would huff, Biff would preen, Ginger would prattle, and so on. But boring or not, one of them had slipped over the line of civilized behavior. And they were willing to step over her to do it. Slowly, from memory, she began to sketch each of her relatives. Perhaps that way, she'd see something that was buried in her subconscious.

When Michael came in, she had sketches lined in rows over her spread. "Quite a rogues' gallery."

He'd come straight from the garage, where he and Randall had found the still-wet brake fluid on the concrete. Not all of it, Michael mused. Whoever had tampered with the brakes had left enough fluid in so that the car would react normally for the first few miles. And then, nothing. Michael had already concluded that the police would find a hole in the lines. Just as they'd find one in the lines of Pandora's, to match the dark puddle beneath her car. It had been every bit as lethal as his.

He wasn't ready to tell Pandora that whoever had tried to kill them had been as close as the garage a day, perhaps two, before. Instead he looked at her sketches.

“What do you see?” she demanded.

“That you have tremendous talent and should give serious thought to painting.”

“I mean in their faces.” Impatient with herself, she drew her legs up Indian style. “There’s just nothing there. No spark, no streak of anything that tells me this one’s capable of killing.”

“Anyone’s capable of killing. Oh yes,” Michael added when she opened her mouth to disagree. “Anyone. It’s simply that the motive has to fit the personality, the circumstances, the need. When a person’s threatened, he kills. For some it’s only when their lives or the lives of someone they love are threatened.”

“That’s entirely different.”

“No.” He sat on the bed. “It’s a matter of different degrees. Some people kill because their home is threatened, their possessions. Some kill because a desire is threatened. Wealth, power, those are very strong desires.

“So a very ordinary, even conventional person might kill to achieve that desire.”

He gestured to her sketches. “One of them tried. Aunt Patience with her round little face and myopic eyes.”

“You can’t seriously believe—”

“She’s devoted to Morgan, obsessively so. She’s never married. Why? Because she’s always taken care of him.”

He picked up the next sketch. “Or there’s Morgan himself, stout, blunt, hard-nosed. He thought Jolley was mad and a nuisance.”

“They all did.”

"Exactly. Carlson, straitlaced, humorless, and Jolley's only surviving son."

"He tried contesting the will."

"Going the conventional route. Still, he knew his father was shrewd, perhaps better than anyone. Who's to say he wouldn't cover his bases in a more direct way? Biff..." He had a laugh as he looked at the sketch. Pandora had drawn him precisely as he was. Self-absorbed.

"I can't see him getting his hands dirty."

"For a slice of a hundred fifty million? I can. Pretty little Ginger. One wonders if she can possibly be as sweet and spacey as she appears. And Hank." Pandora had drawn him with his arm muscle flexed. "Would he settle for a couple of thousand when he could have millions?"

"I don't know—that's just the point." Pandora shuffled the sketches. "Even when I have them all lined up in front of me, I don't know."

"Lined up," Michael murmured. "Maybe that is the answer. I think it's time we had a nice, family party."

"Party? You don't mean actually invite them all here."

"It's perfect."

"They won't come."

"Oh yes, they will." He was already thinking ahead. "You can bank on it. A little hint that things aren't going well around here, and they'll jump at the chance to give us an extra push. You see the doctor in a week. If he gives you a clean bill of health, we're going to start a little game of our own."

"What game?"

"In a week," he repeated, and took her face in his hands. It was narrow, dominated by the mop of hair and sharp eyes. Not beautiful, but special. It had taken him a long time to admit it. "A bit pale."

"I'm always pale with a concussion. Are you going to pamper me?"

"At least." But his smile faded as he gathered her close. "Oh God, I thought I'd lost you."

The trace of desperation in his voice urged her to soothe. "We'd both have been lost if you hadn't handled the car so well." She snuggled into his shoulder. It was real and solid, like the one she'd sometimes imagined leaning on. It wouldn't hurt, just this once, to pretend it would always be there. "I never thought we'd walk away from that one."

"But we did." He drew back to look at her. She looked tired and drawn, but he knew her will was as strong as ever. "And now we're going to talk about what you said to me right before we crashed."

"Wasn't I screaming?"

"No."

"If I criticized your driving, I apologize."

He tightened his grip on her chin. "You told me you loved me." He watched her mouth fall open in genuine surprise. Some men might have been insulted. Michael could bless his sense of humor. "It could technically be called a deathbed confession."

Had she? She could only remember reaching for him in those last seconds, knowing they were about to die together. "I was hysterical," she began, and tried to draw back.

"It didn't sound like raving to me."

"Michael, you heard Dr. Barnhouse. I'm not supposed to have any stress. If you want to be helpful, see about some more tea."

"I've something better for relaxing the muscles and soothing the nerves." He laid her back against the pillows, sliding down with her. Sweetly, tenderly, he ran his lips down the lines of her cheekbones. "I want to hear you tell me again, here."

"Michael—"

"No, lie back." And his hands, gentle and calm, stilled her. "I need to touch you, just touch you. There's plenty of time for the rest."

He was so kind, so patient. More than once she'd wondered how such a restive, volatile man could have such comforting hands. Taking off only his shoes, he slipped into bed with her. He held her in the crook of his arm and stroked until he felt her sigh of relief. "I'm going to take care of you," he murmured. "When you're well, we'll take care of each other."

"I'll be fine tomorrow." But her voice was thick and sleepy.

"Sure you will." He'd keep her in bed another twenty-four hours if he had to chain her. "You haven't told me again. Are you in love with me, Pandora?"

She was so tired, so drained. It seemed she'd reached a point where she could fight nothing. "What if I am?" She managed to tilt her head back to stare at him. His fingers rubbed gently at her temple, easing even the dull echo of pain. "People fall in and out of love all the time."

"People." He lowered his head so that he could just skim her lips with his. "Not Pandora. It infuriates you, doesn't it?"

She wanted to glare but closed her eyes instead. "Yes. I'm doing my best to reverse the situation."

He snuggled down beside her, content for now. She loved him. He still had time to make her like the idea. "Let me know how it works out," he said, and lulled her to sleep.

Chapter Twelve

Michael studied the dark stains on the garage floor with a kind of grim fascination. Draining the brake fluid from an intended victim's car was a hackneyed device, one expected from time to time on any self-respecting action-adventure show. Viewers and readers alike developed a certain fondness for old, reliable angles in the same way they appreciated the new and different. Though it took on a different picture when it became personal, the car careering out of control down a steep mountain road was as old as the Model T.

He'd used it himself, just as he'd used the anonymous gift of champagne. And the bogus-telegram routine, he mused as an idea began to stir. Just last season one of *Logan's* heroines of the week had been locked in a cellar—left in the dark after going to investigate a window slamming in the wind. It too was a classic. Each and every one of the ploys used against himself and Pandora could have been lifted from one of his own plots.

Randall had pointed it out, though he'd been joking. It didn't seem very funny.

Michael cursed himself, knowing he should have seen the pattern before. Perhaps he hadn't simply because it had been a pattern, a trite one by Hollywood standards. Whether it was accidental or planned, Michael decided he wasn't about to be outplotted. He'd make his next move taking a page from the classic mystery novels. Going into the house, Michael went to the phone and began to structure his scene.

He was just completing his last call when Pandora came down the hall toward him. "Michael, you've got to do something about Sweeney."

Michael leaned back against the newel post and studied her. She looked wonderful—rested, healthy and annoyed. "Isn't it time for your afternoon nap?"

"That's just what I'm talking about." The annoyance deepened between her brows and pleased him. "I don't need an afternoon nap. It's been over a week since the accident." She pulled a leather thong out of her hair and began to run it through her fingers. "I've seen the doctor, and he said I was fine."

"I thought it was more something along the lines of you having a head like a rock."

She narrowed her eyes. "He was annoyed because I healed perfectly without him. The point is, I am healed, but if Sweeney keeps nagging and hovering, I'll have a relapse." It came out as a declaration as she stood straight in front of him, chin lifted, looking as though she'd never been ill a day in her life.

"What would you like me to do?"

"She'll listen to you. For some reason she has the idea that you're infallible. Mr. Donahue this, Mr. Donahue that." She slapped the leather against her palm. "For the past week all I've heard is how charming, handsome and strong you are. It's a wonder I recovered at all."

His lips twitched, but he understood Sweeney's flattery could undo any progress he'd made. "The woman's perceptive. However..." He stopped Pandora's retort by holding up a hand. "Because I'd never refuse you anything—" when she snorted he ignored it "—and because she's been driving me crazy fussing over my wrist, I'm going to take care of it."

Pandora tilted her head. "How?"

"Sweeney's going to be too busy over the next few days to fuss over us. She'll have the dinner party to fuss over."

"What dinner party?"

"The dinner party we're going to give next week for all our relatives."

She glanced at the phone, remembering he'd been using it when she'd come down the hall. "What have you been up to?"

"Just setting the scene, cousin." He rocked back on his heels, already imagining. "I think we'll have Sweeney dig out the best china, though I doubt we'll have time to use it."

"Michael." She didn't want to seem a coward, but the accident had taught her something about caution and self-preservation. "We won't just be inviting relatives. One of them tried to kill us."

"And failed." He took her chin in his hand. "Don't you think he'll try again, Pandora, and again? The police can't patrol the grounds indefinitely. And," he added with his fingers tightening, "I'm not willing to let bygones be bygones." His gaze skimmed up to where her hair just covered the scar on her forehead. The doctor had said it would fade, but Michael's memory of it never would. "We're going to settle this, my way."

"I don't like it."

"Pandora." He gave her a charming smile and pinched her cheek. "Trust me."

The fact that she did only made her more nervous. With a sigh, she took his hand. "Let's tell Sweeney to kill the fatted calf."

Right down to the moment the first car arrived, Pandora was certain no one would come. She'd sat through a discussion of Michael's plan, argued, disagreed, admired and ultimately she'd given up. Theatrics, she'd decided. But there was enough Jolley in her to look forward to the show, especially when she was one of the leads. And she had, as they said in the business, her part cold.

She'd dressed for the role in a slim, strapless black dress. For flair, she'd added a sterling silver necklace she'd fashioned in an exaggerated star burst. Matching earrings dripped nearly to her chin. If Michael wanted drama, who was she to argue? As the night of the dinner party had grown closer, her nerves had steeled into determination.

When he saw her at the top of the stairs, he was speechless. Had he really convinced himself all these years she had no real beauty? At the moment, poised, defiant and enjoying herself, she made every other woman he'd known look like a shadow.

And if he told her so, she wouldn't believe it for a moment. Instead he merely nodded and rocked back on his heels.

"Perfect," he told her as she walked down the main stairs. Standing at the base in a dark suit, Michael looked invincible, and ruthless. "The sophisticated heroine." He took her hand. "Cool and sexy. Hitchcock would've made you a star."

"Don't forget what happened to Janet Leigh."

He laughed and sent one of her earrings spinning. "Nervous?"

"Not as much as I'd thought I'd be. If this doesn't work—"

"Then we're no worse off than we are now. You know what to do."

"We've rehearsed it a half-dozen times. I still have the bruises."

He leaned closer to kiss both bare shoulders. "I always thought you'd be a natural. When this is over, we have a scene of our own to finish. No, don't pull back," he warned as she attempted to. "It's too late to pull back." They stood close, nearly mouth to mouth. "It's been too late all along."

Nerves she'd managed to quell came racing back, but they had nothing to do with plots or plans. "You're being dramatic."

With a nod, he tangled his fingers in her hair. "My sense of drama, your streak of practicality. An interesting combination."

"An uneasy one."

"If life's too easy you sleep through it," Michael decided. "It sounds like the first of our guests are arriving," he murmured as they heard the sound of a car. He kissed her briefly. "Break a leg."

She wrinkled her nose at his back. "That's what I'm afraid of."

Within a half hour, everyone who had been at the reading of the will, except Fitzhugh, was again in the library. No one seemed any more relaxed than they'd been almost six months before. Jolley beamed down on them from the oil painting. From time to time Pandora glanced up at it almost expecting him to wink. To give everyone what they'd come for, Pandora and Michael kept arguing about whatever came to mind. Time for the game to begin, she decided.

Carlson stood with his wife near a bookshelf. He looked cross and impatient and glowered when Pandora approached.

"Uncle Carlson, I'm so glad you could make it. We don't see nearly enough of each other."

"Don't soft-soap me." He swirled his scotch but didn't drink. "If you've got the idea you can talk me out of contesting this absurd will, you're mistaken."

"I wouldn't dream of it. Fitzhugh tells me you don't have a chance." She smiled beautifully. "But I have to agree the will's absurd, especially after being forced to live in the same house with Michael all these months." She ran a finger down one of the long, flattened prongs of her necklace. "I'll tell you, Uncle Carlson, there have been times I've seriously considered throwing in the towel. He's done everything possible to make the six months unbearable. Once he pretended his mother was ill, and he had to go to California. Next thing I knew I was locked in the basement. Childish games," she muttered sending Michael a look of utter dislike. Out of the corner of her eye, she saw Carlson take a quick, nervous drink. "Well, the sentence is nearly up." She turned back with a fresh smile. "I'm so glad we could have this little celebration. Michael's finally going to open a bottle of champagne he's been hoarding since Christmas."

Pandora watched Carlson's wife drop her glass on the Turkish carpet. "Dear me," Pandora said softly. "We'll have to get something to mop that up. Freshen your drink?"

"No, she's fine." Carlson took his wife by the elbow. "Excuse me."

As they moved away, Pandora felt a quick thrill of excitement. So, it had been Carlson.

"I quit smoking about six months ago," Michael told Hank and his wife, earning healthy approval.

"You'll never regret it," Hank stated in his slow, deliberate way. "You're responsible for your own body."

"I've been giving that a lot of thought lately," Michael said dryly. "But living with Pandora the past few months hasn't made it easy. She's made this past winter miserable. She had someone send me a fake telegram so I'd go flying off to California thinking my mother was ill." He glanced over his shoulder and scowled at Pandora's back.

"If you've gotten through six months without smoking..." Meg began, guiding the conversation back to Michael's health.

"It's a miracle I have living with that woman. But it's almost over." He grinned at Hank. "We're having champagne instead of carrot juice for dinner. I've been saving this bottle since Christmas for just the right occasion."

He saw Hank's fingers whiten around his glass of Perrier and Meg's color drain. "We don't—" Hank looked helplessly at Meg. "We don't drink."

"Champagne isn't drinking," Michael said jovially. "It's celebrating. Excuse me." He moved to the bar as if to freshen his drink and waited for Pandora to join him. "It's Hank."

"No." She added a splash of vermouth to her glass. "It's Carlson." Following the script, she glared at him. "You're an insufferable bore, Michael. Putting up with you isn't worth any amount of money."

"Intellectual snob." He toasted her. "I'm counting the days."

With a sweep of her skirts, Pandora walked over to Ginger. "I don't know how I manage to hold my temper with that man."

Ginger checked her face in a pretty silver compact. "I've always thought he was kind of cute."

"You haven't had to live with him. We were hardly together a week when he broke into my workshop and vandalized it. Then he tried to pass the whole thing off as the work of a vagrant."

Ginger frowned and touched a bit of powder to her nose. "It didn't seem like something he'd do to me. I told—" She caught herself and looked back at Pandora with a vague smile. "Those are pretty earrings."

Michael steeled himself to listen to Morgan's terse opinion on the stock market. The moment he found an opening, he broke in. "Once everything's settled, I'll have to come to you for advice. I've been thinking about getting more actively involved with one of Jolley's chemical firms. There's a lot of money in fertilizer—and pesticides." He watched Patience flutter her hands and subside at a glare from Morgan.

"Software," Morgan said briefly.

Michael only smiled. "I'll look into it."

Pandora tried unsuccessfully to pump Ginger. The five-minute conversation left her suspicious, confused and with the beginnings of a headache. She decided to try her luck on Biff.

"You're looking well." She smiled at him and nodded at his wife.

"You're looking a bit pale, cousin."

"The past six months haven't been a picnic." She cast a look at Michael. "Of course, you've always detested him."

"Of course," Biff said amiably.

"I've yet to discover why Uncle Jolley was fond of him. Besides being a bore, Michael has an affection for odd practical jokes. He got a tremendous kick out of locking me in the cellar."

Biff smiled into his glass. "He's never quite been in our class."

Pandora bit her tongue, then agreed. "Do you know, he even called me one night, disguising his voice. He tried to frighten me by saying someone was trying to kill me."

Biff's brows drew together as he stared into Pandora's eyes. "Odd."

"Well, things are almost settled. By the way, did you enjoy the champagne I sent you?"

Biff's fingers froze on his glass. "Champagne?"

"Right after Christmas."

"Oh yes." He lifted his glass again, studying her as he drank. "So it was you."

"I got the idea when someone sent Michael a bottle at Christmastime. He promises to finally open it tonight. Excuse me, I want to check on dinner."

Her eyes met Michael's briefly as she slipped from the room.

They'd set his scene, she thought. Now she had to move the action along. In the kitchen she found Sweeney finishing up the final preparation for the meal.

"If they're hungry," Sweeney began, "they'll just have to wait ten minutes."

"Sweeney, it's time to turn off the main power switch."

"I know, I know. I was just finishing this ham."

Sweeney had been instructed to, at Pandora's signal, go down to the cellar, turn off the power, then wait exactly one minute and turn it on again. She had been skeptical about the whole of Michael and Pandora's plan but had finally agreed to participate in it. Wiping her hands on her apron, the cook went to the cellar door. Pandora took a deep breath and walked back to the library.

Michael had positioned himself near the desk. He gave Pandora the slightest of nods when she entered. "Dinner in ten minutes," she announced brightly as she swept across the room.

"That gives us just enough time." Michael took the stage and couldn't resist starting with a tried and true line. He didn't have to see Pandora to know she was taking her position. "You all must be wondering why we brought you here tonight." He lifted his glass and looked from one face to the next. "One of you is a murderer."

On cue, the lights went out and pandemonium struck. Glasses shattered, women screamed, a table was overturned. When the lights blinked on, everyone froze. Lying half under the desk, facedown, was Pandora. Beside her was a letter opener with a curved, ornate hilt and blood on the blade. In an instant Michael was beside her, lifting her into his arms before anyone had a chance to react. Silently, he carried her from the room. Several minutes passed before he returned, alone. He gazed, hot and hard, at every face in the room.

"A murderer," he repeated. "She's dead."

"What do you mean she's dead?" Carlson pushed his way forward. "What kind of game is this? Let's have a look at her."

"No one's touching her." Michael effectively blocked his way. "No one's touching anything or leaving this room until the police get here."

"Police?" Pale and shaken, Carlson glanced around. "We don't want that. We'll have to handle this ourselves. She's just fainted."

"Her blood's all over this," Michael commented gesturing to the bloodstained letter opener.

"No!" Meg pushed forward until she'd broken through the crowd around the desk. "No one was supposed to be hurt. Only frightened. It wasn't supposed to be like this. Hank." She reached out, then buried her face against his chest.

"We were only going to play some tricks," he murmured.

"First degree murder isn't a trick."

"We never—" He looked at Michael in shock. "Not murder," he managed, holding Meg as tightly as she was holding him.

"You didn't want to drink the champagne, either, did you, Hank?"

"That's when I wanted to stop." Still sobbing, Meg turned in her husband's arms. "I even called and tried to warn her. I thought it was wrong all along, just a mean trick, but we needed money. The gym's drained everything we have. We thought if we could make the two of you angry enough with each other, you'd break the terms of the will. But that's all. Hank and I stayed in the cabin and waited. Then he went into Pandora's shop and turned things upside down. If she thought you did it—"

"I never thought she would," Ginger piped up. Two tears rolled down her cheeks. "Really, it all seemed silly and—exciting."

Michael looked at his pretty, weeping cousin. "So you were part of it."

"Well, I didn't really do anything. But when Aunt Patience explained it to me…"

"Patience?" There were patterns and patterns. A new one emerged.

"Morgan deserved his share." The old woman wrung her hands and looked everywhere but at the bloodstained letter opener. She'd thought she'd done the right thing. It all sounded so simple. "We thought we could make one of you leave, then it would all be the way it should be."

"Telegram," Morgan said, puffing wide-eyed on his cigar. "Not murder." He turned to Carlson. "Your idea."

"It's preposterous." Carlson mopped his brow with a white silk handkerchief. "The lawyers were incompetent. They haven't been able to do a thing. I was merely protecting my rights."

"With murder."

"Don't be ridiculous." He nearly sounded staid and stuffy again. "The plan was to get you out of the house. I did nothing more than lock—her—in the cellar. When I heard about the champagne, I had a doubt or two, but after all, it wasn't fatal."

"Heard about the champagne." It was what Michael had waited for. "From whom?"

"It was Biff," Meg told him. "Biff set it all up, promised nothing would go wrong."

"Just an organizer." Biff gauged the odds, then shrugged. "All's fair, cousin. Everyone in this room had their hand in." He held his up, examining it. "There's no blood on mine. I'd vote for you." He gave Michael a cool smile. "After all, it's no secret you couldn't abide each other."

"You set it up." Michael took a step closer. "There's also a matter of tampering with my car."

Biff moved his shoulders again, but Michael saw the sweat bead above his lips. "Everyone in this room had a part in it. Any of you willing to turn yourselves in?" His breath came faster as he backed away. "One of them panicked and did this. You won't find my fingerprints on that letter opener."

"When someone's attempted murder once," Michael said calmly, "it's easier to prove he tried again."

"You won't prove anything. Any of us might have drained the brake lines in your car. You can't prove I did."

"I don't need to." In a quick move, Michael caught him cleanly on the jaw and sent him reeling. Before he could fall, Michael had him by the collar. "I never said anything about draining the lines."

Feeling the trap close, Biff struck out blindly. Fists swinging, they tumbled to the floor. A Tiffany lamp shattered in a pile of color. They rolled, locked together, into a Belker table that shook from the impact. Shocked and ineffective, the rest stepped back and gave them room.

"Michael, that's quite enough." Pandora entered the room, her hair mussed and her clothes disheveled. "We have company."

Panting, he dragged Biff to his feet. His wrist sang a bit, but he considered it a pleasure. Charles, looking dignified in his best suit, opened the library doors. "Dinner is served."

Two hours later, Pandora and Michael shared a small feast in the library. "I never thought it would work," Pandora said over a mouthful of ham. "It shouldn't have."

"The more predictable the moves, the more predictable the end."

"Lieutenant Randall didn't seem too pleased."

"He wanted to do it his way." Michael moved his shoulders. "Since he'd already discovered Biff had been visiting other members of the family and making calls to them, he was bound to find out something eventually."

"The easy way." She rubbed the back of her neck. "Do you know how uncomfortable it is to play dead?"

"You were great." He leaned over to kiss her. "A star."

"The letter opener with the stage blood was a nice touch. Still, if they'd all stuck together…"

"We already knew someone was weakening because of the warning call. Turned out that Meg had had enough."

"I've been thinking about investing in their gym."

"It wouldn't hurt."

"What do you think's going to happen?"

"Oh, Carlson'll get off more or less along with the rest of them, excluding Biff. I don't think we have to worry about going to court over the will. As for our dear cousin—" Michael lifted a glass of champagne "—he's going to be facing tougher charges than malicious mischief or burglary. I may never get my television back, but he isn't going to be wearing any Brooks Brothers suits for a while. Only prison blues."

"You gave him another black eye," Pandora mused.

"Yeah." With a grin, Michael drank the wine. "Now you and I only have to cruise through the next two weeks."

"Then it's over."

"No." He took her hand before she could rise. "Then it begins." He slipped the glass from her other hand and pressed her back against the cushions. "How long?"

Pandora struggled to keep the tension from showing. "How long what?"

"Have you been in love with me?"

She jerked, then was frustrated when he held her back. "I'm not sitting here feeding your ego."

"All right, we'll start with me." He leaned back companionably and boxed her in. "I think I fell in love with you when you came back from the Canary Islands and walked into the parlor. You had legs all the way to your waist and you looked down your nose at me. I've never been the same."

"I've had enough games, Michael," she said stiffly.

"So've I." He traced a finger down her cheek. "You said you loved me, Pandora."

"Under duress."

"Then I'll just have to keep you under duress because I'm not giving you up now. Why don't we get married right here?"

She'd started to give him a hefty shove and stopped with her hands pressed against his chest. "What?"

"Right here in the library." He glanced around, ignoring the overturned tables and broken china. "It'd be a nice touch."

"I don't know what you're talking about."

"It's very simple. Here's the plot. You love me, I love you."

"That's not simple," she managed. "I've just been accessible. Once you get back to your blond dancers and busty starlets, you'll—"

"What blond dancers? I can't stand blond dancers."

"Michael, this isn't anything I can joke about."

"Just wait. You buy a nice white dress, maybe a veil. A veil would suit you. We get a minister, lots of flowers and have a very traditional marriage ceremony. After that, we settle into the Folley, each pursuing our respective careers. In a year, two at the most, we give Charles and Sweeney a baby to fuss over. See?" He kissed her ear.

"People's lives aren't screenplays," she began.

"I'm crazy about you, Pandora. Look at me." He took her chin and held it so that their faces were close. "As an artist, you're supposed to be able to see below the surface. That should be easy since you've always told me I'm shallow."

"I was wrong." She wanted to believe. Her heart already did. "Michael, if you're playing games with me, I'll kill you myself."

"Games are over. I love you, it's that simple."

"Simple," she murmured, surprised she could speak at all. "You want to get married?"

"Living together's too easy."

She was more surprised that she could laugh. “Easy?”

“That’s right.” He shifted her until she was lying flat on the sofa, his body pressed into hers. When his mouth came down, it wasn’t patient, wasn’t gentle, and everything he thought, everything he felt, communicated itself through that one contact. As she did rarely, as he asked rarely, she went limp and pliant. Her arms went around him. Perhaps it was easy after all.

“I love you, Michael.”

“We’re getting married.”

“It looks that way.”

His eyes were intense when he lifted his head. “I’m going to make life tough on you, Pandora. That’s just to pay you back for the fact that you’ll be the most exasperating wife on record. Do we understand each other?”

Her smile bloomed slowly. “I suppose we always have.”

Michael pressed a kiss to her forehead, to the tip of her nose, then to her lips. “He understood both of us.”

She followed his gaze to Jolley’s portrait. “Crazy old goat has us right where he wants us. I imagine he’s having a good laugh.” She rubbed her cheek against Michael’s. “I just wish he could be here to see us married.”

Michael lifted a brow. “Who says he won’t be?” He pulled her up and picked up both glasses. “To Maximillian Jolley McVie.”

“To Uncle Jolley.” Pandora clinked her glass to Michael’s. “To us.”

* * * * *